WARWOLFE

THE ORIGINS OF THE DE WOLFE PACK
A MEDIEVAL ROMANCE

BY
KATHRYN LE VEQUE

DE WOLFE PACK
THE SERIES

KATHRYN LE VEQUE NOVELS

Medieval Romance:

The de Russe Legacy:
The White Lord of Wellesbourne
The Dark One: Dark Knight
Beast
Lord of War: Black Angel
The Falls of Erith
The Iron Knight

The de Lohr Dynasty:
While Angels Slept (Lords of East
Anglia)
Rise of the Defender
Steelheart
Spectre of the Sword
Archangel
Unending Love
Shadowmoor
Silversword

Great Lords of le Bec:
Great Protector
To the Lady Born (House of de Royans)
Lord of Winter (Lords of de Royans)

Lords of Eire:
The Darkland (Master Knights of
Connaught)
Black Sword
Echoes of Ancient Dreams (time travel)

De Wolfe Pack Series:
The Wolfe
Serpent
Scorpion (Saxon Lords of Hage – Also
related to The Questing)
The Lion of the North

Walls of Babylon
Dark Destroyer
Nighthawk
Warwolfe
ShadowWolfe

Ancient Kings of Anglecynn:
The Whispering Night
Netherworld

Battle Lords of de Velt:
The Dark Lord
Devil's Dominion

Reign of the House of de Winter:
Lespada
Swords and Shields (also related to The
Questing, While Angels Slept)

De Reyne Domination:
Guardian of Darkness
The Fallen One (part of Dragonblade
Series)

Unrelated characters or family groups:
The Gorgon (Also related to Lords of
Thunder)
The Warrior Poet (St. John and de Gare)
Tender is the Knight (House of d'Vant)
Lord of Light
The Questing (related to The Dark Lord,
Scorpion)
The Legend (House of Summerlin)

**The Dragonblade Series: (Great
Marcher Lords of de Lara)**
Dragonblade
Island of Glass (House of St. Hever)
The Savage Curtain (Lords of Pembury)

The Fallen One (De Reyne Domination)
Fragments of Grace (House of St. Hever)
Lord of the Shadows
Queen of Lost Stars (House of St. Hever)

Lords of Thunder: The de Shera Brotherhood Trilogy
The Thunder Lord
The Thunder Warrior
The Thunder Knight

Highland Warriors of Munro
The Red Lion

Time Travel Romance: (Saxon Lords of Hage)
The Crusader
Kingdom Come

Contemporary Romance:

Kathlyn Trent/Marcus Burton Series:
Valley of the Shadow
The Eden Factor

Canyon of the Sphinx

The American Heroes Series:
The Lucius Robe
Fires of Autumn
Evenshade
Sea of Dreams
Purgatory

Other Contemporary Romance:
Lady of Heaven
Darkling, I Listen
In the Dreaming Hour

Multi-author Collections/Anthologies:
With Dreams Only of You (USA Today bestseller)
Sirens of the Northern Seas (Viking romance)
Ever My Love (sequel to With Dreams Only Of You) July 2016

Note: All Kathryn's novels are designed to be read as stand-alones, although many have cross-over characters or cross-over family groups. Novels that are grouped together have related characters or family groups.

Series are clearly marked. All series contain the same characters or family groups except the American Heroes Series, which is an anthology with unrelated characters.

There is NO particular chronological order for any of the novels because they can all be read as stand-alones, even the series.

For more information, find it in **A Reader's Guide to the Medieval World of Le Veque**.

AUTHOR'S NOTE

Finally... it's here!

There's so much to say about this novel that it's hard to know where to begin. So let's start from the beginning.

The details of the Battle of Hastings are accurate but for the fact that I added a group of knights that helped the Duke of Normandy win the battle. Everything else – from the location of the Norman landing to the details of Harold's death are fact. But because there is so little documentation about the details of the battle (surprisingly), that's where I begin to weave my fabric of fiction. A few things of note for the sharp-eyed reader:

Warwolfe is mentioned in *Swords and Shields*. Edward I built massive trebuchets for his battles in Scotland and named the machines Warwolfs *(Lupus Guerre),* after the de Wolfe ancestor (that is mostly true – Edward I really did build machines named Warwolf, but it's the Le Veque imagination that put the backstory behind it). Yes, a Warwolf really is a thing!

William de Wolfe (*THE WOLFE*) comes from the House of de Wolfe – and it was Gaetan who was given the title 1st Earl of Wolverhampton, as explained in *The Lion of the North*. William de Wolfe was the third son of his father, however, and his eldest brother, Robert, inherited the title and passed it down through his children. William was given the title Baron Kilham and eventually Earl of Warenton by Henry III.

King Wulfhere founded the city of Wolverhampton in 659 AD – the Duke of Normandy thought it would be perfect for de Wolfe to subdue and rule because of the name, so that's the how and why of the de Wolfes ending up in Wolverhampton. There is lots of coal in the area of Wolverhampton (called the Black Country), which is how the de Wolfes end up making their money.

Gaetan's name was shorted by his men to "Gate" at times, which is how Gates de Wolfe in *Dark Destroyer* got his name – he was named for Gaetan.

The House of de Shera is born in this book. The Roman origins of de Shera (*Shericus*) were mentioned in *The Thunder Lord*, but in this novel we actually get to see how the House of de Shera came about. They are around Worcester in this novel and it is Gaetan who gives them lands around Chester, which is referred to in the *Lords of Thunder* series.

Fun fact: William the Conqueror and Harold Godwinson were cousins. They had met each other several times before the Battle of Hastings and, at one point, Harold even endorsed William as the next king of England when the current king at the time (about 10 years before Hastings) died. William went to England to take it from Harold because the man had catfished on him, among other reasons.

So, let's talk pronunciation of certain names – because there are some odd ones in this book, genuine "old English" or even older names. Here are a few to note:

Gaetan: GAY-tahn

Ghislaine: GIZZ-lane

Téo: TAY-o

Aramis: Some say Ara-MEE, I say "ARA-miss". Like the cologne.

Alary: Just like it looks – Al-uh-ree

Mercia: MER-sha (Not Mer-cee-uh)

Oh, and the lion images that denote breaks in the chapters? That is the lion of the Duke of Normandy.

With that, I truly hope you enjoy this epic tale of adventure, brotherhood, and, ultimately, a romance like none other. Enjoy the original de Wolfe Pack – they were a joy to write!

Happy Reading!
Kathryn

TABLE OF CONTENTS

Prologue... 1

Chapter One... 16

Chapter Two 34

Chapter Three... 54

Chapter Four... 62

Chapter Five.. 86

Chapter Six.. 90

Chapter Seven 102

Chapter Eight... 110

Chapter Nine 126

Chapter Ten 136

Chapter Eleven 154

Chapter Twelve.. 161

Chapter Thirteen 179

Chapter Fourteen 193

Chapter Fifteen.. 201

Chapter Sixteen 222

Chapter Seventeen... 236

Chapter Eighteen... 250

Chapter Nineteen.. 259

Chapter Twenty.. 275

Chapter Twenty-One... 293

Chapter Twenty-Two 306

Chapter Twenty-Three...................................... 328

Chapter Twenty-Four.. 349

Chapter Twenty-Five... 364

Chapter Twenty-Six... 386

Epilogue... 400

De Wolfe Pack Series.. 409

About Kathryn Le Veque 410

PROLOGUE

ഗ

THE LEGEND OF WARWOLFE

Battle, East Sussex
Two years ago, Present Day

"QUEENIE? ARE YOU home?"

A gray-haired man with a hand-hewn wooden cane opened the old door even as he pounded on it, raining rust from the old hinges onto the floor. The house in which the door was lodged was ancient by any standard, a squat farmhouse built from the pale gray stone that was so prevalent to the area. There were big warped beams running up the exterior walls, however, which suggested late-Medieval architecture, but the shape and design of the house was purely Georgian. Everything was symmetrical from the alignment of the old cracked windows to the roofline, pitched in shape and covered with dried thatching that matched the color of the stone.

It was every historian's dream.

Which was why the young woman behind the gray-haired man was so wide-eyed at what she was seeing, following the man into the cool foyer as her eyes so greedily soaked up all of the ancientness around her. This was pure awesomeness as far as she was concerned and she tried not to be distracted by the time-capsule quality of the old house.

They were in search of someone.

"Queenie!"

The old man banged his cane on the wooden floor, a floor that, at one time, had been finished but now it just looked splintered and dirty. And the smell of the house... God, the smell was that of dust and must and dampness.

It was glorious.

"Do you think he's home?" the young woman asked timidly. "I mean, the front door was open and...."

"He's home," the gray-haired man cut her off with confidence. "Queensborough Browne and I have known each other for many years. My family has lived in a house on Telham Lane adjacent to this house since the turn of the last century. My property backs up to Queenie's property. He's most definitely home, Miss Devlin. He never leaves. Therefore, we simply have to find him."

So they were on a hunt for a man named Queensborough Browne and Abigail Devlin was simply along for the ride, an important path in the course of her research for her Ph.D. dissertation in Medieval History at the University of Birmingham. She'd been to the bucolic village of Battle several times over the past nine months, all of her time spent at the battlefield or the museum that held the artifacts of the Battle of Hastings. During these many visits, she'd struck up a friendship with one of the docents there, a Mr. Peters Groby.

It had been a most fortuitous acquaintance.

Mr. Groby was blind in one eye, half-crippled and had a terrible wet cough that seemed to weaken him when it came on, but the man knew the history of England, and the history of the Battle of Hastings, like nobody's business. He and Abigail spoke weekly and she'd been making the trek down to Battle nearly every weekend to listen to his tales and speak with the curators of the museum. They had artifacts and documentation in their archives that she'd been given access to, thanks to Mr. Groby, and she was very grateful for it, but it seemed like all of that history wasn't telling her much about what she really wanted to know. For Abigail, she was looking for something *very* specific.

The unsung heroes of the Norman Invasion and their impact upon the Conquest.

That was the tentative title of her dissertation. She'd refine it at some point, but right now, that was pretty much the entire focus of her paper – the men other than the Duke of Normandy who had made a difference in the conquest of England. The curators at the museum had been very helpful with suggestions on where else she could find additional material that might tell her of the driving forces behind the Duke of Normandy's army, but the truth was that there was very little documentation about that subject in general. There wasn't a great deal known from period sources about the actual Battle of Hastings and the ensuing conquest.

Nearly a year into the first of three years for her Ph.D. studies, Abigail was starting to become discouraged with just how very little information there was about a subject she was certain held great and deep secrets – the front lines of the Duke of Normandy's army, the knights who would have led the cavalry and would have broken through the English army's mighty shield wall, a shield wall that had held for nearly nine hours on that fateful day. But someone had eventually broken through.

Abigail wanted to know who that was.

Now, she had what she thought might be a breakthrough in finding out. Mr. Groby had a friend, it seemed, whose family had been original land owners in the area in the High Middle Ages. This family was very old and the very last of the line, an old man by the name of Queensborough Browne, lived like a hermit off of Powdermill Road, which was in sight of the battlefield and the demolished abbey. Mr. Groby had made an appointment on this day to go and see him but it seemed that Queensborough was nowhere to be found.

Now, they were wandering in the guy's house like a couple of burglars, hunting him down as Mr. Groby continued to bang his cane on the floor and call his friend's name.

"*Queenie!*"

"Mr. Groby, maybe he's just not here," Abigail said, trying to insist because, even though she was awestruck by the old house, it didn't seem right prowling through it without an invitation. "I can always come back. I'll be back next weekend."

"Nonsense," Groby said. "He is here, somewhere. He's expecting us, I assure you."

Abigail wasn't so sure. They had made their way through the foyer, into what appeared to be a back hall that was cluttered to the roof with all kinds of things, and now they were entering an extremely old kitchen. The floor was stone and the stove in what had been the old hearth had to be a hundred years old. They hadn't made stoves like that for decades, if not centuries. The old sink was iron and the very old spigots were also made of iron, or so it seemed. Truthfully, it was difficult to tell. As they passed through the kitchen and towards what looked like an orangery beyond, an old man suddenly appeared with plants in his hands.

"Queenie!" Groby exclaimed. "Didn't you hear me calling you, old man?"

Queensborough Browne looked rather surprised to see his friend, immediately spying the young woman behind him. A stub of a man with a crown of white hair that looked like cotton and enormous hands now dirty from potting, his old eyes inspected the young woman for a moment before replying.

"Is that the girl?" he asked.

Groby nodded, turning to look at Abigail rather proudly. "An American convert," he said. "She's coming back over to this side of the pond. A very intelligent young lady, actually. This is Miss Abigail Devlin. Miss Devlin, this is my friend, Mr. Queensborough Browne."

Queensborough's gaze lingered on Abigail for a moment before turning to set the plants down on the potting table behind him. In fact, the entire room with glass walls and ceiling, called a sunroom in America but in England it had a variety of names, like garden room or

The Orangery, was full of plants in various stages of growth. Plastic pots littered the table along with gorgeous mums and foxgloves. Queensborough brushed off his dirty hands as he returned his attention to his guests.

"Come on, then," he said, sounding annoyed that he'd been interrupted. "It's all in the dining room."

That was as much of a greeting as the old hermit could muster. Abigail looked anxiously at Groby, who simply shrugged and followed Queensborough as he headed towards the front of the house.

"Queenie, when is the last time you left this place?" Groby asked, trying to strike up a cheerful conversation. "I've not seen you over at The 1066 in over a month."

Abigail knew that *The 1066* was a bar over on High Street, an older place without televisions or games to entice the younger crowd. It was an old establishment for older people who just wanted a pint without all of the noise and hype of today's bars. She was trying to peer around Groby to see how Queensborough was reacting to the question, but the man with the cotton hair didn't give much reaction. He seemed singularly focused on what was in his dining room.

"No time," he told Groby. As they entered the dining room with the dark blue walls of peeling paint, dark wood, and a fireplace that was as tall as Abigail was, he waved his guests in with impatience. "Come, come. Sit down so we can get on with it."

Abigail was coming to think he wasn't the hospitable type but Groby didn't seem to be bothered by it. He sat down in a very old chair with a faded red velvet cushion as Queensborough organized a vast array of items already on the table – papers, things that looked like booklets, and an old box that was fairly nondescript except for the fact that it was ancient like the rest of the house and reinforced with iron strips.

In fact, Abigail was quite interested in that box. She summoned her courage to speak as Queensborough fumbled with the latch on it.

"Thank you so much for agreeing to see us today," she said politely.

"Your home is just exquisite. Mr. Groby said that your family has lived here since Medieval times."

"Henry VIII to be exact," Queensborough said, his manner clipped. "That's not exactly Medieval. The lands were given to an ancestor of mine, a great friend of the king's, but most of it was sold in the eighteenth century and our family retained just this small parcel of land and this house. The rest of it went to different owners."

Abigail looked around the dining room, magnificent in its aged state. "How old is the house?"

Queensborough opened up the top of the box, the iron joints creaking. "These two front rooms were built in the time of William Rufus. It was a house for the abbot of Battle Abbey but legend says that his mistress and their children lived here. The rest of the house was built with stones from Battle Abbey when Henry demolished it during the dissolution." He paused to look at her, his old eyes intense. "Tell me something, Miss Abigail Devlin – tell me why you've really come here. What stories do you intend to tell about us?"

Abigail was a bit taken aback by the question because it bordered on hostile. In fact, Queensborough hadn't shown anything *but* hostility since they'd arrived. He was either an ass or just extremely socially awkward. But something told her it was more than that; there was a look in his eye that suggested... protectiveness... even fear.

An old man with a secret.

Not looking at Groby, Abigail answered calmly.

"I only intend to tell the truth," she said. "Mr. Groby explained who I am. I'm researching my...."

"I know what he said," Queensborough cut her off. "I know you're from university. You want to know about what's been buried."

Abigail regarded him. Having parents who were trial lawyers, she was used to aggressive people. His manner didn't bother her. "I want to give a voice to those who have never had their stories told."

"You? An American?"

"Americans have done pretty well at telling English stories and vice versa."

Queensborough's bushy brow furrowed. "But this isn't your right. You know that, don't you?"

Abigail leaned forward on the ancient table. "Why not? Because I wasn't born on this soil?" she asked, trying not to sound defensive. "Mr. Browne, I have had a fascination with England for as long as I can remember. I probably know more about its history than most Brits do. Just because I wasn't born here doesn't mean I don't have a great love for it. It doesn't mean I can't do justice to telling the story of those whose glory isn't yet known. In fact, I don't see any of your native British students taking a stand and demanding to tell the stories I want to tell. So why not trust me with them? I don't love England because it's in my blood; I love it because it's in my soul."

Queensborough considered her declaration. She was well spoken and passionate, and that impressed him just the slightest. But he was still hesitant.

"All right, Yank," he said after a moment. "Then tell me why you're here. Tell me what you want to know."

Abigail could sense that they were getting somewhere now and she didn't waste the opportunity. "Mr. Groby told me that your family has artifacts that no museum has seen," she said quietly. "Artifacts pertaining to exactly what I'm looking for – the knights and soldiers who were on the front lines of the Duke of Normandy's fighting force when they arrived in England. These are the men who really won the Battle of Hastings, Mr. Browne – the Duke of Normandy was a great commander, but it was these line officers who fought and died for England. It's their stories I want to tell and Mr. Groby says you know something about that. Will you please tell me what you know?"

"And you're going to write a paper about it?"

"I am writing my doctoral dissertation about it, yes."

Queensborough looked like he was considering it. Then he looked at Groby. "You have been begging me to turn these things over to the museum," he said. "Is this how you intend to force my hand? Once she publishes her sources, every Medieval scholar in the world is going to want to see them."

Groby cleared his throat. "I'm not trying to force your hand. But this young woman may be the perfect way to introduce your artifacts to the world."

Queensborough pondered that a moment before finally shaking his head. "I don't know," he said. He'd been hiding the artifacts for so long that he really didn't know any other way. It was a difficult mindset to change. "Maybe... maybe you should come back tomorrow. I must think."

Abigail didn't want to lose control of the conversation, not now. She didn't want to leave and take the chance that she'd never be invited back.

"Mr. Browne, do you have any children?" she asked pointedly. "Children that you plan to pass all of these artifacts down to?"

An expression of regret, perhaps even concern, flickered across Queensborough's face. "Only nieces," he said. "But that shouldn't concern you."

Abigail wouldn't let go. "Do they care about these artifacts?" she asked. "I mean, are they going to take good care of them? Hide them away from the world like you do?"

"I'm sure they'll do what needs to be done."

"Do you really want to take that chance?" Abigail asked, her tone nearly pleading. "Why are you hiding these things away? If what Mr. Groby tells me is true, then you have a story that has never before been told about men whose names have been lost to time. Why are you hiding away these men who lived and died in a battle that changed the course of history? Don't they deserve better than to be hidden away? Don't they deserve to have people know of their bravery?"

Queensborough simply looked at her; it was clear that her words were having an impact on him. She made a good deal of sense. Truth be told, he'd been wrestling with the same thing for years. Next to Abigail, Groby spoke softly.

"That's what I've been telling you for years, Queenie," he said with some regret. "For you not to let these stories be told... they'll die with you. You know that. Your nieces don't care about these family artifacts. They'll probably donate them or just let them rot. Why not let Abby take a look at what you have? At least let someone who will love these artifacts like you do tell the story you can't tell."

Queensborough's gaze hovered on Groby for a few long moments before, finally, he turned his attention to the open box in front of him.

With a heavy sigh, he reached into it and pulled forth what looked like an extremely old cloth covering up something square shaped, roughly twelve inches by twelve inches and maybe four inches high.

In fact, Abigail stood up as Queensborough sat down with the package in front of him, leaning over the table so she could get a good look at the object as Queensborough unwrapped it, revealing a rather thick book with ancient yellowed pages and writing that was more artwork than letters.

Classic Medieval writing.

Abigail's heart started to pound. Having spent many an hour reading through Medieval manuscripts and having studied ancient codices like the *Book of Kells*, she knew a very old book when she saw one. Pinpricks of excitement began to pepper her hands as she began to suspect the magnitude of the object before her.

"This is called the *Book of Battle*," Queensborough finally said. "It was finished in the year 1068 A.D., two years after the Battle of Hastings, by a fighting priest known as Jathan *de Guerre*."

"Jathan of War," Abigail translated, instantly enamored with the book in front of Queensborough. "My God... is that book really almost a thousand years old?"

Queensborough nodded. "It is, indeed," he replied, reverence in his tone. "Jathan came to these shores with the Duke of Normandy's army. I suppose you could call him the first war correspondent because he described the battle down to the last detail and he also relayed a remarkable event following the battle. It was a journey of sorts to regain one of the duke's men who had been kidnapped by the enemy."

Abigail's pounding heart grew stronger as she realized the significance of the book. She was so excited that she was beginning to feel faint. "Oh... my," she breathed. "Actual details of Hastings? But we know so little about it. To have another source – a source who was actually there – that would transform everything we know about the battle."

Queensborough nodded, glancing at Groby, who was sitting back in his chair with his hands resting on the top of his cane. There was some guilt in Queensborough's expression.

"I know it," he said. "My old friend, Groby, knows it, but to his credit, he's never told anyone what he knows. He's been all through this book but he's never told a soul about it. He knows that it is my decision to make it known and if anyone knew what I have, they'd beat down my door to get it."

Abigail was nearly beside herself. "Yes, they would," she agreed fervently. "And rightly so. Surely... surely you know what you have there, what this means to the historians of the world."

"I do."

"But it could be the most significant find of this century!"

Queensborough reached out to touch the old book, affectionately, as one would touch a pet or a child. In a sense, maybe it was his pet or child, something he'd been protecting so long that it was oddly a part of him. But all Abigail could see was the man touching an ancient document with his grimy hands and she resisted the urge to slap his fingers away. Meanwhile, Queensborough was deep in thought.

"It probably will be one of the most significant finds in English history," he finally said. "I don't know why my family never turned it over to the authorities. It was just something we kept, like grandmum's furniture or an old aunt's silver set. It was just part of our family. But I suppose... maybe it's time now. I'm an old man. Maybe it's time to finally let this go."

Abigail left her seat to go and stand next to Queensborough, bending over the manuscript and admiring the craftsmanship. Getting a closer look at it only fed her sense of amazement. "This is just exquisite," she said, awe in her tone. "And it's in remarkable shape for being as old as it is. But how did your family come into possession of it?"

Queensborough was looking at the old book as he spoke. "This house has belonged to the abbots of Battle Abbey since the beginning," he said. "When Henry VIII came along and the dissolution of the monasteries happened, things that were kept safe at the abbey were brought here and buried in the floor beneath the stones so that Henry's men couldn't find them. When my ancestor was granted these lands, this house came with it and when he sold everything, our family still kept the house. That's why these things belong to us. They have for centuries."

It made sense. "And somewhere along the line, you had someone translate this book?" Abigail asked. "Or are were your ancestors able to read it?"

Queensborough shrugged. "Both," he said. "It's written in Latin, which most people learned in the old days, especially if you were Catholic. But back in the nineteen twenties, my grandfather took it over to the Church of the Virgin Mary, right across from the demolished abbey, and asked the priest to translate the entire book for a sizable donation. Until then, all the family really knew were bits and pieces of the story. I supposed no one really cared enough to read the entire thing. But the priest did the translation and it's here, in this box. That was the first time anyone had ever heard tale of the Duke of Normandy's Warwolfe."

Abigail cocked her head curiously. "A Warwolf? You mean those big trebuchets that Edward I had built for his battles in Scotland?" Her eyes suddenly widened. "Did the Duke of Normandy have those war machines, too? Two hundred years before their use was first recorded? Holy Smokes... did he bring those war machines to the Battle of Hastings?"

She was very excited about it but Queensborough shook his head.

"No, not the war machines," he said. "At least, not the ones you are referring to. But those machines were named after the original Warwolfe, I'll wager. Because there was a man known as Warwolfe and, according to Jathan, he led a team of the most powerful Norman knights the world had yet seen."

Those words hit Abigail like a ton of bricks; it was what she'd been looking for, what she'd been waiting to hear all of these months. *The most powerful Norman knights the world had yet seen.*

The unsung heroes whose stories needed to be told.

"Oh, my God, yes," she said, breathless in her glee. "Those are the men I want to know about, men that history has forgotten but the ones who changed the course of history. And you're telling me that the fighting priest wrote about those men?"

"He did, indeed," Groby said, a twinkle in his eye when he saw how excited Abigail was. "When you first came to the museum and spoke of what you were looking for, the first thing I thought of was Queenie and his manuscript. I knew he had it, you see, but I also knew he didn't want the world to know about it. It's taken me nine months to convince him to tell you the story and let you see the manuscript for yourself. I agree with you, Abby – these men need to have their stories told. This Warwolfe – he was the greatest one of all. He very much needs to have his story told."

Abigail listened to Groby, a stunned expression on her face, before looking at Queensborough. "I swear to you that I will only treat this subject with the greatest respect," she said, her voice trembling with excitement and emotion. "Could you possibly let me read the translation?"

Queensborough didn't know Abigail; he didn't know her heart or mind. But at that moment, he could see into her soul, in through those big brown eyes, and he could understand what this meant to her. Maybe Groby was right; maybe it was time for the men buried within the *Book of Battle* to have their stories told. Men of war, of conquest, but flesh and blood men who had risked everything for glory. And

Warwolfe... well, he had quite a story.

It was time.

"You can read it but it stays here with me," he said. "You can come back as many times as you wish."

Abigail nodded eagerly. "I promise, I will never take it out of your house," she said. "I won't even tell anyone about it, at least for now, but when I publish my dissertation, I'll have to cite the source. You do understand that, right?"

Queensborough nodded. His focus was on the old book, thinking of the story he'd read in those pages and of what his grandfather had told him. Settling back in his chair, he kept his gaze on those faded vellum sheets.

"*Lupus Guerre*," he muttered. "That means Warwolf in Latin, but I'm sure you already know that. But I want you to remember these names I am about to tell you, Miss Devlin."

"Of course."

"De Wolfe, de Lohr, de Russe, de Reyne, de Moray...."

"Okay?"

"De Winter, de Lara, St. Hèver, du Reims, and Wellesbourne."

"Who are they?"

Queensborough looked up at her. "The men whose stories you are about to hear."

Abigail could feel anticipation like she'd never felt in her life. A smile flickered across her lips, tugging the corners of her mouth. "I'm more than ready to hear about them."

Queensborough could see the unadulterated happiness in her eyes. That told him that he was doing the right thing.

"Tea first?"

Abigail's expression fell and Groby, with a snort, leaned on his cane and slowly stood up. "I'll get the tea," he told Queensborough. "You tell that young lady what she's been waiting to hear before she explodes."

Queensborough grinned, a surprising gesture. "Make mine with gin," he called after his friend.

"No gin until you finish your story!"

Groby was off, hobbling in the direction of the kitchen and the kettle, as Queensborough returned his attention to Abigail. He pointed to the chair that Groby had vacated.

"Sit down," he said. "This is going to take a while."

Abigail quickly planted herself in the warm seat. "I have all of the time in the world, Mr. Browne."

"What were the names I told you to remember?"

Abigail didn't hesitate. "De Wolfe, de Lohr, de Russe, de Reyne, de Moray, de Winter, de Lara, St. Hèver, du Reims, and Wellesbourne."

His grin returned. "You're very sharp."

"I have an eidetic memory. I see words."

Queensborough was increasingly impressed with the young American. "Then I won't keep you waiting." The smile faded from his face as he settled back, his expression turning into something distant. "While the Duke of Normandy came to these shores aboard the *Mora*, Warwolfe had his own vessels, named for the angels because Gaetan de Wolfe and his knights called themselves *Anges de Guerre*, or the Angels of War."

"Gaetan de Wolfe?"

"Warwolfe."

Now, the man behind the legend had a name. "Go on," Abigail begged.

Queensborough did. "De Wolfe evidently had at least a dozen ships to carry thousands of men, ships named the *Ramiel* and the *Sachael*, the *Raphael* and the *Uriel*. Jathan came aboard the *Ramiel*, which was named for the angel of thunder, and that ship contained all of those men whose names I had you remember. Those were the Angels of War, arriving on a boat named for thunder. Appropriate, considering the storm that was approaching England on that day."

Abigail was already fascinated with the tale. "Just ten knights?"

Queensborough nodded. "Ten knights and thousands of men," he said. "According to Jathan, the knights were experts in warfare. The

Duke of Normandy would use them like a crack group of specialist warriors. Sort of like a modern-day SAS squad. They were, literally, the Angels of War. There wasn't anything Warwolfe and his men couldn't do, the first ones into battle and the last ones out. You've been looking for the unsung heroes of the conquest? These men were it, Miss Devlin."

Abigail had waited her whole life to hear this tale. "Will you start from the very beginning of Jathan's story? And even if you think a detail is unimportant, please don't leave it out. Tell me everything."

Something wistful reflected in Queensborough's eyes. "All I ask is that you do this justice when you write your paper. As you said, these men deserve to have their stories told. But I'll take it a step further – bring them back to life again, Miss Devlin. Will you do that? Will you bring them back to life?"

There was so much delight and passion in Abigail's eyes that she was positively aglow from it all. Leaning forward, she put a hand on Queensborough's dirty fingers.

"I'll make you proud, I swear it. I'll make these men breathe again."
He believed her.

CHAPTER ONE

cȝ

De Wolfe Motto: *Fortis in Arduis*
Strength in Times of Trouble

Year of our Lord 1066 A.D.
Late September
Pevensey, England

THROUGH THE MISTS of time, they came.

Thousands of men disembarked vessels that had brought them across the dark and rolling sea. These titans of war emerged from the surf astride war horses that breathed fire, with eyes that bespoke of their thirst for blood.

The Apocalypse, for the Anglo-Saxons, had arrived.

It was a cloudy day towards the end of the month of September when the transports of the Duke of Normandy's fleet moored off the coast of Pevensey, England in shallow water with hardly a ripple from the waves that came in from the south. The sea spray was minimal, as was the swell, allowing both men and materials to be offloaded without trouble. Horses, who had suffered the uncertainty of a trip across the channel, were led off the ships by their masters, kicking up the water and jumping about, smelling the salt and the sea grass, eager to be on land where they belonged.

As the army came upon the shore in waves of flesh and bone and armor, setting foot in this land for the taking, a beachhead was set up so men could recover from the journey and prepare for what was to come. But they made no secret about their arrival; they had no intention of being covert about their presence. Thousands of men raided the countryside for food and anything else they could carry while their commanders, including the Duke of Normandy, huddled in tents and planned the coming incursion.

A military action unlike anything the world had ever seen before.

With their tactics, manpower, and superior weapons, the Normans had the advantage. Harold Godwinson, the King of the Anglo-Saxons, had been far to the north dealing with another attempted invasion by the Norwegians when the Normans appeared on his southern shore. The Normans knew this, of course, through their network of spies and mercenaries, so their appearance on the shores of Southern England had been no accident. This is what they'd planned for, making sure they were able to make it ashore without any resistance from Harold and his army. Now, they were here – and it was essential that they defeat the Anglo-Saxon army in a mighty display of their power.

A battle to end all battles.

Harold had an excellent army, however, which concerned the Normans, but they were also betting on the fact that many of Harold's ranks were full of farmers and farm workers who needed to tend to their fall crops at this time of year. At least, that's what William's advance scouts were telling him and that was what the duke was counting on. While Harold would lose men to the harvest, William was bringing a massive contingent that was fresh and ready to fight.

And that would be Harold's downfall.

After the first night on the rocky shores of Pevensey, William and his men moved on to Hastings and captured the town, where William began to build the first of many castles he would build in England. From that castle, the Normans continued to raid the surrounding area heavily, gathering supplies for their foray north into England. But that particular move came sooner than expected near the middle of October, only three weeks after the landing at Pevensey.

Word had reached the duke that Harold had marched his army at a crushing pace south and were nearing Hastings, prompting William to move his army out of the safety of Hastings Castle and head north to intercept the Anglo-Saxon army. About six miles northeast of Hastings, they came within striking range and on the night of October 13, William and his army formed lines because Harold's army had been sighted by the duke's scouts about ten miles to the north. It was time to take a stand and the Normans did, doing what they did best as they dug in and awaited Harold.

And that's when Warwolfe was called forth.

Gaetan de Wolfe was the tactical mastermind that the Duke of Normandy relied on. An enormous man with black hair and eyes the color of polished bronze, de Wolfe set up the lines of men and weapons that would face Harold's army in the morning. With his generals, men who had each earned great and crushing reputations on the field of battle, the front lines of the Norman army were positioned so as not to allow any room for mistakes or problems.

The lines were to hold, regardless of the situation, because de Wolfe had given that command and all further battle commands would come down through him and his generals, trickling down to men known as the Companions of the Conqueror. These companions were unimpeachable nobles from the finest families supporting the duke's conquest. Although they were men of battle, they weren't necessarily on the lines like Warwolfe and his men were. Even as there were two factions advising and fighting for the Duke of Normandy – the Companions of the duke versus his Angels of War – even the Companions, these great and noble men of battle, knew well enough to defer to the *Anges de Guerre*, led by Warwolfe himself.

Where Warwolfe went, destruction followed.

The morning of the 14th day of October dawned cold with a hint of rain blowing in from the south. Before sunrise and amidst the snicker of horses and the heavy smell of cooking fires, the cavalry mounted, including Warwolfe and his generals, and these ten great men were separated with the three distinct lines that de Wolfe had formed. Each man had specific orders to ensure the success of the day.

Men that would lead the charge against the Anglo-Saxons.

First into battle was Kristoph de Lohr, a Breton from Lohréac, who was the great motivator of men. He was joined by Aramis de Russe, of Flemish blood, who killed with his fearsome double-blades. Lancelot "Lance" de Reyne, a Breton from Morlaix, was a man that all men would follow, and Marc de Moray, former Sheriff from Rouen, was the master of the spear. Fearsome men who struck terror into the hearts of the enemy.

But there were more – Denis de Winter, whose bloodlines descended from the Visigoths, wielded the sword of his forefathers, l'Espada, with the power of the archangels. His friend and comrade, Luc de Lara, who, with his noble Spanish blood, was a titled lord among them as the Count of Boucau. He was an impenetrable wall of destruction. Kye St. Hèver came next. He was a nephew to the Count of Anjou and man they called "The Hammer".

Finally, Téo du Reims, bastard son of the Duke of Reims, wielded his fearsome morning star, and Bartholomew *Eni yn dda*, or of Wellesbourne, was a Welsh mercenary from the ancient town of Wellesbourne and the man all men feared.

These were the *Anges de Guerre*, men who had served with de Wolfe for as long as anyone could remember. Each man was a cog in a bigger wheel, men who fought together as seamlessly as the rain blended with the clouds. All of the men were leaders but there were those that took more easily to command and those who simply wanted to fight – de Lohr, de Winter, and du Reims were those who commanded with grace and ease. De Reyne, de Lara, and de Russe also had the ability, but they tended to lead by actions rather than words. And the rest – Wellesbourne, St. Hèver, and de Moray – were pure beasts of battle. Nothing – and no men – stood in their way and lived to tell the tale.

It was a collection of knights the world had never seen before, all of them led by the greatest knight of all, the knight known as Gaetan de Wolfe. Norse and Breton on his father's side, Gascon and Saxon on his mother's, de Wolfe bore all of the fighting traits of those bloodlines as a man with no weakness and no faults, only glory. Descended from the kings of Breton, he had more nobility in him than even the Duke of Normandy, a man with whom he was particularly close. They thought alike, which was why William placed so much faith in his Warwolfe. He and Gaetan had fought many battles together, but none so important as the one they were about to face on this day.

Therefore, the Duke of Normandy and his Companion nobles were towards the rear of the lines as the *Anges de Guerre* set up the shield wall. Given that there were three distinct lines – one in the middle and then the right and left flanks, de Wolfe himself took command of the center line while de Lohr and du Reims took the left and the right, respectively. These were cavalry lines with the infantry in the front and the archers to the rear. De Winter, de Reyne, and de Lara had command of the three groups of archers while the rest of them – de Russe, Wellesbourne, St. Hèver, and de Moray positioned themselves up with the infantry. Those men would be the first to see action.

And with the final positions achieved, all they could do at that point was wait.

But the wait wasn't long.

Harold and his army appeared an hour after sunrise, coming over the rise from the north and seeing the Normans dug in on an elevated position to the south. Seeing the thousands of men waiting for him, Harold deployed his army on a similar rise. The armies faced each other as the sun rose and the clouds, which had gathered at dawn, began to flitter away on the sea breeze.

Now, there was a blue sky and bright light illuminating both armies. De Wolfe realized as he watched Harold position his men that somehow, somewhere, the king had picked up fresh men. He could tell because they didn't move like men who had just marched hundreds of miles from the north. There was some energy to their step. But he also noticed that, from what he could see, Harold had very few archers. Mostly infantry, some cavalry, and limited archers.

That would be his fatal mistake.

News of the lack of archers made its way back to Normandy at the rear of the lines along with another message that the Norman archers, as a result, were going to be used sparingly. The reason was obvious – when two armies face one another and rained arrows down upon each other, archers from each side would pick up those arrows from the opposing army from the ground and reuse them. With so few Anglo-Saxon archers, the Normans could use up their supply of arrows quickly. De Wolfe wanted to conserve ammunition.

The duke understood that but he was also impatient. He had a throne to claim and another property to add to his Normandy holdings, and he didn't have much patience. He sent orders to the front of the lines for de Wolfe to begin the bombardment before the Anglo-Saxon lines were set and de Wolfe obliged.

Under fair skies and light winds, the Norman's didn't wait for Harold's army to completely set their lines. The first strike was from the Norman archers, raining spears of death upon the unprepared Anglo-Saxon army and creating a good deal of casualties at the onset. Men panicked, ranks wavered, as the Normans charged with all of their might.

After that, it was bedlam.

Eight hours later

WHOOSH!

The mace barely missed his head.

Into the eighth hour of fighting, de Wolfe was forced to nearly throw himself from his horse as a Saxon cavalryman in close quarters fighting hurled ten pounds of iron and death straight at his head. That didn't please de Wolfe, not in the least. So once he ducked low and as the mace sailed over his head, he thrust his sword upward to block it, then used his free hand to grab it. But the Anglo-Saxon warrior wouldn't give it up so easily and de Wolfe ended up driving his big boot into the man's thigh to force him to release it. When the warrior faltered, de Wolfe used the mace and slammed it right into his opponent's mouth.

It was enough of a jolt to cause the enemy warrior to fall forward, spewing blood, and de Wolfe used a dagger tucked into his tunic to stab the man in the back of the neck. The enemy fell off the horse, but de Wolfe didn't care in the least. He was more focused on the horse, a fine animal, and he immediately claimed the beast as a spoil of war. He grabbed the reins and raced over towards the edge of the field where the priests and squires were gathered, all of them watching the battle and looking for opportunities to rush in to help their masters. One of de Wolfe's squires, a young man with the surname of le Mon, took the fine Saxon horse as de Wolfe's big, gray wolfhound barked excitedly. Restrained by the squire, the dog was forced to remain as its master whirled around and charged back into the fray.

Even though it was late in the battle and the sun was beginning to wane, chaos didn't even come close to describing what they'd endured for hours upon end. Harold's army had set up a significant shield wall that the Norman's had difficulty penetrating. As the day headed into evening, de Wolfe knew that they were going to have to do something radical to break it. Harold's army was weakened and to not capitalize on their weakness would be foolish. Little by little, the Normans had chipped away at the Anglo-Saxons but their mighty shield wall – literally, a wall of shields to prevent the Normans from dividing their ranks – had held.

The horse de Wolfe had confiscated was his reward after a second failed attempt to break through the shield wall. He'd killed an Anglo-Saxon warrior and stolen his horse, punishing the man for the fact that he and his brethren were so stubborn. At this point, the Norman archers had ceased altogether because they'd used up too much ammunition. So it was now a job for the knights and infantry, and the situation had deteriorated badly. It was only a matter of time now before the shield wall broke down, so de Wolfe went back to the lines, swinging his sword and trying to push through the wall of Anglo-Saxon warriors who had so ably held the line.

"*Gate!*"

Someone was shouting de Wolfe's name and he turned to see Kristoph de Lohr pushing his way through the fighting. The man's horse was badly cut in spite of the leather armor the animal wore, but Kristoph seemed to be whole and unharmed. Gaetan was glad; he and Kristoph were closer than brothers and he considered the man his best friend in the world. They'd fostered together and had been knighted together, and there was a bond between them that was stronger than blood.

Gaetan reined his charger towards Kristoph, the excited war horses coming together and snapping at each other until both Gaetan and Kristoph called the beasts off.

"We should have this shield wall breached shortly," Gaetan shouted over the noisy clamor of men. "Where is the duke?"

Kristoph had to slug his horse in the neck to keep it from snapping at Gaetan. "I do not know," he said, his sky-blue eyes visible beneath his great helm. "That is why I have come to you. You must come with me now!"

Gaetan didn't want to leave the front lines but he knew Kristoph wouldn't have made such a request without a very good reason. Looking around, he spied Aramis de Russe nearby, trying to use the weight of his horse to smash through the shield wall. The Anglo-Saxon warriors on the other side didn't take kindly to that and there was a serious sword fight going on. Gaetan shouted at de Russe.

"Aramis!" he bellowed. *"De Russe!"*

De Russe's helmed head turned in his direction as Gaetan shouted again. "You have command!"

De Russe understood that order all too well and he returned with renewed vigor to the shield wall. Confident the lines were in good hands, Gaetan spurred his horse after Kristoph, who was now racing for the east side of the battlefield, where the flanks were weakening. He caught up to Kristoph.

"What is happening?" he shouted.

Kristoph slowed his horse, but only so he could answer. "Some of de Lara's men broke through the shield wall on this weakened flank," he said, pointing out what Gaetan had been unable to see from his position in the middle. "There is some fighting going on back in the Anglo lines and one of de Lara's men came back to tell me that Harold is dead. He saw him fall to the north, behind the lines."

Gaetan was seized with the news. "Dead?" he repeated. "God's Bloody Bones, let us not waste time. Rally the men! We will break through this flank and see for ourselves!"

Kristoph was already working on it. De Lara had already broken through the lines and Kristoph sent a man for Denis de Winter, who was the closest by location to them. Between de Winter and Kristoph, they managed to rally several hundred men, now pushing through the weakened flank like a great and unstoppable tide.

But Gaetan had already broken through, charging through the Anglo-Saxon lines, swinging his massive sword and slicing through anything that moved. If what Kristoph told him was true and Harold was dead, then Gaetan wanted the body. He wanted the prize to present to the Duke of Normandy, the greatest prize of all, like the Holy Grail of battle. It was what they'd all been fighting for and dying for.

He began to suspect that the rumor might be true when he was suddenly attacked head-on by a swarm of infantry, men rushing him with their spears and short swords. The charge slowed Gaetan down but it didn't stop him completely. He grabbed a particularly well-armed soldier and yanked him up onto his horse, using him as a shield against others who were trying to impale him.

"Where is your king?" Gaetan bellowed, his hand on the back of the man's head, entwined in his hair painfully. "Take me to your king!"

The Anglo-Saxon soldier resisted but, suddenly, Normans were everywhere, like locusts, and the Anglo-Saxon line began to crumble. Men were beaten back as more knights swarmed and Gaetan could see that de Winter and Kristoph were joined by de Moray, Wellesbourne, and several other lesser knights sworn to Normandy. The Angels of War had arrived and the tide of Normans pushed onward, towards the rear of the Anglo-Saxon army, only to be confronted by the encampment beyond and scores of Anglo-Saxon wounded.

They'd reached Harold's rear.

This was where Gaetan had limited patience. He yanked on the hair of the soldier he still held. "Tell me where your king is," he snarled. "Your lines are broken and my men will soon be destroying your wounded. We will destroy everything if you do not tell me where your king is. Tell me now!"

Gaetan spoke in the Anglo-Saxon's language, something his bed-slave, an Anglo-Saxon woman he'd purchased several years ago, had taught him. He was rather fluent in it so he knew the soldier could understand him. But the soldier struggled against him, quite literally fighting for his life.

"I do not know!" the soldier insisted.

It was the wrong answer. Gaetan's grip on the man tightened. "Tell me or I will slit your silly throat and find someone else who will tell me what I wish to know," he said. "Where is your king?"

The man didn't answer him. In fact, he was trying to hurt Gaetan's horse by kicking the animal in the knees as his legs dangled off the ground. Using that sharp dagger again, Gaetan held true to his promise and the dead soldier slithered to the ground with a mortal knife wound in his neck. Now, Gaetan needed another victim and he quickly spied one nearby.

This victim was smaller, lining up a bow and arrow on one of Gaetan's knights. Before the arrow could fly, however, Gaetan grabbed the archer from behind and hauled him onto his horse.

"Tell me where your king is," Gaetan demanded. "If you do not, you will end up dead like many of your comrades. Tell me quickly!"

He had the archer by the throat but the sound that came forth from his captive wasn't that of a man. It was a female, now gasping in fear and anger as a Norman had her by the throat. She started to swing her fists.

"Let me go!" she demanded. "Release me or I will kill you!"

Frankly, Gaetan was shocked that a woman had been in the midst of the battle. It was enough of a shock that he stopped trying to squeeze her throat. "A female?" he said, sounding somewhat incredulous. "What foolish commander allows women to fight?"

She twisted violently and he caught a glimpse of her face; dressed as an archer as she was, including a cap, at a distance she could very easily be mistaken for a boy but now that he was close to her, he could see that she was no boy. In fact, her features were quite exquisite.

"I can kill you just as easily as a man can," she hissed. "Let me go and I will give you a fair fight, *poubelle*."

She'd called him rubbish in his own language, which was definitely an insult. She wanted to anger him. The trouble was that he found her challenge rather humorous.

"It would be a two-hit fight," he told her drolly. "I would hit you and you would hit the ground. Now, where is your king? Tell me and I shall show mercy."

"I will tell you nothing!"

"You are brave for a skinny little mouse."

That comment seemed to infuriate her, which amused him. She was in a frantic state between terror and rage, but Gaetan had her over his saddle so that she couldn't move very well and couldn't get to any weapons she might have on her body. Every time she tried to rise, he would slam her head down again. The second time, he'd hit her rather hard and stars had danced before her eyes. The third time, he'd slapped her on the arse and she'd bellowed unhappily. Then came de Lara aboard his bloodied charger.

"*Gate!*" he shouted. "With me!"

A command from Luc de Lara wasn't meant to be questioned. Gaetan tossed the woman over the side of his horse, listening to her grunt as she landed in a heap.

"Not this time, little mouse," he told her, perhaps with a bit of taunt in his tone. "This time, you are spared. Remember Norman mercy the next time you intend to do one of us harm."

As she sat up, rubbing her shoulder where she'd hit the ground, Gaetan spun his horse around and took off after Luc. Quickly, he reached the man's side.

"Kristoph said that Harold has been killed," Gaetan said. "Is there truth in this?"

Luc simply motioned to Gaetan to follow and the two of them skirted part of the Anglo-Saxon encampment to where a contingent of Normans stood in a cluster, fighting off Anglo-Saxon soldiers who were trying to get through them. It was clear that they were guarding something and Gaetan followed Luc as the man pushed through the soldiers only to be confronted by a man on the ground and several others standing over him. Luc dismounted swiftly, followed by Gaetan, and they pushed through the crowd.

"There," Luc said, pointing to the man on the ground. "This has been identified as Harold Godwinson."

Gaetan could only see the legs at that point. "By whom?" he asked.

Luc looked at the Anglo-Saxon soldiers who were trying to fight through the Normans to get to the corpse. "An Anglo-Saxon knight identified him to me right before he took his own life. I am not sure if he was a personal guard to Harold and failed at his duty to protect the man, but it is evident that he no longer wished to live in light of his king's death."

Extreme if not understandable behavior, Gaetan thought, but he wasn't entirely convinced. He shifted positions so he could gain a better look at the body. It was of an older man, well-dressed and well-fed, but that was where any semblance of identification ended. There was nothing on the man that would give an indication as to who he was, no belts or vests or colors.

The corpse had an arrow shaft sticking out of the left eye and the face was battered in general, muddied and grossly swollen. The body looked as if it had been tossed onto the ground because it was lying in a strange position. All around it, men were still fighting. As Gaetan watched, someone even kicked the corpse in the head.

Enraged, Gaetan pushed in to stand guard over the body, broadsword in hand as he leveled it at some of the Anglo-Saxons who were trying to push through his men. But that action didn't seem to do much because men were still struggling against him. So he reached out a long arm, grabbing the first enemy soldier who came near him. Snatching the man by the hair, he dragged him into the center of the circle of tussling men, pointing his sword to the battered corpse.

"Who is this?" he demanded to the man in his language. "Do you fight to regain your king?"

The Anglo-Saxon soldier was torn between panic and defiance. "He is not meant for you," he said, spittle dripping from his lips. "Have you not done enough? Give him to us so that we may properly bury him."

"*Who* is this?"

The soldier faltered, terrified. "Please...."

"Answer me!"

The soldier tried to speak but he vomited instead. Something spewed from his mouth, but Gaetan didn't let go. His eyes narrowed. "I will ask you one question. If you do not give me a truthful answer, then I will kill you. Is this Harold?"

The man closed his eyes, trying not to look at the corpse, but Gaetan had him by the hair. When he yanked, the soldier seemed to lose whatever resistance he had left in his body. More vomit leaked from his mouth, so much so that Gaetan hardly heard his answer.

"Aye."

That was all Gaetan needed to hear. He had the confirmation that he sought and he let the man go, watching him as he stumbled away. There was something triumphant in that softly uttered reply, that painfully spoken word. As Gaetan stood there with de Lara and de Winter, a great cry rose up as a charge of men suddenly swarmed around them, cavalry on horseback led by de Russe, Wellesbourne, St. Hèver, and de Moray.

It was clear that the Normans had broken through the shield wall. There were hundreds of foot soldiers with them as well as hundreds of men on horseback, all of them yelling and hacking and killing anything that wasn't Norman. The wounded were being slaughtered and a hastily-erected encampment, set up when the Anglo-Saxon army arrived for the battle, was being demolished. The end of the battle was near and Normans, fed by exhaustion, could smell victory in the air, a mixture of blood and rot and the very earth they stood upon.

The earth of the country that would soon belong to them.

Gaetan could smell the victory, too. He watched the madness as the Normans swarmed and he could see many Anglo-Saxons fleeing angry Norman swords. The sense of triumph he felt was so great that it nearly weakened him, a complete sense of victory encompassing every bone in his body with relief and delight. Even the Anglo-Saxons who had been struggling around their dead king's body in an attempt to claim it were running off, terrified they were about to be cut down. All around him, the army of England was fracturing.

"Victory, my lord," Luc said quietly, watching the same retreat that Gaetan was watching. "This battle is over."

Gaetan nodded his head slowly, his focus on the Anglo-Saxon withdrawal. "God was with us this day," he said. Then, his gaze moved to the body at his feet. "And Harold is ours. God's Bones, I'd hoped for this ending but did not truly expect it. Yet, the reality is before me. Where is Normandy?"

Denis de Winter was standing on his other side. "The last I saw the duke, he was fighting on the far right flank with du Reims," he said. "I do not know where he is now."

"Find him," Gaetan commanded quietly.

As Denis headed off, Lance de Reyne suddenly emerged through the crowds of dying and surrendering men. He was leading his horse, who had a terrible gash on his left foreleg. De Reyne had been part of the charge that had broken through the shield wall and his horse showed the evidence of the difficult fight. Wearily, Lance came to a pause, pulling his helm off and raking a gloved hand through his dark hair. Exhaustion radiated off of him but, like a true professional, he refused to give in to it. He would remain strong until it was no longer needed.

"There are more nobles dead, Gate," he said. "Two captured soldiers have identified them as Gyrth and Leofwine, brothers to Harold."

Gaetan's sense of satisfaction grew. "Where are they?"

Lance threw a thumb over his shoulder. "Not far from here," he said. "They were among the wounded."

"Executed by our men?"

"Trampled."

Gaetan felt no remorse. Such were the perils of war. "Excellent," he said. "Then there will be no brothers left to avenge the king and contest the duke's throne. With Harold dead, William is now the King of England. We have accomplished our goal, good lords. Take satisfaction in your success."

It was a simple statement but one of great impact. The first true battle that Normans had faced against Harold Godwinson on English soil had resulted in what they'd hoped for but hadn't truly expected. Such a complete victory could have only been supported by God. At least, that's the way Gaetan looked at it.

Even so, he knew there was much more to do before the battle was officially over and the prize at his feet was something that needed to be protected. He motioned to Luc and Lance.

"Wrap him up and return him to camp," he said. "I want one of you to remain with the body. It is too important to leave unguarded. Meanwhile, I will find Normandy and tell him of our great prize."

Luc and Lance nodded and began to tend to the body, looking for some section of cloth or tunic left upon the field of battle to wrap him up in. Luc, seeing the squires and priests hovering over near the edge of the battlefield to the east, sent a soldier running for one of the priests that had been following the *Anges de Guerre*, a fighting priest known as Jathan. He was a big man, with a crown of red hair, and he managed de Wolfe's squires and pages as well as served in a religious capacity to all of de Wolfe's knights. These days, men accomplished many tasks in the service of Warwolfe and Jathan had proven himself a valuable asset.

Gaetan noted that his priest and two squires, including le Mon, were heading in his direction but he was more interested in mounting his horse and finding the duke. As he swung himself up into the saddle, he began to look around, making note of his men as he could see them. Although the battlefield was a vast place, it was his usual habit to take a head count of his men to ensure they were all whole and sound. They had all attended many battles together and, by the grace of God, had emerged unscathed. Gaetan, a particularly religious man, said many a prayer for such blessings.

De Lara, de Winter, and de Reyne were accounted for. He had seen de Moray, Wellesbourne, St. Hèver, and de Russe as they continued to move through the destroyed Anglo-Saxon lines, subduing pockets of fighting. Du Reims was the only one he hadn't seen because he was somewhere off to the west with the duke, so Gaetan didn't worry over him. He knew he would see Téo soon enough. He'd seen de Lohr earlier, as well, and but a perusal of the area showed that Kristoph was nowhere to be found. Before Gaetan spurred his horse off to the west, he turned to Luc and Lance.

"Where is Kristoph?" he asked. "He was right behind me when we broke through the eastern flank. Where has he gone?"

Luc and Lance were in the process of wrapping up Harold's body with a cloak that Jathan had been wearing. It was the priest who spoke.

"I have not seen him, Gaetan," he said, looking around as the knights handled the battered body.

Gaetan was looking off to the south where part of the Norman army still lingered and the encampment beyond. "You did not see him ride away?"

Jathan shook his head, his fat jowls trembling. "Nay, I did not. Shall I send a man for him?"

Gaetan's gaze moved over the field of battle for a moment longer before shaking his head. "Nay," he replied. "He is around here, somewhere."

Jathan simply nodded his head and bent over to help the knights with the corpse. Gaetan, with thoughts of de Lohr quickly fading, headed off to the west where William, the Duke of Normandy, would be told that Harold was dead and that he was now king.

Normandy wasn't difficult to find, in fact. He and Téo were found deep in the Anglo-Saxon encampment rounding up prisoners, a task that Gaetan helped with after he delivered his important news. Oddly enough, the duke wasn't willing to believe his Warwolfe until he saw Harold's body, which was much later in the evening when the battle had ended for the most part and the Norman army trickled back to camp.

It was almost a ceremonial event, this viewing of Harold's body. It took place in a dim tent belonging to de Winter, a body wrapped in Normandy's colors that, when unwrapped, revealed a gruesome sight. As the *Anges de Guerre* and the duke's Companions gathered around in the cold dark tent, William grimly viewed the body of Harold Godwinson and, as such, declared himself king on that very night. It was a night for celebration, for rest and reflection, but for Gaetan, it became a night that would change the course of his life.

Kristoph de Lohr did not return to camp that night. When morning came and he'd still not returned, it became apparent that he was either dead or otherwise missing. The dreadful news began to spread over the duke's camp, the news that no fighting man wanted to hear. They'd brought ten great knights with them to England, men who were the greatest warriors of them all, but now only nine were accounted for.

One *Anges de Guerre* had been lost.

CHAPTER TWO

☙

I MET MY END BRAVELY

THEY'D BEATEN THE Norman knight fairly severely, so much so that she ended up covering the man with her body and chasing away those who were trying to kill him. Although she never thought she would have protected a Norman knight, there was something in her that simply couldn't stand by and watch it happen. When some of her brethren began aiming clubs at the knight's head, she covered his bare head with her arms.

"Enough!" the woman ordered. "You will not kill him!"

She had to fight off those who refused to listen to her, but men who knew and respected her called off those unwilling to obey her command. Slowly, the violence eased and they all stood around, looking at her as she literally lay upon the injured Norman knight to protect him. But still, the men were edgy. It was the end of a most important day and they were all still riding high on the scent of battle.

It had only been a few hours earlier in the battle against the Normans when the rumor began to spread quickly through the Anglo-Saxon ranks that Harold had been killed by a Norman arrow. He'd been close to the lines at the time and when he fell, wounded, he'd been trampled by his own men. It had been a chaotic scene as some of his advisors tried to carry him away, shielding him from the soldiers because they knew that once it was known that Harold had been killed, the Anglo-Saxon army would lose faith and fracture.

Unfortunately, that was exactly what had happened even as some of Harold's army still tried to fight back and hold off the Norman tide. But the shield wall had failed and the Normans broke through, many of them swarming right to the spot where Harold had lain. And the Norman knight on the ground....

He'd been one of those who had seen Harold's body and had called forth more Normans to partake in the triumph of a fallen king. He'd been a well-armed, powerful knight, but as he moved about, confident in a Norman victory, he'd made a terrible mistake – he'd traveled alone and without the company of others. He seemed more intent to linger near the Anglo-Saxon lines that were breaking up. For the Anglo-Saxons fleeing the battlefield, the lone Norman knight had been a target of their vengeance.

Knocked off his horse by a nasty club strike to the back of the head, they'd tied the unconscious knight to a horse by his leg and dragged him away as they'd fled. Now, they were several miles to the west in a vast and dense forest, regrouping with some of their dispirited army. The Norman knight was on the ground, dazed, as men took their rage out on him.

But the woman had stopped them.

Even now as she lay sprawled over him, she'd taken a few blows from her own men who had refused to heed her command. An older soldier, seasoned and trying to gain control of the others, held back some of the more aggressive men.

"He is our enemy, Ghislaine," he said in a calm, even tone. "You cannot prevent what must come about. The men must know some satisfaction on this night."

Ghislaine pulchra ancilla Merciae, or Ghislaine, The Beautiful Maid of Mercia, and sister to Edwin, Earl of Mercia, didn't move from her position over the wounded knight. She knew the men wouldn't strike as long as she was there but, in all honestly, she couldn't understand why she wasn't joining them in their rage. She'd been at the battle from the beginning and she, too, held hatred in her heart for the Normans. But there was something about this situation that spoke to her of something beyond a captured Norman knight.

There was an opportunity here.

"His death would be momentary satisfaction only," she said. "None of you realize that this man is of value to us. Do you not understand? You captured him to kill him but you must not do that – he knows the Norman ways. They are upon our shores and our king has been killed this night. Are you too foolish to realize that he may be of use for our very survival?"

It was very dark in the trees, the shadows from the moon barely piercing the canopy as dozens, if not hundreds, of men lingered below, beaten and bloodied from a day of battle against the Norman invaders. They were also confused and dazed. Even as Ghislaine spoke, the men surrounding her and the injured knight didn't seem to grasp what she was suggesting.

"I would rather feel the satisfaction of his head upon my sword!" one of the men snarled as the others around him agreed.

But Ghislaine shook her head. "Nay," she stressed. "He is of more value to us alive."

"The only valuable Norman is a dead one!"

Men shouted in agreement but Ghislaine put up a hand to plead for understanding. "Killing him would accomplish nothing! We would only be harming ourselves in the end! Can you not see how valuable he could be?"

"He is our enemy, Ghislaine."

The voice came from the darkness. Then, a slender man with a massive scar across his face running from his left temple, across his nose, and ending by the right side of his jaw pushed through the men standing about. When he made an appearance, everyone seemed to fall quiet; where anger and revenge had reflected in men's expressions, now there was uncertainty. *Fear.* Even Ghislaine's features changed at the sight; there was fear there but she was trying not to show it.

At that moment, the mood in the agitated circle of men seemed to plummet.

"Alary," she said calmly. "Greetings, Brother. God has been merciful that you have survived the battle."

Alary of Mercia, a brother to both Ghislaine and Earl Edwin, surveyed the group of men standing around before finally coming to rest on his sister, still spread out over the injured knight. His dark eyes narrowed.

"Aye, I survived," he said. He began to pace a slow circle around his sister and the crumpled knight. "I survived when our good king did not. Why I should be spared and Harold should die, I will never know. God is, mayhap, not favoring the faithful on this night. And you, my sister? I thought you hated the Normans as we all did. Why do you protect this knight?"

Ghislaine eyed her brother until he wandered out of her sight; she didn't like the fact that he was behind her now. Alary was unpredictable at best, an edgy sadist with a brutal streak, so much so that their brother, Edwin, had exiled him from the royal stronghold of Tamworth last year. Too much disobedience on Alary's part and an incident that saw one of Edwin's favorite knights killed had warranted such a reaction. If evil had a name and a face, both belonged to Alary of Mercia. *Alary Obscurum*, he was known.

Alary the Dark.

"I am not protecting him," she said, feeling fearful of her brother even as she said it. "But we should think twice before using him as an object of vengeance. He looks to be a very fine knight. Mayhap, we could ransom him to Normandy or even back to his own family. Mayhap, he even knows of Normandy's plans. Certainly, we should consider such things before the men run him through and we lose any chance we have of understanding Normandy's intentions. He *could* be valuable."

Alary had wandered into her line of sight again. He stood there, looking down at her, and it made Ghislaine very nervous. Undoubtedly, her brother was considering what she'd said but, knowing him, there was some grisly twist to it all. She'd seen what the man could do to his enemies. Therefore, she braced herself.

"That is a very astute observation," Alary finally said. "Can the knight speak for himself? Remove yourself, Ghislaine. No one will hurt the knight. I wish to speak with him."

Ghislaine didn't trust her brother. He'd been known to break bonds before and had a history of telling mistruths to those around him. Still, she couldn't lay on the knight forever so she shifted her body, cautiously climbing off the man. He was crumpled on his side, his dark blonde hair matted with dirt and blood. She remained beside him, bending down to get a look at his face in the darkness.

Truthfully, she couldn't even tell if he was conscious. She peered closer to his face, catching a glimmer of his eyeballs in the darkness.

He was awake.

"What is your name?" she asked him in his language, something she had learned at her parents' insistence because it was the common language of many people in England. "Do not be afraid. Tell me your name."

In the darkness, the knight blinked. "You speak my language."

"I do. Answer me. What is your name?"

"De Lohr."

His voice sounded tight, as he was in pain. Ghislaine rocked back on her heels, turning to her brother. "His name is de Lohr," she said. "What would you ask him?"

Alary moved closer, bending over to get a look at the knight. "I want to know a great many things," he said. "Move away. I would speak with him alone."

Ghislaine shook her head. "I will not," she said. "I do not trust you not to kill him."

Alary's expression tightened and he reached down, grabbing her roughly by the shoulder. "I told you to go."

Ghislaine balled a fist and hit his hand away, hard. "He is *my* prisoner," she declared. "I brought him here. I saved him from death. If you want to speak with him, then do it, but I will not leave."

Alary was exasperated. "Why are you so protective of him? What is he to you?"

His question brought her building rage to a halt because it was something she didn't have a ready answer for. She had a myriad of theories, but no hard truths. Her gaze moved from her brother to the knight, who was looking at her steadily – with resignation. He knew his fate was in her hands. She was his only protection against the mob and he knew it. Why *was* she so protective of him?

Remember Norman mercy the next time you intend to do one of us harm.

Something that big, nasty Norman knight had said to her when he had captured her and demanded to know of her king's fate. He could have killed her but he hadn't and he'd reminded her of that fragile mercy. Therefore, his statement remained with her, whether or not she wanted it to.

Now, it was a matter of honor… in the same situation, would she show mercy also?

Perhaps, that was the real truth behind her protection of the injured knight.

"This man is nothing to me," she said for all to hear, torn between defiance and embarrassment. "But one of this knight's brethren captured me during the battle and could have easily killed me. Yet, he spared my life and he told me to remember Norman mercy. Because of him, I will protect this knight because I always pay my debts. It is a matter of honor now – my life was spared and so shall this man's be. He is to be untouched as long as I have breath in my body."

The men around her understood such a debt. They were warriors, all of them, and mercy was that rare and precious quality that often times was the true test of honor in battle. Ghislaine of Mercia was a warrior woman, raised with her brothers to fight and to protect their lands and people.

When Harold brought his army south, Ghislaine's brother, Earl Edwin, had been far to the north so Ghislaine and the outcast Alary had joined Harold's army to meet the Norman invasion. They were warriors from generations of warriors, born and bred, and that was why she was here – a strong woman who commanded respect from the men around her. And because she was a warrior, she had the capacity to understand what honor and sacrifice meant.

I always pay my debts. She was paying it upon the cause of a wounded Norman knight.

But Alary was different. He didn't understand much beyond his own selfish wants; glory for himself, wealth for himself, and an undying jealousy of his elder brothers' status – he had two elder brothers who were both earls: Edwin of Mercia and Morcar of Northumbria. But Alary the Dark was nothing; perhaps he had hoped that supporting Harold against the Norman invasion would somehow prove to the king that he was worthy of such titles as his brothers held. But after this day, that was not to be and the sting of disappointment was a powerful thing in Alary's heart.

Therefore, he wasn't pleased with his sister's refusal to turn the Norman knight over to him. Without another word, he stomped off into the darkness, taking some of the men with him. Only a few lingered now but with the declaration of Ghislaine's merciful intentions, there wasn't much reason for them to hang around the Norman knight. He was too injured to escape and even if he tried, they could easily catch him. Therefore, they started to move away in a disgruntled weary group.

Ghislaine suspected what the men were thinking and she further suspected that her brother's departure was not permanent. He knew they had a valuable asset in the Norman knight and, greedy as he was, she knew he would be back. But at least for the moment, she could breathe without his ominous presence. She leaned over the knight once more.

"How badly injured are you?" she asked. "Can you move your limbs?"

Kristoph couldn't see much of the woman who was hovering over him, but her voice had a silky quality that was deceptively comforting. Could he move his limbs? He really had no idea. He hadn't tried. He'd rolled himself into a ball once they'd untied him from the horse that had dragged him over miles of rocks and bramble, and that was where he remained. Fortunately, he was wearing mail and protection so he was fairly certain the damage to his skin was minimal. But he'd lost his helm somewhere along the way and his head was painful and swimming. So was the leg they'd tied the rope to. Gingerly, he extended both legs to feel for breaks or damage.

"I seem to be able to," he said, now moving his arms slowly. He ended up flat on his back, gazing up at the dark canopy above and a glimmer of stars beyond that. "But it is difficult to breathe. I may have broken something when I fell off my horse."

Ghislaine looked at the man. He was very big and she could see the size of his arms and thighs even through the heavy padding and clothing he wore. It wasn't much different from what her army wore, but it was better made. The Normans had the latest in armor and protection, but that kind of thing was expensive. The man had money or he came from money, because the protection he wore was very fine.

"Then I will have a healer tend to you," she said, "but I cannot promise it will be any time soon. We have a great deal of wounded."

The knight didn't say anything for a moment, staring blankly up at the sky above. "Where is my horse?"

"I do not know."

"My sword. It was sheathed on my saddle."

"I do not know where your horse or your sword are, but I am sure they are both the spoils of war for one of our soldiers. I would not worry over either if I were you. I would worry about myself."

That was not unreasonable advice. Kristoph knew as much but, still, he had to ask. His head lolled in her direction.

"A pity," he said. "I was rather fond of that horse and the sword... my father gave it to me when I was knighted many years ago. I shall miss them both."

Ghislaine's gaze lingered on him a moment. "Then, mayhap, you should not have come to take our country," she said. "Had you remained on your own shores, you would not have lost either one."

He lifted his eyebrows, slowly, as if she had just said something he more or less agreed with. His eyes left her face, moving down her body, seeing that she, too, was wearing heavy protection but on a smaller scale, built for her woman's body. She was dressed like a warrior.

"Much as you have done, I, too, follow my king," he said quietly, not commenting on the fact that she was dressed like a man. "If it makes you feel any better, my wife did not wish for me to come, either."

"You are married?"

"Aye," he said, his expression softening, even in the dim light. "A woman with skin like cream and hair the color of coal. The angel of my heart. She gives the commands and I obey. But on this occasion, I could not. I was duty-bound to follow my king. She will not be pleased that I have managed to throw myself into the arms of the enemy."

Ghislaine thought on a Norman woman with pale skin and black hair who was now missing her husband, only she didn't know it yet. It made Ghislaine think on her own husband, lost in a shipwreck two years ago. He had been traveling with the king to Ponthieu when the ship had run aground. Her sweet Hakon had drown in the ensuing chaos, only three months into their marriage which had been a very pleasant one.

Ghislaine well remembered the grief from that loss, now fighting off the guilt that some woman she did not know would soon be facing the same thing. She should have turned away from the conversation at this point, unwilling to come to know the Norman knight beyond his hated loyalties. But some deep-seated pity in her now had her seeing the knight not as an enemy but as a man. He had a wife, the angel of his heart.

He knew love.

"Then I will repeat that you should not have come to our country," she said, trying to fight off any compassion she might be feeling towards him. "You should have listened to her."

Kristoph could hear the sharpness in her tone, but it was hollow, as if she didn't really mean it. He had been a warrior long enough to know sympathy when he heard it and he knew very well that this female warrior was the only thing that stood between him and a thousand men who wanted to kill him. He didn't want to anger her, but he needed her loyalty. If there was any chance of him coming out of this alive, he needed her on his side.

"You are right. I should have," he said. "I regret that I did not. Her name is Adalie, in fact. She bore my daughter last year and she was quite disappointed that it was not a son, but I was not disappointed. I was glad to have a daughter who looks just like her mother. You have never seen a more beautiful girl-child with black hair and blue eyes. She will be quite beautiful when she grows up. I... I was hoping to be there when she did."

He was being manipulative now, hoping that the female warrior would feel great sympathy for him with a child he wanted to see grow up. It was a desperate move on his part, but the situation called for it. He couldn't see her face in the darkness now because she had turned away from him. It was a few moments before she replied.

"If that is true, then you should not have left her," she finally said. "You did not need to come here with your army. This country already has a king and now he is dead because of you and your men. What about his wife and children? Did you think of them before you tried to kill him?"

Kristoph could hear the strain in her voice. "Nay," he said quietly, but with honesty. "No one ever thinks on the family of their enemies. But at this moment, my family is the most important thing in the world to me – a wife I love and a daughter I adore. I want to see them again, my lady. Will you not help me?"

Ghislaine turned to him, then. She hissed sharply, shaking her head. "I spared your life because one of your fellow knights spared mine," she said. "Do not ask for more than that."

Kristoph had heard that story as he'd lain upon the ground, balled up and in pain. He'd heard her speak of the knight who had shown her "Norman mercy" and he'd heard that she believed she was paying back a debt in protecting him from her angry kinsmen. But he wanted more than a sense of duty; he wanted help.

"Then what do you plan to do with me?" he asked.

She stared at him a moment before looking away. "If you want to stay alive, I suggest you be as complacent and pleasing as you can possibly be. If someone asks you for information on the Norman army, then you will answer truthfully. The moment you cease to become of value is the moment someone will slit your throat. The only way to stay alive will be by cooperating."

In the darkness, he sighed faintly as he understood what she was telling him. "I will not betray my men," he said softly.

"No one said anything about betraying your men. But if I were you, I would do all I could to ensure that I survived to return to Adalie and your blue-eyed daughter. Are they not worth it?"

Just as he had tried to manipulate her, now she was turning the tables on him. Kristoph was astute enough to realize that and he fought off a smile at a lady who would turn the tables on him. She was cleverer than he gave her credit for.

"They are," he said. He continued to watch her in the darkness, thinking of another angle to take in their conversation. Maybe if he tried to establish a personal relationship with her.... "May I ask your name, my lady? We have had a rather long conversation and I fear that we have not been properly introduced."

She wouldn't look at him when she spoke because there was only a hair's-width separating her from truly sympathizing with him. "Ghislaine," she said, "but I suggest you not use it in front of my men.

They will not take kindly to hearing my name from your lips."

"Ghislaine," he murmured. *GIZ-lain*. "It is a lovely name. Have you always fought with the army, Ghislaine?"

She nodded. "As long as I can recall," she said. Then, she turned to look at him. "Before you ask me any more questions, I will tell you that one of my brothers is the Earl of Mercia and another is the Earl of Northumbria. If you were conscious when you heard me speak to a man named Alary, that is also a brother, but he is a demon who walks the earth in a man's skin. He is wicked and devious, so you must beware of him. I have a feeling he will be back and if he truly wants you, it will be difficult to stop him."

Kristoph had, indeed, heard her speaking to a man with a voice that was low and gritty, like rocks grating against stone. He appreciated that she had pointed out a serious danger to him but in his condition, there wasn't much he could do about it. If Alary wanted him, it wasn't as if he could fight back.

Groaning softly, he rolled to his side and slowly sat up, feeling every ache and every stab of pain in his battered body. His head was throbbing and he winced as he sat there a moment, trying to catch his breath.

"Ghislaine, if I may speak plainly," he said, resisting the urge to put a hand to his aching head. "I am not part of the Duke of Normandy's inner circle. I do not know of his plans or even of his operations. I can tell you his strengths and how many men he carries, but you could see that for yourself today. I am afraid that if your men intend to interrogate me, they will be terribly disappointed. If... if I promise to return home to my wife and stay there, will you please let me go?"

Ghislaine looked at him. He sounded sincere, but it was equally possible that he was lying to her. He was finely dressed and she knew he had money, which meant that he more than likely was more to the Norman duke than he said he was.

"Go?" she repeated. "Go where? Do you even know where you are?"

"You could tell me."

She almost considered it. Ghislaine was having visions of a young mother being informed that her husband was never to return and the same feelings she felt at Hakon's death began to swamp her. But she resisted them with all her might.

He is the enemy!

"I cannot let you go," she said. "If you are captured a second time, I will not be able to protect you. The men will beat you to death."

Kristoph knew that was probably true and he struggled not to feel some desperation in his situation. "They are going to kill me anyway when they realize I cannot tell them anything they want to know," he said. "At least I would have a fighting chance if you let me run. For my wife and daughter's sake, will you not do that?"

Now he was bringing the wife and child into the conversation again. She was starting to grow irritated.

"I do not care for your wife or daughter," she snapped. "They are my enemy, as are you. Stop asking me for favors which are not mine to give. You wielded a sword against my countrymen and now you are our prisoner. Accept your fate as an honorable man would and stop trying to play upon my sympathies."

So, she knew what he was up to. Kristoph could see that he'd offended her. Even so, it was a chance he'd had to take. He was coming to realize that, in all likelihood, he would never again see his wife or daughter and he began to feel sick inside. God help him, his life was in the hands of people whose king had just been killed by his comrades. He'd been part of the murder.

He knew that Death was coming for him, too.

"If I have offended you, then I am sorry," he said quietly, sincerely. "And for protecting me against your soldiers... you have my deepest gratitude. I realize you have risked yourself for me and I am most appreciative."

Somewhere off in the darkness, the could hear men's voices. At first, the discussion was quiet for the most part but it soon began to grow in intensity. Moreover, the voices were growing closer as men with torches were now moving through the trees. It didn't take a skilled eye to know that they were heading in their direction.

Ghislaine could see the torches moving through the darkness, growing brighter and brighter, and a sense of foreboding filled her. She knew that Alary's departure had been temporary but what she hadn't counted on was that he would return so soon. She was hoping he would at least stay away until morning. She turned to Kristoph.

"Remember what I told you," she said. "Answer their questions or they will not hesitate to kill you. Do not try to be clever and do not lie; tell them what they need to know and you may yet live through this."

Kristoph was watching the torches grow closer, too. He was certain that he was watching the beginning of his end and it was difficult to suppress his knightly instincts. These men were his sworn enemy and fighting against them was as natural as breathing. But that same thought came the realization that he was in no condition to fight off a mob. He had no weapons and, from the pain in his chest and shoulder area, he was certain he'd broken a rib or two. While there was still time, he turned to Ghislaine.

"My name is Kristoph de Lohr," he said, his voice low. "My home is in Brittany, south of Rennes in a village called Lohréac. I serve Gaetan de Wolfe. I do not ask you to risk yourself any more than you have already. But if something happens to me, I want someone to know of my ending. You are a brave and gallant lady, and I shall never forget your kindness to me. Mayhap someday, you will send Gaetan a missive and tell him what became of me so that he can tell my wife. I hope that you will tell him that I met my end bravely, for that is what I intend to do."

Ghislaine could see the steely resolve in his eyes, even in the darkness. He wasn't afraid of what was coming, not in the least. In spite of her resistance to him, that resolve greatly impressed her. Not only were Normans capable of mercy, but they were capable of great courage as well.

As the mob with torches grew closer, Ghislaine began to regret that she hadn't let de Lohr run as he'd asked. Perhaps he could have gotten away; perhaps not. Now, they would never know, for as the mob came into view through the weak moonlight, she could see Alary at the head of it.

That could only mean trouble.

Now, that brave Norman knight would never see his black-haired wife again or the daughter with the pretty blue eyes. He would soon be dead all because Ghislaine hadn't shown enough mercy to spare his life. Now, she was starting to question every decision she'd made until this point where it pertained to de Lohr. A man's life had been in her hands and she'd failed him.

She'd failed her sense of mercy.

"I see the prisoner is well enough to sit up," Alary said as he came upon them, flanked by many men. "That is good. We will make use of him."

Before Ghislaine could ask what that meant, Alary snapped his fingers to his men and they swarmed on Kristoph, throwing him back to the ground and using hemp rope to bind his arms and legs. From what Ghislaine could see, he wasn't struggling but they were being very rough with him. When she leapt to her feet to try and protect him, Alary intervened and pulled her away, restraining her while his men trussed up de Lohr and carried him off into the darkness.

"Wait!" Ghislaine demanded. "Where are you taking him? I told you that he was more valuable alive! What are you doing?"

Alary still had hold of his fairly strong sister. "I am not going to kill him," he assured her. "At least, not yet. You were correct when you said he will be valuable to our cause. I am going to see just how much the man knows of the Normans and their plans for our country."

Ghislaine tried to follow the men who were carrying Kristoph away but Alary had a grip on her. "An abused man will be a burden," she said, finally yanking herself out of her brother's grasp. "If you hurt him, he will be of no use at all."

Alary cocked an eyebrow at his sister. "Watch your manner of loyalty, little sister," he said, a hint of threat in his tone. "If one did not know better, one might suspect you to have sided with the Normans. Is that why they were able to defeat us? Because they had information on our weaknesses from someone who knew of our movements?"

Ghislaine's blood ran cold and she yanked her wrist from her brother's grasp, bringing up the other hand to strike him squarely across the face. But Alary was fast and he was able to block her strike, but just barely. She managed to scratch his chin. Ghislaine glared at him.

"I will never hear such an insinuation come from your mouth again," she hissed. "I no more contributed to the Norman victory than you did. But in my case, at least I tried to prevent it while you remained at the rear of the army, letting your men go forth to do the fighting in your stead."

As he insulted her, she insulted him even deeper. Alary's jaw hardened as he faced off against her.

"I will pretend I did not hear you say that," he said. "Watch yourself, little sister. Your protection of the Norman knight does not please anyone here. Word may get back to Edwin."

"As word of your lack of action may get back to him as well. Do not threaten me, Alary. You cannot best me."

Alary cocked an eyebrow. "We shall see," he said, stepping back from her, out of striking range. His sister was a warrior at heart and she was not afraid to attack him and, truth be told, he had a healthy respect for her because, at times, she could be just as unpredictable as he could. "After I am finished interrogating your Norman friend, I shall take him back with me to Tenebris."

Tenebris was a hunting lodge used by the Mercian kings but since Edwin had exiled Alary, it was now the place where the dark brother lived. In the wilds west of Kidderminster and located in an area known as the Far Forest, it was a place that most men avoided now. It had a reputation of darkness and debauchery. Ghislaine knew that if her brother took the knight to Tenebris, no one would ever see the man again.

I would like to see my wife and daughter again.

If de Lohr went to Tenebris, that would not happen.

"And do what with him?" Ghislaine wanted to know, hating herself for sounding as if she cared. "He is my prisoner. I told you that. You have no right to take him with you."

Alary grinned. "Little Ghislaine and her prize," he mocked. "Thank you for capturing the knight. Now I shall take him from you. If you want him back, then your men will have to fight my men for him. I think my men want him more, eh?"

Ghislaine's general attitude towards her brother was one of disdain but there were occasions when she genuinely hated him. This was one of those times. He was teasing her, trying to bait her, and it was difficult not to respond to it. He'd been doing it all their lives and the brother/sister dynamic could be more emotional than most.

"If that is your wish, then I shall order my men to retake him," she said, trembling because she was so angry. "And when they are done defeating your men, I will have them go after you."

Alary was smug in his stance. Before the situation grew out of hand, he went to the truth of the matter. "Let me be plain, little sister," he said. "If you send your men to take him, I will kill him before they can do it and that will be the end of your prize. If you do not wish him harmed, then it would be better if you did not try."

Ghislaine knew it was not a threat. This dark and hateful man would shove a dagger between the Norman knight's ribs purely out of spite, because he would not want his sister to have him and for no other reason than that. The knight would cease to be a captive at that point and simply become a possession. Therefore, the hatred in her heart towards her brother was building.

"Why would you do this?" she demanded, frustrated. "I told you that a Norman spared my life, which is why I spared the knight's. I told you that he was my prisoner. You have no right to take him."

Alary was moving away from her now, heading in the direction his men had taken the Norman knight. "Yet I *have* taken him," he pointed out, taunting. "Come for him if you wish. I will kill him before I surrender him to you."

Ghislaine watched him as he went. "Edwin shall know of what you've done."

It was meant to be a threat but Alary simply shrugged, turning and heading off into the darkness. Her threat had no meaning to him.

Even after he was gone, there was a stench in the air that suggested his evilness had not left at all. It was still there, all around her, his gloating victory in taking her prisoner from her. Infuriated, it was all Ghislaine could do to keep from shouting in anger. She had a bow and a quiver of arrows slung over her back. Had there been any light, she would have sailed one of those deadly darts right into her brother's back and felt no remorse at all. He'd taken what belonged to her.

The Norman knight.

Now, she was thinking of him, the big warrior from across the sea. *Norman knight.* Damn the man. She knew his name now and she knew he had a family; a wife and child he adored. He'd asked her to let him go and she'd refused. Now, he was in Alary's hands and that more than likely would mean his death. Tenebris... indeed, it would mean his death.

Ghislaine could hear sounds in the direction the knight had been taken. There were a pair of fires in the darkness, cooking fires for men to warm a meal out of whatever supplies they happened to have. Not strangely, she could hear what sounded like a fight because there was a good deal of thumping and slapping going on. Men were laughing. It didn't take much imagination to realize that they were beating the Norman knight again, probably because Alary told them to.

De Lohr, his name had been. Regardless of Alary's threat, Ghislaine couldn't let them beat the man to death. She was compelled to protect him again.

As she headed over in the direction of the noise, her thoughts turned to what de Lohr had told her. *Mayhap someday, you will send Gaetan a missive and tell him what became of me so that he can tell my wife. I hope that you will tell him that I met my end bravely, for that is what I intend to do.*

Such noble words from a man who had shown nothing but quiet resolve and bravery throughout his capture. He'd never wept, or begged, or shown weakness in any fashion. Even when he'd asked her to let him go, he hadn't pleaded with her. He'd simply asked. *Norman courage.* She admired it, far more than she admired Anglo-Saxon mercy at the moment. Surely such a courageous man didn't deserve the fate that awaited him.

Something inside of her was screaming to help him.

More than that, something inside her was screaming for vengeance against Alary. Cruel and wicked bastard that he was, he could be erased from the world tomorrow and no one would miss him. With his taunts and actions, he had pushed her beyond reason and there was a large part of her that wanted vengeance against him. Tonight, he took her prisoner; tomorrow, who knew what he would take? Moreover, he'd accused her of siding with the Normans. That was unforgiveable slander because Alary wouldn't keep it to himself. He would tell others about this day and it was quite possible that men would start to doubt her loyalties. It would destroy all she'd worked hard for.

Something had to be done.

Gaetan de Wolfe. De Lohr had mentioned the man as his commander. He had asked her to send a message to him. Perhaps she could do more than that; she could tell de Wolfe just where her brother and de Lohr were. De Wolfe could save his man and Alary would be collateral damage. Odd how that thought brought a smile to her lips. Her greedy, wicked brother would be dead and so would his suspicious mind and uncontrollable tongue. She would be doing her people a favor, in fact, and Edwin might even thank de Wolfe for such a service.

There might be some kind of bond struck between the Normans and the Earl of Mercia because of it.

A bond over Alary's death.

By the time Ghislaine reached the men who were pounding on de

Lohr, she had a firm plan in mind. De Lohr was being beaten badly and she, once again, had to throw herself between him and the men who wanted to kill him. Alary's men wouldn't go out of their way to hit her but they kept trying to strike out at the knight behind her, going around her to grab de Lohr by the hair or club him in his already-damaged ribs. That went on for a while as Alary simply stood back and watched, laughing every time his sister received a blow meant for de Lohr. It was entertainment for him. But for Ghislaine, it only sealed Alary's fate.

She was going to send the Normans right to him.

As the night went on, the beating stopped and men, exhausted from a day of battle, wandered off to sleep in the forest. Left alone with the wounded knight, Ghislaine did what she could for de Lohr, who was a swollen, bleeding mess at this point. She could only hope the men had gotten their bloodlust out and would leave him alone from this point on but she didn't really believe that. Still, she couldn't remain with him because she had something very important to do. It was a task that only she could undertake and, if discovered, could mean her death. If she was caught going to the Norman encampment, then everything Alary had insinuated about her would be believed. She was taking a terrible risk.

But it had to be done.

In the hour before dawn, as the eastern sky began to lighten, Ghislaine moved from her post guarding the Norman knight and knelt down next to him as he lay upon the cold ground, battered and swollen. Leaning over his head, she whispered in his ear.

"I am going for help."

She wondered if he even heard her.

CHAPTER THREE

☙

MORTAL ANGELS

T HE MORNING THAT dawned over the field of battle revealed a scene that was straight out of the pages of every story ever told of hell and suffering.

Clouds the color of pewter hung in the sky as a storm rolled in from the south and a brisk wind whistled over the land. Smoke from the fires of both the Anglo-Saxon encampment as well as the Duke of Normandy's encampment trickled up towards the clouds, only to be dashed away by the breezes.

Still, the clouds and smoke couldn't mask the smell of death that was beginning to fill the air. Even the sea breezes couldn't blow it away. As Gaetan stood in front of his tent and watched the landscape lighten with the rising sun, he knew that, soon enough, men would have to walk about with kerchiefs over their faces to blot out the smell of rotting bodies. Dead animals mixed with dead men, their blood saturating the earth. The gulls had swarmed inland, already picking through the flesh on the ground and squawking at each other angrily.

Death was everywhere.

In the tent behind Gaetan, Harold had been on display for the night as men wandered in to see the corpse of the king. It confirmed to them that the throne of England now belonged to William. In fact, brethren from Rotherfield Abbey and South Malling Abbey had come to view the body, along with Harold's wife, who had evidently been traveling with her husband's army.

As a courtesy, William had allowed Harold's wife to visit her husband's body. It had been a difficult moment when Edith the Fair had identified her husband's battered corpse. Gaetan could still hear the woman's cries although she had tried very hard to be brave. The priests who had come with her had tried to be of some comfort to her but they had quickly dissolved into confusion when the woman threw herself upon the corpse of her husband.

That was when Gaetan had stepped in along with Téo, the most diplomatic of his men, and pulled the woman from the swollen body. At the head of the corpse, Jathan had been praying steadily in spite of the fact that the duke had voiced his displeasure at prayers for his enemy. Between the litany of sung prayers and the cries of a grief-stricken wife, it had all made for an uncomfortable and strained situation.

No one had gotten any sleep that night, for a myriad of reasons. Even as Gaetan stood watch over his prize of Harold's body with all of the confusion related to it, his thoughts lingered on the man that had yet to return to camp. As he, Téo, and Luc remained to watch over Harold's body, the rest of the *Anges de Guerre* and many other men set out to find Kristoph.

Sometime before dawn, Wellesbourne returned leading Kristoph's big bay stallion, a flashy and excitable animal that had been difficult not only to catch but to hold on to. Gaetan had been momentarily excited to see the horse and the fact that all of Kristoph's possessions were still on it, including his sword. But that excitement was short-lived when Wellesbourne said they'd searched the surrounding area where the horse was found to no avail.

No Kristoph.

Now, it was dawn and Gaetan was waiting for the rest of his men to return from the search. As much as he pretended to be stoic about the situation, the truth was that he was sick inside. Kristoph was his oldest and dearest friend, and facing the very real prospect of his death was devastating. Gaetan had no desire to tell his younger sister Adalie, who was Kristoph's wife, that her husband had met his death upon the field of battle. Kristoph was too good for that, too valuable to Gaetan's war machine. He was a man of vast knowledge and wisdom. Gaetan couldn't face the prospect of future battles without the man, his second-in-command and someone he very much depended on.

Already, he was living that nightmare.

As he fought off the phantoms of despair, de Russe and St. Hèver came into view through the mist of smoke and clouds, fearsome men emerging from the fog like demons on horseback. But they were alone and Gaetan tried not to feel another nail in his coffin of depression. The men slowed their frothing, exhausted beasts to a halt, dismounting wearily as they handed the horses over to their squires who had been hovering near de Wolfe's tent in their anxious wait for their masters to return. The knights approached Gaetan, removing gloves and helms as they moved.

"We skirted to the east and to the north, Gate," Aramis said, his voice hoarse from exhaustion. "There is a large contingent of the Anglo-Saxon army off to the east, sheltered in some heavily wooded forest area, but we did not get too close to it. It is possible that if Kristoph is a prisoner, he is there, but we have no way of knowing. The good news is that we did not find his body on our sweep. The bad news is that we did not find him at all."

Gaetan merely nodded, his jaw tight with emotion. "I suppose we should be grateful for that," he said. "How big was the contingent off to the east?"

"Big enough," Kye responded as he pulled his helm off. Blonde curly hair, close-shorn, came into view. "We could see their fires at a distance and there were several."

Gaetan nodded his head in a northerly direction. "Not all of the army is to the east," he said. "A goodly portion of it is still to the north. They have been begging for their king's body all night."

"Has the duke agreed to turn it over?" Aramis asked.

Gaetan shook his head. "He does not want them to have it. He told me to throw it into the sea but I will not do it."

"Why not?"

Gaetan looked at the two men. "Something tells me to keep it. It may be of use to us."

Kye looked at him blankly but Aramis seemed to understand. "If we find Kristoph a prisoner…?" he ventured.

"Exactly."

Aramis nodded his head in approval. "An exchange, then."

Suddenly, Kye understood their meaning and he lifted his blonde eyebrows at the prospect. "What does Normandy think of that?"

Gaetan was unremorseful. "He does not know and I have no intention of telling him. He knows that Kristoph is missing. I am afraid I will have to do something drastic if Normandy forbids me to trade Harold's body for Kristoph."

Aramis couldn't disagree. "If the duke told you to throw the body in the sea then, clearly, he cares not for it. What would it matter to him if you used it to regain Kristoph?"

"Those are exactly my thoughts. And woe to the man who tries to stop me."

It was an extremely touchy situation with Gaetan already planning for the negotiation of his friend's return. Knowing how close the *Anges de Guerre* were to each other, and Gaetan and Kristoph in particular, the duke would be taking his life in his hands forbidding his great Warwolfe from regaining one of his captured men by any means possible – even by using the body of a dead king as an incentive.

Aramis and Kye exchanged glances but neither one of them said anything about it. Whatever happened, they would support Gaetan even if it meant alienation from Normandy. Such were the depths of their loyalty.

"Well," Aramis said, putting a hand on Gaetan's shoulder as he moved past the man in the search for his own tent. "Let us know if we are needed. Right now, I hope to find some food and my bed. It has been a very long night."

Gaetan simply nodded as both Aramis and Kye moved past him, seeking some well-deserved rest. As the knights headed to their shelters, Gaetan heard them speaking with Téo as the man emerged from Gaetan's tent. When the conversation was over, Téo came up beside him, his face pale in the early dawn and his breath hanging in white puffs in the cold air.

"Aramis and Kye have returned, I see," he said. "They did not bring positive news."

Gaetan shook his head. "Nay," he said. He sighed heavily in disappointment; he couldn't help it. "They said that they found a large contingent of Anglo-Saxons off to the east, possibly part of the retreating army, but they did not get too close to it."

"At least they did not find Kristoph's body."

"That is what they said. I suppose I should be grateful for small mercies."

Téo could hear the sadness in his voice and he turned to look at the man. "Do not give up hope," he said quietly. "The others are still out there, still looking – Lance, Marc, and Denis. They may yet find him."

Gaetan's gaze was off to the north where the smoke from Anglo-Saxon fires spilled up into the sky. "I have been tearing myself apart trying to recall where I last saw Kristoph and what could have happened," he said, reconstructing his memory. "I was off to the northeast; we had both broken through the eastern flank because de Lara had sent word that Harold was dead. Kristoph was right beside me. We came upon a group of men standing around Harold's body and that is the last I saw of Kristoph. Eventually, we found his horse, but not him. Not... *him*."

"Then it sounds to me as if someone knocked him off the horse."

"Or he was hit with an arrow or a spear and fell off."

"If that was the case, we would have found his body by now," Téo said. He shook his head. "Nay, Gate; Kristoph has been taken away. If we have searched all night and have not found his corpse, then the logical conclusion is that the Anglo-Saxon army has him as a prisoner."

Gaetan turned to look at him. "Oddly enough, I hope that is true. I hope he is alive and a prisoner. At least if he is alive, there is hope of regaining him and I do not have to tell my sister that I let tragedy befall her husband."

Téo put a comforting hand on his shoulder. "We will find him," he said softly, firmly. "Now, you have not slept in almost two days. You must get some sleep while you can, at least until the others return. If they return without Kristoph, then we will need to form a plan of action and you cannot do that if your mind is desperate for sleep."

Gaetan knew he was right; Téo usually was. He was older than the rest of them and had seen much in life. His wisdom was a blessing. With a heavy sigh, Gaetan turned for his tent, his gaze moving over the structure.

"Then I shall go and sleep with a dead man," he said.

Téo lifted his eyebrows casually. "He cannot be worse than some of the women you have bedded."

Gaetan fought off a smirk. "Cold and smelly. Aye, that describes your sister very well."

Téo burst out laughing. "If I was not so exhausted, I would challenge you for that insult."

"If I was not so exhausted, I would accept."

Gaetan was grinning as he entered his tent, comfortable and well-appointed as usual with the distinct addition of a man in a shroud in the middle of it. Jathan, the priest, was still there, singing soft prayers over the body, reading from a song book he had copied himself in his youth.

But Gaetan had little patience for noise when he wanted to sleep. He motioned irritably to the priest even as two squires burst into the tent and headed for him, helping him to remove his protection.

"Enough prayers for now," Gaetan told Jathan. "I wish to sleep and I cannot do it if you are howling in the background."

Jathan immediately ceased his prayers, eyeing his lord as the man headed straight to his padded cot with his squires trailing after him, pulling things from his body.

"Has de Lohr been located yet, my lord?" Jathan asked.

Gaetan held out his arms so the squires could untie his scabbard and his belted tunic. "Not yet," he replied. "But his horse has been found. And not everyone has returned from the search yet. There is still hope."

Jathan considered that information a moment before standing up, his joints stiff from having been in a kneeling position for so long. Being the spiritual guide for the *Anges de Guerre*, he knew what de Lohr's absence was doing to these men and Gaetan in particular. These were men of war and they knew the consequences of that vocation more than most, but Jathan was convinced that they entered – and exited – every battle believing they were immortal. De Lohr's death or capture was a serious blow to those ideas of grandeur but more than that, it was a blow to the brotherhood between them all. With the removal of one, they were somehow fractured. Weaker.

The *Anges de Guerre* were not immortals, after all.

"Then I shall pray for his safety," Jathan finally said. "And for yours, my lord."

Gaetan looked at him as the squires pulled off the heavy padded vest on his muscular torso. "Why me?"

Jathan was moving stiffly to the tent opening. "Because whoever has de Lohr shall surely feel your wrath, will they not?" he said. "God give you strength to do what you must do in order to avenge him."

He left the tent, leaving Gaetan mulling over what Jathan had said. It was quite true. In fact, whoever had Kristoph would, indeed, be punished. Wiped from the earth and all of his brethren with him. Gaetan hadn't much pondered his sense of revenge because he was more concerned with regaining Kristoph but, now, he was thinking of it a great deal.

Indeed, he would make whoever held Kristoph pay dearly.

He slept.

CHAPTER FOUR

ॐ

A MAN OF DARKNESS

"H E IS DEAD, you know."

The words hung in the air, sharp with their pain, deadly with their accuracy. As three of de Wolfe's knights stood in a clearing on a rise a mile or two north of the battlefield, those words were like a nightmare none of them wanted to acknowledge.

But they were more than likely true.

Aramis de Russe, Lance de Reyne, and Denis de Winter were resting their horses after a grueling day and night and then day again of working the animals into a froth with very little rest. But the animals were growing increasingly sluggish so the knights knew they had to rest them or risk losing them. Even though the knights had brought other horses with them, these were their premier horses, expensive and highly-trained beasts they had taken into battle with them, and no one wanted to risk them.

Therefore, they paused in this hour before dawn when the sky was starting to lighten enough so they could douse their torches. But the mood between them was heavy with sorrow.

"It was so dark last night we could have easily passed him if he was injured and unable to call out to us," Denis replied to Aramis' grim statement. "Just because we have not found him does not mean his is dead."

"If Kristoph was alive, he would have found a way to return already," Lance said what the other two were already thinking. He knew his comrades well enough to know what was on their mind, what they were trying not to say. He looked at the two men, their faces pale in the cold and gray dawn. "You know I am right. If he had any strength left in him, he would have returned to us."

Denis shook his head; he wasn't willing to give up as easily as the others were. "Not if he was too injured to move or speak," he said, increasingly passionate in his stance. "Think what you want, but I will not give up looking for him. He would not give up so easily on us."

"No one is giving up, Denis," Lance said. He was an even-tempered man, rational. "But there will come a point when we must face the facts."

Denis, a bit more emotional than the others, cast his friend a long look. "Until we find a body, he is still alive," he said. "You know Gaetan feels the same way. That is why he has sent us out to look for him. Would you give up on me? Or Téo? Or any of us? Then we rest the horses and we keep looking until we find something."

It was the way the others felt as well, only reality and exhaustion were starting to set in, leading them to depressing conclusions. They were brothers-in-arms, all of them, and the loss of one was a heavy blow to their morale no matter how hard they tried to be logical or philosophical about it. Aramis, the most grimly pragmatic of the three, looked out over the landscape, turning shades of green and gray as the clouds above began to fill with light.

"Wellesbourne is to the east," he muttered. "St. Hèver and de Moray to the west. Téo and Luc are back in camp keeping Gaetan sane, which is no easy feat." He turned to look at his friends and colleagues. "We should split up now that light is upon us. We will cover more ground and be able to see better if we do. I suggest we comb back the way we have come and cover the battlefield from the north. It is even possible that Kristoph is mixed in with the Anglo-Saxon wounded."

The grim man was grasping at strands of hope but no one questioned that. They agreed with him. "I will head into the Anglo-Saxon camp," Denis said. "I will inspect their wounded to see if he is there."

The other two nodded. "Beware you do not end up as part of their wounded," Lance said. "Even wounded men can still kill. We do not want to have to go looking for you, too."

Denis nodded as he inspected his horse to make sure the horse had been given enough rest, at least in the short time they'd had. "I will be cautious," he said. "But if Kristoph is not there and we still cannot find him, then we must be willing to consider other possibilities."

Aramis paused in the process of mounting his own weary horse. "What?"

Denis tossed the reins over his horse's head as he prepared to climb into the saddle. "That he has been taken away," he said. "I would be happier to know that some Saxon lord has taken him away and is preparing to ransom him. Men held for ransom are valuable commodities and not usually injured or abused."

It was a happier thought than the one they were currently facing. As the men mounted their horses, Denis reined in his horse and turned to the others before leaving.

"*Et pro Gloria dei,*" he said quietly. For God and Glory.

"*Et pro Gloria dei,*" the other two repeated quietly.

It was their battle call, something they always said to one another before heading into battle or into a risky situation. It was a blessing to each other, a giver of strength, something that belonged only to them. Never did they bid one another farewell, for that was a finality in a sense. *Et pro Gloria dei* was all they ever said when parting from each other, a parting well-made and encouragement. They were words of hope.

Right now, they needed all the hope they could get.

GHISLAINE WASN'T ENTIRELY sure this was a good idea any longer.

Having made it back to the battlefield before dawn, it was swarming with Normans and she had approached a soldier demanding to speak with a knight named Gaetan de Wolfe. Luckily, she spoke their language but her heavy accent gave her away and the soldier grabbed her by the arm and began to drag her over to some of his cohorts, shouting that he had a Saxon captive.

It wasn't what Ghislaine had expected. She had expected the de Wolfe name to open doors for her, in peace and respect. Therefore, her shock in the Norman soldier's reaction turned into full-blown fear when several Norman warriors headed in her direction, all of them drawn in by the shouts of the man who had her by the arm. He was hurting her. But she knew she would be hurt much worse if she let these Norman hounds paw at her. Therefore, she started shouting louder than the man holding her.

"Kristoph de Lohr!" she screamed. "I have come on behalf of Kristoph de Lohr! I must speak to de Wolfe!"

She had to say it two or three times before it registered to one of the older soldiers what, exactly, she was saying. Her accent was so heavy that they hadn't understood her, but an older man with missing teeth and a nose that had been broken repeatedly understood her. He pulled her from the man who had a death-grip on her.

"What do you know of de Lohr?" he snarled at her, his face in hers and his foul breath filling her nostrils. "Where is he?"

Ghislaine had to admit that she was fairly terrified at this point. The Normans smelled terrible and looked like animals to her; grizzled, dirty, wild-eyed. But she'd come this far and there was no turning back.

Ghislaine had waited until the Anglo-Saxon army was asleep before slipping from the encampment in the woods. Trying to avoid being followed, it had taken her more than an hour to reach the battlefield where the Normans were celebrating their victory. By the time she reached the area, which was already starting to stink of dead men, the sun was barely hinting over the eastern horizon and the heavy clouds above were turning shades of gray. Now, she found herself face to face with men she had been trying to kill the day before.

She was more afraid than she thought she would be.

"I will only speak with de Wolfe," she said. "Take me to de Wolfe and I will tell him."

The old soldier's eyes narrowed at her and, after a few moments, it was clear that he didn't believe her. He shook his head. "A Saxon trick," he hissed.

"It is *not* a trick!"

He would not be swayed. He tossed her towards the soldiers who were gathering. "A gift, lads. Enjoy yourselves!"

The men grabbed at her and Ghislaine screamed, trying to bolt away from them. One man managed to grab the long tunic she wore and he yanked, causing her to fall. As she crumpled to the ground, men were swarming on top of her and she screamed and kicked, fighting them off.

But the men ignored her terror, laughing and grabbing at her, trying to settle her down and tell her not to fear so that they could earn her trust and then destroy it. They seemed to think it was all quite humorous while she screamed and kicked. One of the soldiers had just made a grab for her neck when a booming voice overhead stopped them.

"What goes on here?" It was Lance de Reyne, riding up on his frothing war horse in the company of two more knights. "What are you doing? Who is this woman?"

All of the grabbing and laughter came to a halt as the Normans suddenly had better manners in front of one of their commanders. The older soldier who had tossed Ghislaine towards his men stepped forward.

"A Saxon prisoner, my lord," he said, clearing his throat nervously.

"We were...."

"I must see Gaetan de Wolfe," Ghislaine said breathlessly, struggling to her feet and crashing into de Reyne's leg when she lost her balance. "I come with information on Kristoph de Lohr! Please do not let these men have me!"

De Reyne's dark eyes widened. Reaching down, he grabbed her by the front of her tunic and lifted her off her feet.

"What do you know of him?" he demanded. "Tell me now!"

Ghislaine was so frightened that she was feeling faint. "I will only tell de Wolfe," she gasped, holding on to the man's wrist as he held her off of the ground. "I must speak with him immediately!"

"Tell me what you know this instant or I will cut your throat."

"If you cut my throat, de Lohr will die. This I swear."

De Reyne didn't hesitate after that. He yanked her onto his saddle, throwing her over his thighs as easily as one would toss around a sack of flour. Digging his spurs into the side of his horse, they tore off towards the heart of the encampment.

She was face-down over the knight's armored legs. It was a terribly uncomfortable position to be in and Ghislaine struggled to keep her balance, to breathe, and to not panic. She could see the ground passing swiftly beneath the horse's hooves and then they came to an abrupt halt. She grunted as the knight lifted her off of the saddle and lowered her, probably to set her on her feet but she ended up falling. He dismounted behind her, hauling her to her feet as he began to head towards a cluster of white and crimson tents.

Terrified, Ghislaine allowed herself to be dragged along because she could only assume the knight was taking her to the commander de Lohr had mentioned. *De Wolfe*. At least, she hoped so. She hoped that shouting the name of de Wolfe and de Lohr would get her to the man she needed to see because she was coming to very much regret her attempts at heroics to save the Norman knight's life. Her sense of vengeance against Alary had forced her into making a stupid decision. All of these thoughts were whirling in her head as the big knight took her into one of the larger tents.

Thrust into the cool, dark innards of the structure, she was immediately hit by the smell of death. There was something dead in the tent but she couldn't really see much because there was only the faint glow from the brazier to light the area. She blinked, struggling to become accustomed to the dimness of the tent when the Norman knight released her. As she stood there, frightened and dazed, he headed over to a corner of the tent where there was a cot and a supine body upon it.

The person on the cot was evidently dead asleep because it took the big knight a couple of tries to wake him. Ghislaine's heart was pounding in her ears, full of apprehension and fear, as the body on the cot stirred. The big knight muttered something to the man on the cot and, suddenly, he was sitting bolt-upright and rubbing his eyes. When he stood up, unsteadily, all she could see was this impossibly tall figure in the darkness, bigger than any man she had ever seen. Then he came towards her, his features coming into the weak light.

Her heart stopped.

He was dark, swarthy-skinned, with black hair and eyes the color of bronze. His features were surprisingly even, his jaw square and his nose straight. In fact, he was quite handsome; male beauty like nothing she had ever seen before. But her inspection of him was interrupted when he barked at her, savagely.

"Who are you?" he demanded. "What do you know of Kristoph?"

His voice... that voice that came rolling out at her like molten rock, flowing hot and fast and deep. Had she heard it before? She couldn't be sure. Ghislaine swallowed hard, never so intimidated by anyone than she was at this very moment by him. It was a struggle to find her tongue.

"I... I am Ghislaine of Mercia," she said, trembling. "I have come on behalf of Kristoph de Lohr. He told me that Gaetan de Wolfe is his commander. Are you de Wolfe?"

His jaw was ticking furiously. "I am," he said. "*Where* is Kristoph?"

He asked the question through his teeth. Ghislaine struggled against her fear, but in the same breath she was offended by his reaction. Considering she came with news of his knight, she thought he might have been happier to see her. No such luck.

God, what had ever possessed her to come?

Still, she was here and, unless she wanted the Normans to walk all over her, she had better start showing some of the courage she was born with. If Ghislaine had one great quality, it was her boldness in the face of most any given situation. She was a strong woman from strong stock. It was time to show the Normans that.

She was finished playing the fearful little lamb.

"As I said, my name is Ghislaine of Mercia," she said, her voice a little stronger now as de Wolfe and the other knight, the one who had brought her, glared at her quite seriously. "My brother is Edwin of Mercia. I have another brother, Morcar of Northumbria. Do you recognize these names, my lord?"

She had a very heavy accent but she seemed fluent in their language. De Wolfe nodded. "I do," he said, displeased. "I recognize the names very well and I can only assume de Lohr has been abducted by your brothers." Knowing these powerful men were her brothers, he had a suspicion as to her true identity. He would think on that later. For now, he had to know about Kristoph. Have you come to deliver terms of his ransom? Whatever it is, I will pay it."

Ghislaine could see the man thought that his knight had been abducted only to be ransomed. That was a fairly normal practice in warfare, where men were taken and then returned, unharmed, for a price. She shook her head.

"It is far more complex than that, my lord," she said. "I am not here to deliver a ransom demand. I am here to tell you that your man is in terrible danger."

De Wolfe's brow furrowed. "Danger?" he repeated. "What do you mean?"

Ghislaine sought to explain. "Another brother, known as Alary of Mercia, has taken your knight as a prisoner," she said. "It is his intention to interrogate your man for information about the Norman army. At least, that is his intention at the moment. I do not know what his intention will be tomorrow or the next day. Already, he has beaten your knight. He is wounded and, if you do not rescue him quickly, I fear he will not survive."

De Wolfe simply stared at her at moment. But at least his expression wasn't as hostile as it had been. In fact, he seemed to ponder what he'd been told quite seriously and, in truth, with some disbelief. In warfare, where men were captured and ransomed, to mistreat a prisoner was almost unheard of. Knights, and especially men of wealth, were almost treated as guests in some cases until the ransom was paid. Therefore, de Wolfe was naturally perplexed.

"No ransom?" he clarified.

"No ransom."

"But he is alive?"

"Alive but wounded. Did you not understand? He is in danger."

De Wolfe nodded. "I understand," he said. "So your brother will not demand ransom. What does he want, then?"

"I am not sure if there is anything he wants."

De Wolfe was growing increasingly confused. "Then why have you come?"

That was a question with a complicated answer, something she didn't want to divulge at the moment. She thought it might make her appear weak. But the truth was that she had a difficult time coming up with a reasonable explanation.

"It does not matter why I have come, only that I have," she said. "Do you want your man back or not?"

De Wolfe nodded, slowly, eyeing her most critically, as if he couldn't quite figure all of this out. "I want him back and I shall have him," he said. "But if you are the sister of the man who has captured him, as you claim to be, then you will tell me why you are here on behalf of your brother? Why have you even come if he does not wish to ransom my knight?"

Ghislaine averted her gaze, realizing she was going to have to tell the man something of the truth. She suspected he wouldn't rest until he received some kind of reasonable answer from her, something to satisfy his curiosity. Therefore, she tried not to sound too embarrassed as she spoke.

"I am here because... because I hate my brother," she muttered. "He is a vile and terrible man. He is so despicable that Edwin exiled him from Mercia for reasons I shall not go in to. But Alary joined with King Harold's army to fight for the king against the Duke of Normandy and find royal favor, but when that did not happen... now I believe that he views your man as everything he hates."

De Wolfe wasn't moved by her speech, but a good deal was becoming clear to him. "Then you come to betray him."

It wasn't a question. It was a statement of fact, and a true one. Frustrated that he was pushing her into a more personal confession, her eyes snapped up to him. "I do," she said angrily. "Your knight was originally *my* prisoner. I fought with the Saxon army yesterday and I was there when your knight was knocked off his horse. The fall rendered him unconscious so my men and I dragged him away from the field of battle, tied him to a horse, and sent the horse running. But when the horse finally stopped running and many men from Harold's army were trying to beat your knight to death, I stopped them. I stopped them because... because a knight captured me during the battle. But instead of harming me, he let me go and told me to remember Norman mercy. And I did – I spared his Norman compatriot because of it. Mercy was shown to me, so I showed mercy to the Norman knight. But Alary took your knight away from me for his own devious purposes. Now he has him and I can no longer protect him."

De Wolfe was simply staring at her but it was apparent that something was going on in his mind. After a moment, he bent over as if to look at her more closely.

"Then I understand why you have come," he said simply. "But in listening to you speak, something else has occurred to me. I recognize your voice. I believe it threatened me once."

Ghislaine wasn't sure what he meant. "We have not met before."

De Wolfe continued to stare at her until, suddenly, his eyebrows lifted. "The little mouse," he said as if an idea had occurred to him. "When we broke through the eastern shield wall, I captured you. You called me rubbish."

Ghislaine's eyes widened. She well remembered the knight she called *poubelle* and her mouth popped open. She hadn't seen his face but now she recognized that voice. Of course she'd heard it before – when he demanded to know where her king was.

It was her merciful knight, in the flesh.

"*You!*" she gasped. "The Norman knight!"

De Wolfe simply looked at her. "Aye, it is me, the Knight of Rubbish," he said with some disdain in his voice. "And look at the little mouse; you are punier than I had imagined. Take off that cap and show yourself. You look like a man dressed as you are. Let me see what you really look like."

Ghislaine looked down at herself. She was, indeed, dressed in a tunic and leather, a belt around her slender waist and hose on her legs. Her hair was still caught up in a heavy leather cap. But that was intentional. It was easier to fight with men if they thought she was one. It was also easier to move among them. As she hesitated to remove her cap, de Wolfe reached out and pulled it from her head.

And that's when things changed.

Gaetan was quite surprised, really. Off came the cap and out flowed the most beautiful hair he had ever seen. It was mussed and a little dirty. But he could still see the shine even in the dim light as nearly-black hair tumbled over her shoulders, glinting with red. Moreover, once he got a good look at her face, he could see that she was quite beautiful – she had a round little face with rosebud lips and wide blue eyes. When she blinked, her lashes fanned against her pale cheeks. Aye, she was quite beautiful if one could look beyond the muss and dirt. Exquisite, even.

A seed of interest sprouted.

"Why do you fight?" he asked after a moment. "Are the Saxons so desperate for men that they permit their women to fight?"

Ghislaine eyed him, a faint blush of embarrassment coming to her cheeks. "I fight because I have been trained to fight," she said, lifting her chin at him. "I fight because I am good at it. My mother was a warrior, as was my grandmother. I do what I want to do."

"And no one says otherwise?"

"No one dares."

Gaetan scratched his head. "I would believe that," he said. Then, he looked to Lance, who was still standing next to him. "Gather the men and bring them to my tent. We have word of Kristoph that they will want to hear."

With a lingering glance at the disheveled Saxon woman, Lance quit the tent, heading out to find the rest of the *Anges de Guerre*. When he was gone, Gaetan turned to Ghislaine.

He was far calmer than he had been when she'd entered the tent, with less rage and more curiosity. He wasn't panicking at all, no matter how much she tried to stress that Kristoph was in danger. Perhaps, he didn't really grasp what she was saying. Perhaps, she wasn't communicating it properly in his native tongue. Whatever the case, Ghislaine eyed him with some trepidation now that they were alone.

"Now," he said steadily. "Let us return to the subject of my knight and away from a woman warrior who has no business being on a battlefield. You said that you showed mercy to Kristoph so I suppose I should thank you. You also said he was knocked from his horse – did you do it?"

Ghislaine shook her head even though she wasn't quite over his comment about warrior women having no place in battle. She hadn't had a man speak to her in such a way since she had been very young. No one dared dispute Ghislaine and her right to battle.

"It was not me," she said, miffed. "I saw him after he was on the ground."

"But it was you who tied him to a horse and took him away?"

"My men did it." She watched him for a moment before confessing the rest. "I knew he would be a valuable prisoner and I thought as you thought, that mayhap we could ransom him. But Alary had different ideas on that."

Gaetan's gaze drifted over her as she spoke. He could see that he'd offended her. Her answers were very clipped. He didn't much care, however, and he rather liked her husky little voice with the heavy accent. There was something about the woman that was inherently intriguing, unlike the fine and pampered women he knew. She was strong and she had spirit. Those were admirable qualities.

She was also clever; he could sense that. He didn't want her to think that she was more clever, or smarter, than he was. Therefore, he switched to her language simply to prove to her that he wasn't an idiot who did not know the language of the Saxons. Perhaps, she would understand that he was more than a warrior, capable of only fighting.

His mind was as sharp as a razor.

"I have not heard of Alary of Mercia," he said, watching her eyes widen because he spoke in her tongue. "Why was he exiled by Edwin?"

Ghislaine heard the question but she had one of her own. "How do you know my language?"

"How do you know mine?"

"Because my mother insisted we learn the language of our servants so we would know if they were to rise up against us."

Gaetan lifted an eyebrow. "It is always wise to know the language of an enemy. *That* is why I know your language."

Enemies. They were most definitely enemies. Therefore, Ghislaine couldn't disagree with his statement. But the fact that he could speak her language gave her pause. There was something cunning behind those intense eyes. She eyed him for a moment.

"You want to know why Alary was exiled?" she asked. "He was exiled because he was foolish enough to get one of Edwin's men killed, among other things. He has no conscience, nor does he have any understanding of things outside of his wants and needs. If you do not serve a purpose for him, then he will just as easily kill you."

"And you fear that is what he will do to Kristoph?"

"I know he will." She could see the concern ripple across Gaetan's face so she sought to impress upon him how serious she was. She had to get through to him. "He will not want your money, I do not believe. He will demand to know everything about the Norman army and their plans to advance into England from your knight. If he does not get what he needs, then he will have no use for him."

Gaetan pondered her statement. It was clear that she had some concern for Kristoph, which Gaetan thought was rather odd. There was no reason why she should have any concern for the enemy. It was true that she showed the man some mercy, evidently, by protecting him from those who sought to kill him, but beyond that... something about this didn't sound right. There was something else that she wasn't telling him.

As he considered that suspicion, the tent flap flew back and men began entering; de Russe, de Winter, de Lara, and de Moray followed by de Reyne, St. Hèver, du Reims, and Wellesbourne. Half-dressed, or sleepy-eyed from having been roused from their precious moments of sleep, big men were filling up the entry. They didn't look pleased, either, glancing between Gaetan and the Saxon woman with a mixture of anxiety, frustration, and hostility.

The hostility was definitely palpable and Ghislaine instinctively stepped back, away from the seasoned warriors that were spilling into the tent. She also saw a squire or two, and maybe even a priest. Too many men were suddenly piling into the shelter and she backed away without looking where she was going, abruptly tripping over a bundle in the middle of the tent.

As she tried to pull her feet out of it, the fabric came away and she found herself looking at Harold's corpse. He was tinged purple and green, his skin waxy like tallow. A scream left Ghislaine's lips when she realized what she was looking at, struggling to pull the shroud away from her ankles. The more it wouldn't come free, the more she panicked. Gasping, she finally freed herself, crawling over to the edge of the tent.

In spite of the fact that the tent was filled with fighting men, Ghislaine only had eyes for the pasty face of the dead king. *Her sister's husband.* But she wouldn't tell the Norman's that, fearful that it might somehow seal the suggestion of taking her a hostage if they knew she was related to the man. That fear alone kept her silent.

In fact, she'd tried to push Harold's death out of her mind because there was so much more of the situation demanding her attention. But the sight of his lifeless body brought tears to her eyes. Her sister had been rather fond of the man and she had accompanied him on his battle march from London. She was certain that her sister had already been informed that she was a widow and Ghislaine wished she could be of some comfort to the woman. But she had her own problems at the moment.

Poor Edith....

As Ghislaine stared at Harold's remains, hand over her mouth in distress, Gaetan went to the body and tossed the fabric back over the face. He could see how startled and unbalanced she was but it was of no matter to him; war was war and if she was going to fight like a soldier, then she would know that death went along with such a vocation. He never imagined that her shock and grief was for another reason entirely. His gaze hovered on her for a moment before turning to the men standing behind him.

"This is Ghislaine of Mercia," he told his knights in their language. "She is the sister of Edwin of Mercia, Morcar of Northumbria, and Alary of Mercia. She has come to tell us that Kristoph is now the prisoner of her brother, Alary, and that he is in a good deal of danger."

Various expressions of surprise and concern spread across the faces of his exhausted knights. "Where is he?" Denis de Winter asked, to either Gaetan or Ghislaine. "Has ransom been demanded?"

Gaetan shook his head. "That is the strange part," he said. "According to Lady Ghislaine, her brother seeks no ransom. He is using Kristoph for information and she fears that when Kristoph is no longer useful, Alary will kill him."

"*Where* is he?" Luc de Lara asked, far more unpleasantly than Denis had. "We searched far and wide and did not find him. Where is he being held?"

Gaetan looked at Ghislaine, who was struggling to pull herself together. When she saw that their attention was on her, she labored to speak coherently.

"Part of the retreating army gathered to the east in a forest," she said in their language, mostly looking at Gaetan because those angry, huffing knights intimidated her. "Your knight was there when last I saw him but Alary said he would be moving him north to Tenebris, which is where he lives out his life these days. Tenebris used to be a hunting lodge for the kings of Mercia but now... now it is a terrible, dark place with a dark reputation. Alary rules over it like his own little kingdom and Edwin simply looks the other way. Men go in to Tenebris but they do not come out again. You cannot permit your man to go there because, if he does, you will never see him again."

The knights were trying to decipher her heavily-accented speech. "Tenebris?" Aramis repeated, looking at Gaetan. "I've not heard of it. Where is it?"

Gaetan shook his head. "I do not know." He turned to Ghislaine. "Where is this place?"

Ghislaine found her feet, rising unsteadily on shaky legs. "To the north, somewhere west of Coventry," she said. "There is a good deal of wild land between here and Tenebris. It is a perilous journey that will take many days."

"I know where it is."

Bartholomew Wellesbourne spoke and all eyes turned to him. He was a man of few words, big and blonde with eyes so dark that they were nearly black. He was the only one of the group that hadn't been born in France. As a mercenary, he'd been hired by Gaetan years ago and had simply never left the man even though his loyalty to the man far outweighed any monetary compensation these days. His focus was on Ghislaine, however.

"A ydych yn deal Cymraeg?" he asked her. *Do you speak Welsh?*

Ghislaine nodded her head hesitantly. "Ychydig yn." *A little.*

Bartholomew eyed her, somewhat suspiciously, before turning to Gaetan. "I was born in the village of Wellesbourne, as you know," he said. "It is very close to Wales and I spent my youth there. I traveled with my father, who was also a mercenary, and I have seen much of the land she speaks of. There is a forest there called Far Forest that is rumored to be haunted. Mercia borders several Welsh kingdoms and she is correct; it is very wild. If he takes Kristoph there, we will quite possibly lose him forever."

Gaetan didn't like the sound of that. Now, all of the warnings of Kristoph being in danger were starting to sink in as he was coming to realize what, exactly, she had meant.

"Then we must go and get him now," he said, turning to Ghislaine. "You say that he is being kept to the east of here?"

Ghislaine nodded. "Aye," she replied. "But there are several hundred men camped there. If you intend to rescue him, then you must take many men with you. My men will not so easily give up their Norman prize."

As the knights considered that option, Marc de Moray pushed through the group and went straight to the body of Harold in the center of the tent. Big, gruff, black-haired de Moray was a no-nonsense kind of man. He tossed back the fabric across the king's face, exposing the slightly green features to the weak light.

"Will they give it up for this?" he asked, looking at Gaetan. "Normandy told you to toss the body in the sea but you did not. You have held on to it, mayhap for just such an event? Because if you have, I will ride in to that encampment this very moment with the body and demand Kristoph's release in exchange for their king. If they do not accept the terms, then we will exchange the lady for Kristoph. Surely this Alary of Mercia will want his sister back."

Ghislaine's eyes widened. Now, *she* was to be a hostage? "He does not know I have come," she said. "Alary has no love for me, as I have no love for him. You would be offering him nothing that was of value. It would be useless."

Gaetan eyed de Moray for a moment, perhaps considering his offer to deliver Harold's body, before looking to Ghislaine. "What were your plans after you told us of Kristoph, then?" he asked. "Did you think we would simply let you return to your Saxon brethren? You *do* realize that you have left yourself open to the enemy, do you not?"

Truth be told, Ghislaine hadn't considered any of that. She looked at the big men in the tent, all of them blood-thirsty warriors who had come to her lands seeking glory. They were her enemy and they did not trust her. It took her a moment to realize how very foolish she had been. Her thoughts of mercy, of vengeance against Alary, had her singularly focused. She hadn't considered what she would do after telling the Norman's of her brother's plans for their comrade. Now, she was feeling cornered, frightened in more ways than she could comprehend.

"I came with peaceful intentions," she said, having visions of all of these men swarming on her at once and being pulled limb from limb. Her gaze was fixed on Gaetan. "You showed me mercy once before. Do I wrongly assume you would show it to me again?"

Gaetan merely shrugged. "It is possible," he said ambivalently. Then, he turned to de Moray and his men. "I had the same idea as Marc suggested – using Harold's body to exchange for Kristoph's freedom. Téo and I discussed it earlier with just that possibility in mind. We will send the lady back with a message – Kristoph for their king."

Ghislaine was quickly growing agitated. "Alary cares not for Harold's body," she insisted. "He served the king only to gain his favor because he has two brothers who hold great lands while he himself has none. Now that the king is dead, believe me when I tell you that he has no use for the man. And sending me back to him with a message from you will only sign my death warrant. My brother will want to know how I became a messenger for Norman knights."

Gaetan turned to her but, before he could speak, the big knight, de Moray, spoke again. "Then I will ride into the encampment and exchange myself for Kristoph," he said. "I have no wife to mourn me. If the man wants a prisoner, then he will take me. Kristoph has a child and a wife who need him."

Gaetan put a hand on de Moray's shoulder. "Although I admire your sacrifice, I will not lose you, too," he said. "We will regain Kristoph without anyone sacrificing himself. I need my *anges* intact. I will lose no man and I will leave no man behind. You know this."

It was true that they did. That had been their mantra from years back; *no man left behind, no man lost*. It was part of the bond that kept them so strong. It was that faith in their unit as a whole that gave them the illusion of their own immortality. As the men pondered the next step in regaining Kristoph, a round, dirty figure pushed himself forward from behind the row of knights.

It was the priest. Jathan had heard de Reyne summoning the men to Gaetan's tent and, even half-asleep as he had been, he scrambled up from his pallet and followed the tide of exhausted men into Gaetan's quarters. Now, he'd heard the reason they'd been summoned and he sought to lend his aid. He, more than anyone, understood the loyalty that bonded these men together and he knew that de Moray would sacrifice himself without question.

"My lord," he said to Gaetan. "Surely they would not harm a man of the church. I will go into the Saxon encampment and see to Kristoph myself. Mayhap, I can negotiate for his release."

Gaetan turned to his priest, as did the rest of them. Jathan had been a knight before he'd been a priest and was therefore an excellent fighter, but he still had the look of a killer about him. He'd preach the good word in one breath and snap a neck in the next. Gaetan shook his head, sadly.

"You still look like a warrior no matter how much you pretend to be a priest," he said. "Although I appreciate your offer, I fear they would not believe you were a man of the church."

Jathan wouldn't be deterred. "Then I shall go to the nearest abbey and solicit assistance from the priests," he said. "They can go to the Saxon encampment and negotiate for Kristoph. If one of us cannot go, then the church must intervene."

Again, Gaetan shook his head. "That would take time," he said. "The Saxon army is not going to remain to the east forever, as the lady has mentioned. They will be moving out soon and I suspect the only thing we can do is go now ourselves and bring Kristoph back. Not with a great army as the lady suggested, but just the nine of us – this is either a job for a great many men or just a few. We can slip in and take him without raising an alarm."

"Then let me at least offer myself as a prisoner," Jathan insisted. "Surely they would not harm me. Mayhap they would even take me to where Kristoph is and, from that position, I can help him when you come to free him. You will need a man on the inside if he is as injured as the lady has said."

De Wolfe didn't look entirely convinced. "There may be truth in that," he admitted. "But we would have to coordinate that carefully so as not to create a great alarm. We must be stealth, whatever we do."

Still over by the edge of the tent, Ghislaine nodded eagerly. "They are in the forest where there is a good deal of cover for your movements," she said, relieved that they were finally understanding the seriousness of the situation. "I will take you there and I will show you were I last saw your knight. Mayhap, they have not even missed me these few hours and will not have even known I have left, so I will be able to move about the encampment freely."

As Gaetan considered her offer, de Moray spoke up again. "How do we know you weren't sent here to take us all to our deaths using Kristoph as bait?" he asked, somewhat savagely. "I do not like that you are so eager to help us regain him."

Ghislaine could see their point, in a sense. Therefore, she tried not to be too offended by it. "I swear by my mother that I have not been sent here to lure you to your deaths," she said steadily. "I have given my reasons to your lord for coming; among them is the fact that my brother is a wicked man who holds your friend captive. When you rescue your friend, if my brother falls victim to your sword, I will not mourn him. I will thank you for doing me and the rest of Mercia a great service."

Now, the situation had a bit of a twist on it that was unexpected – a Saxon woman seeking the assassination of her terrible brother, who just happened to hold a Norman knight captive. It was difficult not to believe her sincerity and even de Moray's hostility had banked somewhat. He looked at Gaetan.

"Is this true?" he asked. "She has come seeking her brother's murder?"

Gaetan's gaze was on Ghislaine as she stood on the other side of the tent, looking at all of them with a mixture of fear and hope. He was a good judge of character because his life depended upon such things and he was coming to think that the lady was sincere. A bit foolish, perhaps, but sincere. She seemed a little too naïve about the ways of men to be anything else. Strangely, he was starting to feel the least bit of compassion towards her.

"There is something you should know," he told his men. "Towards the end of yesterday's battle, I captured what I thought was a Saxon archer. It turned out to be Lady Ghislaine. I spared her life and, in turn, when Kristoph was captured, she spared his. Of course, there is no way of knowing if she is being truthful until we regain Kristoph and speak with him, but given that we have no other alternative, I am willing to trust that she is a lady of her word. I am willing to trust that Kristoph's situation is as she says it is and that we can depend on her for her assistance in regaining him. But at the first sign she is lying, I will not hesitate to slit her throat. Make no mistake."

Deadly words from de Wolfe and Ghislaine had no doubt that he meant them. But she didn't show her fear. She simply looked him in the eye, steadily, to emphasize the fact that she wasn't lying about anything. They needed their knight returned. She needed vengeance against her brother.

There was an old saying... *my enemy's enemy is my friend.*

Perhaps this would work out, after all.

"That will not be necessary," she said. "I have been completely truthful."

Gaetan's eyes glittered at her in the weak light of the tent. "That remains to be seen," he said. Then, he turned to the knights standing behind him. "Prepare yourselves. I intend to go to the Saxon encampment as quickly as possible, so dress accordingly. Travel lightly. We will need to slip in and slip out, and we cannot do that if you are heavily armored or burdened with many weapons. Take only what you will need."

De Reyne, standing closest to him, frowned. "Why not wait until darkness?" he asked. "It will make it much easier to move about."

Gaetan shook his head. "We cannot take the chance that they will move out this morning and take Kristoph with them," he said. "Unfortunately, operating in the day will leave us exposed, but we will simply have to double our efforts of caution."

The knights understood. The plan was set and they were more than ready to see it through, feeling anticipation in regaining their lost man. Surely it would be a simple thing against the beaten Anglo-Saxons who had taken Kristoph prisoner. They quit the tent, heading back to their own shelters to prepare for the coming incursion into the enemy encampment, but Téo lingered behind.

He waited until the men were gone before speaking to Gaetan. "Will you tell Normandy what you intend to do?" Téo asked. "And what of Harold's body?"

Gaetan turned to look at the corpse, the face still exposed. He sighed heavily. "Normandy does not want it," he said. "If Kristoph's captor will not take it in exchange, then I suppose it is of no use to use. Seek out William Malet and see if he will assume the burden. Although he is close to Normandy, I do not believe he wishes to see the body thrown into the sea, either. He did not seem to approve of those orders when Normandy gave them to me. See if he will give the body back over to the king's widow or even to his mother. I heard she had offered gold for it."

"I heard that also. Do you think Normandy will turn it over to them?"

"That is difficult to know. But I no longer have any use for it."

Téo understood; William Malet was a trustworthy man, one of the duke's many Companions. He was as reasonable as any of them to handle the disposal of the body. As Téo headed out to find Malet, Gaetan was left with Ghislaine, once again, alone in the large cluttered tent, but that didn't last long. Soon, there were squires entering the tent again to assist Gaetan in dressing for his coming mission and Ghislaine was all but forgotten.

Still standing over near the edge of the tent, Ghislaine watched the activity and she was, in truth, grateful to have been forgotten. This entire incident had been a nightmare, one of frustration and fear. She didn't even feel much relief that the Normans would soon be doing as she had hoped by rescuing their comrade and, hopefully, killing Alary in the process. Whatever hope she did feel in that action had taken a blow when she'd heard de Wolfe mention that the Duke of Normandy had wanted Harold's body thrown into the sea. She was even more surprised to hear that her sister, Edith, had evidently already been to view her husband's body but had left without it.

So much had happened to a family so devastated.

But, perhaps, the worst was yet to come. At this point, nothing was certain. Exhausted, shaken, Ghislaine sank down to her buttocks on the cold ground as de Wolfe went about dressing. But she wasn't watching the big knight. She was looking at Harold's exposed face, seeing the damage by the arrow, heartsick over the loss of her sister's husband. He had been a good man for the most part and very kind to her. Not only was her family devastated, but the country as well. There was a new king, a duke from across the sea. And already, Ghislaine was in league with his men to have her brother killed.

Was it survival?

Was it treason?

Either way, she'd made a deal with the devil. She hoped the price wasn't too high, whatever that was to be.

CHAPTER FIVE

cß

WAR DOG

"WHERE IS YOUR little protector?" Alary asked in Kristoph's language. "She has been so determined to shield you from the rest of us that surely she would not leave your side. Where has she gone, Norman?"

It was daybreak on the day after the battle to end all battles and Kristoph wasn't in the mood for this line of questioning. On top of the initial injuries he'd had from being knocked off his horse, now he had the pleasure of damaged organs from the kicking he'd taken, a swollen face, probably a broken nose, and loose teeth. There was coagulated blood all in his mouth and down his throat, making swallowing difficult. His head was killing him and he couldn't see out of one eye because the swelling was so bad. Therefore, the questions being posted to him were not welcome.

"I would not know," he said through his swollen lips. "I have not exactly been alert as of late."

Alary was crouched beside the fallen knight. He could see how badly the man was injured but he had no sympathy. He grunted.

"None of my men have seen her, either," he said. "What did she say to you when she left you? My men said she whispered something to you before she disappeared."

Kristoph lay there with his eyes closed for a moment before, slowly, opening his eyes as Alary's question registered. "The last I spoke with her was last night sometime," he said. "At least, that is the last I recall."

Alary didn't doubt the man. The knight had been beaten into unconsciousness last evening and was only now, at daybreak, becoming lucid again. Still, he was hoping to find a clue as to his sister's whereabouts.

"No one can find her," he said. "But knowing my sister, she is probably lingering around the edges of the Norman encampment, picking off Normans with her bow. She is quite good with it."

Kristoph's eyes remained open for a moment longer before closing; it was too exhausting to keep them open. "It seems to me that she is a seasoned fighter."

Alary thought on his strong-willed obnoxious youngest sister. "She does as she wishes and no one has stopped her," he said frankly. "I have two sisters, one of whom is the widow of Harold. Did you know that? The king you killed was my sister's husband."

Kristoph didn't know that and he surely didn't care. "Many husbands are killed in battle," he muttered. "It is the way of things."

Alary's eyes narrowed. "It is the way of Norman conquest," he said. "These are not your lands. You should not have come here."

"Your sister said much the same thing."

"For once, she was correct."

"Much as you have followed your king, I too was simply following orders."

Alary snorted. "I follow no orders."

"Then why are you here?"

Alary cocked his head. "An excellent question. I suppose the answer is because I deserved something from all of this. Edwin, my brother, is not here, nor is Morcar, my other brother. They did not come south with Harold, but I did. I wanted something for that loyalty."

"Like what?"

"The Earldom of Wessex, mayhap. I would even take Sussex."

"But you were not given anything for your show of loyalty?"

Alary sighed heavily, shaking his head. "You and your Normans killed Harold before that could come about."

"Were it in my power, I would give you what you wanted. I can give you lands in Brittany if you release me. I will give them to you without hesitation."

Alary looked at him. "Rich lands?"

"Very."

"Are you titled, then?"

"My father is," Kristoph said, hearing a sprout of interest in Alary's voice. "He is the Count of Rennes. He would give you much for my return."

Alary considered that, but only for a moment. "I do not wish to live in France," he said. "I was born in England. This is where I will stay."

Kristoph's heart sunk. "Then what do you want to release me?"

Alary leaned over him, getting a good look at that swollen face. "You do not seem to understand that I do not want anything at the moment. I am far more interested in your value to me as a Norman."

"What does that mean?"

"It means that through you, I shall know what the Duke of Normandy has planned and I shall use that to my advantage. Where Harold could not defeat your army, mayhap I shall."

Kristoph was feeling sick, disillusioned. He was also quite hungry and thirsty. "If you give me something to drink, I shall tell you what I know, but I warn you that it will not be very much. I am not privy to Normandy's plans."

Something in Alary's expression suggested he didn't believe the man one bit. "I would suggest you reconsider that statement," he said. Then, he glanced up at the sky, which was beginning to lighten as the sun began to rise. "A new day is upon us, *kriegshund*. It is time to return to my home in the north. We shall become good friends, you and I. And you will tell me all you know."

Kristoph didn't say anything more after that. He could hear Alary moving around, calling out to his men and telling them to gather their possessions and horses in preparation for returning home. It was exactly what Kristoph didn't want to hear. He knew the Normans were only a few miles to the west and if Alary took him away, then the gap would grow and no one would ever find him. They would have no idea where he had gone.

As he lay there listening to the Saxon soldiers gather, visions of his wife filled his head as Gaetan told her that she had become a widow. He thought of his daughter, who would be without a father. There was nothing more he wanted out of life than to return home to his wife and child. Panic set in. He couldn't leave; he *wouldn't* leave. He had to get back to Gaetan.

He wanted to go home.

As wounded as he was, he still managed to roll onto his belly and push himself up onto his hands and knees. Then he tried to stand, but his body was so battered that it made it very difficult. But he ignored the pain, the swimming head; all he could think of was running all the way back to the Norman encampment. He simply had to get there. But just as he lurched to his feet, someone hit him across the back of the head again and he went down like a stone.

Before he blacked out completely, he thought he saw Alary standing over him, laughing.

He was in the grip of the Devil.

Merciful darkness enveloped him.

CHAPTER SIX

❦

A MAN LOST

THEY'D TAKEN THE horses as far as they could go before leaving them in a thick copse of trees about a quarter of a mile from the Saxon encampment.

But they didn't move on from there, at least not immediately. Gaetan and his men, dressed in clothing that blended with their surroundings – faded greens, browns, natural colors – and certainly none of the brightly colored heraldry that the Normans tended to favor – took pieces of the bushes and trees around them and shoved them into their clothing so that they blended in with their surroundings even more. It was a stealth operation and given that they were going in daylight, they wanted to take every precaution not to be seen.

In truth, it was impressive to watch. Ghislaine had seen her own people do such things, especially when hunting, and this was hunting in a sense. They were hunting for their comrade, and for Alary, and they were trying to make themselves as inconspicuous as possible. But it wasn't simply the manner in which they were dressing – it was also their attitude in general. There was a professionalism that Ghislaine had never seen before. They worked as a unit and acted like a unit, each man looking out for the man next to him as well as himself. She knew virtually nothing about these men but she could see how much they cared for one another. They were quiet, efficient, and swift.

Impressive, indeed.

Ghislaine was already dressed in a manner that made her blend with the land and trees – she was wearing a long tunic made from wool that had been dyed with onion, making it a dull shade of brown. She crouched in the bramble that smelled heavily of earth and compost, away from the men who were preparing to stalk the Anglo-Saxon encampment, alternately watching the camp in the distance and the men around her.

If they felt any trepidation, they didn't show it, which kept her from showing any as well. She wouldn't give them the satisfaction of seeing that she was genuinely frightened to have returned to her own encampment.

Alary was here, somewhere, and she wasn't looking forward to seeing the man.

But she was also alternately watching de Wolfe in the midst of all of this or, at least, trying to pretend like she wasn't. Even if she hadn't known he was the man in command, simply from the way he dealt with his men and the way they reacted to him would have told her that he was. He wasn't heavy-handed. In fact, she'd not heard him raise his voice or give any real measure of direction, but a word here or there and his men knew exactly what was expected of them. She'd heard of men commanding simply by their sheer presence but she'd never seen it before until now. De Wolfe literally commanded simply by being there. Men obeyed.

But it was more than his overwhelming presence that had her impressed; it was his appearance as well. The more she looked at him, the more she realized that he was unlike any man she had ever seen. The men she knew, for the most part, were pale, with light or dark hair, a few of them muscular, or tall, and, on occasion, she had come across a man she thought was handsome.

But de Wolfe looked like he'd stepped out of some other world. He was a big man, bigger than any man she'd ever seen, with fists the size of her head. He had a square-jawed face that was handsome enough but when he smiled – and she'd only seen it once, just a flash to one of his men – his face changed dramatically. It was enough to make her heart skip a beat.

But those were foolish thoughts, to be sure, and she was frustrated at herself for thinking them. She refused to admit that her Norman enemy had her intrigued. Therefore, she returned her focus to the encampment in the distance, watching men move about, trying to single out anyone she knew, especially Alary. It was mid-morning by now and she knew he would be up and about, prowling, scheming. What worried her the most was what had become of de Lohr. She couldn't see him from where she sat. It was imperative she locate him.

"Lady Ghislaine."

Startled by her whispered name, Ghislaine turned to see de Wolfe standing behind her with one of his men alongside. It was the same man who had offered to negotiate for de Lohr, as a man of the church, although she didn't know his name. She didn't know any of their names. De Wolfe and the man crouched down a few feet away to be more on her level.

"This is Jathan," de Wolfe said quietly. "He is my priest. Jathan offered himself up as a prisoner once before and he has done it again, so I have agreed. I believe the best plan of action would be for you to enter the encampment with Jathan as your captive. If your absence has been discovered, you can simply say you were hunting for Norman prisoners on the battlefield. Is that something your men would believe?"

Ghislaine nodded. "I believe so," she said. "I mentioned that it is possible my absence has not even been noticed, but if it has, it will make it seem as if I am telling the truth when I bring a Norman captive with me."

De Wolfe lifted an eyebrow in agreement although he didn't seem to be overly enthusiastic about his priest offering himself up as a prisoner. That much had been obvious earlier in the tent when the same discussion had come up, but clearly, de Wolfe had reconsidered that. He glanced at the priest as he spoke.

"It is hoped that Jathan will be taken to where de Lohr is so he can help Kristoph when the time comes to free him," he said. "Mayhap, you can tell your brother you have brought him another prisoner. A gift, as it were. Surely he would take him to where his other prisoners are being held."

Ghislaine looked at the priest. "That is a reasonable certainty," she said hesitantly. "But Alary will not care that he is a priest. He will treat him like any other prisoner."

De Wolfe nodded. "That is the hope."

Ghislaine cast him a long look. "You must be careful what you hope for. You do not know how my brother is."

De Wolfe cocked his head. "Nay, I do not, but I have been a warrior my entire life and I have seen the wicked souls of men. Jathan knows the risks."

Ghislaine's focus settled on the priest, who seemed resolute about the situation. There was no fear in his eyes and Ghislaine was sure the man had no idea what he was getting in to, but she didn't argue. It was a plan that made sense and now it was time to act, for time was growing short. The longer they waited, the more chance there was of Alary leaving the camp and taking de Wolfe's knight with him. Rising to her feet, she brushed the dirt and leaves off her leather hose.

"Then I shall take him and discover where my brother is keeping your man," she said, pulling the leather cap that de Wolfe had yanked off her head, now tucked into the belt at her waist. "I will return as soon as I can."

De Wolfe and Jathan stood up, too, and de Wolfe's other men began crowding around now that the first move on the Anglo-Saxon encampment was about to be made. Ghislaine gathered her long hair in one hand and wounded it up sloppily on her head, pulling the cap down over it. Hair stuck out all over the place even as she pulled the ties down around her neck and secured it. Then, she unsheathed a long, sharp dagger that had been tied to her belt and pointed it at Jathan.

"Come with me," she said to the priest. "And you'd better make it look as if you are afraid of me and my dagger, or this will not go well."

"Pretend I'm holding a dagger on you, Priest," Wellesbourne growled from behind de Wolfe. "That should make you scared enough."

Jathan gave him a rather droll look. "The only thing that scares me about you is your lack of piety, Wellesbourne," he muttered. "God is going to strike you down one of these days and when he does, I do not wish to be anywhere near you lest we both go up in flames. Shall we depart, my lady?"

Ghislaine could see that the threats bouncing about weren't serious. Wellesbourne had a hint of a smile on his lips, as did a couple of the other knights, but de Wolfe had no humor on his face. He simply pointed through the bramble.

"Go," he commanded quietly. When Ghislaine moved forward, he suddenly grabbed her by the arm. "And if you think to betray me and my men by telling your brother that we are gathered in the bramble, know that I will have St. Hèver in the trees with an arrow pointed right at you. He can kill you from quite a distance, so do not make any foolish moves."

Ghislaine looked at him, a hulking presence in the shadowed trees, and her irritation rose. "So we are back to threats, are we?" she asked, offended. "The fact that I came to you with information about your knight wasn't enough. The fact that I have risked my life and continue to risk it for a Norman enemy still means nothing to you. Then, by all means, keep your man trained on me and if you believe I am betraying you, then kill me. But you had better make sure you kill me with the first shot because if you do not, I am fairly good with a bow myself and you will be the first one I will come for."

With that, she shoved Jathan forward, her dagger at his back, and pushed him right through the trees. When he stumbled, she pushed him again, kicking him right in the arse when he turned around to see why she was beating on him so. Together, they burst through the trees and into the clearing beyond, in full view of the Anglo-Saxon encampment about a quarter of a mile away.

Gaetan and his men watched them head off and St. Hèver moved into position with his crossbow, using a tree trunk to steady himself and his weapon. He was aiming right at the lady and her prisoner as the rest of Gaetan's men slowly moved up to gain a better view of them through the trees.

"I do believe she threatened you," Luc de Lara muttered to Gaetan.

He snorted. "Aye, she did," Gaetan replied. "But no more than I threatened her."

Luc simply nodded, his gaze tracking the woman and the priest, as they all were. "Do you really believe she will betray us?"

Gaetan lifted his big shoulders, vaguely. "We shall soon know," he said. "You and Denis flank them as they move. Stay to the trees, however, and stop when it is no longer safe to travel. Keep an eye on the pair for as long as you can."

Luc nodded, moving through the other knights until he came to Denis. Young and excitable, Denis was more than agreeable to the orders and the two of them suddenly took off into the foliage, pushing through the heavy bramble and trying to remain silent as they moved. Gaetan watched them head off until he lost them in the shadow. Then, he moved up beside Téo and Aramis, standing between them as the men watched the Saxon warrior lady and the priest head towards the enemy encampment.

All they could do now was wait.

GHISLAINE KNEW THEY were being watched as she and the priest headed into the Anglo-Saxon encampment and it was difficult to choose just who she was more afraid of at the moment – her brother or the Norman knight pointing an arrow at her back. None of this venture had gone as she had hoped but the problem was that she couldn't stop the forward momentum now. She couldn't simply walk away; she was becoming more and more entrenched in a situation of her own making and struggling not to lose control of it.

She was in it until the end.

As she and Jathan came to the edge of the encampment, several exhausted men around a weakly-smoking fire caught sight of her and began gravitating in her direction. Seeing that she was now noticed, she took action. She grabbed Jathan by the back of his tunic and shoved the tip of the dagger into his back.

"I am sorry if I hurt you," she whispered to him. "But I must make this convincing."

Jathan could see the enemy soldiers heading in their direction and he kept his eyes on them. "Understandable, my lady," he murmured. "Good luck to us both."

With that, the conversation died but Ghislaine's apprehension was full-blown. The blade pressed into Jathan's back was trembling so that she suddenly kicked his knees out and forced him on to the ground so her men would notice the prisoner and not her quivering hands. Besides… she didn't want her shaking hands to jiggle that sharp blade right into the priest's back.

"Look what I have found!" she said triumphantly. "Another Norman dog!"

Men were gathering around her, peering at the man on his belly, his face pressed into the cold, wet grass because Ghislaine had her foot on his head. She was beaming from ear to ear, as if genuinely happy with her captive, but it was all for show – she wanted her men to see how hateful she was towards the Normans and how gleeful she was in the capture of one. She had to be convincing.

And it worked.

Men began to congratulate her, peering down at Jathan only to spit on the man when they looked their fill of him. They had a Norman in their midst now and it seemed to rejuvenate whatever defeat had settled in their hearts and minds. A few of them even kicked Jathan as they circled him, like vultures going in for the kill.

"Another Norman bastard!"

"Kill him! Harold demands it!"

"Wait!" Ghislaine threw up a hand to stop the mob mentality before it truly started. "I will not kill him. I would put him with the other Norman prisoner, the one my brother took from me. Where is he?"

A man with dark dirty hair went to stand with her. He was one of her own soldiers, sworn to her, as were most of the men standing around her. In an age where men controlled the army and the country, it was extremely rare for a woman to command men but Ghislaine did. These men were gifted to her by her brother, Edwin, because he wanted her protected in battle. He knew he couldn't keep her out of a fight so he had gifted her with about a hundred men and the means to support them.

Ghislaine's men were extremely loyal to her, as evidenced by the fact that they'd remained in the encampment even when she'd turned up missing. A few had even gone out to look for her, but most of them were certain that Lady Ghislaine would return. She tended to be a loner at times, and a wanderer, but they knew she would not leave them. Even if she was a woman, she understood the heart of the warrior and the mentality. She would never leave her men if she could help it.

They had been correct.

Therefore, the man with the dirty hair was glad to see her and not surprised she'd brought back a prisoner. Lady Ghislaine was brave that way.

"Alary took his men and left just after dawn, my lady," he told her. "That was a few hours ago."

Ghislaine's smile of triumph turned into something of a grimace and it was a struggle not to openly react to the news. "He left?" she asked, unable to keep the astonishment from her tone. "He... he is gone?"

"Aye."

"And he took his army?"

"Those who could move, aye. At least two hundred men, mayhap a little less."

"But… but what of my Norman prisoner? Did he take my knight, too?"

All of the men were nodding to varying degrees. "He was searching for you before he left, my lady," another man said. "He would not wait for you to return."

So Alary knew I was missing, Ghislaine thought. "So he took my prisoner and ran off?" she asked. "Did he not know I would return?"

The man with the dark hair shrugged hesitantly. "He did not say, my lady," he said. "He looked for you. But when he could not find you, he took his men and his prisoner, and he left."

It was unhappy news, indeed. It wasn't as if Ghislaine could have stopped Alary had she been here, but to run off while she was away seemed underhanded somehow. Still, she was astute enough to realize that there was an unspoken question hanging in the air between her and her men at the moment – the fact that she had gone missing for quite some time. Yet, she was not troubled by it. The answer was on the ground at her feet.

"My brother is a fool," she said, her disgust real. "Had he only waited, I would have had another Norman captive. Did he think I had run off? He knows me better than that." She started to look around, realizing that there weren't as many men around as there had been the night before. In fact, the area seemed rather empty and her disgust turned to puzzlement. "Where did everyone go? Has everyone fled for home?"

The men were looking around because she was. "Most," the man with the dirty hair said. "Lord Leofwine's men departed before the sun rose to return home to his wife in Kent. And everyone else… there is no reason to remain, my lady. It is best to return home and brace for what is to come."

Ghislaine looked at the man. He was young and she could hear the fear in his voice. He'd suffered through the worst of the battle, just as they all had. It made the situation a bit more heady for her, a bit more sad. Beyond her scheming to have the Normans kill Alary lay the very real defeat of the Anglo-Saxon army and the destruction of her people.

And there was nothing any of them could do to stop it.

"It is the Normans that will come," she said, feeling somewhat hollow and depressed even as she said it. "The Normans are already here."

"Aye, my lady."

"And my brother… he had fled them."

"Aye, my lady."

She cast him a sidelong glance. "I would assume that Alary is returning to Tenebris?"

The man shook his head. "He did not say."

Ghislaine sighed faintly, her thoughts moving from the defeated army to her brother's departure. It was what she had feared but honestly hadn't believed would happen, at least not until tomorrow. She had believed they had time before he left the encampment but she'd been wrong.

"Alary had many wounded," she said, looking back over to the east, through a debris field of cold fires and the remnants of makeshift camps. "You said he took those who could move with him? What about his wounded?"

The man pointed off to the east. "He left them," he said grimly. "They are over beyond that row of trees. Brothers from the small priory at Winchelsea have come to take them back to the priory for tending."

So much hopelessness in the dead, the wounded, and the departed. Looking out over the makeshift encampment was like looking at a graveyard. Ghislaine couldn't help but feel more grief. This was what was left of her people, her country. It would never be the same again. But her focus soon moved to the men who were standing around her, men that were loyal to her, men waiting for her orders. While others had fled, they had remained. She knew they were waiting for direction from her and she took a deep breath, summoning the bravery that she was known for. She couldn't let her men down.

"Wytig, have the men pack what possessions they have," she said. "We will go back to Tamworth Castle. Edwin will want to know what has happened and he will want to hear it from us."

Wytig, the young man with the dirty hair, nodded. "Aye, my lady," he said. Other men had heard the order and they were already starting to move, to collect what little they had in preparation for going home, but Wytig was looking at the prisoner beneath Ghislaine's foot. "What of him? Do we take him?"

Ghislaine looked down at the priest. It reminded her that she needed to return to de Wolfe and tell him what had happened. Taking her foot off of the priest's head, she yanked the man to his feet.

"Nay," she said. "I will do what needs to be done with him. Gather the men and, once they are ready, go. I will catch up to you."

Wytig nodded and turned to the dirty, beaten Anglo-Saxons, encouraging them to gather their possessions. As the men prepared to depart, Ghislaine put her knife in Jathan's back and turned him back in the direction they had come.

"Go," she barked.

Her men heard her, watching as she marched the prisoner back towards the trees in the distance. They all assumed that their lady was going to execute the prisoner but no one wanted to interfere. Ghislaine of Mercia could be rather unpredictable and deadly, especially when questioned, so they returned to their task and continued gathering their possessions for the march home. It was time to leave this place of defeat and destruction, and there wasn't one man who wasn't eager to do so.

But she wasn't going to execute the prisoner. She was going to tell de Wolfe that Kristoph had already been taken away. Alary's departure had been unexpected but he was only a few hours ahead of them, at most. Moreover, most of his men were on foot so it would be slow travel for the most part, time enough for Normans on horseback to catch him. Even if Alary had two hundred men, nine Norman knights on horseback could do a good deal of damage, especially if they first removed Alary with the same arrow de Wolfe had threatened her with should she betray them. Once Alary was dead, his men would be leaderless and it would make it very easy to take back their comrade and depart.

At least, that was her theory, one that Ghislaine wouldn't hesitate to put to de Wolfe when she told him that her brother had left and had taken de Lohr with him. Alary of Mercia would be no match for angry Norman knights who wanted their friend back.

Would Ghislaine feel any remorse that she had instigated her brother's demise? About as much remorse as he would feel if the situation was reversed. But one thing was certain; Alary had to die soon or the Norman knight's life would be forfeit.

So would hers if Alary realized what she had done.

CHAPTER SEVEN

cg

GO FORTH AND CONQUER

"HE HAS TAKEN Kristoph and headed north," Gaetan said. "My lord, you know that I cannot let him go. I must retrieve him."

It was nearing noon on the day after the battle north of Hastings that saw Harold Godwinson killed. Unlike the previous day, which had been wrought with inclement weather as the battle was fought, this day was clearing up and the sun was shining, warming that land. But that also meant the bodies of the dead were heating up. The stench at midday was nearly unbearable as scores of Normans hurried to clear up their dead while, to the north, Saxon dead continued to lay spread out over the ground. Rumor had it that Beddingham Priory had sent most of their priests and servants over to clear the Saxon dead, but from the Norman encampment, there seemed to be very little movement.

Yet, it was of no consequence, at least to Gaetan. He stood in the spacious tent of the Duke of Normandy, alone because he'd asked for privacy, and was even now addressing the man. After explaining what had happened to Kristoph and the subsequent attempt to rescue him, Gaetan was now further explaining to the duke that he and his men intended to follow Alary of Mercia to regain their lost man. Unfortunately for Gaetan, or the duke, or both, the duke didn't seem to be apt to readily agree.

A potential problem was looming.

"Alary of Mercia," William of Normandy rolled the name over his tongue thoughtfully. "I know of him. I've not had direct dealing with him, of course, but I know of him. His reputation is rather unsavory."

Gaetan nodded. "According to the man's sister, unsavory is a kind way of putting it, my lord," he said. "Surely you can understand my need to remove Kristoph from his custody as soon as possible."

"And this sister has been the only one to bring you news of Kristoph's disappearance?"

"Aye, my lord."

"Is she telling the truth?"

Gaetan sighed heavily. "I have wondered the very same thing. But in the absence of any other eyewitness to Kristoph's disappearance, I have no choice but to trust her," he said. "However, when Jathan accompanied her to the Saxon encampment, he heard her men speak of the Norman knight that Alary held prisoner. That seems to prove that she was telling the truth."

William lifted his eyebrows in reluctant agreement. A large, muscular man with bushy auburn hair and dark eyes, he was a larger-than-life commander with a temperament to match. He was an exacting master and a skilled one, and he lavished praise and rewards upon his favorites. But he was also very selfish. He wanted his subordinates' attention on him and his needs.

To hear that his great Warwolfe was focused on retrieving a lost man had him somewhat unhappy at the moment. He understood very well that the *Anges de Guerre* were a close-knit group and the loss of one of them was disturbing for all, but he was very reluctant to allow Gaetan to leave him now when he needed him the most.

There was the conquest of a country at stake.

"Then it would seem she has been truthful thus far," he replied belatedly. "But there is no guarantee that she is not leading you into a trap, Gate."

"That is very true, but Kristoph is clearly with her brother. We have no choice but to follow him."

"But why risk all of your men? I do not believe you are thinking clearly."

Gaetan knew that William was reluctant to let him go and he knew why; the duke was inherently selfish. He didn't like that Gaetan wanted to do something other than contribute to the glory of the conquest. Warwolfe, as far as William was concerned, belonged to him and so did his wants and ambitions. Anything that went against what William wanted was met with resistance. Therefore, Gaetan was very careful in his reply.

"I am thinking clearly enough, my lord," he said steadily. "The longer we discuss it, the further away Alary of Mercia travels and the longer it will take me to retrieve Kristoph. You must look at it this way – when I catch up to Alary, he will be the first man to fall under my sword. For abducting Kristoph, make no mistake – I will kill the man. With this brother gone, Edwin and Morcar and the others will be, mayhap, more willing to negotiate with you or even support you rather than resist because they realize their lives will be at stake. Alary's death will send a definitive message to those nobles who choose to resist. So, in a sense, I will be sending a message of Norman dominance to the entire country."

It was a manipulative statement but the duke seemed to agree, reluctant as that agreement was. "That is true," he admitted. "Sending my *Anges de Guerre* to blaze the trail before me will, indeed, send a message."

"Aye, it will, my lord."

"But I do not want all of you to go."

Gaetan cocked an eyebrow. His patience was growing thin. "You know that we travel as a unit," he said. "We work as a unit. If I must choose to leave some behind, you will have extremely unhappy men on your hands. Besides... you have plenty of knights and more than enough support for a further incursion into the country. You do not need me and my men at the moment. We must bring back one of our own, my lord. Surely you understand that."

William eyed him a moment before going to the pewter pitcher of wine and pouring two cups. He brought one over to Gaetan, all the while pondering the situation and what needed to be done. Truth be told, he knew he couldn't deny Gaetan's wish to save Kristoph de Lohr from Alary of Mercia's clutches. Gaetan and Kristoph were like brothers and to deny Gaetan would only incite rage in the man. He didn't need his Warwolfe directing hatred against him. Therefore, he had to be clever about this so they could both get what they wanted out of the situation. He had to make this work for them both.

"You know I do not want you to leave me, not now," he said, grasping at the last vestiges of resistance. "I have great need of you, Gate. But I understand that you must rescue Kristoph. I understand that all too well, for Kristoph is a great knight and a loyal friend. I have tremendous respect for him. What if I wish for you to leave du Reims and de Russe here?"

"They will want to go."

"But I have great need of them. If I cannot have you, then at least leave them with me."

"I must respectfully refuse, my lord."

William frowned. "Then let us say I deny your request to go at all. What would you do then?"

Gaetan took a drink of the sweet red wine. "If you were in my position, what would *you* do, my lord?"

William's frown turned into a sly grin, knowing that Gaetan had him cornered. "I would disobey."

"So would I."

William laughed softly. "That would not do for either of us," he said. "I am far too fond of you to punish you if that were to happen, so I suppose that it is best that I do not deny you. Are you sure I cannot change your mind?"

"Alas, my lord, you cannot."

"Then I will, therefore, give you permission to go, but you will do something for me when you do."

"Anything, my lord."

William's dark eyes glittered. The man was a grand opportunist. Since he couldn't hold Gaetan back, he knew he had to make the best of it. If Gaetan wanted something from him, then he wanted something from Gaetan.

"Take a quarter of my army with you and subdue Mercia and the Midlands when you go," he said. "After you find Kristoph, you will begin the conquest of the heart of England. I intend to remain to the south to claim what I can before moving on London, but you... you will go into the heart of England and you will subdue it. With my army claiming the south, including Winchester where the royal treasury is situated, and you in the heart of England to bring it under Norman control, we can bring the Saxons to their knees. Think on it, Gate – we shall have this entire country subdued within the year."

It was an enormous responsibility and an enormous honor William was asking of Gaetan. It was a task that only a commander of Gaetan's caliber would be capable of and Gaetan didn't take the responsibility lightly. He knew this was the kind of directive that would have a man leaving a great mark on his legacy – beyond his Warwolfe persona, beyond his great reputation as a knight, lay a man who hoped to leave a legacy for his children one day that didn't involve memories or reputations one couldn't use to buy food or clothe men. His children, when they came, would need something tangible for that.

This was the opportunity to get it.

"I am grateful for your trust, my lord," Gaetan finally said. "When I do this thing, what shall be my reward?"

William snorted at his ever-shrewd Warwolfe; they thought very much alike, indeed. "As great a reward as I can give you," he said. "There are great riches to the north, you know. I have studied this country and I know her well. There is an area north towards Chester called the Black Country, as it is rich with coal and other elements that can make a man extremely wealthy. The largest town is called Hamtun where there is a large abbey, I am told. The town deals in coal and sheep. Do what I ask of you and I shall make you the Earl of Hamtun and all of the riches that belong to her. I want my Warwolfe to be happy."

Gaetan liked the sound of that. In fact, it was extremely generous. "No man will know it is my town unless we call it Wolfeshamtun," he said, unable to let go of his pride, not even for a moment. "If I am going to rule, then let all men know *who* rules."

William nodded, seeing the gleam of satisfaction in Gaetan's eye. "Agreed," he said. "Call it Wolfeshamtun or Wolverhamtun, or whatever you wish. It shall be your domain, Warwolfe. Go north and conquer."

Gaetan was feeling increasingly eager to get on with what needed to be done, now fueled by a substantial reward from the man who would be king. Sensing that their conversation was coming to a close or, at the very least, wanting it to come to a close, he bowed his head respectfully to William before turning for the tent opening.

"I will need to depart today, as quickly as possible, my lord," he said. "If you are agreeable, I will have du Reims and de Reyne select men from the army to accompany us. I have been so involved in Kristoph's disappearance that I am ashamed to say that I do not even know the strength of our remaining army other than my own men."

William watched him as he walked away, a very busy man, indeed. "And how many of your men survived?"

Gaetan paused by the tent opening. "I brought two thousand men with me," he said. "I have lost nearly two hundred with nearly the same number wounded."

William nodded as he absorbed those statistics. "You fared better than some," he said. "Select no more than one thousand men to fill in your ranks. That will give you a sizable army with which to infiltrate the heart of England."

"I am taking archers."

"You already have a goodly amount of archers, Gate."

"I need more."

William sighed at his stubborn commander. "Then, God's Blood, take them," he said, annoyed. But the annoyance quickly cleared away. "And this sister of Mercia – where is she?"

"In my tent, my lord. She is awaiting my return."

"As your captive?"

Gaetan wriggled his dark eyebrows, a somewhat ironic gesture. "As my guide," he said. "She does not know it yet, but it is she who will take me to Alary. If she thinks to lead me into a trap, then she will be the first one to step into it. Every step we take northward, she will be in the lead."

William simply nodded. "Send me a message to keep me abreast of your progress," he said. "I have a suspicion this will be a long and perilous journey."

"So do I," Gaetan admitted.

"Gate?"

"Aye, my lord?"

"*Et pro Gloria dei.*"

The words that the *Anges de Guerre* used to send each other into battle were now murmured from the duke's lips. There wasn't much more to stay at that point because he knew that his Warwolfe would take all precautions necessary to ensure a successful mission which, in William's estimation, was turning out to be a blessing in disguise. Now, de Wolfe had a reason to head into the heart of England and it had nothing to do with the lands and title he was promised, but everything to do with a missing comrade… and that was most powerful motivator of all.

Nay, William wasn't genuinely upset about de Wolfe's intention to head after Alary of Mercia but he wanted the man to be cautious and thoughtful. The last thing he wanted to do was lose one or more of Gaetan's men but, ultimately, this undertaking would work to everyone's advantage.

At least, that was the hope. But God help the lords of Mercia if something happened to Kristoph de Lohr. William knew, as he lived and breathed, that the beast would be unleashed if that happened, and that beast would tear apart Mercia and the Midlands like nothing anyone had ever seen before.

God help them all.

CHAPTER EIGHT

ɔ

UNLIKELY ALLIES

G HISLAINE WAS SITTING in de Wolfe's tent because that was where
he put her and told her to stay. He needed to speak with the Duke
of Normandy, he said, and his other men had disappeared, including
the priest. The squires, however, were crouched outside of the tent like
watch dogs, cleaning mail and waiting for their master to return.

Making sure the Saxon woman didn't escape.

As if they could stop her but, frankly, Ghislaine was too tired to run
at the moment. After she had delivered the news that Alary had left the
encampment and taken Kristoph with him, Gaetan had gone to seek
permission to pursue Alary northward and Ghislaine was left wondering what de Wolfe intended to do once he received that permission.
Would he try to follow with only his few men or would he bring an
army with him?

At this point, Ghislaine wasn't entirely sure what her role was in all
of this. She'd told de Wolfe about his abducted knight. One of his other
knights, a Welshman, knew the area and knew where Alary's lair of
Tenebris was, or at least the proximity thereof.

Now, de Wolfe had a mission to attend to in order to rescue his
man but Ghislaine wasn't part of that mission, or so she thought. There

wasn't any reason for her to go with the Normans as they headed into enemy territory. Perhaps the best thing for her to do would be to catch up with her men and return to Tamworth to tell her brother, Edwin, what had transpired near Hastings. It was time for her to return to her family and pray that de Wolfe and his men killed Alary in their quest to regain their man.

So she waited, impatiently, for de Wolfe to return. Seated on her bum in the middle of the tent with her legs hugged up to her chest, she lay her cheek on her up-bent knees, hearing the sounds outside of the tent, the unfamiliar conversation of Norman warriors. She was cold, and hungry, and wondering where her next meal would come from. Surely the Normans would not feed her, although she had hoped for something. He stomach was growling painfully.

More waiting and wondering as the minutes dragged on. At some point, she must have dozed off because when next she opened her eyes, it was because someone was sniffing around her. Or, more accurately, some*thing* was sniffing around her. When her sleepy eyes came into focus, it took her a moment to realize she was looking at a very big dog.

Brown doggy eyes stared aback at her. Startled, Ghislaine refrained from making any sudden movements, afraid the dog might attack her. He was absolutely enormous, with shaggy gray hair and a long snout. And big teeth; definitely big teeth.

As she stared at him, unmoving, he licked his chops and lay down beside her, all the while looking up at her rather expectantly. But Ghislaine had no idea what to do with the monstrous dog looking at her. Perhaps, it was a death watch and he was waiting for her to die first so he could eat her. What else did Norman dogs eat but prisoners? When her stomach growled, loudly, the dog lifted his head and licked his chops again. Ghislaine resisted the urge to scream for help.

It seemed like she spent an eternity watching the dog as it stared at her. It was an odd standoff. Her limbs were becoming cramped from being folded up like they were but she didn't dare move. Just when she thought she could take no more, she heard the tent flap slap back.

"Gather my things." It was de Wolfe, snapping orders to the squires as he entered the tent. "Our army will depart within the hour and I want to be ready. You will also make sure de Lohr's belongings are packed up but we will leave those with Normandy for safekeeping. Even now, du Reims and de Winter are mustering the quartermasters so make sure my trunks are loaded onto the wagons."

The boys were scrambling; Ghislaine could hear them. The dog, lying next to her, suddenly popped up and moved away, rushing to his master when he heard his voice. Ghislaine, too, lifted her head about the time de Wolfe came into view. He glanced at her as he began pulling off gloves.

"We will be leaving as soon as my men can be mustered and the army organized," he addressed her. "We will be heading north within the hour."

Ghislaine struggled not to yawn. "The duke has given you his permission to go after your knight?"

"He has," he said, throwing the gloves into a large chest. He went to work on removing his tunic. "How much do you know of this country, Lady Ghislaine? What I mean to ask is how well you know the path to this Tenebris that you have mentioned as Alary's stronghold."

Ghislaine, fuzzy-minded from hunger and the lack of sleep, had to ponder his question for a moment before answering. "I know it well," she said, rubbing her eyes. "You must travel north from here and then veer northwest when you come to London. There is a main road, a Roman road, that will take you north all the way to Chester, but you must go west when you come to Kidderminster. That will take you to the Far Forest where Alary's stronghold is."

One of de Wolfe's squires suddenly rushed into the tent, racing to help his master. The dog, who had been hovering by de Wolfe in the hopes of being petted, finally received a pat and, satisfied, moved away. Unfortunately for Ghislaine, he was coming in her direction again and she leaned away from the animal as it came near. She eyed the beast as it sat right down next to her as if they were the greatest companions in the world.

"Then what would you estimate as the time it would take for an army to travel to the Far Forest?" de Wolfe asked, oblivious to Ghislaine and her fear of the dog that had cozied up to her. "My concern is that we reach the Alary's lair before winter sets in completely. Weather will hamper a mission such as this one."

Ghislaine alternated between eyeballing the dog and de Wolfe. "It will be cold through Christmastide but winter usually does not set in until after the new year." She inched away from the dog, who lifted his head to see why she had moved. "May I leave now? There is nothing more I can do for you. You know where Alary is taking your knight. I have told you all that I can."

De Wolfe turned to her, his gaze appraising her, as if he knew something she didn't. In fact, that wasn't far from the truth. It was obvious by his expression that he was about to say something he was quite sure Ghislaine wouldn't like.

"You are not going anywhere," he said quietly. "You will be accompanying me and my men north as we follow your brother. You will be our guide."

Ghislaine's hunger and exhaustion were forgotten. She staggered to her feet as the dog next to her did the same, standing up because she was. But Ghislaine wasn't looking at the dog; her gaze on de Wolfe was wide with shock.

"I cannot be your guide!" she said. "I must return to Tamworth Castle, to Edwin, and tell him what has happened. I am no longer of any use to you – I have done what I set out to do. I told you of your knight's abduction and I told you where to find him. You must do the rest yourself!"

De Wolfe went back to unlacing his tunic, ignoring Ghislaine's distress. "You are of great use to me," he said, "and you shall not return home until I am finished with you."

Ghislaine had no idea how to respond. Leading the Normans to the Anglo-Saxon encampment to find their knight and leading them on a perilous journey northward to follow her brother were two different things. The longer she gazed at de Wolfe, the more panic she began to feel. She couldn't go northward; she had to go home. She *wanted* to go home. With that thought, she made a break for the door.

Gaetan was on her in a minute. He could see the bewilderment, the terror, in her eyes and he suspected she might try to run. It was just a feeling he had. When she suddenly darted for the tent entry, he was ready for her. He was bigger, stronger, and faster than she was and he grabbed her around the torso before she could get to the opening.

When she turned into a wildcat, Gaetan was not surprised; he simply held tight and tried not to get kicked in tender places. He turned away from the entry with her in his arms as his terrified squire bolted from the tent. The lad didn't want to be caught up in any fight, which was wise of him. Even the dog scampered away, hovering nervously at the edges of the tent.

"Stop fighting," Gaetan said quietly and somewhat calmly into her ear. "Cease your struggles, little mouse. It will not change the way of things."

But Ghislaine was too overcome to respond. She did, however, feel his mouth by her right ear and she slammed her head in that direction, head-butting his jaw in what was a fairly hard blow. When he tried to move his head away from her, she stiffened up, threw her head back again, and caught him in the chin. The ensuing strike caused him to bite his tongue and he could already taste the blood.

"Release me!" she howled. "You have no right to hold me! Let me go!"

Gaetan had to admit that she put up a hell of a good fight. His little mouse may have been rather small and slender, but she was very strong for a woman. He was impressed. Moreover, she had a warrior's instinct and she knew just how to hit him to break his hold on her, but he was more experienced than she was. He shifted his grip on her so she could no longer head-butt him, but he hadn't taken into consideration her powerful, slender legs. She managed to wind her legs all around his somehow and, before he could catch himself, he ended up tripping and falling forward.

Ghislaine's momentary victory in tripping up her captor ended in pain as she hit the ground and he fell atop her. He was a big man, his weight more than double hers, so when he fell on her, it knocked the wind from her. Her struggles slowed dramatically as stars danced before her eyes.

But for Gaetan, it was infuriating. He didn't care if he fell on top of her or not. Once he was down, he rocked back on his knees and grabbed her by the arm and flipped her over onto her back.

"Foolish wench," he growled. "What made you think you could win that fight? And what made you think that the moment you came into my encampment that I would not do with you as I pleased? Are you truly so naive?"

Ghislaine lay there, halfway on her back, as Gaetan knelt over her. She was panting heavily, having had the wind knocked out of her. But unfortunately for Gaetan, the wheels of her mind were still spinning. This fight wasn't over by a long shot. Realizing that Gaetan was straddling her, she brought up a knee and managed to catch him in the groin.

It wasn't a hard blow but it was enough to cause him some pain. She'd put a boney knee right into his manhood and he grunted in both surprise and pain, furiously grabbing her as she tried to use his momentary shock to crawl away. He had a leg, yanking her back to him even as she tried to claw her way from beneath him. But pulling her along the ground had lifted her tunic, exposing her legs and buttocks that were encased in the leather breeches. Her buttocks drew his attention; bringing down a trencher-sized hand, he spanked her hard.

Ghislaine howled in pain as he spanked her at least three times, harder than she'd ever been spanked in her life, but his swat had the desired effect – she stopped trying to escape him. She lay there and kicked her legs angrily, effectively trapped beneath him.

"You deserve all that and more," Gaetan hissed, his groin still throbbing from her knee. He spanked her again, a sharp slap echoing off the walls of the tent. "And that is for trying to damage my legacy."

Ghislaine had stopped trying to escape him because she knew she couldn't win; he had her tightly, now with her buttocks exposed to his big hand. "You beast," she breathed. "You Norman barbarian! I am not surprised you take pleasure in hitting a woman!"

Gaetan had a temper; his men knew it and soldiers who had served with him knew it. He was quick to temper when seriously displeased and, in this instance, he was more than seriously displeased. The little Saxon wench had tried to injure him and she was going to pay the price.

"We Norman barbarians only strike animals, of which you are most definitely one," he said, his grip tightening on her when she twisted angrily. One hand had her pinned while the other reached down to yank on her breeches, pulling so hard that the ties either broke or pulled loose, sliding them down to expose her naked arse. "And disobedient little mice must be punished."

With that, he slapped her nude flesh with his palm again, leaving a perfect hand print across both already-reddened buttocks. Ghislaine screamed as if he were killing her.

"You are... *evil!*" she cried. "How do you dare do such a thing? *Let me go!*"

Gaetan wasn't about to let her go. She had a few more spankings coming as far as he was concerned. Any woman who would try to shove her knee into his manhood would get nothing less. But when he lifted his hand to slap her buttocks again, a strange thing happened; he hasn't really looked at her arse before but now that he got a good look at it, he wasn't sure he wanted to slap it again.

He'd never seen anything so perfect.

White, heart-shaped, and smooth, her buttocks were exquisite. Mouth-watering, even. It was utterly strange that as he sat there and stared at them, he could actually feel his aching member becoming aroused. More than aroused, in fact – *hungry*. It had been a long time since he'd had a woman, since his first bedslave had not accompanied him from Brittany. He was, in fact, a man with an insatiable sexual appetite and he had more than one bedslave, but only one that he bedded with regularity. He called her *Prima*.

Now, gazing down at Ghislaine of Mercia's perfect naked buttocks, he could imagine sliding his aroused member between those perfect cheeks and finding great satisfaction in the warm folds. Perhaps he'd found a Saxon bedslave now that he was in their country. If that was his intention, then perhaps he shouldn't beat her so hard.

He didn't want damaged goods.

"You deserve nothing less than a good beating," he said, but his spanking hand had ceased. Shifting his body weight, he yanked her over onto her back again so that he could see her face. But the moment he looked at her, he could see the tears on her face. He peered at her curiously.

"Why do you weep?" he demanded. "If you are going to fight like a man, then you must take your punishment like a man. And those who are defeated do not usually weep unless they are idiots who have no business fighting in the first place."

Ghislaine was trying very hard not to burst into tears; she was hungry, exhausted, and now with the added pressure of being embarrassed on top of it. He was dealing her a ration of insults, which she more than likely deserved at this point for trying to knee him in the groin. It was a struggle to keep her composure.

"You have no right to keep me a captive," she said hoarsely. "I have only tried to help you find your knight and, for that, you hold me captive and beat me. I should have never come to you, Norman. I should have kept my mercy to myself."

Gaetan looked down into that sad little face. He couldn't agree with her because had she not come to him, he would still be wondering what had happened to Kristoph. So, in that sense, he owed her a great deal. It was enough to soften him, just the slightest, but not too much. She was still the enemy as far as he was concerned.

"You came to me to betray your brother," he pointed out. "I wonder if there were really ever any altruistic intentions on your part."

She scowled. "I told you that I showed your knight mercy because you had shown it to me upon the field of battle. But now I wish I had not!"

He nodded faintly. In truth, he didn't want to start a big battle with her again, but she had to know who was in control. He could tell that she was used to being in command and not being contested. That being the case, this was going to be a harsh lesson for her because he intended to dominate her any way he could.

She would *not* get the better of him.

"Mercy is the mark of a true warrior," he told her, hoping that she would respond to reason. He was growing weary of wrestling with her when he had work to do. "I want you to listen to me and listen carefully, because what I tell you will be of importance to you. You did right by showing Kristoph mercy. You will never know how grateful I am to you. I understand that you came to me to tell me where he was but you also confessed that you hoped my drive to rescue my knight would result in your brother's death. Therefore, you have a dual purpose. I have no problem killing Alary once we catch up to him. In fact, I demand it – he has taken my knight and my vengeance knows no bounds. But your task with me is not completed. Telling me of Kristoph and your brother was only the first part of it. Now, I need your help to find your brother so that you may finish what you have started. If my mission is to be a success, then I need your help. Will you do this?"

From fighting and spanking one moment to calm, rational conversation the next, Ghislaine found herself staring up at the man and watching his mouth when he spoke. He had full lips, curvy, and big dimples in each cheek when his mouth moved. And his voice... it was that liquid metal again, searing and smooth, filling her ears with its heat. Something about that voice made her heart lurch strangely. Or was it simply him in all of his male glory that did it? She honestly didn't know. All she knew was that when he spoke to her in that tone, she felt like doing anything he wished, like she had no mind of her own.

Witchcraft!

"You do not need my help," she said, her voice raspy. "I told you where Alary lives. You can easily find him."

Gaetan shook his head. "I do, indeed, need your help. You know this land, the people. You will be of great service to me and my men as we navigate into the heart of the country."

Ghislaine could tell that no matter what she said, he was still going to force her to accompany him. It wasn't as if she had to return home because anyone was waiting for her; there wasn't anyone any longer. She'd spent the past two years trying to find something to fill that hole that her sweet Hakon had left in her; whether it was helping Edwin or commanding her men, no matter what she did, that hole lingered. She had no reason to believe that assisting the Normans would help her find what she was looking for, but it wasn't as if she really needed to return home. There were only bittersweet memories there, and if she was considered a traitor for aiding the enemy, she really didn't care. She knew the truth.

Perhaps now, she was being presented with another purpose in life. A Norman purpose.

"Very well," she said after a moment. "I will take you. I will finish what I started. But you had better kill my brother or he will kill me when he sees what I have done."

Gaetan had to admit he was rather relieved that she was willing to cooperate. "Do not trouble yourself over your brother. When I catch up to him, he will not survive my wrath."

"I hope that is true."

"If I release you, you will not try to run again?"

"I will not try to run again."

Gaetan immediately climbed off her, reaching down a hand to pull her up. But Ghislaine ignored the hand; she wasn't willing to forgive him yet for everything he'd done to her. She wasn't willing to fall so easily for his chivalry. Instead, she sat there, trying to pull up her breeches discreetly.

As she fidgeted with her clothing, unwilling to look at him, the big dog came up beside her again, sitting down and leaning against her. Ghislaine had completely forgotten about the dog, who had scampered out of the way when the fighting began, but now he was back again and practically sitting on top of her. She tried to scoot away from him.

"I do not like dogs," she said. "Can't this beast find someone else to sit next to?"

Gaetan had been watching her as she tried to straighten her clothing out, but he'd just turned for his chest again when she spoke. He looked over his shoulder at the big wolfhound as it practically sat in her lap.

"That is Camulos, named after the Gaul god of war," he said, turning back to his trunk. "He will answer to Cam."

"I do not like dogs."

"That is unfortunate because he likes you."

"Is he your dog of war?"

Gaetan sighed heavily. "Nay," he said flatly. "Cam is like my child; loyal, affectionate, and demanding of my attention. He will lick you to death before he would try to kill you. It is unfortunate that a dog with that size is so docile, but I do not have the heart to leave him behind. He goes where I go."

Ghislaine managed to pull her breeches up again, re-tying them with part of a leather strip that had been broken when Gaetan had yanked them down. She moved away from the dog only to have it cozy up to her again. She sighed with frustration as the dog looked at her with longing in its doggy eyes.

"My men packed my possessions and took them when they left the encampment," she said, ignoring the dog who wanted her affection. "I have nothing but the clothes on my back, my bow, and my knife. I have nothing else."

Gaetan pulled the tunic over his head, revealing a padded tunic beneath. "I will supply you with what you need."

"I need something to eat," she fired back softly, noting his disapproving expression when he glanced up at her. She softened her demand, not wanting to anger him because she wanted something from him. "I... I have not eaten since yesterday."

Still casting her that expression that suggested he didn't like a demanding woman, Gaetan made his way over to the tent flap even as he unfastened the ties on the padded tunic. He stuck his head out of the opening and ordered one of the squires to bring food. When the boy went off, running, Gaetan came back into the tent and pulled off the padded tunic.

"I will have food brought to you," he said. "What else do you require?"

Ghislaine didn't answer right away, mostly because she found herself looking at a naked man from the waist up. And what a naked man... Gaetan's skin was tanned from having worked and practiced beneath the sun's rays and he had a fine matting of dark hair over his chest. His neck was thick, his shoulders broad, and the muscular design of his arms and chest were a size that Ghislaine had never seen before. The man was positively enormous. Her heart started to do that odd leaping thing again and, this time, she realized that her breathing was coming in strange gasps as well.

Of course, she'd seen men with their tunics off and in an intimate situation. She well remembered Hakon's sinewy torso and long limbs. He was the only man who had ever touched her naked flesh until Gaetan had so rudely spanked her naked buttocks. But in looking at the attractiveness of the Norman as he tossed the padded tunic into the chest... she almost didn't care that he'd spanked her.

Maybe if she was lucky, he'd do it again.

Foolish wench, what are you thinking? She scolded herself, tearing her eyes away from Gaetan as he practically stripped naked in front of her. Good God, is that where this was heading? Was he simply going to take off of his clothing right in front of her? The thought titillated her and terrified her at the same time. She tried to distract herself by focusing on the question he'd asked her.

"I... I require a bedroll, something to sleep on when we travel," she said. "Mayhap a cloak because mine was with my men when they took my possessions away. I will also need a horse and some arrows for my quill. I used most of mine in the battle yesterday."

Gaetan was rummaging around in the big chest. He didn't answer her because he seemed to be quite intent on finding something. Ghislaine kept her gaze averted from him, mostly because she was afraid that if she looked at his naked chest again she would never be able to look away. But as she listened to the rustling behind her, the dog put his big paw on her lap. She picked it off.

"Here," Gaetan said, tossing a few things at her, garments of some kind. "See if these will fit. If I am to travel with a woman, I prefer she look like a woman. See if any of that is serviceable to you."

Offended, Ghislaine turned to tell him so but he tossed another garment and it hit her in the face. Sputtering, she pulled it off, eyeing him unhappily a moment before turning to inspect it.

Surprisingly, it was a very fine shift. Curious, she looked at the other things that were landing around her as he tossed them out of the chest. More shifts and even two heavy *cotes*, or long tunics that went all the way to the ground. These were made of wool but it was of a very fine type. More things came flying out at her, including scarves, and at least one belt that was woven with leather and had tassels on the end.

Truthfully, Ghislaine had never seen such fine things. Worse still, she'd never dressed as a fine lady in her life and had never had the need for this kind of clothing. Feeling the softness of these garments, however, she was greatly tempted. It was the first time in her life that such clothing had tempted her. She looked at Gaetan in astonishment.

"Where do you get these things?" she asked.

He stood up from his chest with a leather satchel in his hand that seemed to be full. "They belong to me," he said. "My... let us say my companions wear them and sometimes they travel with me, so I have those possessions mixed with mine."

Ghislaine didn't understand his reference. "Companions?" she repeated. Then, it occurred to her. "You mean whores?"

He shook his head. "Women that belong to me," he said. "Call them servants if you will."

She looked at one of the cotes, dyed a dark blue. "Your servants wear fine things such as these?" she asked, awed. "You must be a very generous master."

Gaetan watched her as she rubbed her hand on the soft woolen garment. Truth be told, those things belonged to his first bedslave, *Prima*, whose real name was Adéle, an Anglo-Saxon woman he'd stolen from a Breton baron whose home he'd overrun many years ago. Adéle was bright, sensual, sexually experienced, and older than him by a few years. He was fond of her, just like he was fond of Camulos the dog, but there wasn't anything more to it. There never had been, even when she'd given birth to his two sons. He'd almost lost her in the last birth but she had recovered, still to adorn his bed where or when the mood struck him.

For some reason, he hadn't brought her on this trip, mostly because none of the usual camp followers were coming because of the limited space on the cogs that brought the men to the shores of England. Therefore, Adéle remained behind in Brittany along with the rest of the non-military retinue he usually brought, mostly servants, but Adéle's clothing was still intermingled with his.

Now, Ghislaine would wear it. There was a part of him that was slightly eager to see what she looked like when dressed as a woman. As beautiful as she was, he could only imagine what fine clothing would do for her.

"I can be generous when it is warranted," he said. Then, he unslung the satchel that was over his shoulder and dropped it onto the ground beside her. "I am not entirely sure what is in there, but you may use the satchel to keep your possessions in."

Ghislaine picked it up and put it on her lap, peering inside the leather sack. "More possessions for your servants?"

"Aye."

Possessions, indeed. There was a small hand mirror, a comb, a horsehair brush, tweezers, an alabaster pot that contained some kind of balm made from wax and honey, a lumpy white cake of soap that smelled of rosemary, and a glass phial tucked inside a small leather pouch, stuffed with dried grass, that was half-full of oil that smelled of roses.

It was more feminine things than Ghislaine had ever seen, like a treasure trove of silly things she'd never cared for, perhaps because she'd never had the money for them. But now, someone was giving her these things.

Selfishly, she wanted to keep them, even if other women before her had used them. Wondrous, magical things that Norman women used.

As the dog lay down beside her and kept trying to put his paws on her, Ghislaine forgot about the fight and the general reluctance to accompany the Normans northward as she inspected and then neatly folded all of the clothing that Gaetan had thrown at her. Three shifts, two cotes, a scarf, a belt, and even a pair of what looked like short braes, or fine woolen trousers that stopped right above the knee.

Ghislaine had never seen such a thing before and held them up, inspecting them curiously. But one thing she noted as she went through the possessions – de Wolfe's "servants" were heavier than she was. She didn't have the round bottom to fill them out, although her breasts were rather full. She knew the items were going to hang on her somewhat but, in truth, she didn't care. Looking at the rags she wore compared to the clothing she had in her hand… she was willing to let it hang. It was a benefit to the situation that was unexpected, indeed.

The food came after that as did a bucket of cold water that Gaetan had requested to wash with. He was still over by his chest, alternately watching Ghislaine as she sat there with the attention-demanding dog and Adéle's clothes spread around her, and pulling forth items to take with him on their journey.

Outside the tent, his men were packing their possessions and the army was amassing. But inside the tent, Gaetan was quite curious about the young woman in whose hands he would soon be placing his life and the lives of his men. Had he not been so desperate to regain Kristoph, he more than likely wouldn't have forced the lady into his custody. But the truth was that he wanted his knight returned, and in one piece, and the lady on the ground seemed to be his best option. As he'd told William, every step they took northward, Ghislaine of Mercia would be in the lead.

He didn't know if he was anticipating this trip or coming to dread it.

Either way, there was little choice but to go.

CHAPTER NINE

☙

THE HUMANITY BENEATH

Two days later
Outside of Chipstead, 52 miles north of the battlefield

G HISLAINE DIDN'T MIND travel, for she was heartier than most women. She was used to traveling with men and suffering hardship of cold and weather and limited food, but traveling with over two thousand Norman soldiers and nine Norman knights was something of an experience for a woman who thought she was well-seasoned for such things.

Dressed in one of the cotes that Gaetan had given her and wearing a cloak that one of the men had loaned her, a heavy thing that wasn't very clean but it was very warm, she rode a shaggy stout mare and was relegated to riding just behind the knights at the front of the column. There were soldiers behind her, mounted cavalry, foot soldiers behind them, and the provisions wagons bringing up the rear with a small contingent of soldiers to protect them from behind.

There was crisp organization to the movement and the structure of the army, something Ghislaine found quite fascinating. She'd been a warrior most of her life but the Normans had a different type of philosophy when it came to their troops than her people did. She would admit that her people weren't nearly as organized in some aspects, nor as well-armed. The Normans seemed to bring everything with them – smithies, leatherworkers, quartermasters, cooks – everything to possibly keep an army of this size going.

Then, there were the knights themselves. That was where Ghislaine's attention was most of the time, on the elite knights who served de Wolfe. *Gaetan*. That was where it all started; she'd spent two days watching the man from the rear, his proud posture as he rode his charcoal-colored beast and the way he commanded his men with such ease. There was something hugely impressive about it and she was coming accustomed to her fluttering heart when it came to Gaetan de Wolfe. The man did nothing but make her heart flutter.

She was finished being angry at herself for it. Now, she was actually coming to enjoy the sensation. It wasn't as if Gaetan had given her any encouragement or even anything suggestive; far from it. Maybe that was the most attractive thing of all about him. He was a challenge in every sense of the word. And in her world, he was forbidden. Perhaps that was the most appealing thing of all.

An enemy knight who made her heart lurch.

But there were other knights around him, men who were clearly powerful and seasoned in their own right, men she'd been exposed to from the beginning of her association with Normans, but now she knew their names even though they didn't have much to do with her. These were all friends of Kristoph, the man she'd come to know briefly, the man who had started her entire association with de Wolfe, and she knew their drive to rescue Kristoph was as strong as Gaetan's was. She could see it in their eyes.

Casually, her gaze drifted over to her right. A knight named de Reyne was there, a big man with shaggy dark hair and eyes that were a murky shade of blue. He was somewhat quiet but when he did speak, it was loud and booming. Nothing he did was soft of volume. To her left was a knight named Aramis de Russe, a seriously frightening specimen of a knight. He simply had a look about him that suggested great pain and destruction to his enemies, so Ghislaine tried to stay clear of him. Even now, she was afraid to look at him.

Riding slightly behind her, back with the cavalry, were two more knights, Marc de Moray and Denis de Winter. De Moray was terrifying like de Russe was, with black eyes and an angular face, while de Winter had that same handsome look about him that Gaetan did and seemed a bit more friendly. At least he would dip his head politely at her when their eyes met.

The rest of the knights were somewhere back behind her with the rest of the army, men she'd only become acquainted with as far as their names were concerned – Luc de Lara, a titled knight as Count of Boucau. Kye St. Hèver was blonde and pale but perhaps one of the most muscular men she had ever seen. Then there was the Welsh mercenary, Wellesbourne, who was quite possibly as frightening as de Russe and, finally, Téo du Reims, the only knight other than Gaetan who had actually spoken to her. He was polite but distant, a handsome man with copper curls and dark eyes.

And there was Gaetan....

He'd hardly said anything more to her since that day in his tent where they'd battled to the death. Well, not exactly the death, but certainly to her submission. He kept himself at the head of the pack, away from his men for the most part, riding alone except for his big gray hound because that was the way he preferred it. His squires, and other squires, also rode near their masters and, every so often, Ghislaine would see a squire rushing up to de Wolfe, who would speak briefly to the lad before sending him back to his men or back to the rear of the convoy. Strict protocols were observed at all times.

Unfortunately, it made for a boring journey because there was very little conversation between the knights that she could overhear to amuse herself. The priest, Jathan, rode directly behind her but he did not strike up any conversations with her although he had smiled at her once or twice during the course of their journey, smiling at the woman who had put her food on his head and shoved a knife into his back.

Ghislaine would have liked to have spoken to him, at least, just to pass the time, but there were no such opportunities, so she spent the time gazing up at the sky, watching the birds, or the clouds, or the scenery in general. They were still south of London by several miles but they passed near a cluster of several small villages grouped together off to the east. Smoke from the villages hung in the sky in a brown layer, haze from a thousand cooking fires.

As they moved further north, the road narrowed and the foliage around them began to thicken and become more wild. Ghislaine knew this road since it went between Edwin's holdings and London, and she knew the area slightly only because there was a great lord's house not far ahead where Edwin had often stopped to rest during his travels. It was later in the day at this point and the clouds, which had stayed away since they began their journey two days ago, were threatening to return and dump their watery load on them. Ghislaine could see the clouds off to the east.

"My lady." One of the squires was suddenly beside her, his young face flushed with urgency. "Sir Gaetan wishes to speak with you."

A little surprised, and more than a little concerned, Ghislaine spurred her horse forward, pushing between de Russe and de Reyne as she went. Her animal had a rather bumpy gait as she bounced around on the fat horse until she reached Gaetan. Reining the beast to a walk, she looked at up Gaetan expectantly.

"You wished to speak with me?" she asked politely.

He was wearing a great helm with a band of metal that went down the length of his nose. He had on a mail hood so most of his face was covered with mail, but the eyes were exposed. He turned to look at her and, once again, she could feel her heart lurch. She was coming to expect that reaction to the man as of late.

"When we are in the presence of my men, you will address me as 'my lord'," he told her. "You seem to be rather relaxed on the respect you show those above you."

Ghislaine blinked in surprise. She hadn't expected a tongue lashing, nor did she like it. "If that is the case, then you will address me formally as well, my lord," she said, unwilling to submit to the man's pride. "I am the sister of two earls and the sister-in-law to a king. I do not believe I am beneath you in rank."

Something flickered in those bronze eyes. He suddenly remembered that he had a suspicion of her true identity when they first met. He had a feeling that those suspicions were about to be confirmed. He decided quickly that he wouldn't let on. "What king?" he asked, dubious.

It took Ghislaine a moment to realize that, in fact, she hadn't told him anything about her relation to Harold. She had purposely not told him, but his ego-driven scolding had brought forth her tongue which, at times could be unrestrained. But she realized there was no point in trying to deny it. In fact, it was probably better if he did know so he didn't go on thinking she was "beneath" him.

"My sister is married to Harold Godwinson," she said, somewhat softer. "*Was* married to Harold. Now, she is his widow."

Gaetan had a strange look on his face. "Your sister is Edith the Fair?"

Ghislaine nodded. "Aye," she said. "She is my older sister."

"How many sisters do you have?"

"One."

Now his expression became suspicious. "Edith the Fair has a sister only known as The Beautiful Maid of Mercia," he said. "At least, that is all I have ever heard about her. *Pulchra ancilla Merciae*, they called her."

Ghislaine nodded, not at all impressed with the name. "I was given that moniker as a young girl, but people still use it," she said, looking away. "It remains with me."

Now it was Gaetan's turn to be surprised. Even beneath the helm, Ghislaine could see his eyebrows lift from the shape of his eyes.

"Why did you not tell me any of this?" he asked, somewhat aghast. "I have heard of The Beautiful Maid of Mercia but I never heard a name associated with it."

"I am curious as to why a Norman should hear of me."

"Much as I know your language, it is wise to know one's enemy, and that includes family members. We Normans are not so ignorant as you would like to think."

"I never said you were. But you seem to know a lot about us."

He cocked an eyebrow. "Mayhap that is so, but I did not know enough to know that you were The Beautiful Maid of Mercia."

Ghislaine wondered if he was on the edge of ridiculing her the way he said it or if he had already known her identity. "I am," she said, then quickly added: "My lord."

Gaetan stared at her a moment longer before finally shaking his head. "Now I can see why you have been given that name," he said. "You have beauty that is beyond compare, but your manner of dress and behavior leaves something to be desired. You could command the finest husband in all of England if you would only brush your hair and dress like a woman should."

It was a compliment and an insult at the same time. Ghislaine felt more than a little self-conscious. Reaching up a hand, she touched her hair as if to feel how messy it was; it was plaited into several braids that were gathered up at the base of her skull by a strip of leather. Her hair was very long, and somewhat thick, so she often braided it up tightly to keep it out of the way. But from the way Gaetan spoke, he made her feel as if she did nothing at all to make herself attractive, as a woman should. Not that she'd ever really cared... until now.

"I *was* married," she said before she could stop herself. "I do not wish to be married again, so you need not be concerned over how I dress."

Gaetan's attention lingered on her. "What happened to your husband?"

She was feeling embarrassed at her outburst, even a little wounded. "I thought you knew everything about my family."

"I did not know you had a husband. What became of him?"

She thought she heard some concern in his tone. Was it even possible that he would be concerned with such a thing? Even so, she wasn't sure she wanted to answer him but she supposed it didn't much matter. Hakon was gone and talking about him would not make the longing for him any less.

"He drowned," she said simply. "But surely you did not call me up to the front to ask me personal questions. Did you have business to discuss with me?"

There was a rebuke in her statement. Snappish, even. Gaetan would have dismissed her immediately for such a thing but he didn't and he truthfully had no idea why. Any snappish woman deserved to be sent away. But he'd sent for her because he wanted to discuss their surroundings and any potential allies or enemies up ahead, but now they were on the subject of her relationship to the dead Anglo-Saxon king and the fact that her husband was dead.

Gaetan wasn't a man to get too close to people and especially not too close to someone he considered the enemy, but he couldn't help his curiosity about Ghislaine. *The Beautiful Maid of Mercia.* He'd spend two days not talking to her, trying not to look at her or think about her, but he found that she lingered heavily on his mind no matter what he did. Even when he rode at point as he was, knowing she was back behind him, his thoughts lingered on the woman with the perfect buttocks. But it was more than his obsession with that body part; it was an interest in the woman herself.

It was foolish and he knew it.

It could even be deadly.

"I summoned you to discuss the area we are in and to ask what you know of it," he said, reining in the curiosity of her that had gotten the better of him. He felt foolish for it. "We are east of London now and this is the Roman road you have indicated we follow. What can we expect from here on out?"

He was back to business, away from a personal conversation, and Ghislaine wasn't sure how she felt about it. It was true that she essentially told him that her life, her past, was none of his affair, but the truth was that it felt rather good to have someone interested in her for once. Even if he thought she didn't dress like a lady should, or even if he had made remarks she considered rude, there was still something about the man that didn't make him completely boorish. She'd seen glimpses of the humanity beneath.

"This is the road that runs between Edwin's holdings and London, so we have traveled it many a time," she said. "Up ahead, there is a great lord known as Lord Boltolph and his domain is Westerham. He has a large home and a very large hall."

Gaetan was interested in this lord. "Did he go to war with Harold?"

Ghislaine shook her head. "I did not see him there," she said. "The last I heard, he went to fight in the north with Harold when the Danes were causing trouble, but I do not know if he has returned."

The thought of sleeping in a home and not a tent or on a moving ship was appealing to Gaetan but he had over two thousand men with him and accommodating such a crowd by a generous lord would be difficult and expensive.

"Is he a powerful lord?" he asked.

Ghislaine nodded. "He has a great house that has tiled floors, left from the Romans, and there is a large village that he both supports and protects."

"How many men does he have?"

"Five hundred, mayhap. I do not exactly know."

Gaetan pondered that. It would be a good opportunity for him to try to make an alliance with a local lord, something that would benefit William in managing the land that would soon become his kingdom. He had come north for a reason, after all, and that was to help subdue the natives for William. He may as well start with a local lord.

"Then mayhap we shall call upon him," Gaetan said. "Mayhap he shall accept my offering of peace if he will support William."

Ghislaine cast him a long look. "And if he does not?"

Gaetan was looking at the road ahead. "Then I have two thousand men to raze his home, kill his people, and steal his wealth. It would be in his best interest to cooperate."

It wasn't a threat, simply a statement of fact. Ghislaine knew the Normans had come to conquer but, still, it was difficult to hear that conquest put into words. It was the scorched earth mentality she was coming to see.

"Then let me go ahead and tell him of your approach," she said. "He knows me, as Edwin's sister. Perhaps I can convince him to cooperate so you do not have to destroy the man. His daughter has always been very kind to me. I would hate to see her fall to your men."

Gaetan looked at her, then, seeing the woman in the weakening light of the day and his thoughts began to wander again. She was wearing one of Adéle's cotes, too baggy on her frame, but she looked markedly better than she had since he'd known her. At least she was out of that tunic and men's hose she liked to favor. Her face was a little dirty but, on her, it looked rather charming.

He had to shake himself of those thoughts, however, and remind himself that she was the enemy. She had made an offer to contact a local lord, a Saxon nobleman, on behalf of the Normans but he didn't entirely trust her. Men who were too trusting often ended up dead.

"I will send you with Jathan," he finally said. "Convince this lord that being a pleasant host to me and my men will only be to his benefit."

Ghislaine pondered his words. "He is a good man, my lord," she said, deliberately addressing him formally because she wanted him to soften a bit. "In fact, he is known as Boltolph the Sane. He is known for his just and fair ways, so you need not threaten him. Show him a man of good will and I am sure he will react in kind."

Gaetan wasn't used to be questioned or lectured, which was what Ghislaine seemed to be doing. Part of him wanted to listen to her because she made sense but the other part of him was incensed. "Men of too much good will often end up dead," he told her flatly. Turning to the nearest squire, he had the lad summon Jathan. As the boy went charging back into the column, Gaetan returned his focus to Ghislaine. "How far ahead is this lord's home?"

Ghislaine could see that he wasn't apt to take her advice. She sighed sharply. "Less than an hour ride, I think," she said, looking at their surroundings. "We should start seeing the outskirts of the village shortly."

"Then waste no time. Tell Boltolph the Sane that Harold Godwinson was killed three days ago and that William, Duke of Normandy, is now the king. Tell him that I come in peace but if he thinks to dispute me, I will burn everything he owns to the ground."

Ghislaine resisted the urge to roll her eyes. "Is that how you make peace? By threatening a man with death unless he submits?"

There was an unexpected twinkle of mirth in Gaetan's eyes. "How else should I make peace?"

Ghislaine could see the mirth and it both confused and infuriated her. Was he making light of her concerns? "Not by threatening men with death and destruction," she said. "Can you not simply be polite?"

"No."

It was such a stubborn answer that, now, Ghislaine was in danger of grinning. She looked away before he saw it.

"I am not surprised," she muttered.

"What did you say?"

She cleared her throat, noticing that Jathan was coming forward on his old hairy horse. "I said that you are wise," she said, lifting her voice. "I shall do my best to convince Boltolph to give you and your men shelter for the night."

That was the last thing Gaetan heard from her as she dug her heels into the side of the horse, spurring it down the road with the priest following. Camulos was, too, rushing after the pair as they tore off down the road.

Gaetan let the dog go, knowing the beast had developed something of a great affection for Ghislaine over the past couple of days.

Truth be told, he didn't blame the dog in the least.

CHAPTER TEN

cg

A WARRIOR'S HEART

Westerham, home of Boltolph the Sane

FORTUNATELY, BOLTOLPH HADN'T resisted the Norman incursion. In fact, the man wasn't even home.

But his daughter was. Gunnora had been very glad to see her friend, Ghislaine, as the woman entered the walled courtyard of Westerham. Having been called forth by the men guarding the entry to the complex, Gunnora was a tall, lovely woman with long blonde hair and an ample girth. She was, quite simply, a big woman with a big heart, and she embraced Ghislaine warmly.

Through a few minutes of friendly chatter, Ghislaine was distracted by the fact that Westerham was nearly devoid of soldiers. There were a few guarding the walls and milling about, but it was very clear that the army was gone. When she asked Gunnora about her father, the woman confirmed that, indeed, her father was still in the north. Ghislaine didn't know if she felt worse about that or better, because now there would be no resistance to Gaetan and his army. Gaetan intended to stay here for the night so, perhaps, it was best that there be no chance at resistance. Westerham would remain intact and the Normans would continue on their way come the morning. But because Boltolph was not in residence, it meant that Gaetan would not be able to establish an alliance with him.

But Gunnora saw things differently.

Truth be told, the woman didn't have much of a head for warfare. Harold's death and the advent of the Normans meant little to her. She had been twice married, and twice widowed, and she was constantly on the hunt for another husband. So when Ghislaine asked if the Norman army could lodge at Westerham for the night, Gunnora was more than willing to let them come. Saxon or Norman made little difference to her; if they were men, they were welcome.

Gaetan and his men were literally welcomed with open arms by the people of Westerham. The gates to the enclosure were wide open and the soldiers on the wall, what little there were of them, simply watched them enter without any reaction whatsoever. But a large woman with a mass of blonde hair, standing near one of two long houses in the compound, seemed quite excited to see them. Ghislaine was with the woman and introduced her as Gunnora Boltolphdotter, Lady of Westerham.

As Ghislaine introduced their hostess to de Wolfe's knights, who seemed less interested in Gunnora and more interested in their surroundings, Jathan pulled Gaetan aside and explained that Boltolph was still in the north with the majority of his army.

With that information, Gaetan understood that he could have had a very quick submission of Westerham if he wanted to, confiscating the lands and riches for himself, but he thought better of it. Better to be allied with the Saxon lord than to steal from him at this point, especially if he wanted the man's cooperation with other Saxon lords.

Therefore, in the interest of being a polite guest, he only had his knights and the provision wagons come into the bailey to be protected during the night while the rest of his army camped outside the walls. They were permitted to hunt in the forest or fish in the river for their food but they were not permitted to raid the village, which was quite unprotected. It would have been like lions hunting lambs.

God's Bones, when did he become such a polite guest?

He wasn't going to admit it. Under no circumstances would he admit it. But… perhaps, there was a chance that Ghislaine's words had some impact on him. Had he truly become so soft and foolish that he was actually listening to a woman? Or was it the fact that he had no choice but to trust her advice in this strange new world?

Or, perhaps, he simply wanted to please *her*.

He was an idiot….

As night fell and black clouds gathered for a storm that soon unleashed its ferocity, Gaetan's army settled in for the night courtesy of Lady Gunnora. Westerham was actually quite vast and comfortable as far as homes went; there were two longhouses, or what looked like longhouses, with one of them being made from waddle and daub with a heavily-thatched roof, and the other was made from stone until about midway up the wall when it abruptly turned into another kind of stone, very rough-hewn and jagged. This structure, too, had the heavily-thatched roof and it was into this building that Gaetan and his men were ushered.

It was a busy place, crowded with servants and tables that were oddly low to the ground. The benches looked like they were meant for children. It was also incredibly smoky and Gaetan and his men realized that it was because the cooking fire was at the far end of the hall, spitting thick smoke into the roof where it would struggle to escape through holes in the walls. There were several people cooking over this very large fire, a pit dug into the ground. A cauldron sat upon one side of it, steaming heavily, while an entire pig was roasting over the center of it, turned on a spit.

In all, it was a bustling place. Chaotic, even. Gunnora and a man the presumed to be her majordomo indicated for the knights to sit at a table near the door and they did. As the knights settled down, they were followed by their squires who removed weaponry and anything else that made it difficult to sit. From that moment forward, it was a meal unlike anything Ghislaine had ever seen before.

The men were weary; she knew that. They were all weary from battles and travel. Gunnora and her servants brought out drinking vessels which were, in some cases, hollowed-out horns from cattle. Those went to most of the men while Gaetan and Téo received glass bowls to drink from, evidently quite an honor. Gaetan thanked Lady Gunnora in her own tongue as she and her servants filled their cups to the rim with sweet beer, literally beer sweetened with honey. It was fermented for quite a long time and had quite a bite to it, but the knights drank it gratefully as food was brought to the table.

It was simple fare for the most part but it was plentiful – cabbage potage flavored with garlic, onions, white carrots, butter, and copious amounts of bread. The knights dug in to the food as Gunnora and her servants catered to them, delivering the first of the roast pig before anyone else was served. There was an entire leg on the table that the knights began cutting from with their daggers, pulling off big slabs of roasted pork. It was a feast fit for a king.

Only when they had sliced off their fill did Ghislaine even try to take any food. She was on the end of the table where Jathan was, both of them seated far down the table from the knights. For Jathan, that was where he usually ate and for Ghislaine, she didn't want to put herself in the middle of feasting knights who only days before had been her enemy. Perhaps the still were. She assumed they would want to sup without her seated amongst them. In any case, she sat at the opposite end of the table with Gunnora and enjoyed her meal.

In fact, she was enjoying it immensely. It was more food than she'd had in several days but Camulos had followed her into the hall and she found herself sharing her meal with the dog because she couldn't avoid his pathetic doggy stare. As she stuffed herself with the succulent pork, Gunnora seemed to be paying more attention to the Norman knights.

"My dear, they are quite attractive, aren't they?" Gunnora hissed at her giddily. "Are they all married?"

Ghislaine glanced down the table at the group. "I would not know," she said. "I do not know that much about them."

"Then why are you with them? Are you a liaison on behalf of Edwin?"

Ghislaine shook her head. "Nay," she said, not wanting to tell Gunnora about their missing man because the woman, as kind as she was, had a big mouth. Ghislaine didn't think that was the type of thing Gaetan would want spread around. "I... I am their guide. They do not know Mercia as I do, so I am helping them find their way."

"But where are they going?"

"North."

Gunnora's curiosity wasn't satisfied but she could sense that Ghislaine didn't wish to speak of why she was accompanying the Normans. She leaned into the woman and whispered.

"Are you their prisoner?" she asked. "Are they forcing you to do this?"

They were, in fact, but Ghislaine didn't tell her so. Gunnora wouldn't understand why, exactly, she was being forced, so it wouldn't do to upset the woman. Therefore, Ghislaine simply shook her head.

"Of course not," she said. "Have you been well, Gunnora? I have not seen you in a very long time."

She was deliberately trying to change the subject but Gunnora, who didn't have much female company, was glad to tell her of her life since the two last saw one another.

"I have been well," she said. "Papa has a man he wishes for me to marry but nothing can come of it until he returns from the north. I believe he said that he was going to fight with Edwin. They were to hold off the Danes."

Ghislaine nodded. "That is true," she said. "But that was some time ago. Your father should be returning very soon."

Gunnora shrugged, turning to her food. "I wish it would be soon. Why did you not go north with Edwin, Ghislaine? You always fight with your brother."

Ghislaine was focused on her food as well, hearing the soft laughter of the knights down the table and wondering what they were laughing about. Glancing at them, she could see their camaraderie, the warmth in their expressions when they looked at each other. She wondered what it was like to know such companionship, for it was something she'd never experienced.

Certainly, she had men she commanded and family around her, but she'd lived a rather lonely life as the youngest child of a powerful family. Both of her parents were dead and her siblings had lives and families of their own. Hakon had been the one she'd been closest to and his death had not only left a hole in her heart, but it had left her with mind-numbing loneliness. She was alone, unwanted, and unloved. Listening to the knights down the table as they laughed and conversed, she wondered if she would ever know companionship like that.

To belong.

"I have not felt like fighting for my brother since my husband's death," she said quietly. "When Edwin left for the north, I did not want to go with him."

Gunnora's mouth was full of pork. "Yet you went with Alary to fight off the Normans?"

Ghislaine looked at her queerly. "Who said anything about fighting with Alary?"

"Because he was here only yesterday. He said he had fought with Harold but he did not have Normans with him like you do. Are you *sure* they are not forcing you to accompany them?"

So Alary had been at Westerham. Ghislaine didn't know why she was shocked to hear that. Since Westerham was an ally, certainly he would have stopped for the night for lodgings. It would have been completely normal and expected.

He did not have Normans with him like you do.

That statement concerned her greatly.

"I told you that they are not," Ghislaine said casually. She didn't want to tip Gunnora off about the real situation between Alary and the Normans that were, even now, in Gunnora's hall. "Alary would make a terrible ally to the Normans and you know that, so he left the field of battle before I did. But… but you did not see a Norman knight with him?"

Gunnora cocked her head thoughtfully. "I did not, but his men did not come into the hall," she said. "In fact, they feasted in the bailey and left in the morning. Alary did not seem to want to be sociable. Why do you ask?"

Because he has a Norman captive, Ghislaine thought. Alary knew, as Ghislaine knew, that Gunnora couldn't keep her mouth shut about such a thing so he had kept his prisoner hidden. Rumors of a Norman captive would, in fact, possibly reach the Normans. Now, Ghislaine was starting to understand that Alary was being very careful with his prisoner and she knew that Gaetan would want to know that Alary was only a day ahead of them. In fact, she was very eager to tell him.

"That is typical of Alary," Ghislaine said casually as she turned back to her food, although her attention was really on Gaetan, down at the end of the table. "He was never very social, at least not with women. Had your father been here, he more than likely would have supped in the hall."

Gunnora shrugged. "Mayhap," she said. "He did say he was returning home."

"That is where we are going, also."

Gunnora lifted her head, puzzled. "Then why did he not wait for you?"

Ghislaine simply shrugged and turned back to her food. In hindsight, she should have given the woman an answer because, in Gunnora's mind, perhaps Alary would have waited had he known his sister and a contingent of Normans were only a day behind him. She opened her mouth to speak but her majordomo was at her side, whispering in her ear, and she excused herself from the table.

Ghislaine continued to eat, rather glad that her hostess had vanished. She didn't want to talk about Alary anymore because any further conversation might lead to the real reason Ghislaine was accompanying a large Norman army northward. Some might think that was treacherous, and it was true that Gunnora might as well, so it was best to be off the subject.

Now, all Ghislaine could think about was the fact that Alary was only a day ahead of them. Gaetan had to know but the more Ghislaine watched him with his men, the more she was hesitant to interrupt him.

"My brother was here yesterday," she said to Jathan, sitting across from her. "I must tell Gaetan."

Jathan had eaten so much pork that he was close to bursting with it but, much like Ghislaine, he'd not eaten much over the past several days. Still, he wouldn't stop eating and pushed another piece of pork into his mouth. His gaze moved down the table to the men he'd known for years.

"I heard," he said, shrugging when she looked curiously at him. "Our hostess' voice carries. I heard what she said."

"Then Gaetan must know."

Jathan sighed, cutting another piece of pork with his knife. "I know you must tell him, and I do agree, but this is the first time in weeks I have seen these men relax," he said. "Let them enjoy a little more of this peaceful time before telling them what you know. Once you do, it will keep them up all night as they plan tomorrow's travel to catch up to your brother. So for now... just wait. At least give them the night to enjoy and then you can tell them in the morning."

Ghislaine could see that he was concerned for the knights and their state of mind. Men like this had little time to relax and those moments were precious. He was right; there wasn't anything they could do about it tonight. Tomorrow would be soon enough. She returned to her food.

"They look as if they do not have a care in the world," she said.

Jathan chewed loudly. "Thoughts of Kristoph are not far from their minds, I assure you. They miss him."

Ghislaine had a perfect view of Gaetan from where she sat and she watched the man, greedily drinking in his male beauty. "One would not know that by looking at them."

Jathan's attention moved to her, his expression something between thoughtfulness and genuine concern. "I will tell you something of these men so that you understand them, my lady," he said quietly. "You will understand why they are so determined to regain their comrade and why moments like this, when they are relatively carefree, are more valuable than gold. Do you see de Wolfe? He is the man they call Warwolfe, the greatest knight in the Duke of Normandy's arsenal."

Ghislaine cocked her head curiously. "Warwolfe?" she repeated, still looking at Gaetan. "An intimidating name. Yet… it suits him."

Jathan drank deeply of his mead. "Aye, it does," he said. "The man is immortal and I have seen him in enough battles to know. And these men that are sworn to him, they are all great knights in their own right, men who have fought together for many years. They have seen much of life and death together, and Warwolfe is the man that binds them all together. The Duke of Normandy calls these knights his *Anges de Guerre*."

Ghislaine looked at him then. "Angels of War," she translated softly. "I *have* heard of them. I have heard the men speak of Normandy's Angels but I wondered if they were simply telling stories."

Jathan shook his head. "They were not," he replied. "These men have been at the forefront of most of the Duke of Normandy's wars, going back years. If the duke did not have them, it is difficult to say if he would have even won the battle against Harold Godwinson for, in truth, these were the men who led the charge. You are looking at the front of the duke's army."

Ghislaine's attention returned to the men at the end of the table, feeling some awe now as she looked at them. "Tell me about them," she asked, sipping at her mead, a very strong drink that was already making her head swim. "They will not speak to me but I would know something of these men I have been tasked with guiding north."

Jathan's tongue was loosened by the mead in his veins. Ghislaine was not Norman and he more than likely should not tell her what he knew, but he couldn't help himself. This serious, solemn lass needed to be aware of the greatness of these men, far greater than any knights she had ever heard of.

Legends in the flesh.

"Their rally cry is *et pro Gloria dei*," Jathan said. "De Wolfe is their leader, as you know. He is a descendant of the kings of Breton. The family name is Vargr, which means a monstrous wolf in the Breton tongue, but Gaetan's father changed the family name to de Wolfe in the Norman fashion. Although born a bastard, Gaetan is the only son of a great warrior father, William, and when his father died, Gaetan inherited the de Wolfe lands and titles. From his mother's mother, he inherited control of Lorient and the ports, which makes him a very wealthy man."

Ghislaine was fascinated to learn something of the man she was becoming quite attracted to. "*Et pro Gloria dei,*" she murmured. "For God and Glory."

"Aye."

"Is... is de Wolfe married?" she asked because she found she had to know.

But Jathan shook his head. "He is not married, but he has two sons through a woman who has warmed his bed for many years," he said. "He also has a daughter by another bedslave."

Ghislaine looked at him as if shocked by the word. "He has bed-slaves?"

Jathan lifted his eyebrows as he took another drink of his mead. "Women he has acquired by conquest," he said simply. "Much to his mother's distress, I might add. She wishes him to marry and produce legitimate children. But do not look so shocked; surely Saxon warriors have slaves who warm their bed."

They did, but Ghislaine didn't like the thought of a slave woman in Gaetan's bed. Not that it was any of her concern, but the fact that he had women to service him meant that had no need for another woman. *Her.*

Sweet Mary, what had she been thinking?

"They do," she said dully, tearing her gaze from Gaetan and feeling incredibly disappointed now that she knew he had other women. "What of the others? Are they all as wealthy as de Wolfe?"

Jathan nodded. "Being a noble knight is an expensive undertaking," he said. "De Lohr, the man we seek, comes from nobility. His family owns most of western Brittany. De Russe's father is from Flanders, the Count of Roeselare, but the family itself is very old and originally came from the realm of Kievan Rus, which is far to the east."

"He is very frightening."

Jathan gave her half-grin. "Aye, he is, but there is no man more fearless or loyal in battle."

"Go on."

Jathan turned to look at the group. "De Reyne is from Morlaix in Brittany, the son of a great landowner, and...."

"But how do they all know one another? And what makes them so loyal to de Lohr?"

Jathan could see that she was studying the group quite intently, understandably curious about these men she found herself traveling with. But there was something more in her tone, as if she were deeply puzzled by their association because she didn't understand the kind of bond they shared. Women usually didn't.

"They all fostered with other knights who fought together on the field of battle," he said. "That is how I met them, too. I was a knight before I turned to the church. These men go back to their childhood in some cases and bonds were forged that cannot be broken. That is why they go after de Lohr; these men are brothers, my lady. And they will not leave one of their own behind."

Ghislaine drained her mead, reaching for the pitcher to pour herself more even though she knew she shouldn't. The buzz in her head was growing stronger and when that happened, it meant she would sleep heavily and wake up with an aching head. But she didn't much care this night; her world had changed drastically over the past few days and she was trying very hard to make sense of it all. But there was one thing she could already make sense of and that was the strength of the relationship between these men. She wished she had someone who cared about her enough to go after her should she be abducted. But the truth was that there was no one. Depressed, she took another gulp of mead when she heard someone call her name.

"Lady Ghislaine!"

She could see Gaetan waving her down the table to where he was sitting and, startled, she immediately set her cup down and got up from the bench. The great and handsome Gaetan was summoning her and she was more than willing to go to him, if only to be in the man's midst for only a moment. She was halfway down the table when Gaetan pointed to her as he spoke to his men.

"We have a goddess among us," he told them. "I am sure none of you knew that The Beautiful Maid of Mercia was our guide. Lady Ghislaine is the sister of Edith the Fair, who was the wife of Harold Godwinson. Truthfully, I have never been this close to a lady of legendary beauty before, although it is difficult to tell by the clothing she wears."

Ghislaine was horrified by the compliment once again paired with an insult from Gaetan's lips. He never seemed to do anything else. Wide-eyed, she looked at the Norman knights who were all looking at her quite curiously now. De Russe and de Moray were the closest to her, the men she was the most frightened of, and when she saw them turn to her, she moved away quickly, tripping over her own feet as she did. She stumbled right in to de Lara, who grabbed her before she could pitch into their food.

"Steady, my lady, steady," de Lara said, carefully righting her. He had noticed her discomfort with the proximity of de Russe and de Moray. "But I do not blame your reaction to those two. See their dark eyes? That means the devil is upon them. De Moray will belch loudly enough to knock cups from the table and, although it is not frequently spoken of, de Russe is known as the Lord of Flatulence to his friends. He will fart a tune if he is drunk enough."

The table erupted in laughter, all except Aramis. Being insulted in front of men was one thing, but being insulted in front of a woman was quite another. "I see that I have not beat you nearly hard enough, de Lara, for your mouth continues to runneth over," he growled. "Next time I shall cut out your tongue."

The table was still laughing but Ghislaine wasn't so sure why when de Russe was leveling threats. She believed him even if the others did not. "I do not believe that about you, my lord, truly," she said to de Russe because she didn't want him spewing threats at her, too. "I am sure Lord de Lara is mistaken."

Luc was grinning even though Ghislaine was very nervous. "Do not fear him, my lady," he said, putting an arm around her waist to pull her closer to him and away from de Russe. "He would not dare strike me with you as my protector."

Aramis simply shook his head, sighing heavily as he turned back to his drink. "Only de Lara would have a woman as a protector."

"I would not discount her so easily," Gaetan, across the table, pointed out. "I have seen her fight. She is not to be trifled with."

Aramis cast Ghislaine a long glance. "Is that so?" he said. He then looked her up and down with those dark murky eyes. "How many men do you command, my lady?"

Ghislaine was growing increasingly uncomfortable with the discussion and the fact that de Lara had his arm around her waist. Although seemingly a kind enough man, and a handsome one, she was vastly uncomfortable with him touching her. In fact, the entire situation had her wanting to run for cover.

"Two hundred men," she said, wondering if her voice sounded as nervous as she felt. "Mostly archers."

Aramis seemed to turn more of his attention to her, now seriously inspecting the lady warrior they'd brought with them. The highly alcoholic mead was loosening them all up, even those who normally didn't speak much, de Russe included.

"I see," he said. "But do they fight in hand to hand combat?"

Ghislaine nodded. "They have."

"Have you?"

Again, Ghislaine nodded. "Aye, my lord."

Aramis rolled his head sideways, looking at the men around the table. "This is something I must see for myself," he muttered, a flash of a grin on his face. "Someone give her a sword. I want to see how she can fight."

There was jest and joviality to the conversation and the knights around the table were grinning as one of them turned to the squires sitting against the wall by the door, demanding a short sword.

Ghislaine, however, was mortified. Terrified *and* mortified. Was it really possible that the enormous knight wanted to fight her? Worse still, she could see men pulling out their coin purses and plopping silver coins onto the table, evidently betting how long it would take for her to either surrender or be disarmed by de Russe.

Ghislaine couldn't decide if she was more insulted by what was going on or more frightened. De Lara still had a grip on her as one of the squires ran up and handed her a beautifully made sword that was fairly lightweight, but it was something Ghislaine had never fought with before. It wasn't her weapon and she wasn't used to it. So they expected her to fight with this, did they?

She could hardly believe this was happening.

But it was happening, indeed, and men were putting money out to bet on the spectacle. Feeling increasingly frightened, Ghislaine looked to Gaetan to see if he would stop the fight but he was looking at her most appraisingly over the rim of his cup, his bronze eyes dark in the dim light of the hall. As de Russe collected his sword and came away from the table, pulling her out of de Lara's grip, Gaetan stood up and came around the end of the table.

Ghislaine was standing near de Russe, having absolutely no idea what she was going to do, when Gaetan put himself between her and the massive figure of de Russe. *Thank God!* Ghislaine was relieved beyond measure that Gaetan was showing some sense but that comfort lasted only briefly. Gaetan pulled her away a few feet and put his hands on her upper arms, bending over to speak to her in a calm, quiet voice.

"He has a blind spot below his chin," he muttered. "He is used to fighting big men or men near his eye level, not a small woman. He will lift his sword and when he does, go underneath it and put your blade to his belly. Do not puncture him but let him know you will not stand for his foolery. I have seen you fight, my lady. Your bravery knows no bounds."

Ghislaine was looking up at Gaetan, trembling in his grip. "Does he really want to kill me?"

Tears filled her eyes when she said it and Gaetan could see, at that instant, that she did not see this as a joke. She saw it as a very big man trying to kill her, her enemy. Gaetan shouldn't have felt anything towards her at that moment but he did; he felt a great deal of pity for her. She was frightened and they were all making a joke about it.

But it wasn't funny anymore.

Gaetan had been watching her all evening as she sat with their hostess, Lady Gunnora, and the truth was that it was difficult for him to take his eyes off of her. Something about Ghislaine was drawing him to her more and more but it was interest unlike anything he'd ever experienced before. He'd known beautiful women – he owned beautiful women – but Ghislaine was different. There was something about this serious, courageous woman that had captured something inside of him. He wasn't sure what yet, but she stirred something within him, and right now he was feeling a good deal of compassion for her fear.

And a good deal of protectiveness.

"Nay, he does not," he answered after a moment, his voice soft with sympathy. "He is making a joke with you because he does not believe you can fight. I know better, but he does not. If it frightens you, I will not let him do this."

I know better, but he does not. Ghislaine could see Gaetan's respect for her in his eyes as he said those words, respect that he'd never shown her before. It was so strange how those few words suddenly dashed her fear for the most part, fortifying her because she realized that Gaetan had faith in her.

She blinked away her tears, looking at de Russe standing a few feet away, toying with the sword in his hand. It occurred to her that if she fought de Russe, even in jest, then it might make Gaetan's knights respect her just a little as well. Perhaps they would even talk to her. As Jathan had said, these men had fought together for many years and there was an inherent respect for one another because of it. They knew what each man was capable of. But they didn't know what *she* was capable of. She'd spent the entire meal marveling at their bond, even being jealous of it.

Perhaps this was her chance to earn a little of their respect, too.

"I will fight him," she said, sniffling. Then her gaze returned to Gaetan. "And I shall win."

"Are you certain?"

"I am."

Gaetan could see that she was dead serious. She'd overcome that fear he'd seen in her eyes and now all he saw was determination. It had happened quickly, like a flame being doused, but there was no doubt that she would now meet de Russe head-on. It was a rather astonishing transformation but one he admired. He couldn't help the lick of a smile that crossed his lips.

"I believe you."

With that, he moved back to the table and pulled out his own coin purse. As his men were vying for control of the pot, he slapped a gold coin right into the middle of it.

"That is for the lady's win," he said.

His men looked at him with some astonishment as more coins began to come forth, turning the pile on the table into a significant sum. De Wolfe had upped the ante and his men responded in kind. De Russe, meanwhile, could see what was happening and his brow furrowed as he marched over to the table to see that Gaetan had bet against him.

"You do not think I can subdue her?" he asked Gaetan, incredulous.

Gaetan had to fight off the giggles at the sight of Aramis' insulted face. "I think you can try."

Aramis scowled. "You are going to lose your money, de Wolfe."

Gaetan thought it was quite humorous to toy with Aramis' pride, which was considerable. "We shall see."

In a huff, Aramis turned back to Ghislaine, who had set the sword down and had pulled out her dagger. It wasn't a big dagger and certainly a lot smaller than the sword that Aramis held. He looked at her in disbelief.

"Is that what you intend to use?" he demanded.

Ghislaine nodded. "Aye, my lord."

Exasperated, Aramis shook his head. "Then you are either the bravest woman alive or the most foolish," he said, lifting the sword defensively. "Then let us get about this, my lady."

"Make your move, my lord."

Aramis couldn't believe it. Was she actually challenging him? Shaking his head in disbelief, he lifted his sword and headed straight at Ghislaine, who was simply standing there with her dagger in her hand. He took about five steps when she suddenly fell to her knees, well under his range, and latched on to his left leg.

As Aramis faltered because Ghislaine threw him off balance, she wedged herself between his legs and brought the dagger to bear straight up, pointing right into his manhood. Aramis was forced to freeze in position because he could feel the tip of the blade through his trousers. Moreover, she had her free hand braced against his left buttock so if she truly wanted to ram that dagger into his privates, it would give her the leverage to do it.

In less than a few seconds, he was beaten and he knew it. Damnation, he knew it all too well. His sword clattered to the ground and he lifted his hands slowly in surrender.

"I concede, my lady," he said steadily. "I have yet to have a son, so I would be grateful if that dagger did not go any further."

It was a swift and clever victory on the part of Ghislaine and, after a moment's disbelief at what she had done, the table of knights and half of the room erupted in cheers and laughter. Other men had seen what had happened and their laughter joined the knights'.

Still wedged between Aramis' legs, Ghislaine could hear the revelry but she refused to take her eyes off of Aramis, who was looking down at her with those dark cloudy eyes. She wasn't entirely sure he wouldn't try to grab her or otherwise try to snatch this victory from her if she lowered the dagger, so it remained in place until the corner of Aramis' mouth began to twitch. When a slow smile spread across his lips and, perhaps, even gave a faint nod of approval, Ghislaine smiled back.

The dagger swiftly came away.

After that, Ghislaine spent the rest of the evening seated between Aramis and Gaetan as the knights drank and told stories of the man they were going to rescue. She didn't really participate in the conversation, but she was permitted to listen. De Russe even filled her cup with mead. It would seem that besting the man had the effect she had hoped for; now, they weren't nearly so indifferent to her. Enemy or not, she had proven herself in some small way to the *Anges de Guerre*. It was a night she would never forget.

Little did she know that while she was enjoying her evening, Gunnora's majordomo had sent a message, at Gunnora's request, to Alary, who had been easy to track because of the size of his group and the lone wagon and oxen that was pulling it.

Near dawn, Alary received a missive from a Westerham rider that Lady Ghislaine had arrived at Westerham for the night with an escort of Norman soldiers and Lady Gunnora suggested that Alary wait for her to catch up with him.

Puzzled and panicked, waiting for Ghislaine was the last thing Alary had in mind.

CHAPTER ELEVEN

CB

MESSAGE RECEIVED

The Village of Oxshott

KRISTOPH WAS HEALING slowly but his misery lingered.

It was just before dawn on the fourth day after the battle that saw Harold Godwinson lose his life and Kristoph was awake, standing beside the horse that Alary rode because his bound hands were tied to the saddle. Alary wouldn't permit him to have his own mount, even though his battered body screamed for it, instead making him walk beside him as they traveled. If Alary spurred the horse into a trot, then Kristoph ran beside him and if he happened to stumble, which he did once, then Alary would drag him for as long as he found pleasure in his suffering.

But Kristoph was strong, which probably irked Alary. He never begged for mercy and he hardly said a word about anything, not his pain nor his suffering nor his hunger, which was substantial. He'd hardly been fed since his capture but the previous night, one of Alary's men had taken pity on him and brought him half a loaf of bread from the inn where Alary was staying, bread that Kristoph had taken gratefully and wolfed down. He had no idea when he'd be fed next and, even now, as the sun began to peek over the eastern horizon on this damp, cold morning, he wasn't sure when he would eat this day, *if* he would eat this day. But his strength was returning for the most part and he suspected he'd be able to escape in a day or two.

That was the plan.

Therefore, he didn't let his depression in the situation get to him. He'd been watching Alary for the better part of four days, analyzing his enemy. The man was petty and suspicious, but he didn't seem particularly bright. Kristoph was fairly certain he could outsmart him at some point.

As he stood by the horse this chill morning with a few of Alary's men standing around on guard, he noticed when a rider on a weary horse arrived and began asking questions of some of Alary's men. Someone pointed to the inn and the man disappeared inside, which led Kristoph to wonder if the rider was looking for Alary in particular. It seemed to him as if the man was looking for someone from the way he was behaving.

But Kristoph didn't give the rider any more consideration than that as the same man who had given him the half-loaf of bread untied his hands and gave him watered ale to drink and another cup full of a barley gruel, which Kristoph sucked down in one big swallow. He smiled gratefully to the man and handed back the wooden cups about the time another of Alary's men came bolting from the inn, heading in his direction. Kristoph heard a reference to himself, twice, and his curiosity piqued. Soon enough, he discovered that he'd been summoned.

Fighting down his trepidation, Kristoph's four-man escort took him to the inn, which was essentially one long single-room building and little else. There were people sleeping all over the hard-packed earthen floor although at this time in the morning, men were rising as serving wenches moved among them, delivering food. Coughing, snorting, and farting abounded as men woke to a new day.

Kristoph hadn't slept in the inn the previous night. He'd slept on the cold ground next to the cart, so the stale heat of the inn was welcoming as his escort took him over to Alary, who was sitting next to the blazing hearth. Alary was breaking his fast for the day, eating his bread and cheese as he sat at the table with the rider who had so recently arrived on the weary horse. Kristoph had been correct in his assumption that the rider had been looking for Alary. When Alary looked up from his food to notice that Kristoph had arrived, he indicated for the man to sit.

"Join me," he said, mouth full. "Have you eaten?"

That was more than Alary had said to him their entire journey north. Kristoph was instantly on his guard.

"I was given a ration," he said.

Alary shoved bread and cheese at him. "Eat," he said. "You and I must have a discussion and you cannot do it on an empty stomach."

Kristoph was increasingly wary. He eyed the man sitting with Alary; a pale, young man dressed in rags with a running nose and bushy hair. He looked cold and hungry. He didn't know the lad but that didn't mean anything; something was amiss. He could feel it. Being that he was still starving, however, he took the food where he could get it. Breaking off a big piece of the warm bread, he took a healthy bite.

Alary looked up from his meal. "How are your injuries healing, *kriegshund*?"

It wasn't the first time Alary had called him by that name. Kristoph spoke several languages and he wasn't particularly insulted by being called a war dog. He was one.

"As well as can be expected," he said, swallowing the big bite and taking another.

"Do your ribs still hurt?"

"Aye."

"Your face is not so swollen anymore."

"I will heal."

Alary nodded, sopping up gravy on his trencher with his bread. "Tell me something," he said. "Why would my sister be following us with a Norman army?"

Kristoph was puzzled by the question. He had to think a moment. "Your sister?" he repeated. "She is following us?"

"Aye."

"Who told you this?"

Alary indicated the weary rider. "He did."

Kristoph looked at the young man, who was gazing back at him with a good deal of anxiety. That was the only thing Kristoph could read from his expression. He returned his focus to Alary.

"I would not know why she is following us," he said. "She is *your* sister."

Alary nodded. "Aye, she is, but I have never known what is in her mind," he said, rather casually. "This rider has come from Westerham. We were there the two evenings past, if you recall. This rider says that my sister is at Westerham with an army of Norman soldiers and she has told Lady Gunnora, the lady of Westerham, that they are following us. I have been asked to wait for her to catch up to us. Now, why do you suppose my sister is coming after us?"

Kristoph was astonished to hear this but, in the same breath, he was thrilled. His mind began to work very swiftly. The woman had been more than concerned for him when Alary and his men were beating him. She protected him and tried to stop them. Even after he'd been beaten unconscious, she'd evidently spoken to him because Alary's men had seen her, although Kristoph had no memory of what she'd said. But she clearly had believed he was her prisoner and she had been furious with Alary for taking him from her. That much, he remembered.

My prisoner, she'd said.

If I had something I wanted back very much, wouldn't I try to find help from a sympathetic source?

Kristoph pondered that very question which led him to a myriad of possibilities, not the least of which was the fact that he knew Gaetan would not give up looking for him. He knew that Gaetan would spend his entire life searching for him. That was truly the one hope that kept Kristoph brave in this dire situation.

What if… what if the lady warrior had somehow found an unlikely ally in Gaetan? The lady had been enraged at her brother when he'd taken Kristoph. Was she enraged enough to seek revenge against her brother by summoning the Normans to rescue her prisoner? And Gaetan, of course, would be happy to comply.

It made perfect sense to Kristoph.

"If your sister is in league with my countrymen, then that is not something I would know," he said, skirting the subject. "I only met the woman once she'd captured me. I think that if she had been a Norman collaborator, she would not have captured me at all, so what you are telling me makes little sense."

Alary swallowed the bite in his mouth, reaching for his cup of watered ale. "I agree," he said. "But, then again, Ghislaine has never made any sense. She is a foolish woman, even more foolish once her husband was killed. I think his death did something to her mind because she was not the same afterward. Now I am wondering if she is not bringing the Normans to exact some kind of vengeance against me for taking you away from her. Would you not agree that is logical?"

That was exactly what Kristoph was thinking but he didn't want to admit it. "My countrymen are not so easily swayed," he said. "It is more likely that she is *their* prisoner."

He was trying to throw Alary off the scent but Alary was sharper than he'd given him credit for. "Lady Gunnora did not seem to think so," he said. "If my sister is following me, then it is for a reason. She wants you returned. And she wants to punish me."

Kristoph could sense something foreboding coming about. He didn't like the look in Alary's eye. "My countrymen are not so foolish that they would follow a woman," he said. "I would not worry over it."

Alary shrugged. "Mayhap," he said. Then, he turned to the young man sitting at the table. "Do you know who Ghislaine of Mercia is?"

The young man was wide-eyed with fright in the face of Alary's question. "I… I think so, my lord."

"You have seen her before?"

"I think so, my lord."

It wasn't much of an answer but it seemed to satisfy Alary, at least moderately. "Then I want you to take something to her and you will also deliver a message for me."

As the young man nodded nervously, Alary turned to Kristoph.

"Give me your hand."

Kristoph's blood ran cold. "Why?"

"Give it to me or I shall force my men to give it to me. It is your choice."

Kristoph studied him a moment, trying to determine why he wanted to see his hand. *Give me your hand.* Nay, he didn't want to see his hand. He wanted *the* hand. He began to feel the familiar rush of battle because he knew, no matter his injuries, that he was going to resist with everything he had. If Alary wanted his hand, then he was going to have to fight for it.

"If you tell me what you are going to do, I will consider it," he said evenly.

Alary's eyes narrowed. "I have given you a command, prisoner. You will obey!"

"Nay."

With that, Alary stood up and made a grab for Kristoph's arm, but the knight stood up and dumped the table over, tossing the remains of the meal back on to Alary. He then threw a big fist at the first man who charged him. As that man went sprawling, a second man charged and Kristoph slugged the man in the nose, sending him to the ground. The third man who charged him was the soldier who had been kind to him and had given him food, and that momentary hesitation cost him. The fourth soldier, seeing the fight, got his hands on one of the big iron pots near the hearth and struck Kristoph across the back of the head with it.

The knight fell like a stone.

Within a few minutes, the terrified rider from Westerham was back on his mount, carrying the top portion of Kristoph's left pinky finger with him. The message he was told to deliver to Ghislaine of Mercia was simple:

Follow me and the next time I will send a bigger piece of the Norman back to you. His life is in your hands.

CHAPTER TWELVE

cs

A PRICE TOO HIGH

H E MET THEM on the road.
A frantic young man, a portion of a finger, and a message to Ghislaine from her brother was all it took to bring a two-thousand-man army to a standstill.

Setting out from Westerham, Ghislaine had been permitted to ride up near Gaetan, which was evidently quite rare. Aramis rode behind her and off to the left so every time she looked over her shoulder, he was there glaring at her. And then he would flash a smile and look away, letting her know that he really wasn't glaring at her. Something about besting the man the night before had made him something of her watch dog, or worshipper – Ghislaine couldn't really tell but she thought it all rather wonderful. These Norman knights were starting to warm to her and it was something of a comfort.

But that all ended when the frenzied rider heading down the road towards them very nearly crashed into Gaetan and would have had de Russe and Wellesbourne not rushed out to intercept him. The young man was hysterical, asking for Ghislaine of Mercia and she was brought forward, but Aramis made sure to stay between her and the young man, who proceeded to pull out a coin purse that he handed to Aramis, who in turn handed it to Ghislaine.

She recognized the purse.

There was a star carved into the leather, the same kind of star that Alary had on a seal that he used to sign missives. As the young man babbled and sobbed the message that Alary had given him to relay, Ghislaine's stomach was in knots as she timidly opened the pouch to peer inside. She couldn't see much, however, so she shook out the contents into her palm.

The bloody tip of a finger appeared.

Horrified, she shrieked as Gaetan, who was now standing next to her, plucked the finger chunk from her palm. As Ghislaine stood there with both hands over her mouth, utterly appalled with what she was seeing, the young man spat out the message a second time when Gaetan demanded it. The lad added the circumstances under which the finger had been taken and Gaetan's face turned pale.

It was Kristoph's finger.

Follow me and the next time I will send a bigger piece of the Norman back to you.

With her hands still over her mouth, Ghislaine watched Gaetan make his way to the side of the road, the finger still in his hand, before promptly doubling over and vomiting the contents of his stomach. The rest of the knights were beside themselves when the reason for Gaetan's illness was relayed to them, the revolting fact muttered from one man to another.

Even the knights from the rear of the column – today it was de Reyne, de Lara, and St. Hèver – heard from their comrades what had happened and they stood, as the others did, in a tense group, watching Gaetan struggle with his composure.

It was a horrific turn of events.

It was Téo who finally went to stand next to Gaetan, putting a hand on the man's shoulder in a comforting gesture before taking the finger from him and going in search of the original pouch it had been delivered in. Ghislaine still had it and she handed it to him, watching the man grimly seal up the finger in the leather pouch before glancing to de Russe and de Lara. Something had to be done; they all knew it. Téo finally muttered to Aramis.

"Get the men off the road and into the trees," he said quietly. "I do not want the army standing vulnerable if that Saxon bastard knows we are following him. Do not have the men set up camp but tell them to sit and wait. It is clear that something new has been added to the situation that the commanders must discuss."

Aramis nodded, gathering Wellesbourne, de Moray, St. Hèver, and de Reyne to him, all of them the great movers of men, and the five of them began moving the column off the road and into the trees to the west. Horses, wagons, and men plowed through the thick wet grass and into the trees beyond. Meanwhile, Jathan had come forward and when Téo whispered what had happened, the priest took the leather pouch and began to pray earnestly over it.

Everyone was clearly in shock but they were working through it as their training kicked in. Moving the men off the road until the situation could be discussed was how some of them dealt with it while others, Téo and Luc and Denis, stood near Gaetan, waiting for a command to come forth. The hysterical messenger stood near Ghislaine and she pushed her revulsion aside long enough to pull the man away from Gaetan, pulling him back down the road towards his exhausted mount. When they reached the frothing horse, she grabbed the man by the collar.

"By all that his holy – what has happened?" she hissed. "How did my brother know I was following him? And how did you know to find me here?"

The young man had fluid leaking from every part of his face; mucus, tears, saliva. "Lady Gunnora sent me to find Lord Alary," he told her. "She sent me last night. She said your brother had gone ahead of you and she wanted me to tell him to wait for you to catch up."

That wasn't what Ghislaine had expected to hear. Witchcraft or the devil's own work had been on her mind, but not Gunnora's intervention. Not her friend. When Ghislaine realized what the woman had done, her eyes widened dramatically.

"She did *what*?" she shrieked. "She told you to find my brother and tell him I was coming?"

The young man could see that the message he had carried from Gunnora had evidently not been welcome and, given what had happened this morning, he wasn't surprised.

"Aye, my lady," he said, now fearful of Ghislaine and her bulging eyes. "She said he should know. But Lord Alary... he was angry when I told him. He... he cut that poor man's finger off."

Hearing those words was like a blow to her gut, a sickening roll of nausea washing over her. "You were there?" she hissed. "You saw it?"

The young man nodded, wiping at his face. "Lord Alary... he was calm at first," he sniffled. "He wanted to know why you were following him. He asked the man but the man did not know."

"You mean he asked the knight why I was following him?"

"Aye, my lady. But the man could not tell him."

"So he... he cut off his finger?"

The messenger nodded unsteadily. "The man fought against Lord Alary but in the end, he was subdued. Alary cut the finger himself."

Ghislaine wanted to vomit. Little by little, the situation was becoming clear and she was aghast beyond words. Gunnora's well-meaning gesture had ended up in a man losing part of a finger. She could hardly believe what she was hearing, now terrified for Gunnora when Gaetan found out what she'd done.

But that wasn't the worst of it. She hadn't told Gaetan yet about Alary having been at Westerham two nights past. They'd moved out of Westerham in the darkness of pre-dawn and she'd not even seen Gaetan until they began traveling on the road and the sun was rising. But the most tragic part of all was that she'd briefly forgotten about telling him because she's been so swept up in the fact that Gaetan and his knights were warming to her, making her feel as if they were not entirely opposed to her presence, that Alary's visit to Westerham had completely slipped her mind.

She'd been a fool.

"God in heaven," she breathed. "What has she done? What has she –?"

"Lady Ghislaine!"

It was Gaetan. He saw her speaking with the rider and was making his way over towards her with Téo and Luc in tow. When Ghislaine turned to him, startled, she could see the fury and desperation in his eyes. Selfishly, she wasn't only worried for Gunnora now; she was worried for herself, fearful of what these knights would now think of her. She had no idea how this situation could possibly be salvageable.

"My lord," she said, feeling incredibly nervous as she spoke. "This messenger is not from Alary. He is from Westerham."

Pale and slightly wild-eyed, Gaetan looked between Ghislaine and the messenger. "Westerham?" he repeated. "I do not understand."

Ghislaine took a deep breath, praying that Gaetan wouldn't strike her down where she stood when he found out what had happened. She had no choice but to tell him everything.

"Last night at the feast, Lady Gunnora told me that Alary had visited Westerham the previous night," she said, watching his eyebrows lift in surprise. "I… I was going to tell you, as I knew you would want to know, but you… you seemed to be enjoying yourself so much during the meal that I did not want to ruin your mood. Jathan said that it was very rare when you were able to relax and we thought it best to tell you this morning. You could not do anything about the information last night even if I had told you. I thought…."

Gaetan didn't let her finish. He was on her in a flash, looming over her, those bronze eyes flashing with rage.

"You sought to withhold this information from me?" he snarled. "By what right do you make a decision like that?"

"It was my fault, my lord."

Jathan, who had been praying over the severed finger, had heard Gaetan's rage and came to Ghislaine's rescue. He quickly came alongside Ghislaine as he saw his lord was close to breathing fire upon her. He knew Gaetan's moods and what he was seeing wasn't good; the man had been known to strike out for lesser things. But something like this, something involving one of his men, could set him off to new levels of anger.

Nay, this wasn't a good thing in the least.

"She wanted to tell you but I told her to wait, my lord," he said calmly, quickly. "It is not her fault. It is mine. Even now, she did not put the blame on me as she explained why she had not told you, but the truth was that it was my fault entirely. You must not blame her. You and your men were enjoying a rare evening of relaxation and I told her it would be acceptable to tell you on the morrow, as you could not do anything about it last night."

Gaetan was still enraged, his focus completely on Ghislaine as a hunter would stalk prey. He wasn't even blinking as he stared at her. Ghislaine stared back at him, trying desperately to remain strong, but the truth was that she was terrified. The was Warwolfe, the Duke of Normandy's greatest knight, and he had not achieved such fame by being weak.

He achieved that fame by being deadly.

Truth was, Gaetan was struggling with shock and revulsion such as he'd never experienced. Kristoph's partial finger was bad enough, but in hearing that Ghislaine had known something about her brother she'd not confided in him – even if she'd wanted to but was discouraged by Jathan – told him that she was still not to be trusted. He wasn't sure he could forgive her for the oversight.

In truth, there was an odd measure of disappointment and hurt mixed up in his outrage. Disappointment in Ghislaine, in himself, and hurt because he was coming to like the woman, just in the slightest. Last night when she'd bested de Russe, he'd found himself drawn to her more than he'd even been drawn to any woman he'd ever known. He'd spent all night seeing her in his dreams and when he'd awoken, he'd even had her ride near him as the army moved northward simply because he wanted her nearby. He didn't even want to speak with her, as conversation was not usual on a battle march. He had simply wanted her nearby for the comfort it had given him.

Now, that comfort had been damaged.

"My lord?" Jathan said when Gaetan didn't reply to his explanation. "Did you hear me? It was not the lady's fault. It was mine. Punish me if you will, but do not blame her."

Gaetan was still staring at Ghislaine, unblinking, and she was doing the same. But as he watched, he could see tears filling her eyes. She suddenly blinked, quickly, to chase them away, but they returned, playing on his sympathies no matter how hard he tried to resist. He didn't want to feel compassion for her. He didn't want to feel anything for her.

But he was.

Damnation... *he was.*

"What did you tell Lady Gunnora that made her send a messenger to your brother," he finally asked, his voice quiet and raspy. "Explain this to me so there is no misunderstanding in my mind as to what you have or have not done."

Ghislaine was trembling with fear, with emotion. "I certainly did not tell her to send a missive to Alary if that is what you are thinking," she said, her voice quivering. "She asked many questions about your army and she wanted to know if I was your prisoner. I told her that I was your guide and that we were heading north. She told me that Alary had stopped at Westerham the night before and she said he was returning home. I said that we were also heading home as well because she asked and I did not want to tell her the truth. She wondered why Alary did not wait for us but she said no more than that. I can only surmise she believed she was helping when she sent the rider northward to tell Alary that I was behind him. The messenger said that she told him to tell Alary to wait for us to catch up."

Her words were quiet and she looked him in the eye with every one spoken, which told him that she wasn't lying. He'd seen his share of liars and they did not stand against him, strongly, as she was doing. In truth, her explanation made a good deal of sense and his gut reaction told him that there was no mal intent involved on the part of either Ghislaine or Gunnora. It was just a miscommunication and a woman who took initiative when she should not have. He looked at Jathan.

"You were sitting with the women last night," he said. "Did you hear this conversation she speaks of?"

Jathan nodded. "I heard it all," he said. "Lady Ghislaine never told Lady Gunnora to send for Alary. In fact, she did her best to avoid the subject. Whatever Lady Gunnora did was completely on her own."

Gaetan had no reason to disbelief his priest. Much like the rest of his knights, he trusted the man implicitly but it was a good thing the man had heard the conversation. Otherwise, Ghislaine would be cast into the shadows of mistrust quite easily. Gaetan had to admit that he was relieved, at least for Ghislaine's role in all of this. But Lady Gunnora's role was something else altogether.

The woman acted when she should not have and she had cost Kristoph.

Swiftly, Gaetan turned away from Ghislaine and made his way back to Aramis and Téo, who were standing on the road with the others. His jaw was ticking furiously as he faced them.

"It was Lady Gunnora who betrayed us," he muttered. "Aramis, you will return to Westerham with five hundred men. Take Wellesbourne and St. Hèver with you."

Aramis nodded grimly. "What would you have me do?"

Gaetan had no mercy in his eyes. "Burn Westerham and the surrounding village to the ground," he muttered. "Have half the soldiers confiscate anything of value, including livestock and stores, but the rest of it... burn it. And you make sure Lady Gunnora understands that sending that message to Alary last night was the catalyst. I will tolerate no traitors towards me or my men. She will understand that. What she did cost Kristoph a finger."

Aramis didn't flinch at the harsh order. "And the lady? What will you have me do with her?"

Gaetan sighed sharply, turning to look at Ghislaine, who was still standing where he had left her. He could have quite easily have given a harsh order for Lady Gunnora but because Ghislaine had spoken kindly of her, and because she was a friend of Ghislaine, he backed off his usual command of execution.

"Leave her alive to watch what her foolish mouth has brought upon her people," he said. "She can see the results of her loose tongue."

Aramis nodded, whistling over Wellesbourne and St. Hèver so he could relay their orders. The other knights were gravitating in their direction also. Before Aramis could move away to complete fulfill his orders, Téo stopped him.

"Wait," he said, looking to Gaetan. "Before they go, there is much to discuss, Gate, not the least of which is the fact that Alary of Mercia now knows we are following him. He told Lady Ghislaine through the messenger that he would send a bigger piece of Kristoph back to us if we continue to follow."

Gaetan had to pull his thoughts away from vengeance against Lady Gunnora and focus on the situation at hand. He depended on Téo to be his rational self sometimes because the man was inherently wise in all situations. He mulled over the man's words but in the same breath, he realized his men didn't know the entire story as to why Alary of Mercia had sent back a piece of their colleague and a threat. Taking a deep breath, he struggled for calm.

"You are right, as usual," he said to Téo, but his focus moved to his men, all of them now huddled in a circle around him. "You should know why this has happened. Last night, as we feasted at Westerham, Lady Gunnora told Lady Ghislaine that her brother, Alary, had stopped at Westerham the night before. It was Lady Gunnora who sent word to Alary that we were following him and that is why he sent back a piece of Kristoph. I have ordered Aramis and Bartholomew and Kye back to Westerham to burn it to the ground. Treachery will not go unpunished, especially now as we embark in a strange new country. We must be seen as the law and the lords of this country now, and that means we punish those who act against us. If we are perceived as weak, we may as well return home. We cannot hold a country with weakness."

By the time he was finished, the rest of the knights were nodding in serious understanding. The situation now made more sense to them than simply a random act of brutality.

"What *of* Ghislaine of Mercia?" de Moray wanted to know. "Surely she knew what Gunnora was doing. They sat together during the meal, whispering between them. Surely Ghislaine has something to do with this."

It was an accusation, but not an unexpected one. Gaetan fixed on de Moray, who could be a malcontent at times.

"Jathan was with them the entire time, as you all saw," he said for the benefit of all of his men so there would be no doubt. "He heard their entire conversation and said that there was never, at any time, any hint of subversion or treason on the part of Lady Ghislaine. I want to make that clear. If I thought there was, I would be the first person to punish her and I think you know that."

De Moray's jaw ticked faintly as he simply lifted an eyebrow and looked away. That wasn't good enough for Gaetan.

"Marc," he said to the man. "Is this in any way unclear?"

"It is clear."

Gaetan didn't believe him but he didn't dispute him, at least not at the moment. "We need Lady Ghislaine if we are to find her brother," he said for de Moray's benefit and for the benefit of the others. "Nothing is to happen to her. If I discover that any one of you have moved against her, I will consider that an intentional disruption against this mission and a direct threat to Kristoph's life. She knows these lands and we do not. Right now, she serves a purpose."

Before de Moray could reply, Aramis stepped towards the man menacingly. "I know you," he growled at Marc. "I know that once you believe something is true, you will believe it until the end. If Jathan said that Lady Ghislaine had nothing to do with warning her brother that we were coming, then I believe him. If you make any attempt against her, you will have to deal with me personally."

He reached out to grab de Moray by the shoulder when he finished, but it was not a friendly touch. It was one of threat. De Reyne was between them and, with a couple of the others, he sought to separate them before a brawl started. But Gaetan entered the fray and slugged de Moray so hard that the knight went stumbling backwards.

"Make a move against Lady Ghislaine and you will have to deal with me as well," he said. "Whatever you think you suspect about her, forget it. That is my command. If you do not wish to follow that command, then you can ride back to Normandy and stay with him. I have no use for you."

De Moray was a man of great pride but he was no fool. If his comrades, men he loved like brothers, were so convinced of the woman's innocence, then there was no reason for him not to believe it. But he was a naturally suspicious character and it was difficult for him to move past that. Still, he wasn't suspicious enough that he would walk away from his brothers. He sighed heavily and threw up his hands in a gesture of surrender.

"If you believe she did not instigate this treachery, then I will take you for your word," he said, though it was difficult for him to back down. Then he pointed a finger at Gaetan. "But men who trust too easily are often made fools of."

Gaetan was still glaring at him, as was Aramis, but they backed off, moving away to stand with the others. Téo, the peacemaker, went to de Moray and pulled the man back into the group.

"We need Marc to see things we may not," Téo said evenly. "There have been times when his suspicious nature has been of great use. Let no one condemn him for it. But at this moment, we need everyone's level head. Gate, Alary will be watching from now on to see if we are following him. We cannot be a day behind the man with a two-thousand-man army; he will know it is us and we will risk Kristoph greatly if we continue to follow him on this path."

Gaetan raked his fingers through his dark dirty hair, laboring to collect his thoughts on the matter. "That has occurred to me," he said. "It seems to me that we must leave the army behind while we continue onward. We cannot follow him with so many men because we would make a very big target. Alary would quickly know we have disregarded his threat, so we will have to leave the army behind."

"Leave them where?" Téo asked. "Right here? Or do we send them back to Normandy?"

Gaetan shook his head. "Not back to Normandy," he said. "Part of our mission heading north is to subdue Mercia. I cannot do that if I send the army back to Normandy. Therefore, we must leave them here."

"What about leaving them at Westerham?" Aramis asked. "I realize you have ordered us to burn the place, but what if we simply confiscate it for our army? There are plenty of supplies and a village to sustain us. That would make more sense than burning it and leaving our army to fend for themselves in the wilderness of Mercia."

Gaetan liked that idea. "An excellent suggestion," he said. "That will be punishment enough to Lady Gunnora to have a Norman army confiscate her home."

The others seemed to like that idea a good deal. "Westerham could become your first outpost in Mercia," de Winter suggested. "But what of Lady Gunnora's father, Lord Boltolph? Were we not told that he was soon to return? He may not like that the Normans have stolen his property."

Gaetan lifted his eyebrows. "The man cannot compete with two thousand Normans, dug into his holding like a tick on a dog," he said. "I am happy to allow him to return to Westerham so long as he lives alongside us in peace. I would rather have him as an ally and not an enemy, but I will let him choose what his relationship will be. It will be up to him."

A plan was formulating, something that made the knights feel more in control of the situation. It wasn't as if they would give up pursuing

Kristoph, so leaving the army behind – and confiscating the property of Westerham in the process – seemed like a logical solution as the nine knights continued onward in the quest for their colleague.

No one was about to back away, no matter what Alary had threatened.

"So, it will be only the knights moving forward," de Reyne said. "I think that is an excellent solution but I do not believe it is wise to continue on this road. Alary will have his spies watching his retreat and, if they see us, that would also jeopardize Kristoph."

It was a true statement. Gaetan turned to Ghislaine, still standing over by the rider from Westerham, and emitted a whistle between his teeth. When she looked at him, startled by the sound, he motioned to both her and the messenger and then beckoned both with a crooked finger. Ghislaine understood, immediately grasping the messenger and pulling him with her over to the collection of enormous knights. The messenger was clearly dragging his feet but Ghislaine had a good grip on him. As they drew near, Gaetan spoke to the messenger.

"Where did you find Lord Alary last night?" he asked.

The messenger stumbled in the lady's grip before answering. "In the village of Oxshott, my lord," he said.

"How far from Westerham?"

The messenger shook his head. "Not far, my lord. Ten or twelve miles."

Gaetan glanced at his men. "Then he moved quite slowly yesterday," he said. "We have been making nearly twenty-five miles a day with an army and he has only traveled ten or twelve since Westerham? That seems odd."

Téo addressed the messenger. "Has Lord Alary seen a battle or something that would slow his travel? Did you see wounded among his men?"

The messenger shook his head. "Nay, my lord. No battle, at least not from what I could see. But his men did seem weary from what I saw and, although Lord Alary ate well, I did not see his men eat while I was there."

Next to him, Ghislaine sighed with disgust. "That is typical of my brother," she said. "He would live in comfort while his men starve."

Gaetan scratched his head. "That can only work to our advantage when we catch up to them. Starving men will not fight strongly, nor are they particularly loyal to the lord who starves them." He paused a moment. "Still, it would only take one of them to get to Kristoph and do great damage to him if they discovered we were still following. Is this the only road north that will take us to Alary's stronghold?"

Ghislaine shook her head. "There are others, but not nearly as well traveled."

"Could we parallel Alary's travel and intercept him at some point?"

Ghislaine cocked her head thoughtfully. Then, as the knights watched, she went in search of a stick, bringing it back to the group and then dropping to her knees in the center of the knight's circle. She began to draw with the stick.

"I have been traveling Mercia my entire life," she said, wanting to be helpful now that they had seemingly given her the chance to do so. Perhaps they would even forgive her for this incident at some point. "We are north of the sea right now and close to London. Alary is not far ahead of us and since he more than likely departed this morning, just as we did, he is probably somewhere west of London right now along the road we are currently traveling on. Just to the north of us, intersecting this road, is another road that leads west. If we take that road, we will travel about five miles before we come to another road that leads north. This is a small road, more of a path really, but it runs deep into Mercia and all the way to the village of Worcester, which is far to the north."

Gaetan liked the idea. "How close is Worcester to Tenebris?"

Ghislaine made a mark on her crude map. "Not far at all," she said. "Tenebris is northeast of it, mayhap two or three days. If we travel swiftly enough, we can be waiting for Alary before he reaches his stronghold."

From a day that had suffered from a terrible moment of darkness,

Gaetan was starting to see some hope. Perhaps nothing was lost, after all, in their quest to save Kristoph. He turned to Wellesbourne, who knew this area considering he was from the village whose name he bore, which was in the borderlands between Wales and Mercia.

"And you?" he asked. "What say you? Do you know the road she speaks of?"

Bartholomew nodded, eyeing the map in the mud. "It has been a long time since I have traveled that road, but it will take us north, as she says."

That was good enough for Gaetan. His attention returned to Ghislaine. "And your brother will not know we are following him?"

Ghislaine shook her head as she drew the approximate location of the road Alary would be traveling upon. "My brother is intelligent but not experienced when it comes to warfare," she said. "He will only think to look behind him to see if he is being followed. He will not think to look alongside him, on the road to the west."

"Then that is how we shall travel."

Ghislaine nodded but there was something in her expression that suggested she wasn't entirely thrilled with the plans. "I must suggest caution, however," she said, glancing at the knights as she spoke. "Although this is the most likely path to travel, this road moves through some of the most fearful places in Mercia. It is rife with danger. Even those of us who live here and know the road will not travel upon it."

Gaetan didn't see much threat in what she was saying. "We are heavily armed," he said. "I do not think there will be anything upon that road that we cannot fight off."

He was confident but Ghislaine was not. The road she suggested wasn't safe in the least but it was the only solution. There were other roads but it would take time to reach them, which would see Alary possibly make it to Tenebris before they were able to reach him. Therefore, there was little choice. If they still wanted to follow Alary with the hope of rescuing the man, then this was the only way. As Ghislaine pondered the coming journey north on that road of many dangers, Gaetan turned to his men.

"Prepare the army to return to Westerham but abandon the order to burn it," he said. "For now, we will use it. Aramis, make sure Ansel of Guise is in command. Tell him to return the army, settle in, and wait for us to return."

Aramis nodded to the command. "And when Lord Boltolph returns?"

Gaetan was resolute. "As I said – the man may coexist with our army peacefully. If he does not, Ansel has permission to do what is necessary to maintain control of Westerham."

With a plan set, the knights seemed far more composed than they had only moments earlier. Even de Russe and de Moray were moving off together, talking between them. Tempers would flare at times between the men but, like any close family, those things were quickly forgotten.

As they moved away, Ghislaine was left crouching down over her map in the mud, realizing that Gaetan hadn't moved away with the others. He was still standing there, probably looking at her, his mind filled with doubts about her. His presence made her vastly nervous but she also viewed it as an opportunity to convey her sorrow in the situation. He was calmer now and would, perhaps, be more apt to accept her condolences. Dropping the stick, she brushed off her hands and stood up.

"Shall I send the messenger back to Westerham?" she asked.

Gaetan's gaze had been on his men in the distance, now moving to her. He pondered her question for a moment.

"Nay," he replied. "I will send him back with the army. I do not need him returning before them to warn Lady Gunnora that the Normans are returning to stay."

"Very well." Ghislaine paused a moment, summoning the courage to say what she felt was necessary given the circumstances. "I wish I had known what Gunnora was thinking last night in regard to my brother. If I had known, I would have most certainly stopped her. But on behalf of the children of Aelfgar, I must apologize for what Alary has done. He has always had an evil streak in him, something my father saw long ago when Alary was a child. That is one reason, among many, that Alary has no lands or titles. Everything he has, Edwin has given to him because he feels pity for the man who is a bastard from his father's loins."

Gaetan wasn't feeling nearly the rage he had been earlier and, in truth, he appreciated Ghislaine's attempts at an apology. She seemed sincere about it, but he was still feeling the hurt and disappointment from the fact that she'd been told not to tell him about Alary and she had obeyed. The more he thought on that, the more he supposed that his disappointment was in the fact that she had listened to Jathan and not to her loyalty to him.

She *did* have loyalty to him... *didn't she?*

"I was not aware that Alary was a bastard," he finally said.

Ghislaine nodded. "My father had concubines," she said, thinking of Gaetan's bedslaves and finding distress in the thought. She didn't like to reminded that he had women that were close to him. "Alary is the son of a woman my father kept company with for years. I was told by some that he loved her. When Alary was born, he insisted my mother treat him as one of the family, which was a difficult thing for her to do. It seemed that my mother had trouble conceiving more children and in an attempt to give my father another son, I was born several years later. I was not a welcome child, by either parent. Therefore, Alary and I have always had a strange bond between us. I do not love him and he does not love me, but we understand one another. We are both forgotten children of a powerful House."

Gaetan was listening to her, perhaps more closely than he wanted to. With every day, every hour, showing him more interested in her, he was naturally curious about her background. Yet, this was not the time nor the place. Perhaps at some later date, he would know about her birth and upbringing, but not now. Now, he had a knight to rescue.

And her brother to kill.

"Then if you understand your brother so well," he said, "tell me if he will follow through on his threat to harm Kristoph even more if he discovers we are still following him."

Ghislaine averted her gaze when he asked the question, mostly because she knew he wasn't going to like the answer. Already, she didn't like it. But she knew, in her heart, that it was the truth.

"The finger is only the beginning," she said quietly. "Alary of Mercia never says anything he does not mean. That is why it is imperative for us to stay away from him unless you want de Lohr sent back to you in pieces."

Gaetan believed her, word for word.

CHAPTER THIRTEEN

cs

DOGS OF WAR

THE NEXT FIVE days of travel had seen Ghislaine, Gaetan, and the knights making at least twenty-five miles a day, sometimes more if the pushed the horses. They'd been making excellent time without the army to drag them down, and the war horses were hearty and well-fed. They rested every night for several hours before beginning the trek in the morning again. There was a drive behind their swift travel, something felt intently by every man – they had to make it north before Alary did to intercept him before he could make it to Tenebris.

It was the fuel that fed their fire.

Now that it was just the eleven of them, including Jathan, travel had been a different experience than it had when the army was all around them. The knights still rode in formation – men on point, men in the middle, men covering the rear, but there was more conversation. Quiet snippets of it bounced around and the travel, in general, was more relaxed but no less determined. Also of note was the fact that they rode with their shields slung over their left knees, which they hadn't done before, and they rode in tight quarters with Ghislaine in the middle. It was a defensive formation in case they were attacked. But so far, their travel had been thankfully uneventful.

After the incident five days ago, Ghislaine was no longer riding up near Gaetan, as he remained in the front, but de Russe never left her side. He remained on her left while Wellesbourne was on her right. Even when the other men changed positions, those two remained the same. Ghislaine was coming to think that they'd been appointed her protectors or they were simply keeping an eye on her just in case she really did have something to do with tipping off her brother. She was the enemy, after all. Ghislaine kept having to remind herself of that.

But she never asked them because the men really didn't talk to her. She was genuinely disappointed that they had taken a step or two back in their relationship. They were back to simply tolerating her again because of what happened with Gunnora and Ghislaine wasn't sure what more she could do to change their minds. There seemed to be some debate among them as to who trusted her and who didn't, something that left her feeling sad and uncomfortable. Now, all she could do was take comfort in the big gray dog that seemed to follow her every move.

Camulos the dog had taken a liking to her and, try as she might, she couldn't shake the beast so she'd stopped trying. He was the only real companionship she had now. He even slept with her, a great big smelly dog who loved to cuddle, and she found herself overcoming her dislike of dogs because of it. She found it very strange that so seasoned a knight should have a dog that wasn't a killer, but she was glad for her sake. The dog gave her camaraderie when no one else really did.

But her disappointment wasn't only in the situation, or what had happened with Kristoph's finger. Her most heartfelt disappointment was in the fact that Gaetan seemed removed from her now, hardly speaking to her these past few days. He would only address her if it had something to do with the road or their travel in general, but that was where it ended.

Even at the end of the day when they would stop and camp for the night, with Wellesbourne and St. Hèver building massive bonfires to keep the darkness away, Gaetan would stay clear of her as she ate with

Jathan and the dog while Gaetan and his men sat around one of the big bonfires. She was so very sad that she was no longer privileged enough to sit and talk to Gaetan. She kept reflecting back to the night at Westerham when they'd included her in their drinking and revelry. It was the best night of her life.

She missed, very much, what she would no longer know.

Therefore, Ghislaine was resigned to this journey, so quiet and so lonely even though she was surrounded by men. He heart felt like a rock, heavy and weighty, cold and crumbling. Once, Gaetan had breathed a little bit of life into it but that momentary light had been fleeting. Thoughts of him and the sight of him, still made her heart flutter but it was like the death throes of a dying beast.

Quiver, quiver...

Quiver....

Like anything else that wasn't nurtured or fed, soon enough, her heart would flutter no more.

Therefore, she distracted herself as they moved along, pretending to study the land when her mind teetered on the edge of self-pity. More and more, however, her focus on the land surrounding them was occupying her time because they were entering an area known for its strange people and dark customs. Even if Gaetan didn't want to speak to her, it was time she speak to him because they were entering an area he needed to know something about and she didn't want to be blamed again for withholding information.

Coming off of a slight rise with a vast valley spread out below in the distance, they were quickly approaching the shadowlands.

"Jathan," she turned to the priest. "I must speak with Gaetan. It is important. Would you ask permission?"

The priest, who had riding next to her quietly for the past few days, nodded his head and kicked the sides of his shaggy horse, forcing the animal to move faster than it wanted to. He made his way up to Gaetan at the front and Ghislaine could see the priest speaking to Gaetan and pointing back to Ghislaine. Gaetan didn't respond, or at least she didn't see him respond, until several moments later when Jathan finally came back to her and invited her forward. Digging her heels into the sides of her shaggy mare, she cantered forward until she came to Gaetan.

He was riding tall and proud astride his big war beast as Ghislaine came up to ride beside him, but he didn't look at her. He kept his eyes on the road ahead.

"What is so important that you must speak with me?" he asked.

His voice sounded so unkind. Ghislaine's heart sank and she sighed heavily, unsure how much of his coldness she could take. Her disappointment and sadness in his treatment of her was starting to turn into something else.

Resentment wasn't far off.

"I thought you should know that we are entering the realm of the shadowlands," she said, her manner as unfriendly as his was. "The people who live here are secretive and dark, and have been known to eat their enemies. Although there are a few abbeys here, the church has not been able to change their ways. In fact, several years ago, we heard that they ate the priests who had tried to convert them to Christ. An old name for them is the *Cilternsaetan*, but before that, it was something worse. They were known as *caro comdenti*."

Gaetan turned to look at her, translating the Latin. "Flesh eater?"

Ghislaine nodded, meeting his gaze briefly before looking away. "I told you there was danger on this road."

Gaetan was looking at her even when she looked away. It was a stolen look as far as he was concerned, a moment in which he could look at that angelic face and have a reason to do so. He'd spent the past two days struggling with what he was feeling for her, trying to tell himself that she was disloyal to him, an untrustworthy enemy, but what his mind told him and what his heart yearned for were two different things.

He didn't want to talk to her. He didn't want to look at her. He'd kept himself well away from her, and she'd kept herself away from him as well. He was content. Not happy, but content. But now, here she was, and in looking at her he realized just how much he'd missed her. Something about this woman was growing on him, inside him, just like a parasite, and he couldn't shake her no matter how hard he tried.

In fact, he was thinking more about missing her than the words she was speaking, so it took him a moment to shake off his daydreams to realize she was telling him something quite serious. He reined his horse to a stop and the entire group came to a halt behind him, but Gaetan motioned for the group to come near and they closed in around them. He gestured at Ghislaine.

"The lady has told me something about the people in this area," he said. "The ancient name for them is *caro comdenti*. It seems that when she warned us of danger along this road, it includes a people who eat the flesh of their enemies."

Everyone, especially Jathan, began looking around them with some concern. They were in a light collection of trees to the east while off to the northwest was an expanse of flat, open grass as far as the eye could see. In fact, the entire area was flat and a mighty river ran off to the west; he could see the glistening of the water now and again.

But the land looked empty of people and oddly empty of animals or birds. In fact, all was quite still, which was troubling. It was easy to get an uneasy feeling about it, especially now with what the lady had told Gaetan.

"Has Edwin had any run-ins with these people?" Téo asked. "We are in Mercia, after all. These are his lands."

Ghislaine shook her head. "Edwin's seat of Tamworth Castle is to the north in an area of more civilized people. He does not spend much time in this area if he can help it. Some say these lands are cursed."

"But you suggested this road," Gaetan pointed out. "If you knew this area was so terribly dangerous, why did you suggest it?"

Ghislaine looked at him. "Because it would have taken us much longer to reach the only other road that leads to the north," she said. "You wanted to parallel Alary and that is exactly what we are doing, but it does not come easily. I warned you the day we left the army back at

Westerham. Do you not recall?"

Gaetan did. He remembered saying something about the fact that they would be heavily armed, so he couldn't blame Ghislaine for taking them down a dangerous path. She had, indeed, warned them. Rather than admit that, however, he simply brushed it aside.

"Is there a town or somewhere to stay the night?" he asked. "Dusk will be upon at some point and I am not entirely sure I wish to sleep in the open tonight if there are men waiting to harvest my flesh."

Ghislaine pointed down the road, northward. "Evesham is not too far away and Worcester beyond that," she said. "We could make it to Evesham but it would be after dark. There is an abbey there where we could seek shelter."

Over near Gaetan, Wellesbourne snorted. "The abbey is a beacon in a sea of darkness," he said as the knights turned in his direction. "Remember that I am from the Marches between Mercia and Wales. I have been about these lands before with my father and what she says is true. It is a cursed land but it is also our only option if we want to make north before Alary does. I would strongly suggest we make it to Evesham, as the lady has suggested, as quickly as we can. Legends and ghost stories abound in this land. Some say it is not only cursed, but haunted."

Jathan crossed himself fearfully as the other knights looked at Wellesbourne with varied levels of amusement. "Since when did you become so superstitious," St. Hèver wanted to know. "Ghosts do not exist."

Wellesbourne looked at him, pointedly. "Have you ever seen one?"

Kye shook his head. "I have not. Show me one and I will believe. In fact, I'd rather like to see one."

Wellesbourne shook his head, a gesture of regret. "If we do not make it out of this land, then you may *become* one. Gate, I suggest we get moving. There is no time to waste."

There was some urgency to Wellesbourne's statement, which spurred the other knights forward. The man didn't show concern for no reason at all, which meant he must have, indeed, been wary about their surroundings. No one wanted to discount that. As the group began to move out, Camulos suddenly began barking.

The lazy sweet dog of their liege wasn't one to bark, which immediately put everyone on edge. He was trotting up ahead of them, into an area that was fairly dense with trees. They could see the end of the tree line beyond where the road opened up again into fields, but in order to get to that open space, they had to pass through a thicket of trees that lined both sides of the road. The dog was wandering up into that sheltered area, barking at the trees.

Gaetan didn't like that in the least. Camulos may have been a lazy, good-for-nothing dog, but he was nonetheless alert and, at times, had been an excellent warning system. Silently, he lifted a balled fist and immediately, every knight unsheathed his broadsword or at least put a hand to the hilt of their weapon. Up towards the front of their group, Denis de Winter already had *l'Espada* out, the metal blade gleaming in the weak light.

They were ready for a fight.

But Ghislaine was very suspicious about what was going on. The tribes around here were unorganized and rough, but they were cunning in that they used the land to their advantage. The Normans did not; heavily armed, they believed they could withstand anything because of their superior weapons and armor and tactics. They didn't even try to hide themselves. Perhaps their superiority was true in an open battle, but in covert warfare, it might not be so effective.

Ghislaine couldn't stand the thought of Gaetan being cut down because he fought one way while the *caro comdenti* fought another. He hadn't seemed to be apt to really listen to her on this journey, instead, relying on his men or on Wellesbourne who, it seemed, hadn't been home in almost twenty years. Times changed, as did areas and towns in that time. Gaetan and his men were entering this land like warriors on a quest when what they needed to do was be as unobtrusive as possible.

That arrogance was going to cost them if they weren't careful.

The dog was milling around up on the road, sniffing the ground, but he'd stopped barking. He even stopped to look back at the knights behind him, men who had slowed their forward progression considerably. But Ghislaine's warrior instincts were taking over; she had little doubt that there was someone, or something, waiting for them up in those trees. She could feel it. Men with arrows, perhaps, or axes, both of them sharp projectiles that would come sailing out at the Normans as they passed through. A glance at Gaetan and the others showed that they were ready for a fight, tensed up and prepared. They were waiting for it to come to them.

But Ghislaine couldn't wait. Better to draw out what was lying in wait and remove the element of surprise to give the Normans targets to strike at. If there was, indeed, someone waiting in the trees, then it would take away their advantage if she was able to draw them out. And if there was no one waiting… well, she would look like a fool. But it was better than permitting Gaetan and his men to be cut down.

She had brought them along this road. Perhaps, in a sense, she needed to protect them from it.

When the dog began barking again, Ghislaine kicked her mare as hard as she could and the horse bolted, tearing up the road and into the collection of trees. She could hear someone shouting behind her, men shouting out her name, but she ignored them. She was about halfway down the shaded path when the arrows suddenly began flying from the trees and she heard men in the foliage, barking like dogs. They were howling and hooting, and an arrow zinged by her head. Gasping with fright, she lay down on the mare, putting her head next to the horse's neck for protection. More arrows, more barking, and then sounds of a fight behind her.

And then, an arrow struck her.

A large yew arrow with a barbed iron head went straight into her right thigh, straight through it, and embedded itself in the mare's body. Startled by the pain, the mare came to a sudden halt but Ghislaine didn't fall off because she was pinned to the horse by the arrow. She tried to control the horse with one hand while trying to remove the arrow with the other, but she couldn't get a good grip on the shaft. Without a weapon, she was vulnerable to the men who were now rushing her from the trees. Terrified that she was about to be captured, she tried to get the mare moving but the horse wasn't cooperating.

Her terror was replaced by great surprise when two war horses suddenly appeared and the men who had charged her from the trees were cut down by broadswords that were singing a deadly song as they sailed through the air. The attackers were still barking and Ghislaine caught sight of them, dirty men in leather and loincloths, faces painted with mud and twigs in their hair. Some had iron-head axes and still others had bows and arrows, but even in their greater number they were no match for the Norman knights on horseback.

Still, it was a battle from the start as Gaetan and his men cut down the savage tribe that ambushed them from the trees. Soon, the road was littered with headless bodies, bloodied limbs, and carnage, but the dog-people didn't give up. They were tenacious, but so were the knights. There were far more of the dog-people than the Normans and they seemed to come in waves, but the Norman knights handled them easily.

Meanwhile, Ghislaine and the two knights who had ridden to her aid seemed to be boxed in by a swarm of the dog-men but, in short order, the attackers fell away and someone grabbed hold of her horse's reins, tearing off down the road to get her out of harm's way. Ghislaine simply held on to the horse's neck, in anguish with the arrow still through her thigh.

She watched the road pass beneath the mare's feet, praying they would make it to safety as the ground whizzed by and rocks kicked up in her face. Time seemed to have little meaning as they ran, but jostling her leg was sheer agony and with every move the horse made, she struggled not to cry out. But soon enough, the horse came to a halt and hands were reaching out to steady her. Someone pulled her into a sitting position and when she looked around, she saw Gaetan bailing off his horse and rushing to her side along with de Moray, his bloodied sword still drawn. De Moray stood guard to make sure they weren't attacked again as someone slid onto the back of her horse and held her steady.

"Easy, my lady." It was Aramis behind her, bracing her right thigh against his enormous right thigh to keep it steady as Gaetan tried to get a look at what had happened. "We shall remove this quickly, have no fear. Stay still."

Ghislaine was in pain, in distress. "I am sorry," she gasped. "I knew there was someone in those trees, waiting for us, and I thought if I drew them out, they would lose the element of surprise."

Gaetan looked up at her, an oddly compassionate expression on his face, something Ghislaine hadn't seen in days. His focus moved to Aramis, sitting behind her and holding her fast, before returning to the arrow.

"It was a clever move, little mouse," Gaetan said as he tried to get a look at the underside of her thigh where the arrow had her pinned. "It was also astonishingly brave. But had you told me your plans, I would have sent an armored man in your stead so we would not find ourselves in the position we do now."

He was back to complimenting her and rebuking her in the same breath. "Had I told you my plans, you would have stopped me," she said frankly. "I took you along this road, de Wolfe. It was my duty to protect you when I sensed danger. You do not know these lands; I do. I know what these people are capable of and I could not... I would not...."

She trailed off, unable to finish. Gaetan didn't say anything after that. He had his hand on her leg, which was covered with those leather trousers she liked to wear, even beneath the cotes he had given her. In truth, he didn't trust himself to speak because he still wasn't over the shock of seeing her risk her life for him and his men. Never in his life had he met a woman of such bravery, but in that bravery there had been great danger. Now, she had an arrow through her thigh, anchoring her to the horse. He could see that it was embedded fairly deeply and he pushed aside any emotion he was feeling to logically address the injury.

But it was a struggle.

"It will cause you more pain if I try to pull it out and I am not entirely sure I can because of the way it is embedded in the mare," he said, hating the fact that he was starting to feel queasy at the sight of her with an arrow in her. "I am going to break the shaft and then we will lift you off of it."

Ghislaine was looking at him steadily, pale-faced, with beads of sweat on her upper lip, but her expression was one of faith. *Total faith.* Gaetan locked eyes with her and, at that moment, something changed for him. This strong noble woman had been trying to do the right thing since nearly the moment they met. Not including their brief encounter on the battlefield, she had been trying to help men she didn't even know save their comrade. Her motives weren't entirely altruistic; she wanted to be rid of a half-brother who had made her life miserable. But more than once, she had gone above the call of duty to help men who were, in theory, her enemy.

But not anymore.

At this moment, she had proven herself to him.

"We need more hands to help, Gate," Aramis said, his voice tense. "I can lift her up but we must have more hands to steady both her and the leg."

Gaetan could see his point. He turned to see de Moray standing behind them, sword in hand and legs braced, prepared for anything that might come charging out at them. Back on the road beneath the canopy of trees, he could see his men on horseback and several bodies on the ground. There was still some fighting going on but, as he watched, Jathan and Luc de Lara came shooting out of the chaos, heading in their direction.

Jathan and Luc were on them quickly but their rush caused the injured mare to dance about nervously and Ghislaine gasped in pain as Aramis tried to hold both her and the horse steady. Gaetan, too, was trying to keep the mare from moving around as Luc and Jathan rushed up to see her injury.

"I cannot remove this arrow, as it is embedded in the horse," Gaetan explained to them, quickly. "It has her pinned. I am going to break the shaft and then we will try to lift her off of it. Luc, get on her other side and prepare to help lift her up on my command. Jathan, find something to stanch the blood flow. We will need to bind the wound."

The priest, pale-faced with the rush of battle, went running back to his horse to collect bandages from his saddlebags as Gaetan prepared to break the shaft. He looked up at Aramis to see if the man had Ghislaine properly braced.

"Do not let her move," he told Aramis quietly, steadily. "Hold her fast. Luc, help him steady her while I break this."

Ghislaine had her head turned away, hearing Gaetan's words. She had never been more terrified in her life. She was in excruciating pain as she felt hands on her left leg and thigh, holding it still, while Aramis wrapped his enormous arms around her to keep her from bolting once Gaetan jostled the arrow. They'd all had their share of wounds enough to know how painful something like this was, so once Aramis nodded briefly to Gaetan to signal he had a good grip on the lady, Gaetan went quickly to work.

Grasping the shaft of the arrow just above her thigh, he snapped the shaft in half. As Ghislaine bit off her cries of pain, he took hold of her right leg and, with Aramis shifting his grip and lifting, pulled her leg off the arrow that was still stuck into the side of the horse. Ghislaine screamed in pain as they did so, made worse by the fact that it wasn't a clean removal; something had her leg stuck to the arrow so the first attempt at removal was only partial. Gaetan had to grasp hold of the underside of the arrow to hold it steady and had his men lift again, this time with de Moray's help, to pull her right leg completely off of the shaft. Finally, her leg came free.

Aramis handed her down to Gaetan, who cradled her against his chest as Jathan rushed up with a wad of boiled linen and a bladder of wine that was part of their provisions. As Luc and Marc went to work removing the remainder of the arrow from the poor little mare, Aramis went to assist Gaetan and Jathan in wrapping the lady's leg. Aramis took a close look at the wound before he let the priest put bandages on it.

"'Tis a dirty wound, Gate," he said grimly. "I can see bits of her cote and other debris in it. It must be cleaned."

Gaetan shook his head. "Not now," he said. "We must get her to safety before we clean the wound. Douse it with the wine and wrap it. We must get out of here."

Aramis knew that; they all did. He eyed Ghislaine, who was trying very hard to be brave, before taking the wine bladder and dousing the liquid onto the wound. It was the only thing they had to clean it at the moment but the sting of the alcohol had Ghislaine biting off her screams in her hand. It was horrific battlefield medicine. With great haste, Aramis and Jathan then proceeded to bind the leg tightly as the rest of the knights began trickling down the road.

"How is the lady?" Téo asked, pulling his worn horse to a nervous halt.

Aramis was binding the leg so tightly that Ghislaine was weeping softly in pain, hand over her face and her head against Gaetan's shoulder. Gaetan turned to glance at Téo, an expression on his face that suggested he was becoming ill.

"Injured," he said simply. "The arrow has been removed but the wound must be tended. We cannot do that here. Has the fighting stopped?"

Téo nodded. "For the most part," he said. "St. Hèver and Wellesbourne are dispatching the wounded, but many of those fools ran off. They will return for their dead and we do not want to be here when they come back."

"Agreed. Is anyone injured?"

"Only the lady."

Gaetan was relieved, at least in the aspect that none of his men had been wounded. "De Moray!" he barked.

Marc appeared at his side. "Aye, Gate?"

"The mare?"

De Moray turned to look at the little animal as Luc patched up the puncture. "The mare's wound is deep but it did not puncture anything vital," he said. "But that was not an arrow from a tree-dweller. It had a heavy iron head on it that had barbs to embed it in whatever it struck. That is why you could not remove it easily."

An iron arrowhead with spines in it was a dastardly piece of equipment, designed to maim. "Our tree-dwellers have had some contact with tribes who know how to make weapons to not only kill but to inflict great pain in doing it," he said ominously. Then, he shifted Ghislaine in Marc's direction. "Now that we know that, we will be more careful bringing an army into this land. Here, take the lady while I gather my horse. You will take charge of the mare."

De Moray gently took Ghislaine from Gaetan, holding her in his big arms as Gaetan went for his war horse and Aramis finished binding the leg. By the time de Russe was finished with the dressing, all of the knights had joined them, all of them greatly concerned for the lady who had taken the arrow to her leg. As they jockeyed for position to see the extent of the damage, Gaetan vaulted onto his war horse and rode alongside de Moray, extending his arms for the lady. When she was carefully handed up to him, he settled her across his big thighs and gathered his reins, digging his spurs into the sides of his animal and tearing off down the road as his men followed closely.

At breakneck speed, the knights made their way to the safety of Evesham Abbey.

CHAPTER FOURTEEN

cs

THAT DARK SKY

Tavern of the White Feather
Bicester

I T COULD HAVE been worse.

That's the way Kristoph looked at the situation with his finger. It was healing very well thanks to the wine he soaked it in almost every night, given to him by the same man who had been giving him food and drink this entire time. At night, wherever he was chained – usually on the wagon and with the livestock – the soldier would bring him food and sit next to him. For the first few nights, the man didn't say a thing, especially after the episode that saw Kristoph lose the tip of his finger, but a couple of days ago, the man actually began to speak to him.

At first, it was small talk, but last night, it was an entire story about daughters he had lost to the Danes. Mostig was the man's name and Kristoph listened to the man tell a horrific story about watching his daughters' abduction and his home going up in flames. Injured, sick, he'd wandered until he'd been found by Edwin of Mercia's people, who took him in and sheltered him in exchange for his service as a soldier.

Mostig didn't mention how he came into the service of Alary and Kristoph didn't ask. In fact, Kristoph didn't ask anything because he didn't want his curiosity to get back to Alary. The less antagonizing the man, the better. Kristoph didn't want to lose another finger.

It was a misty night in the village of Bicester, a densely-populated berg with poorly constructed homes crowded in around each other and torches burning near the town square in a vain attempt to stave off the darkness. The mist was creating a wet coating on everything but the torches had been soaked in fat, which meant more heavy black smoke than flame was pouring from them on this night. It was a very dark night, in fact, with the moon obscured by the clouds. All was eerily quiet and still as the residents of the town huddled behind their locked doors, preparing for sleep.

Kristoph sat on a bed of old straw beneath the wagon, watching the night beyond the livery yard where Alary had stabled his horses for the night. There was a tavern across the street, simply called The White Feather from the sign scratched above the doorway, and he'd seen Alary disappear inside when they'd arrived in town earlier that evening.

Kristoph was expecting his soldier friend to come out of the tavern at some point to give him something to eat but the man hadn't made an appearance yet, so he sat beneath the wagon and watched the mist fall, his thoughts wandering to his wife and daughter as they so often did these days. Hardly an hour went by that he wasn't thinking of Adalie and their daughter, Chloe.

It was the only thing that kept him strong enough to stay alive.

Kristoph glanced at his left hand, his long and strong fingers beneath the weak light. The little finger was the one that Alary had cut and he'd been mercifully unconscious when it had happened so he never felt a thing. He'd awoken to a bandaged hand and a little finger that had the top knuckle removed. It really wasn't all that bad as far as amputations went; it could have been the whole hand and he wouldn't have known until it was too late, so he was grateful for small mercies.

Still, he wasn't feeling so merciful towards his captor.

He tried not to think of Alary at all, a man who kept him heavily chained at all hours of the day and night. Alary might have been an arrogant arse with delusions of grandeur, but he wasn't a fool. He guessed that his captive would try to escape so he kept him tightly bound, always secured to something that was heavier than he was so he couldn't easily run off. Even now, as Kristoph tested the chains that were secured to the axel of the wagon because testing the anchor of his chains had become a habit, he heard the door to the tavern open.

Men were spilling out into the night, heading over to the livery, and he recognized several of Alary's men, drunken and loud. He didn't like when they got drunk because one or more of them always wanted to fight him, challenging the great Norman invader. He didn't feel like getting into a fight this night so he tried to stay out of sight, sliding back behind the wagon wheel to obscure his form. His ribs were still damaged, his beaten body was slowly healing, and the hand with the half-missing finger was still very sore from the injury.

But one thing was for certain – his strength was returning and, with that, so was his drive to escape these Saxon bastards.

Surprisingly, Alary was one of those who had come from the tavern. Kristoph could see him crossing the road, talking to his men, laughing with them, and drifting in his direction. Since Alary didn't usually socialize with his men, this was of concern to Kristoph and he watched very carefully as the man crossed the road, hanging on one of his men and laughing uproariously. Unfortunately for Kristoph, Alary seemed to be heading in his direction.

Damnation, he thought. He wasn't ready to lose another finger, or worse. Alary managed to stay clear of him most of the time, but with drink, he became more aggressive. The closer Alary drew, the more Kristoph braced himself.

Unfortunately, he wasn't quite as concealed as he'd hoped. Alary spied him under the wagon bed, tucked back by one of the wheels. He bent sideways to see him more clearly and almost ended up falling over. He laughed.

"Norman?" he called. "What are you doing under there? I can see you. Come out from there!"

Kristoph debated whether or not to obey but he knew if he didn't, things would go badly for him. He didn't want to agitate a very agitable man. Slowly, he pulled himself out from beneath the wagon bed. Alary made his way over to him as he came out from beneath, the mist drifting down onto his face and head.

"Look at you," Alary said drunkenly. "You look terrible."

Kristoph couldn't very well disagree. "I do not smell very good, either."

Alary laughed. "That is to be expected," he said. He gazed at Kristoph a moment, sobering. "We must speak, you and I. There is much to tell."

The last time Alary had been friendly like this, Kristoph had lost part of a finger. Therefore, he was extremely wary as Alary plopped down beside him, sitting in the old straw as he gazed up into the misty sky, blinking his eyes because he was getting water in them. But he kept staring up into that dark sky, reflecting the darkness of his troubled mind.

"You will be happy to know that my spies tell me that your Norman friends are no longer following us," he said. He cast Kristoph a sidelong glance. "Does that surprise you?"

Kristoph wasn't surprised because of one primary factor – he didn't believe Alary in the least. He suspected the man was trying to play some kind of demoralizing mind game with him but he wasn't about to let Alary get the better of him. If the man was trying to cause him grief, then he was in for a disappointment.

"You sent them the tip of my finger," he said after a moment. "If it were me, I would take your threat seriously. They did what they had to do so that you will not cut off something more vital."

Alary nodded thoughtfully, as if they were having a perfectly normal conversation. "But to back off completely?" he asked. "They must not be very loyal friends if they have abandoned you."

"You are probably correct."

"Is that what Norman loyalty is worth?"

Kristoph wasn't sure if he was trying to antagonize him or ask a genuine question. Kristoph knew it was safer, for him, to simply agree with him.

"You told them to stay away, and they have," he said. "I should think you would be pleased."

Alary nodded, looking up at the sky again as the soft mist fell on his face. He closed his eyes, feeling the cool cleanse of the mist upon his face but he also began to tip backwards because of the drink in his system. He ended up bumping back against the wagon.

"Norman," he said after a moment. "Why have you come here? What will your people do now that they have killed my king?"

Kristoph had heard variations of this question since his abduction and, for once, he sought to take charge of the conversation. Much as he did with the lady warrior that first day he'd been abducted, Kristoph viewed this moment as an opportunity to make himself less of an object of hate and more of a man who had simply been obeying orders. It had worked with the woman, but Alary... he was different. There was something not quite right about the man, which made Kristoph proceed very carefully.

But it had to be done. If had any chance of survival, he would have to take it, in any form.

"I was only following the commands of my liege," he said, leaning forward to look Alary in the face. "But what of you? Are you frightened now that the Normans have come to the shores of England? Truthfully, England has had many enemies come to her shores, men who have taken chunks of the country for themselves. The Danes, for instance. They continue to raid and loot, not only in England, but as far south as Breton. We have had our troubles with them. Why do you fear the Normans so?"

Alary blinked as water pooled in his eyes. "Would you not also fear men who came to your shores and killed your king?"

It was as vulnerable and truthful as Kristoph had ever seen Alary. He knew it was the drink talking, but it didn't matter. It was a surprisingly weak question as the wine removed all of Alary's inhibitions and controls. Perhaps there was something human inside the man, after all, and it was to that human part of him that Kristoph intended to appeal to.

"You want to know what the Normans will do?" he asked. "I will tell you quite simply – they will come. They will continue to come and abducting me will not make them stop coming. If you want to survive this conquest, then you must ally yourself with the Normans and holding me hostage will only make you the enemy in their eyes. You can cut off my hands, my feet, my ears, and send it all back to them with threats, but I am one knight who is meaningless in the grand scheme of things. They will not care if you cut me to pieces and send me back. It will only make you more of an enemy in their eyes and they will come for you. They will not stop until they have you. Do you want to survive? Then you will listen to me. I will tell you how to survive."

By this time, Alary was looking at him, his drunken expression rippling with concern. "How many men have come with Normandy?"

"Tens of thousands. You were on the field of battle; you saw how many there were."

Alary had. Suddenly, his drunken state wasn't quite so pleasant. It was magnifying his emotions, fear or jubilation or sorrow. He looked at Kristoph, his brow furrowing.

"If they keep coming, I will send you back to them in a puzzle that no man could put back together," he said, growing agitated. "That will keep them away!"

"I told you it would not. They do not care about a solitary knight when it comes to conquest."

"They must not come to Mercia!"

"They are already *in* Mercia."

Alary's eyes widened as he realized what the Norman said was true. He groaned, as if becoming ill. "They are crawling all over the south of Sussex and Wessex," he hissed. "Of course they are in Mercia!"

Kristoph watched the man closely, hoping this didn't mean he was about to lose another body part. "Do you want to keep them away?"

"They must stay away!"

"Do you want to keep them away?"

Alary labored to climb up from the dirty straw, staggering because he couldn't quite catch his balance. He ended up leaning against the wagon to steady himself.

"How do I keep them away?" he finally asked. It sounded like a plea. "Tell me!"

Kristoph felt a huge surge of hope in that question. Maybe – just maybe – he could keep himself alive and in one piece until he had the opportunity to escape. If he could convince Alary that he was of help, that he could help him keep the Normans away, then perhaps that opportunity would come at some point.

Kristoph could only pray.

"I will tell you the secret on how to keep the Normans away," he said. "But you cannot threaten me any longer. You cannot cut off any more fingers and, for God's sake, feed me and let me sleep in a bed. Keep me alive and I will tell you how to keep the Normans away."

Alary was so drunk that he didn't have his usual steadiness of mind. What Kristoph was offering was quite attractive to him. Even though Tenebris wasn't actually his but a fortified lodge belonging to his brother, still, it was the only thing he had. He didn't want to relinquish it. The fear of losing it to the Normans was wreaking havoc within him.

"I will," he finally said, wiping his running nose with the back of his hand. "What will you tell me?"

"Feed me and we will discuss it."

One of the best moments of Kristoph's life was when Alary ordered his equally-drunken men to unchain the prisoner, but he wasn't so drunk that he left Kristoph unattended. With a drunken four-man escort, Kristoph was escorted over to the smelly, low-ceilinged tavern where he sat on the floor by the hearth and enjoyed a feast of boiled mutton and bread.

But to Kristoph, it was the best meal he'd ever tasted.

He tasted hope.

Maybe he would live through this, after all.

At least, that was what he thought until the next morning when Alary woke up with a headache and no memory of their conversation.

CHAPTER FIFTEEN

⊗

A FIRE WITHIN

Nearing Worcester

WORCESTER WAS A city that was partially in ruins.

Surrounded by a massive forest and bisected by the River Severn, a waterway that flooded the city now and again, Worcester had seen better days. Tribes had attacked it from the south some twenty years earlier and burned a great deal of it, and reconstruction had been slow because of continued tribal battles that had been going on since the great burning. But the cathedral stood, soaring into the cloudy sky, like a great bastion of hope and faith amidst the ruins of the struggling city.

After leaving Evesham, she was back to riding her shaggy mare, Ghislaine led the knights through trees and meadows towards this downtrodden city. Three days since the arrow strike that had nearly crippled her, she was wasn't feeling particularly well but she wasn't one to give in to illness or injury of any kind. The Normans had learned that about her. She'd only ridden with Gaetan the night of her injury when he'd rushed her to Evesham Abbey where the knights had proceeded to tend her – all of them, in fact.

Every one of them knew what she had done to draw out the enemy and save them from an ambush, so in that one swift motion, she'd changed the minds of them all. It had been an act of bravery by a woman like none other. Even de Moray, who had always been so suspicious of her, was now a believer in her honesty and intention to help. Although the price of proving her worth had been high, it had been worth it in Ghislaine's opinion. It was worth it even more in the way that Gaetan was now being so attentive to her.

But he wasn't the only one. When it came time to tend her wounds, it was like having nine physics while Jathan simply stood by and watched, praying furiously while the knights dealt with the wound. When they'd reached Evesham after the attack, the priests from Evesham's cathedral were very helpful and brought boiled linen and medicines, herbal remedies, that promised to help the wound.

Once they were able to take a close look at the damage, they could see that the arrow had missed her bone. It was a clean puncture straight through her leg. Unfortunately, Aramis has been correct – it was a dirty wound. The arrow had pushed leather and fabric into her leg as it traveled and that was something that needed to come out. The knights knew it and so did Ghislaine. As she bit off her groans of pain on a rag, Gaetan plucked out the debris by candlelight with a long set of iron tweezers provided by the priests.

It had been a rather harrowing experience but one that had understandably bonded Ghislaine to the knights. They'd all been wounded at one or more points in their lives so they well understood her agony when it came to cleaning out a wound.

But Ghislaine was strong. She didn't faint or go into hysterics even when Gaetan put stitches in her leg, and Aramis patted her on the shoulder more than once during the procedure. The big knight with the muddy dark eyes remained by her side until Gaetan's eyesight began to give out in the weak light and then he took over, cleaning out what Gaetan had missed. When both Aramis and Gaetan were satisfied they'd sufficiently cleaned the wound, it was doused again with wine to cleanse it and honey was applied as a salve to keep away the poison.

Gaetan then wrapped it up tightly.

But Ghislaine didn't stay awake long enough to suffer extended pain. Exhausted to the bone from the events of the day, the monks had given her a draught of wine with poppy powder in it to make her sleep, and sleep she did. She slept well into the morning and no one bothered to wake her up.

In fact, as she slept against the wall of the cathedral covered up by several cloaks that the knights had so thoughtfully deposited on her during the course of the night, Gaetan and his men secured all entrances into the cathedral and refused to let anyone in while she slept. They threatened anyone who tried. For that day, the priests of Evesham had to hold mass on the steps at the front of the church.

When Ghislaine finally awoke well into the morning and realized what Gaetan and his men had done, she had to admit that she was very touched. Aramis and Lance de Reyne brought her food, simple gruel and watered wine, but she slurped it down as Aramis went to check her wound. But that brought Gaetan around and he pushed Aramis aside as he checked his handiwork on her leg personally. Little did Ghislaine know that he was getting a bit of a thrill at the tender white flesh of her thigh and, Gaetan thought, so was Aramis.

There was a competition afoot.

In fact, Gaetan became somewhat territorial over her, especially around de Russe whom, he suspected, was becoming rather enamored with the woman who bested him at Westerham. He'd known Aramis for years and he'd never shown much attention towards women, considering them a necessary nuisance and nothing more. So for Aramis to show Ghislaine the concern he was, in fact, had Gaetan concerned.

It shouldn't have, but it did.

Gaetan wasn't entirely sure why, other than the fact his attitude towards Ghislaine was different since the arrow strike. He'd been pulled towards her from the start but now, that pull was stronger than he could control. He'd once considered taking her as his bedslave but, somehow, she was too good for that. She didn't deserve to be relegated to a man's bed. She was courageous, beautiful, and strong. So very strong. A woman like that deserved to be a queen.

Or the wife of a great warlord.

That thought had occurred to him while he was cleansing her wound again with wine. She flinched but she didn't utter a sound, not like she had before. She was steeling herself to the pain, becoming accustomed to it, and the more he held that tender white thigh in his hands and tended the arrow wound, the more he admired a woman who should bear her pain so stoically. But when that word crossed his mind... *wife*... he'd almost dropped her leg and probably would have had de Lara not been holding the ankle to steady it.

It was a foolish notion that had startled him. He wasn't meant to have a wife. He had three bedslaves, three children, and he didn't need a wife. At least, those were his usual thoughts, thoughts he'd had for years. But in the same breath, it occurred to him that he had never wanted a wife because he'd never met a woman he considered worthy. What better wife to take than the sister of Edwin of Mercia, linking Norman and Saxon, cementing alliances? But he wouldn't marry her simply for the alliance.

He would marry her because he was coming to think she was something very special, indeed.

But Ghislaine was oblivious to Gaetan's thoughts as he checked her wound twice more that day before she went to sleep. The knights had delayed their journey for two full days to tend to the woman who had sacrificed herself for them. But the morning of the third day, they set out for Worcester through dense forests and a road that narrowed so much, at times, that they had to pass through in single file. The weather had been rainy one day, sunny the next, and as they neared the city, the temperature rose to the point where the water in the ground and in the trees turned into steam and the air became heavy with moisture. Compounded with the humidity from the river, it made the air rather uncomfortable.

The knights were sweating beneath their mail and tunics and even Ghislaine was feeling hot as the air around them turned into a steam bath. She was wearing layers of clothing and she rolled her sleeves up as much as she could, trying to find some relief from the sticky warmth. She kept wiping the sweat from her forehead but she soon came to realize that her cheeks were also very hot – unnaturally hot.

Riding behind Gaetan as they passed through a stretch of trees that, once again, had them riding single file, she touched her cheeks discreetly, realizing with dismay that she had a fever. She'd felt rather queasy all day but she has attributed it to the fact that she was taxing her body by traveling with a nasty wound to her leg. It didn't occur to her that it was because she was beginning to run a fever.

Fear kept her silent as they continued to travel, fear of becoming a burden, of even being left behind as the knights continued on to Alary's lair. This was her quest, too, and she didn't want to surrender this moment of moments, when she finally felt as if she was a part of something, accepted by men she'd proven herself to. It had been a difficult and long fight, and she wasn't about to relinquish it. She prayed fervently that the fever would be mild and that it would quickly pass. It was simply her body's way of dealing with the poisonous humors that were inside of her as a result of the arrow wound.

God, please rid me of this fever, she prayed silently. It was a prayer she said repeatedly as they traveled beneath the bright sun, which was only compounding the problem. When the road would widen and the knights would spread out, Gaetan would end up on one side and someone else, usually de Russe, would end up on the other. She was terrified they would see how red her cheeks were so she tried to keep her head down and not speak with any of them, as much as it pained her. Gaetan was finally showing her the attention she had been hoping for and she very much wanted to show that she was receptive to it, but now she was afraid to.

Afraid he would see her illness in her face.

After several hours of travel, they stopped to rest the horses along a small creek in a thicket that was heavy with moisture. The water bubbled down the rocks as the horses drank. Wellesbourne and St. Hèver even went so far as to pull their horses into the water, splashing them to cool them off. Ghislaine, meanwhile, had wandered upstream a bit, kneeling down with her painful leg beside the crystal-clear water to splash some on her face. It was cool to her skin and felt wonderful. As she dried her face off with the sleeve of her cote, she heard footsteps next to her. Turning slightly, she caught sight of Gaetan's boots.

"Is the weather always ridiculously hot in October?" he asked.

She kept her head down, pretending to still splash water on her face. "Nay," she said. "A day like this is most unusual."

Gaetan moved up beside her and crouched down as well, putting a big hand in the water and drinking from it. "How does your wound feel?"

She nodded. "It aches," she said, an understatement. She paused a moment before continuing. "I... I have not had the opportunity to thank you for tending it so carefully. I do not think any physic could have done a better job."

He wiped the cold water on his face. "It was the least I could do, considering you risked your lives for all of us."

"I did what I believed needed to be done."

"I know."

A brief silence followed, but not uncomfortable. It was rather warm, in fact. Gaetan remained crouched next to her, now watching the stream bubble as water dripped from his hands. "We are near Worcester."

"We are."

"How far to your brother's stronghold?"

Ghislaine cocked her head thoughtfully but, in doing so, she realized that she lifted her head and exposed her red cheeks to his scrutiny, so she quickly lowered her head again.

"Very close," she said. "We will be there by tomorrow."

He grunted. "I had not realized we were so close."

She nodded. "We are quite close," she said. Then, she sighed thoughtfully. "I have been thinking of my brother and of his travels. If he continued to travel as slowly as he was when we first began to follow him, then he would be at least three days behind us, mayhap more. Even with our delay in Evesham, I do not think he has caught up to us. On the road he is traveling, unless he has deviated, he will come through Kidderminster. The road our party is on will come up west of Kidderminster and it is my assumption that we will reach Tenebris before he does."

Gaetan shifted so he was sitting on his buttocks now, resting his weary body. "I have been thinking the same thing," he said. "We will be waiting for him when he arrives."

"It would make for a perfect ambush if we can single out de Lohr and steal him away before my brother can hurt him."

It was a bit of covert tactics and he looked at her, approval in his eyes. "You are a clever little mouse," he said, grinning. "I have never met a woman who thought so logically. Mayhap, you should have been the one to command Harold's army. On second thought, it was a good thing that you did not. We more than likely would have lost."

Ghislaine fought off a modest grin. "I am not a pampered Saxon lady, as you well know. I think like a warrior. It is how I have been trained."

Gaetan was looking at her, the way her dark hair draped over her shoulder, the shape of her body beneath the cote that clung to her in places. But he also noticed she was sitting oddly with her right leg favored. He knew, from experience, that injuries like that hurt a great deal to the point where even routine movement was excruciating. But she bore it stoically; not even a whimper.

A strong lady, indeed.

"Your training has been invaluable in our quest to find our comrade," he said. "In fact, I cannot imagine having made this journey without you."

It was close to a compliment from Gaetan, as far as compliments went. He wasn't the kind to give an encouraging or positive word, or so he seemed. Ghislaine dared to glance over her shoulder at him, her red cheeks partially obscured by her hair. "I would say that it is unfortunate that we had to make it in the first place, but somehow... somehow I am not. I believe some understanding has come out of this. Understanding for Normans. Mayhap you even understand my people more as well."

He shrugged. "I understand that they are proud," he said. "I understand that they are skilled but not organized."

Before she could reply, more than likely to dispute his comment, Camulos wandered up, tail wagging. Instead of going to Gaetan, he went straight to Ghislaine and licked her on the chin with a big wet tongue and wet fur around his mouth. She groaned, wiping the slobbery kiss away.

"And I understand that Normans have smelly dogs that they treat like children," she said, trying to move away from Camulos as he sat down next to her. "Why does this dog like me so much? Does he not know that I despise him?"

Gaetan laughed softly as his dog leaned against her. "He has good taste in people," he said. "If he likes you, take it as a compliment."

"I want him to go away."

"Do you really?"

She thought better of her initial reply, which had been an affirmative. The dog had been her only companion when the knights had taken to ignoring her. Making a face that suggested surrender, she shook her head.

"I suppose I do not," she said, putting a hand on the dog's big head. "He is annoying but ridiculously sweet. I have never seen such an affectionate dog."

Gaetan reached out to slap the dog affectionately on the back. "I acquired him with the hope that he would help me in battle," he said. "Alas, that was not to be; the first battle I took him to, he ran right towards the enemy with his tail wagging. They almost stole him from me."

Ghislaine looked at the dumb dog, grinning in spite of herself. "I would believe it," she said. "I suppose he is not entirely annoying."

Gaetan watched her pet the animal, who lapped up the attention. "He likes you a great deal," he said. "In fact, you may have to take him with you when you return home. I am not entirely sure he will be happy with me any longer."

Return home. Ghislaine pondered those words. In truth, she hadn't even thought of returning to Tamworth since this quest started and now that the eventuality was on her mind, she realized that she couldn't return to her lonely life. She would miss these arrogant, powerful knights who had made her feel more companionship than she'd ever felt in her life. She would miss this silly dog, the jittery priest, and the sense of purpose they all had. She didn't want to lose any of it.

Her movements slowed as she continued to pet the dog.

"I do not think I should return home," she said.

Gaetan's eyebrows lifted. "Oh?" he asked. "Why not?"

She shrugged, feeling very bold with what she was about to say. "Because I do not think I should leave you alone in this country," she said. "You do not know the people or the customs, but I do. I... I think I would be of great value to you."

Gaetan watched her for a moment before a faint smile began to tug at his lips. He was quite glad she'd made that suggestion because the thought of her returning home, of leaving him, didn't sit well with him either. The thought of losing his little mouse was a sad thought, indeed.

"You think so?" he said. He pretended to think on it. "Once I reclaim Kristoph, I am moving on to the north. I have been asked to secure it."

She looked at him, then. "Then you need me," she said firmly. "The north is a wild place with tribes and customs you would not understand. I understand them and I could be of great help to you."

His smile grew when he realized she was eager to do it. *Eager to go with him.* God, was it really possible that she might be feeling something for him as he was feeling for her? It seemed like an impossibility given how they'd met and the trouble they'd had during their association, but there was no denying the magnetism between them. He looked at her, she looked at him, and the world seemed to stop for a moment. He couldn't remember when it hadn't always been like that.

He couldn't imagine never seeing her again.

"You have already been of great help to me," he said. "But what of your home? Won't Edwin miss your presence? Surely he cannot do without you, either."

Ghislaine shrugged, looking back to the silly dog. "There is nothing for me at Tamworth," she said. "With Hakon gone these two years, there has been nothing there for me ever since he died. That place is a tomb for me. I do not want to go back, not ever."

Gaetan was curious about the dead husband, the man she'd only mentioned once. "Hakon," he repeated. Now the husband had a name. "You said that he had drowned?"

"Aye."

"May I ask how it happened?"

It was a polite question. Strangely, she didn't feel the angst she usually felt when answering it. "There was a shipwreck two years ago at Ponthieu when Harold tried to take men into France," she said. "Hakon, as my husband, was one of Harold's knights. He was one of the few to drown in the shipwreck."

Gaetan remembered the incident, mostly because one of his allies had taken Harold hostage for a time after the shipwreck. "There were several ships, as I recall, tossed about by a storm."

Ghislaine nodded. "Aye."

"Did you have children?"

"Nay."

"But you miss him."

It was a statement, not a question. Ghislaine nodded, once. "Every day."

She left it at that and Gaetan didn't push her. He was starting to understand her sorrow at a dead husband she was evidently fond of, but it seemed more than that. No more husband, a home she didn't want to return to... was that why she was willing to escort his knights north-ward? Because it helped her forget the memories of a dead husband? She was a lady with secrets and sorrows. Perhaps she was running from them; perhaps not. In any case, he appreciated that he was coming to know her a little more, as moments of conversation like this on this journey had been rare. But as he looked at her lovely face, he caught a glimpse of her red cheeks as she was looking at the dog. He'd been leaning back on an elbow but now he sat up.

"Why are your cheeks so red?" he asked. "Come here. Let me feel your face."

The smile vanished from Ghislaine's lips when she realized he was on to her secret. "That is not necessary," she said quickly. "It... it is the sun. It has burned my face."

Gaetan's eyes narrowed suspiciously. "That does not look like a burn from the sun to me."

"It is."

He didn't believe her; that was clear. In an instant, he was reaching around the dog and grabbing Ghislaine by the arm, pulling her over to him so he could put a hand to her face. She tried to pull away but he laid a big palm against her forehead and, immediately, his eyes widened.

"You have a fever," he said seriously. "How long has this been going on?"

Ghislaine looked at him fearfully. "I am sure I do not have a fever," she insisted weakly. "It is simply too much sun."

Gaetan sighed faintly. "Mousie, you do, indeed, have a fever," he said, somewhat gently. "I must look at your wound. There is poison in it."

Ghislaine was looking at him with great distress, completely over-looking the fact that he'd called her *mousie*, a pet version of the "little mouse" term that he seemed to like so much when addressing her. Had she not been so afraid of his discovery of her fever, she would have been very touched. Flattered, even.

Giddy.

"It can wait until we reach Worcester," she insisted. "Truly, I feel fine. I simply think I have had too much sun."

Gaetan acted as if he hadn't heard her. "We must get you to Worcester immediately and seek a physic," he said. "They do have physics in this barbaric country, don't they?"

She nodded. "Aye," she said. As Gaetan began to rise, she grabbed him by the arm, preventing him from moving. When he looked at her, curiously, she gazed up at him with teary eyes. "Promise me you will not leave me in Worcester while you go on without me. I do not want to be left behind."

Gaetan had never been one to be swayed be feminine wiles or tears but, at this moment, he was quite swayed by the tears. He didn't like to see them on her face. "I cannot make any promises," he said, though it was gently done. "If you are ill, you cannot travel. You know that."

Her features crumpled. "I do not want to be left alone," she wept as tears streamed down her face. "This mission is as much mine as it is yours. I must see it through."

Gaetan felt a good deal of pity for her. Taking the hand that was on his arm, he lifted it to his lips for a tender kiss simply to comfort her. "You are very dedicated and I appreciate that," he said patiently. "But if you are ill, you cannot…"

Ghislaine was so distraught that she couldn't even spare the thrill for the kiss he'd just given her. "*Please!*"

She was weeping louder now, attracting attention. Gaetan sighed heavily as he rose to his feet, lifting her up to stand. De Russe, the ever-present protector, was immediately at her side, appearing quite concerned with her tears.

"What has happened?" he asked her. "What did Gaetan say to you?"

Gaetan rolled his eyes. "I did not say anything to her," he snapped quietly. "She is running a fever. We must get her to town and locate a physic. If her leg is becoming poisoned, then it must be treated."

The concern on de Russe's features grew. "I knew it was a dirty wound," he muttered, reaching out to take Ghislaine's right arm as Gaetan took the left. "Come along, my lady. We will go and find you a physic."

Ghislaine was feverish and unhappy. She pulled her arms from their grips even though they were only attempting to help her. "I can walk alone," she said, incensed. "I am *not* feverish. It is simply the sun."

Gaetan looked at Aramis' questioning expression over the top of her head, shaking his head faintly to indicate that the lady was wrong in her assessment of her illness.

"Then let us at least get you out of the sun," Gaetan said patiently.

By this point, the other knights were gathering around her, drawn by her weeping. De Moray and de Winter, in particular, were looking at her with great concern.

"My lady?" de Moray asked. "What has happened?"

Gaetan prevented her from answering. "The lady is ill," he said. "Get the horses. We must leave for Worcester immediately."

"I am *not* ill!"

"Of course not."

Gaetan had an amazing amount of patience with her as they headed for the horses. He wanted her to ride with him but she balked, insisting she ride her own horse, so de Lara brought the mare around and helped her to mount. Her leg was very tender, making it uncomfortable to ride, but de Lara was clever. In helping her mount, he was able to get a hand on her leg, pretending to help her but what he really wanted to do was feel the limb to see if it had any temperature to it. Once he helped the lady settle, he turned and walked past Gaetan, muttering in the man's ear.

"Her leg is on fire."

Gaetan's heart sank. Gesturing to his knights to mount up, soon they were all moving in the direction of Worcester, which was less than an hour away. They could see the top of the cathedral as soon as they left the thicket and passed onto the road, and then on to the city that was still devastated by tribal wars and a flooding river.

Now, as they entered the outskirts of the beaten city and headed towards the city center, the fever that Ghislaine had been trying to ignore was growing worse. She could tell because her eyeballs were growing hot, a sure sign that her fever was worsening. She also felt strangely weak and her head was swimming and rather foggy. It was an increasing effort for her to stay upright on her mare because she wanted nothing more than to lay down and sleep.

Behind her, she could hear small talk from the knights as they passed into the town. De Russe, riding behind her, came up beside her and handed her a purple flower that he'd ripped from a vine they'd passed. The flower brought a weak smile to her face and she held on to it as they continued into the town proper, past the waddle and daub buildings and the inhabitants of the town who, at just past noon, were winding down their business for the day.

Children ran about, playing, and Camulos found a dog friend to sniff at but the dog ran off, leaving poor Camulos rather bewildered. But Ghislaine didn't notice any of it; she was starting to feel dizzy as her flaming cheeks and burning eyes raged. It hurt to even keep her eyes open, so she closed them, briefly, to bring them some relief.

Up ahead, Gaetan was speaking to Téo and Wellesbourne about the town and the possibility of finding a physic for Ghislaine. But as they chatted, a shout from behind stopped them.

Gaetan turned around, swiftly, just in time to see Ghislaine hit the ground as she fell from her horse, unconscious.

"WHEN DID YOU say she was injured?"

All nine knights, Jathan, and the silly dog were crowded into a small, grossly dirty one-room hut that was near the Worcester cathedral. Mannig was the man asking the question. The abbot at Worcester had referred the knights to him when they'd shown up at the cathedral door carrying a feverish, half-conscious woman. Mannig was actually an apothecary, not a physic, but he was known to treat the sick and injured and, at the moment, he was the best option they had. The abbot didn't know of a local physic to refer, so they had to go with the apothecary. Gaetan, greatly distressed by the turn of events, answered the man's question.

"Three days ago in an ambush," he said. "What will you do for her?"

Mannig was a tiny man with a bushy beard and a bald head. He was also very old and had seen a great deal in his life, which meant he lacked tact at times. He simply spoke what was on his mind because he had no time for pleasantries.

Moreover, he was looking at nine very big Norman knights and was quite puzzled as to their presence, especially in the heart of Saxon England, but that curiosity would have to wait. He had a sick woman on his hands and the knights wanted answers. When the knight who seemed to be the leader of the group asked the question, Mannig turned back to the bed where the woman was sleeping feverishly and fitfully.

"She has the poison in her," he said. "It is a matter of taking the poison out and healing her humors. She is in very bad humor."

He was speaking with a strange mix of his language and Latin terms, which gave the knights pause when listening to him. They were all multi-lingual, as was necessary in these times, but it took them a moment to decipher what he was saying. Even so, Gaetan already knew what the old man was telling them. He was impatient with a fool who spoke the obvious.

"What will you do for her?" he asked again, trying not to sound angry or desperate about it. "And what can we do to help?"

The old man glanced over his shoulder at the patient. "Everything depends on how much poison is in her body. If it is too much, then I can do nothing. But if there is a chance...."

Gaetan cut him off. "Then examine her now. Waste no more time."

The old man dutifully went to the bed and bent over Ghislaine, peeling back the layers of clothing on her leg. The movement jolted her awake and she slapped her hands over the leg that the old man was trying to uncover, trying to stop him from moving her painful limb. Gaetan, Aramis, and Téo went to the bed, quickly, to calm her.

"Be at ease, little mouse," Gaetan said quietly, kneeling down by her head and pulling her hands away from her thigh. "We have brought you to a healer. He wishes to inspect your wound."

Ghislaine looked at him, her eyes big in her pasty face, and shook her head. "Nay," she breathed. "It is nothing. I must go now."

She tried to get out of bed but many hands stilled her as the old man finished peeling back her cote and shift to get to the trousers she wore beneath. The entire time they'd been traveling, she'd never parted ways with her trousers, which she was comfortable with, but she'd continued to wear the cotes that Gaetan had given her, making for many layers and an awkward mix of clothing for the lady warrior who had never dressed like a lady.

It had also been part of the problem when the arrow penetrated; there had been many layers to go through, taking many layers with it into her leg. There was a binding around her right thigh, stained with seepage, which the old man carefully unwrapped. All the while, Gaetan kept eye contact with Ghislaine to keep her calm.

"We are in Worcester," he told her softly. "The priests at the abbey sent us to this man. He will help you."

In just the past few hours, Ghislaine had gone from lucid and feverish to hardly lucid and burning with fever. The poison in her body was creating a muddled mind and her thought processes were affected.

"The abbey?" she repeated. "Where is the abbey?"

Gaetan smiled faintly at her. "Not far," he said. "We took you there first."

"The abbey is still here?"

He nodded to the odd question, stroking her forehead simply because he couldn't help himself. She was so very sick and he felt so very miserable for her, an odd reaction from a man who had little compassion for anyone other than his men. Even when Adéle had been giving birth to his sons, he'd been away at the time and had spared little thought to the woman who was struggling to bring forth his children. It was cold of him and he knew it, but it was of no matter. There was no emotion involved when it came to his bedslave, a mere possession and nothing more.

But with Ghislaine, the situation was much different. She brought forth emotion from him that he never knew he had, a depth of pity that he didn't know he was capable of, but he was afraid to show any of it, afraid it might look like weakness. Still, seeing her so ill made him sick to his stomach and he felt foolish for it, wrestling with this sense of compassion he was unused to.

She made him feel.

"The abbey is still there," he murmured. "Quiet, now. Let the apothecary look at your wound. He will know what to do."

Ghislaine simply nodded, her eyes never leaving his. There was that faith again, reflected in her gaze, faith he'd seen before and faith that made him feel stronger than anything he'd ever known. He continued to hold her attention as, down below, the apothecary took a sharp knife and cut away her trousers to inspect the wound better. Aramis and Téo hung over the man's shoulder to see the wound for themselves.

"You will not leave me here?" Ghislaine asked, her voice hoarse and weak.

Gaetan continued to stroke her forehead as he gazed down at her. "I will not leave you here. You are part of us, Mousie. I would not leave you behind, not ever. Put your mind at rest."

Ghislaine sighed, relieved by his words. She clutched his hand tightly as if afraid to let him go. She was just starting to doze off again when the old man touched the arrow entry wound and she nearly came off the bed, shrieking in pain. Even de Moray and de Reyne rushed forward to keep her still because she was kicking so, throwing a knee right into

Aramis' chest as he stood over her. The man grunted as the wind was knocked from him. Now, everyone was rushing to still her as the old man peered more closely at the wound.

"Keep her leg still," he commanded quietly. "She is raging with fever and the leg is full of poison. Who cleaned the wound after she was injured?"

Gaetan looked at him. "I did," he said without hesitation. "It was doused repeatedly in wine before we stitched it."

"Did you remove any debris?"

Aramis answered before Gaetan could; he was very worried for the lady. "It was a dirty wound," he said. "We took out what we could find but there is always a chance that more was pushed deep that we could not get to."

The old man bent over the leg, inspecting the wound very closely as Ghislaine was all but pinned to the bed by the knights. When the old man touched the cat gut stitches that Gaetan himself had put into Ghislaine's leg, pus began to seep out from between the strands.

The knights all saw it and it was something no one had wanted to see. Pus meant poison, and poison would kill. The leg itself was swollen, the area around the stitches red and angry. The old man pushed again on the wound and more pus came forth.

Now, everyone was looking at the apothecary, waiting for a brilliant answer on how to cure the woman, but the apothecary remained silent as he continued to inspect. He had de Reyne help him bend the knee up so he could get a look at the exit wound, which didn't have the pus or swelling that the entry wound on the top of the thigh did. De Reyne lowered the leg down as the old man stood up.

"There is poison in the wound, of that there is no doubt," he said, "but the wound on the back of the leg is clean. That tells me that the poison has not spread."

It was good news as far as news of the wound went, but she was still in grave danger. He moved away from the bed as the knights watched him with a mixture of curiosity and impatience. He just seemed to be puttering around at that point. Even Wellesbourne, who hadn't shown much interest towards Ghislaine one way or the other, was unnerved by it.

"Well?" he finally demanded. "What do you intend to do?"

The old man went to one of the long dilapidated tables in his hut and began knocking things around, evidently looking for something. Mice scuttled off of the table as he banged about.

"I intend to cut the leg open and clean out the poison," he said. "If I do not, she will die."

It was a simple statement, to the point, but it was something no one wanted to hear even if they already knew that fact. The mood of the room had gone from one of great concern to one of sadness now as they realized their guide, the woman who had become part of them in spite of their rocky relationship with her, was seriously ill.

As it often was with wounds, if the initial injury didn't kill then the chance of poison after the fact often did. Now, they were facing that very situation and there wasn't one man who wasn't feeling pity for Ghislaine.

Their little warrior was facing her most difficult challenge yet.

"How will you clean out the poison?" Gaetan wanted to know, although he already suspected the answer. He simply wanted to hear the old man's process. "What medicaments will you use?"

The apothecary didn't answer right away; he was pulling the items he needed off of his table. In fact, he had a handful of what looked like strips or straps, and when he rounded the table on his way to a second table over near the door, he held out the straps to de Winter, who was the closest to him.

"Tie her down," he instructed. "She cannot move while I am cutting her wound open."

Denis looked at the straps in his hand with a good deal of apprehension before looking to Gaetan for instructions. Would they tie her down? Or would they do as they were doing now, which was holding her down themselves. Gaetan saw Denis' expression and he shook his head, faintly.

"Nay," he said. "We will not tie her down. We will hold her. Tying her down would only terrify her."

The old man was casual in his reply. "As you like," he said, "but if she moves, I may cut more than needed. I may do further damage. Do you understand?"

"I do."

"Straps will not touch her," Aramis said in that threatening tone he used so often. "We will make sure she does not move."

Gaetan's gaze moved to Aramis, who was standing down by her feet. He was reminded, yet again, that his knight, his longtime comrade, might be feeling the same thing for the lady that he himself was. Gaetan was starting to think that he needed to have a word with Aramis about it if Ghislaine survived all of this. If he was going to stake a claim, then he'd better do it quickly.

Providing she lived.

That was all Gaetan cared about at the moment.

The old man wandered between tables, picking up what he needed by way of a cracked wooden bowl. He tossed a few things into it; a large needle, cat gut, two knives of different sizes, and a wad of boiled linen. He picked up a second bowl that had a cloth covering it that, when removed, filled the air with the stench of vinegar. Then he came back over to the lady on the bed, and the knights surrounding her, and began to hand things to the men who weren't involved in pinning the lady to the bed. Wellesbourne and Jathan ended up holding the two bowls.

"Now," the old man said as he settled himself between de Reyne and de Moray, who were on the right side of the bed and pinning down the right side of her body. "This will be painful and she will not like what I am doing, but it is necessary. You must hold her as still as you can else she will do more harm to herself. Are we clear?"

De Moray responded. "We are not fools, old man. Get to it."

Gaetan shot de Moray a disapproving expression; he didn't want the apothecary insulted just when they needed the man to do a job. But the old man seemed not to notice. He simply peered closely at the infected would and held out a hand.

"Bring me my knives."

Wellesbourne came around and knelt down next to the old man, extending the bowl that had the knives and other sharp objects in it. Taking forth the larger of the two knives, he didn't even warn them when he immediately began to cut the sutures on the entry wound of her thigh.

Ghislaine stiffened with pain and those holding her clamped down. The apothecary went to work on his screaming patient.

CHAPTER SIXTEEN

cg

I CANNOT TAKE THAT WHICH DOES NOT BELONG TO YOU

I T WAS EVENING.

The door to the apothecary's hut opened and men began spilling out, forming a group of exhausted knights that gazed up into the clear cold sky as the world outside remained dark and still.

It was in stark contrast to the screams and groans inside the hut. They'd come outside for a breath of air after the harrowing procedure on Ghislaine's wound. Not one man had watched the event unfold and not felt a twinge of queasiness about it, though none would admit it. Men were meant to take such pain from wounds, but watching a woman go through it – and a strong woman at that – had been inherently wrong in many ways. She shouldn't have put herself in harm's way. She shouldn't have taken an arrow on their behalf.

But she had and she was paying the price.

No one felt very good about that.

The streets of Worcester were abandoned at this time of night, the only sounds those of nightbirds in the distance as they hunted near the river. The knights were weary and hadn't eaten since morning, but that didn't seem to matter at the moment. They were concerned about their little guide, who had only now quieted down and had fallen into a heavy sleep. She'd passed out during the cutting and scraping that the apothecary had done to her, only to be awakened by excruciating pain that she'd had to endure because she didn't lose consciousness a second time.

There came a point towards the end where she couldn't even scream anymore, only flinching as the old man stitched a wound that was now at least three times as big as it had been before. He'd had to cut the wound to get down into it, so now there was quite a hole in her leg, but it was as clean as the old man could get it. He'd cut away, scraped away, and even found a small piece of leather that he believed had been causing the poison. He'd removed it, rinsed the wound with vinegar, and stitched it up with surprisingly small and neat stitches.

After that, everyone breathed a sigh of relief.

Once the operation was finished, so was their task of holding Ghislaine down on the bed. The knights released her but they didn't leave right away, watching her as the old man had her drink something he called "rotten tea", a foul potion, before she fell into an exhausted sleep. Or, perhaps she had even passed out again. It was difficult to say, but at least she was reasonably at peace once the horror of the procedure was finished.

St. Hèver and Wellesbourne were the first to wander away, the tough and most heartless of the group who ended up being the most sickened by the experience. They were eager to leave. Gradually, they all went outside except for Gaetan, Jathan, Téo, and Aramis. Those four lingered for a few minutes, perhaps to prove that they weren't as squeamish as the others, until Téo and Jathan, finished with his prayers for the lady, finally went outside.

That left Gaetan and Aramis, but Gaetan wasn't going to leave before Aramis did. He sat at Ghislaine's head, still holding her hand because she'd been squeezing it throughout the procedure. He was fairly certain she'd broken bones but he didn't much care about that.

He was only concerned with her.

"That was an exceptionally brutal thing to watch," Aramis finally muttered when they were alone. "I have been exposed to battle wounds my entire life but that was... rough."

Gaetan was looking at Ghislaine's sleeping face, thinking he imagined something more than normal concern in Aramis' tone. He struggled to keep his jealousy at bay, an unusual thing, indeed, when it came to his men.

God, how he hated feeling this way, swamped with feelings he'd never experienced before. The last thing he wanted to do was upset Aramis but the man had to know how he felt. He couldn't be upset with the man if he'd not been forthcoming about his feelings.

He cleared his throat softly.

"She is the most courageous woman I have ever known," he said. Then, he tried to look at Aramis but found he was unable to. This was going to be a difficult admission. "I appreciate your help with the lady. In fact, you have been most kind towards her since that evening at Westerham."

Aramis nodded, his gaze on Ghislaine's ashen face. "She was very clever, your little mouse."

"You wondered if she could really fight. You received your answer."

"I did, indeed."

Gaetan paused. "Aramis," he said. "I have been thinking about something. I do not wish to offend you, my friend, but I must ask. Do you have feelings towards the lady other than simple friendship?"

It was a blunt question that filled the air between them. Aramis tore his gaze away from Ghislaine's face. He didn't look particularly surprised by the query. In fact, he'd been expecting it. Therefore, his reply was calm and truthful.

"I know you do," he said quietly.

Gaetan looked at him, then. He felt foolish that his friend was more observant than he gave him credit for but, in truth, it wasn't as if he'd been hiding it as of late. "Does it show?"

"To me, mayhap."

"Do the others know?"

Aramis shrugged. "I have not asked. No one has said anything if they do."

Gaetan wasn't sure how he felt about that except that he felt as if he'd been keeping a secret from his men and that was something he'd never done. He didn't like withholding information from them but, in this case, he wasn't even really sure what he was feeling for her. How was he supposed to verbalize it to others?

"You have not answered my question," he said after a moment. "Do *you* feel something for her?"

Aramis' gaze lingered on Gaetan a moment before returning to Ghislaine. "Would it matter if I did?"

"I would appreciate an honest answer."

Aramis was quiet for a moment before the answer came, soft and hesitant. "It is possible that I do."

Gaetan pondered the reply. Oddly enough, he felt relieved by it. Now, he could deal with it. It was the unknown that had him unbalanced. "I do not blame you."

"Nor do I blame you."

"I believe I will marry her."

Aramis sighed faintly; Gaetan could hear him. "I see," he said after a moment. "May I ask you something, Gate?"

"Of course."

"What about Adéle and your other women? Do you believe Lady Ghislaine would like to be brought into a household where there are other women to share your bed?"

Gaetan shook his head. "I am sure she would not," he said. "I will send Adéle and the others away. I do not need them any longer."

"*Need* them?" he repeated. "You sound as if they were something to be tossed away. You are speaking of the mothers of your children."

"I realize that."

"There is also that goldsmith's daughter who bore you a son years ago. What about her?"

Gaetan thought on the first illegitimate son he'd had, a fine lad named Estienne. Truth be told, he forgot about the child at times because the boy's mother died the previous year and he'd done his duty to send the boy to squire, but he'd not seen him since. Now, Aramis had him thinking on the son he'd only seen once or twice in his lifetime. Another child from another woman he'd bedded. He was starting to feel the least bit uncomfortable with his behavior for the first time in his life.

"His mother died last year," he replied after a moment. "She is no concern."

Even though Aramis knew Gaetan and how the man conducted his personal life, it had never been any concern of his until now. Now, he was coming to wonder if Ghislaine wouldn't be yet another conquest in the ongoing annals of Warwolfe.

"But Adéle and your other women are quite alive and, I would imagine, quite inconvenient to you now that you are contemplating taking a wife," he said. "Now you would cast them all aside simply because you feel something for another woman?"

Gaetan sat back, mulling over the question. "Adéle knows that I hold no feelings for her," he said. "She has been with me many years. She knows my thoughts and she knows that marriage was never a possibility. She is a slave, Aramis, and nothing more. And my sons… I adore my sons but to have legitimate heirs with a woman like Ghislaine would make me the proudest man alive."

Aramis understood that because he was having the very same feelings. But Gaetan was his liege; it wasn't as if he could fight the man on this and his disappointment was deep. The noble thing would be for him to back away. Perhaps he could; perhaps he couldn't. He wasn't exactly sure what he felt for the lady, either. And in that respect, what he would verbalize would be much the same as Gaetan. Both of them career knights, unused to emotional attachments.

Until Ghislaine entered their world.

"She would produce magnificent sons," he agreed. "But you do not see her as simply the mother of your heirs, do you? She is much more than that."

Gaetan nodded slowly, a bobbing of the head that was both thoughtful and hesitant. "It is strange, Aramis," he said. "I never wanted to marry. You have known me for years and you know I have avoided marriage as if it were poison. I suppose I never met a woman I considered worthy of marriage but in Ghislaine, I see a woman more worthy than I am. Now, I am afraid she will not want me because I am not good enough for her."

Aramis lifted his eyebrows thoughtfully. "Then you should ask her."

"What if she denies me?"

"Then I will be there to ask her if she feels I am worthy of her."

Gaetan looked at him. "You would take her from me?"

"I cannot take that which does not belong to you. But I will give you the first opportunity to marry her. If she refuses you, then you will not begrudge me if I do."

It was a fair enough bargain. Gaetan didn't like the thought of Aramis married to Ghislaine but it wasn't as if he could prevent it. He was quite worthy of her, as well. Aramis would inherit his father's title, Count of Roeselare, someday. So he would be a most worthy man with titles and wealth. Moreover, Aramis was a man of good character. Perhaps a little rough around the edges, but he was of good character. Gaetan considered him a close friend.

"I appreciate your honesty," he said. "And I appreciate that you will give me the first opportunity to express my feelings for her. I shall not forget your generosity."

Aramis lingered by the end of the bed before coming around and laying an enormous hand on Gaetan's shoulder. "You have been a great and true friend to me, Gate," he said. "I could not live long enough to repay everything you have done for me. Although I had hoped I was wrong and that your attention towards the lady was nothing more than duty, I understand that you feel something for her. That is a rare thing, my friend. What is affection and love in our world?"

Gaetan looked up at him, appreciating his words, his reaction to the situation. "It is a curse or it is a blessing," he said. "I have seen it curse men until they were ghosts of their former selves but, in the case of Kristoph and my sister, I have seen the blessings between them. I have always envied that bond but never thought I would know it for myself. Mayhap I shall not. If the lady does not return my feelings, then I will not begrudge you if she finds comfort in you. She could do worse."

Aramis snorted, patted his shoulder one last time, and left the hut. Gaetan felt a great deal of relief when the man was gone but not for his absence; it was for the understanding between them now, something he knew he had to get out in the open before it festered. He had too much respect for Aramis not to clear the air. Although he wasn't happy that Aramis had some feelings towards Ghislaine, he knew Aramis was a man of honor. In fact, he felt some pity for the man, expressing feelings for a woman he would probably never have.

Hopefully, he wouldn't.

Gaetan looked down at Ghislaine, sleeping heavily beside him. She was still holding on to one of his hands that, by this time, was numb. He couldn't feel his fingers any longer. He studied her face in the weak light, the way her lashes fanned out against her cheek, the tiny little scar she had on her forehead near the hairline, and the rosebud lips that were pale but still quite kissable. Here in the darkness, with no one watching, he did, indeed, kiss them tenderly.

They were as sweet as he had imagined.

But he wasn't entirely alone; he knew that. He could hear the old man over in the darkness behind him, rummaging about. The old man who had heard the conversation between him and Aramis, although he didn't much care. It was done. Still holding Ghislaine's hand, he looked over his shoulder towards the rustlings sounds.

"My men and I have not eaten since this morning," he said. "Is there a tavern nearby?"

The old man was cleaning off his knives with vinegar. "Aye," he replied. "Down the road is a place called The King's Head. They will provide a meal for a price."

"And a bed?"

"You can sleep there, also."

Gaetan turned to look at Ghislaine. Gently, he stroked her forehead with his free hand. "I must leave her here, at least for the night," he said. "I will pay you well for your services and the use of the bed."

The old man wandered in his direction, peering down at his patient. "She will sleep until tomorrow," he said. "Go and eat. She will be here when you return."

Gaetan didn't want to leave her but the apothecary had a point; she was dead asleep. She wouldn't know if he'd left to eat, something he and his knights very much needed to do. Reluctantly, he nodded.

"You will watch over her?" he asked.

The old man nodded, turning away to put his knives away. "I will not leave."

Carefully, Gaetan disengaged his fingers from her grip, pulling the dirty woolen blanket up over her. His gaze lingered on her even as he stood up and stretched the kinks out of his big body.

"Then my men and I will find something to eat," he said, turning for the door. "I will return shortly."

The old man simply nodded, busying himself at his table as Gaetan slipped from the hut.

Once outside, Gaetan stretched out his body again, rubbing at a spot on his back that was sore from having sat hunched over for so long. His men were standing around, weary and waiting.

"Has she awoken?" Téo asked.

Gaetan shook his head. "She sleeps like the dead," he said. Then, he looked around. "Where are the horses?"

"There is a livery on the other side of the cathedral," St. Hèver told him. "When you took the lady inside the apothecary, Lance and I took the horses to the livery. They are well tended."

"And our possessions?"

"I paid the livery keep to watch over them but we took your money purse from your saddlebags. I have it."

Satisfied at the way of things for the moment, Gaetan pointed down the road. "The apothecary said there is a tavern down the road called The King's Head where we can find food," he said. "I could use something to eat now that the apothecary is watching over the lady."

Everyone agreed on that account. The King's Head, in fact, was only a few doors down from the apothecary's hut. So, in short order, the knights found themselves faced with a tavern that was only half-full, which meant there was a good deal of food to go around. Beside a roaring fire pit that sent a heavy layer of smoke into the room, the knights stuffed themselves on boiled pork, carrots, and apples.

All the while, however, they felt as if someone was missing and, more than once, made a comment about the lady warrior besting Aramis that night in Westerham. It was a favorite story to tell. It seemed as though Ghislaine was more a part of them than she'd ever hoped to be and it was a sad thing she wasn't here to see it. Gaetan kept thinking how much she would have enjoyed the meal and the fact that de Moray burped out a tune after having too much ale, nearly rupturing eardrums. Nothing was heard from the Lord of Flatulence this night, but the Lord of Belch was in fine form.

Even Gaetan was able to laugh at it. He felt relieved and hopeful, praying that morning would find Ghislaine much better. A praying man, he found himself giving thanks to God several times during the night and finding a sense of peace because of it. He couldn't believe that God would have brought Ghislaine to him only to take her away when he realized his feelings for her. As the night went on, he was becoming more and more convinced that everything was going to be all right.

He couldn't have been more wrong.

WHERE AM I?

That was Ghislaine's first thought when she opened her eyes into a dark and unfamiliar room. It smelled odd, too, something between rot and death and smoke. It was a frightening smell, one that immediately had her on-edge.

Fear filled her veins. Ghislaine genuinely had no idea where she was. She tried to look around without moving her head but she saw no one at all. Then she tried to think back to her last coherent memory and she remembered being in a wooded area, beside a creek, with Gaetan, but little else.

The fear began to take over. *Why can't I remember anything?* She knew there was more; clearly, more had happened. Then it came to her… there *was* something else… sickness… *a fever!* Aye, she remembered that she had a fever. Instinctively, she put a hand to her cheeks to feel if they were still hot. They were warm, but not overly. Certainly not as hot as she had remembered. Perhaps the fever had gone away.

But *what* was she doing here?

Timidly, she lifted her head, looking around what seemed to be a tiny hut that was cluttered with tables, broken chairs, and a myriad of things she couldn't identify. There was untidiness everywhere, piles in the corners from what she could see, as well as covering the floor. Having no idea where she was, or why, she was starting to feel some panic.

Where were Gaetan and the other knights? Tears filled her eyes when she realized they had left her behind when they'd gone on to intercept Alary. Gaetan had promised her that he wouldn't leave her, but he'd obviously broken that promise. Ghislaine couldn't see any other reason for his absence.

Perhaps he had only lied to her so she wouldn't suspect what he was planning to do. No one wanted to travel with an ill companion, someone who would drag down the entire party. Gaetan and his knights had a mission to accomplish and when Ghislaine told him how close they were to Tenebris, she had rendered herself no longer necessary. Perhaps if she hadn't been ill, she could have continued with them, but they'd left her off somewhere and gone on without her.

Angry as well as frightened, she wiped at the tears. She wasn't going to stay behind, not in the least. She'd come this far and risked her life for those ungrateful knights, and she was going to see this through, too. It was her right just as much as it was theirs.

Cautiously, she sat up a little more but shooting pains raced through her right thigh and she gasped, her hand flying to the leg as if to still the pain. It hurt so much worse than it had before and she was confused by the level of pain but she wasn't stopped by it. As she gasped again, trying to move to the edge of the bed, Camulos' head came up and big brown eyes looked at her anxiously.

Ghislaine sighed heavily when she saw the dog. There was great irony in the realization that Gaetan had left the beast with her. What was it he had said? *You may have to take him when you return home.* Evidently, he'd left the dog behind.

He didn't want to take the dog, just as he hadn't wanted to take her.

That understanding fed her determination. Now, she was more angry than she was frightened. She intended to catch up to Gaetan and tell him exactly what she thought of a man who broke his promise. She'd helped him, risked her life for him, and when she no longer was of use, he took the first opportunity to leave her behind like rubbish.

He wasn't going to get away with it.

Biting off groans of pain, she pushed her right leg over the side of the bed. The thigh was heavily bandaged and her trousers on that leg were in tatters, but it didn't matter. She was going to leave this place and track down Gaetan de Wolfe and his thankless men. She was going to show them that they couldn't treat a Saxon that way. Treat *her* that way.

A woman who clearly adored him.

Perhaps, most of what Ghislaine was feeling was hurt and disappointment. A man she was coming to have feelings for had lied to her. He'd made her feel what she thought she'd never feel again and then he'd run off like a coward. Was that the extend of Norman bravery?

Only on the battlefield and not of the heart?

She was going to catch up to him and tell him what she thought of him.

Both feet came to rest on the uneven dirt floor and she struggled to regain her balance. She was in so much pain that sweat was beading on her forehead, but she fought it. She was determined to leave and nothing was going to stop her. But as she pondered that thought, she caught sight of a body hunched over one of the tables.

Startled, she froze, watching the figure in the darkness for a few moments only to realize that whoever it must have been sound asleep. The figure hadn't moved in spite of the noise she'd made. Terrified that it was someone Gaetan had paid to keep her confined, she knew she had to run before they captured her and tied her onto the bed. She had to run from that dark smelly place and never look back.

Carefully, she rose to her feet but it wasn't easy; the pain in her right thigh was beyond measure. It didn't work particularly well, either, so it was very difficult not to make noise as she hobbled towards the door. Once, the body sprawled on the table shifted and made a noise, like snoring, and she froze, waiting to see if he awoke. Fortunately, the figure didn't move again, so she continued straight out the door and into the dark night beyond.

Camulos was right behind her, pushing past her as she headed out into the dark street. She didn't even know where she was; her mind was still cloudy, but she didn't realize it. To her, she was thinking perfectly clearly but the truth was that she wasn't thinking straight at all.

She was... somewhere. Some town, somewhere, and she had to find Gaetan and his ungrateful knights. Was she in Worcester? She could see an abbey to her right, looming big and dark against the night sky, but she didn't recognize it. She was almost in a dreamlike state where things were familiar but not exactly as she remembered. Nothing made any sense at the moment.

There was a road beside the church, however, heading out of the town and across a river. Perhaps it *was* Worcester, after all. Worcester had a bridge across the Severn, a well-traveled bridge. If she took the road out of town, then she would be able to find safety in the trees or in a field before looking to the night sky to find her bearings. She didn't want to stop in the town, fearful that there were more people Gaetan had paid to keep her there. She couldn't trust anyone, not even the priests.

There were some clouds, however, and the sky had shifted because of the lateness of the hour, which caused Ghislaine some concern. If she couldn't use the night to guide her way, then surely she would find her bearings when the sun came up. She would recognize the landscape or perhaps even ask someone if she didn't.

Dragging her bad leg and being followed by the big dog, she made her way out of town as quickly as she could, clinging to the buildings, staying in the shadows, fearful she'd be caught. Camulos remained right by her side but she couldn't pay any attention to the dog. She was too concerned with making a break for freedom and ignoring the pain from her throbbing leg. It was slow going, made worse by the fact that she had to duck into the shadows on more than one occasion because there was someone in the street. She didn't even have her dagger with her, stripped by de Wolfe, no doubt.

She was defenseless.

With the nightbirds singing to their mates as the only sound in the dark, she made her way around the side of the cathedral where she could hear the gentle trickle of the river. She could also smell the dampness. There was a rock wall and she clung to it, making her way up a path that ran between the wall and the river, trying to walk with that painful leg and having no idea where she was really going, only that she was going to find Gaetan.

But pain and exhaustion soon overwhelmed her. Ghislaine came to the point where she really didn't have any thoughts in her head other than the searing pain in her leg. *Just one more step*, she told herself. *Just one more step....* She began to live for that one more step, limping severely because it hurt so badly to walk. But she would push through it. She had to make it to freedom!

Somewhere up ahead, she could see a bridge, lit by torches against the blackness of the night. There were men up there, too, even though it was very late and they were more than likely protecting the crossing. Perhaps they were even there to keep her from crossing, men that Gaetan had paid to keep her inside this dark stench-filled city.

If Gaetan has paid those men to keep me here, then I must take their attention away from the bridge!

Ghislaine could only think of sneaking past those men. She could see two, at least, as she drew closer. The river was surrounded by foliage and grass and, before she sank down into it to hide, she picked up several small rocks from the path she was walking on. As she faded into the foliage to watch the bridge at close range, Camulos wandered after her.

The bridge itself was wooden and not very well made. It looked as if it had been the victim of too many repairs. As the men at the mouth of the bridge huddled around a fire and drank from a wooden pitcher, Ghislaine began to throw rocks under the bridge, sometimes hitting the wood, sometimes hitting the water. She wanted those men to go down and see what it was so that she could slip across the bridge. Her leg may have been weak, but her arms were strong. She was able to throw the rocks far enough to adequately hit the wood of the bridge.

As she hoped, the men on guard were startled by the sounds of the rocks and immediately went to investigate. Ghislaine hurried out of her hiding place and onto the rickety bridge, hearing the men down below by the river as they spoke to one another, unable to find the source of the sounds that had drawn them away from their posts.

But to Ghislaine, it was the sound of hope – hope that she would escape that terrible town where Gaetan had left her. Even with her bad leg, she was able to shuffle across the bridge quickly enough so that by the time the guards returned to their warm fire, she was already on the other side, in the trees where they couldn't see her.

Now, she had a fighting chance to find Gaetan.

In the dark, in the dead of night, she simply began to wander.

CHAPTER SEVENTEEN

୪

THE HUNTED

"**Y**OU KNOW HE'S in love with her."

It was a statement, not a question, coming from Luc de Lara. He was standing with Wellesbourne, de Reyne, de Moray, and St. Hèver in front of the tavern where the knights had spent several hours eating, drinking, and having a rare and relaxed conversation. They were currently waiting for the rest of the men – de Wolfe, de Russe, du Reims, de Winter, and Jathan to finish relieving themselves back behind the tavern in a communal toilet. They'd all had a few visits to it during the course of the night but now that they were leaving, there were those who needed to make one final visit.

Those who didn't were standing in the dark street and it was de Lara's quiet statement that hung in the air between them now. The mood had gone from warm and satisfied to uncomfortable all in a split second.

"Who?" Wellesbourne said. "De Russe? That much is obvious. I have not seen him pay so much attention to a woman since Abbeville, at least two years ago. Do you remember? The potter's daughter."

De Reyne snorted. "His father would never permit it," he said. "The Count of Roeselare would never stand for his son to marry such a low-born woman."

De Lara nodded. "He puts a great deal of pressure on Aramis to marry well. No wonder the man tries to stay away from women; his father has all but turned him off of them. But the Earl of Mercia's sister is another matter altogether."

"He will never have her," de Moray, the grumpy old man of the group, spoke softly. When the others looked at him, curiously, he simply shook his head. "She will marry another."

"Who?" de Reyne wanted to know.

De Moray looked at the collection of men, his brow furrowed. "Have you not seen the way Gate behaves with her? It is not only de Russe who is in love with her, but de Wolfe. I have seen lesser women tear apart strong men so I would be lying if I said this does not concern me."

De Reyne cast a long glance at St. Hèver, who simply shook his head. "Gaetan is not in love with her," Kye said quietly. "Interested, I would believe, but the man is not in love with her. I do not believe he knows how."

"Gate has Adéle warming his bed," de Reyne put in. "She has already given him two sons. He has no need for anyone else, least of all a Saxon woman."

St. Hèver nodded in agreement. "If anything, he will take her as a concubine."

"Until he tires of her," de Reyne said knowingly.

"Exactly."

Those two seemed to agree but the others did not. De Lara put up his hands in a supplicating gesture.

"Are you two so blind that you do not see it?" he asked. "Watch how he behaves around her and then you will understand what I mean. De Russe may be in love with the woman but I can promise you that Gaetan is as well. Did you not see how he held her hand when that fossil of an apothecary was carving into her leg? That, good knights, is a man who feels something. Mark my words."

"Why did you let me drink so much?"

The question came from around the side of the tavern as de Winter suddenly appeared, groaning, followed by Aramis, Gaetan, and the others. The group at the front of the tavern instantly quieted their gossip as the others came to join them. Now, Denis de Winter was evidently miserable and was blaming everyone but himself, so the subject shifted from talk of Gaetan and Aramis to de Winter's spinning head.

"I can feel the world rock when I close my eyes, which means to-morrow my head will be swollen," Denis said. "Someone should have stopped me."

Téo, walking beside him and grinning, slapped the man on the back. "Your head is already swollen and misshapen no matter what you do," he said. "You have the biggest head I have ever seen."

De Winter put both hands on his head, outraged. "I do *not*."

"It's the size of a full moon, Denis. I am surprised you can get it into your helm."

De Winter scowled at him. "Then my head must reflect the size of my manhood," he sneered. "I can hardly get it into my trousers."

"That's not what she said."

Soft laughter erupted from the group but Denis didn't like that fact that he was evidently being insulted on his most important body parts. "Who is *she*? I demand to know."

Téo simply laughed at him, shaking his head at a drunken de Win-ter who had a big head and an even bigger manroot. He looked at Gaetan, who was smirking at de Winter as the man looked down into his trousers to make sure he was as well-endowed as he thought he was.

"God's Bones," Gaetan muttered, yawning because of the late hour. "The conversations we have among us are most enlightening. Denis, stop looking at yourself. There is something inherently vulgar about that."

De Winter shrugged but he stopped looking. Then he turned his back on Téo, farted loudly, and walked away. Téo, under a gas assault, waved his hands to chase off the stench and moved well away. In fact, all of the knights shifted, shoving de Winter back into the area of his own smell. Gaetan rubbed at his forehead, knowing they were all weary and somewhat inebriated, and that sleep was in order before all of the farting and insults grew out of hand.

"I am going back to the apothecary's hut," he told them. "I will take Téo and Jathan with me. The rest of you can either sleep in the tavern or in the livery, but return to the apothecary at dawn."

The men nodded to the orders. "But what if Lady Ghislaine is not well enough to travel?" de Moray asked. "What then?"

That was the question all of them were asking. Gaetan folded his enormous arms in front of his chest in a pensive gesture.

"I suppose we shall decide that tomorrow," he said. "If the fever is broken, then we shall continue with her. But if it is not, then I suppose she will have to remain. We are close enough to Alary of Mercia's lair that we more than likely do not need her any longer. The lady and I were speculating earlier today that if Alary is still traveling as slowly as he was when we departed Westerham, then he is a few days behind us, if not more. There will be plenty of time to intercept him and reclaim Kristoph. I am sure the lady would like to be there when we do."

"She is only our guide, Gate," Wellesbourne said, which caused everyone to look at him in various stages of disapproval. He grew defensive. "All I am saying is that she has served her purpose. The lady was gravely injured because of us so, mayhap, it is time to relieve her of this burden. I have been in this land enough to be able to find Tenebris, so we do not need her any longer. Moreover, when we meet up with her brother, there is going to be a fight and it does not seem fair to drag her into our battle when she is already injured."

Gaetan remained even tempered as the others frowned at Bartholomew. "She saved Kristoph from death the day he was captured," he reminded the man. "We have gotten this far because of her. She has served a valuable purpose and I would no more cast her aside than I would cast one of you aside. Unless anyone has any objections, she will continue to be a part of our contingent while we are on this mission."

No one seemed to have any objections and Wellesbourne remained silent, fearful that saying any more would only antagonize the group that was clearly sympathetic towards the lady. But Gaetan's words only seemed to underscore what de Lara had said earlier, about Gaetan being in love with the woman. The Gaetan he knew would have never spared such concerned for a woman. Now, the knights were starting to see it, or at least some of them were.

Gaetan wasn't aware of their thoughts, of course, but he was eager to get back to the apothecary because he'd been gone longer than he'd anticipated. It had been cathartic to sit with his men over hot food and enjoy good conversation. Even so, his thoughts were never far from Ghislaine. He'd relived that stolen kiss a few times, wondering what it would be like when she actually returned his kisses. The thought had made him smile.

Now, he glanced up in the sky, seeing that the stars had changed because of the late hour. The moon was sitting low on the horizon as clouds drifted across the heavens.

"If no one has anything more to say, then seek your beds, all of you," he said. "I will see you on the morrow."

As he turned in the direction of the apothecary's hut with Téo beside him, Aramis stepped forward. "I would like to go with you to see if the lady's condition has changed," he said politely.

Gaetan's gaze lingered on him a moment. Even though there was an understanding between them about Ghislaine, he didn't want Aramis hanging around her. He wanted that right reserved for himself. But he couldn't deny the man because everyone would wonder why he had, so he simply waved him on. As he started to walk, he realized that the entire group was following him, even Wellesbourne, because they all wanted to see how the lady was faring.

Realizing this would now be a group effort, Gaetan simply led the way. In truth, he was pleased that his battle-hardened men were showing their compassion and concern. They'd been through so much death and destruction together that sometimes he wondered if they still had that capacity. He'd often wondered if he still did, but the past several days had shown him that they all did, still. Beneath the warrior facades, there was still something decent beneath although, when in action upon the field of battle, it was difficult to see otherwise.

The apothecary's hut was an odd-shaped structure that was attached to more structures that belonged to the avenue behind him, which was a street of bakers and grain brokers. In fact, Gaetan had almost missed the apothecary's door the first time because it was lodged in a half-moon-shaped annex that attached to his hut, all of it set back from the street. This time, he knew exactly where he was going and, putting a finger to his lips to silence the conversation behind him, he opened the door and ducked inside.

That earthy, musty smell was the first thing Gaetan was aware of as he came through the door. It was so dark that he literally couldn't see anything and he stumbled in the general direction of the bed where he'd left Ghislaine.

Behind him, he could hear his men bumping around and he shushed them, irritated that there wasn't so much as a taper lit in the room. As he put his hand out, knowing the bed was somewhere nearby, someone struck a flint and stone behind him. A soft yellow glow flickered in the room and he turned to see the apothecary light the taper by his head.

"Apologies, my lord," the old man said. "I fell asleep and did not realize the candle had gone out as well."

He was lifting the taper as he spoke but when his gaze fell on the bed, he suddenly came to a halt. Seeing the old man's puzzled expression, Gaetan whirled around to see what had the old man stumped and he, too, saw the empty bed. So did the other knights. After a moment's shock to digest the unexpected sight, everyone was suddenly dropping to their knees, looking on the floor, searching for the lady who had evidently fallen from the bed. That included Gaetan; he lifted the bed up to get a look underneath.

But it only took a few moments to realize that Ghislaine wasn't on the floor. She hadn't fallen off and rolled under one of the cluttered tables, nor was she rolled up in a corner. She wasn't anywhere to be found. Now, the realization set in that she was not in the hut at all. She was gone.

Gaetan turned accusing eyes to the apothecary.

"Where is she?" he boomed.

The old man wasn't easily rattled, but he was showing some concern. "I was here the entire time, though asleep," he admitted. "But she could not have left. I could not have been asleep for that long."

Gaetan threw the bed to the ground, breaking off two of the legs. "You were asleep long enough that someone came in and took her," he snarled. In a rage, he reached out and grabbed the old man. "You said you would watch over her!"

The old man was fragile and in danger of being crushed. "Kill me and I cannot help you!" he cried with more emotion than they had seen from him since the beginning. "Let me go!"

De Lara, nearest Gaetan, reached out to ease the man's hands off the old man's bird-like arms. When the old man stumbled back, finally freed, he picked up a stick that was laying on the table next to him and backed away, holding up the stick in front of him defensively as de Lara, and then Téo, pulled Gaetan back so he wouldn't kill the old man.

There was horrible tension in the air with the realization that Ghislaine had disappeared. Apprehension fed rage. Sensing this, the apothecary knew he had to explain himself or risk being torn apart by nine angry-looking men.

It would be a terrible death.

"I would have heard if someone had entered," the old man said, shaken. "The lady would have made noise, at least. And that big ugly dog you left would have barked. No one took her!"

That big ugly dog you left would have barked. That sentence stopped Gaetan's rage, at least for the moment. "The dog," he said, looking around frantically. "Did anyone see Cam?"

The knights were all shaking their heads, tensed up and waiting for the next command. But de Russe was already moving for the door.

"We cannot stand around and discuss this," Aramis said, his voice edgy. "If no one took her out of here, then she must have left under her own power and the dog went with her. The old man is right; Cam would have barked had there been a struggle and I'm sure the old man would have awoken as well. With that leg, she could not have gone far. We must find her."

That made as much sense as anything else and Gaetan was struggling not to panic. He'd never been so rattled in his entire life. "How could she walk out with her leg as injured as it was?" he wanted to know. "Walking would have been impossible."

De Russe, near the door, looked at him. "You have said yourself she is a determined brave woman," he said. "It must not have been impossible, for she is clearly gone."

She was, indeed, and they had to find her. There was no more time for speculation. Gaetan moved away from the old man, following de Russe out of the door as the rest of the knights followed. The last person out was Jathan, who felt rather badly for the terrified old man. He'd nearly been torn apart limb from limb for falling asleep. As the others ran out, he paused.

"Be calm, my friend," he said quietly. "Those men are the *Anges de Guerre*. They are fearsome, but they are not reckless. You have saved their Saxon guide and although they are fearful for her safety, they will respect you because you helped her. It is their fear for her safety that causes them to behave so. If she returns, keep her here."

The old man still kept the stick up between him and the rather round knight who looked more like a priest in the brown robes he wore. He couldn't even find comfort in the words. All he knew was that a very big man had just tried to kill him, so he kept the stick up in front of him even as the man in the brown robes quit the hut.

After they were gone, Mannig threw the wooden bar across the door and locked it.

But no one heard the bar being set; they were focused on finding Ghislaine. As Gaetan, Téo, de Reyne, de Moray, and Wellesbourne began milling around the apothecary's hut and branching outward, searching the buildings surrounding the hut and every little crevice they could find, de Russe, de Winter, and St. Hèver went running towards the livery to collect their horses and search on horseback. They could cover more ground that way.

There was a huge sense of urgency among them, each man concerned for the safety of their little guide. Up by The Kings Head, where they'd recently eaten, there were fatted torches outside of the establishment, shoved into iron sconces and smoking heavily, but it was the only bit of light on the street so de Reyne and de Lara went to steal them. With the moon low in the sky, the city was in near darkness and they very much needed the light.

Now, with something to light their way, the knights went about calling Ghislaine's name in the darkness, trying doors and, if unlocked, sticking their heads inside to see what was beyond. They startled more than one person that way. As de Russe and the others disappeared into the livery across from the cathedral, de Lara followed behind them with his torch. He was just crossing the road when he suddenly came to a halt.

Something in the muddy road had his attention.

There were footprints, but they weren't normal footprints – the left one was normal but the right one looked like only half a foot, as if whoever they belonged to was favoring the right leg. It looked very odd. Better still, there were dog tracks beside it. Peering closely, Luc could see that the footsteps led all the way down the avenue that ran next to the church. It was a clue as far as he was concerned so he put his fingers in his mouth and emitted a piercing whistle that had the knights in the stable emerging.

He pointed to the ground.

"Here!" he shouted. "I think I have found her trail!"

That had de Russe, de Winter, and St. Hèver running from the stable, clustering around de Lara and looking at what he was pointing out. St. Hèver crouched down, touching the foot imprints and looking at the paw prints that ran alongside.

"This must be her," he said. "It is a small imprint, a woman's imprint, and I would know those dog prints anywhere. Denis, run and find Gaetan. He will want to know."

De Winter ran off into the darkness, following the sounds of men calling for Ghislaine in the distance. But Aramis snatched the torch from de Lara and began to follow the footprints. When Luc and Kye went to follow him, he waved the men off.

"Nay," he said. "Remain here and wait for Gaetan. I am going to see where these lead."

Luc and Kye simply nodded, watching de Russe as the man practically ran alongside the footprints before taking a sharp right turn to follow them back behind the cathedral. At that point, he disappeared from their sight, but they knew why he was running. Better to make it to the lady before Gaetan did. All of that talk about both de Wolfe and de Russe being in love with the same woman was starting to play true, but both de Lara and St. Hèver simply looked at each other knowingly and shook their heads; if de Russe wanted to risk Gaetan's wrath, then that was his business.

They weren't going to get involved.

In truth, they were absolutely right – Aramis wasn't going to wait for Gaetan. He wanted to find the lady himself because he was as concerned for her as Gaetan was, if not more so. He'd graciously agreed to stand aside because of Gaetan's interest in the woman but that didn't mean he wasn't going to show Ghislaine how much he cared about her. He would be the first to find her, the first to show her that he was the one, out of all of them, who was the most concerned. He was obsessed with locating her as he followed the imprints along the west side of the cathedral until they suddenly disappeared into a cluster of foliage next to the river.

That was where they ended. Now, he was stumped, trying to find her foot impressions in the mud beneath the canopy of trees but it was impossible. Even with the torch in his hand, there simply wasn't enough light. Therefore, he came to an unhappy halt, unwilling to enter the cluster of bushes any further because he didn't want to step on any of her imprints that might be there. Daylight would make them more visible and he didn't want to tramp on anything.

For the moment, his search seemed to come to an end but a flicker of flame caught his attention. Isolated the source, he could see two men on the bridge several yards away, huddled around a fire to stave off the night and an idea occurred to him. Quickly, he climbed the slope to the road above where it connected to the bridge. Approaching the men on guard, he held out his hands to show that he had no weapons.

"Gentle men," he said evenly. "I am searching for an injured woman. Have you seen a limping woman pass this way?"

He had startled the men, evidenced by the fact that one of them jumped up so fast that his three-legged stool toppled over. They didn't have swords but they had clubs, and they grabbed at their weapons as the enormous Norman knight approached. Frightened and suspicious, they wielded the clubs, ready to strike.

"Woman?" one of them spouted off. "There's been no woman tonight!"

Aramis came to a halt. "I believe you," he said. "But I am tracking her footprints and they lead off over there near the river. She may be under the bridge. Do you mind if I look?"

The pair didn't move, looking at him very apprehensively. "Where did you come from?" the second man demanded. "Who are you?"

Aramis knew they'd picked up on his accent. "I mean you no harm. As I said, I am looking for a woman who is injured. It is possible she is even under the bridge, hiding."

As he said it, a group of men came charging up behind him, running along the path between the river and the cathedral. The thunder of their feet was enough to terrify the bridge guards completely, who suddenly began banging on a bell that was perched on the end of the bridge. It was obviously some kind of warning system because all around them, lights began flickering on in the homes. The toll of the bell carried and Worcester was coming alive.

That was not what Aramis had wanted to see. Quickly, he whirled around to the knights who were running up behind him, including Gaetan, and threw up his hands.

"Stop!" he roared. "You have just alerted the entire town!"

Winded, Gaetan came to a halt, looking around to see that, indeed, lights were appearing in windows and voices of alarm could be heard. The bridge guards were still banging on the bell and he could see, very quickly, that the situation was deteriorating rapidly. He grabbed Aramis by the arm.

"Did you find her?" he demanded.

Aramis shook his head, running back to the spot where the foot imprints had disappeared into the bushes near the river. He was pointing at the mud but no one could really see what he was talking about; the torches were burning out and the moon had sunk over the horizon. It was far too dark to see anything.

"The imprints disappeared here," he pointed out. "Either she went into the river or she hid beneath the bridge, but you startled those fool guards before they would allow me to see."

Gaetan and Wellesbourne made their way into the foliage, ripping it apart as they came to the river's edge but it was simply too dark to see very much. People were now starting to come out of their homes with weapons, with shouts of alarm going up. Gaetan knew they had to get out of there or risk fighting off the entire town.

"Damnation," he hissed. "We must get out of here. We cannot do battle against everyone in the village."

Jathan, standing aback behind the knights who were hunting around in the foliage, looked about fearfully at the townspeople, up in arms. "We can seek sanctuary in the cathedral," he told them. "We can explain to the priests that we are looking for a lost woman!"

Not seeing a figure in the water, or even near it, Gaetan made his way out of the bushes as the others looked about as well. "How long would it be before the priests, loyal to the Saxons and not the Normans, opened the doors to the cathedral and let the mob take us away?" he asked, eyeing the people now coming out onto the road by the bridge. "Nay, we must leave now. We will cross the bridge to the other side of the river and...."

A shout cut him off. "Gate!" It was Wellesbourne. "On the bridge! *Look!*"

Everyone strained to see what he was pointing to and, beneath the starry sky, they could see the outline of a big shaggy dog at the opposite end of the bridge.

God's Bones, Gaetan knew that shape. He knew that dog.

Camulos!

"Cam!" he hissed. He began grabbing men, pulling them from the foliage even as he was running himself. "Come on! We must get across the bridge! She is on the other side!"

There wasn't one knight among them who had ever moved faster in his life. In short order, they were plowing through the crowds on the bridge, riding as fast as they could for the dog, who turned and ran up the road, through the dark fields and black forests beyond.

They followed.

GHISLAINE WASN'T SURE how long she had been walking, only that it seemed like endless hours in an endless night. The sky above changed with the hour and she'd lost her bearings some time ago, but she refused to turn back. She refused to go back to that town where Gaetan had left her.

So she continued to walk in the dark, limping heavily on her bad leg. She was confident that once daylight came, she'd be able to discover where she was and go from there. Tenebris wasn't far from Worcester and, knowing that's where Gaetan and his men had gone, she was certain she could catch up to them.

Those were her thoughts, anyway.

But the reality was that she was still running something of a fever and her body was near to the point of collapse because of her injury. She was weak and the more she walked, the more muddled her mind became. It was oh-so-dark now that the moon had set, making it difficult to go any further. The sky blended with the land and Ghislaine's rational self, the one that was being suppressed by the illness taking over her mind, knew that it was time to stop. She simply couldn't go any further.

Stumbling off the road, Ghislaine pulled the coat she was wearing up around her head, protectively, and wandered into a forest that stretched as far as the eye could see. There was protection here from the road and from the elements, for the most part. Around her were the sounds of the night, of nocturnal creatures looking for food, but she wandered and wandered until something tripped her and she fell forward, into a flooring of leaves that had fallen from the canopy as winter approached. It was rather soft, if not very cold, but Ghislaine wasn't one to be choosy. With the skirt of her cote wrapped up around her head for warmth and protection, she toppled over into the leaves, exhausted, wounded, and muddled.

Sleep claimed her immediately.

CHAPTER EIGHTEEN

ɔɛ

CAPABLE OF KILLING

Near Warwick, 40 miles from Tenebris

TRAVEL HAD BEEN slow with Alary and his men, something Kristoph had been exceedingly grateful for considering the injuries he'd sustained during his capture those weeks ago. His ribs were much better and he was feeling as close to normal as could be expected given the circumstances. He still wasn't getting enough to eat and with all of the walking he'd been doing, because Alary still wouldn't allow him to ride a horse, he'd lost a significant amount of weight. His trousers were hanging on him now. His wife wasn't going to even recognize him.

He'd also grown a fairly bushy beard and his blonde hair, usually cut short, had grown. It was shaggy and dirty, something that bothered him because he was usually well-groomed. But that was of little consequence considering his circumstances, circumstances he soon intended to change.

He was working on a plan.

Alary didn't know he was feeling as good as he was. He was still walking hunched over, pretending to be in pain, and he had generally been acting ill. There was a reason for this; Alary kept him in irons and he was hoping that, at some point, the irons would be removed and he would be able to escape. He was essentially trying to lull his captors into a false sense of security and, so far, it was working.

He'd been concocting a plan for the last several days. He knew they were far to the north, nearing Alary's stronghold, and his soldier friend had spoken freely about their path and the towns they'd traveled through, so he had a fairly good idea of where they were and where they were going.

It was also true that he never doubted for a moment that Gaetan and his comrades were somewhere nearby, perhaps not following him on the same path, but Kristoph knew they were planning to rescue him. Even after Alary's threat, when news had come from Alary's spies that they were no longer being followed, Kristoph knew that wasn't true. His longtime friends and brothers would come for him.

He would stake his life on it.

But it was difficult to wait them out, hence the plan he'd been formulating. If he could simply break free of Alary, he could run and hide and the man couldn't find him. Then he could make his way south, back the way they'd come, and, hopefully, find traces of Gaetan and the men to follow. If they were looking for him, perhaps he could look for them. It wasn't the best plan, but he simply couldn't remain Alary's prisoner any longer. He was afraid that one more day, or even one more hour, might see Alary cut something else off or decide to beat him again. He wasn't going to stand by while that happened.

He had to make his move.

Tonight, they were on the outskirts of Warwick, a fairly large town that had seen its share of traffic throughout the evening. Once again, Kristoph was in the livery with his guards and the animals, cushioned by surprisingly fresh hay this night as the sounds of the tavern across the yard filled the air. There was laughter and the smell of meat in the air, and he could even hear what he thought was a citole. Someone was playing and singing.

As he lay back and listened to the sounds that were comforting and friendly in nature, and not reminding him of his dire situation, his friendly guard, Mostig, came out of the back of the tavern with a trencher of food in his hands.

Kristoph saw the man enter the livery and he sat up, eagerly awaiting his only meal of the day. Mostig approached him and delivered the food at his feet. There was a hunk of boiled meat on it and a heaping pile of boiled vegetables, and Kristoph began eating like a man who had never seen food in his life. He shoved it in his mouth, devouring it, as Mostig loosened his chains.

"It is crowded in the tavern tonight," Mostig said. "There is a great Saxon lord inside, traveling with his daughter. Lord Alary has told him of you and he is interested."

Mouth full, Kristoph looked at Mostig with curiosity. "Interested? What do you mean?"

"In you."

"Why?"

"For his daughter from what I heard."

Kristoph stopped chewing, struggling to swallow what was in his mouth. "For his daughter?" he repeated, puzzled. "I do not understand."

Mostig shrugged. "The homely girl is not married yet."

"But… *I* am already married."

"That will not make the lord happy."

Kristoph frowned. "You *know* I am married," he said. "We have spoken of my wife and daughter frequently. I cannot and will not marry another woman."

Mostig wasn't unsympathetic. He and the Norman knight had been together constantly and they'd formed an odd bond of sorts. Mostig even considered them friends, as strange as that seemed. In a sense, he was concerned for his friend's safety because he knew Alary. He knew what the man was capable of. A worried expression rippled across his face.

"But the lord offered to pay Lord Alary a great deal for you," he said. "Lord Alary is considering it. Norman, if you marry her, then you will no longer be subject to Lord Alary and his whims. He can no longer cut your finger off or beat you or harm you. If you are sold, then you must go for your own sake. Get out of here while you can."

Kristoph couldn't believe what he was hearing. He stopped eating completely and fixed Mostig with a serious glare. "I told Alary my family would pay him well for my safe return but he would not take it," he said, incredulous. "Yet, he will sell me to a Saxon lord as a husband for the man's daughter?"

His voice was growing loud and Mostig hastened to quiet him. "Do not speak so loudly or Lord Alary will hear," he hissed. "If you are sold, it will be the best thing for you. Do you understand? They will more than likely not keep you in irons. You will be... free."

It was a hint to escape, as clear as the subject had ever been spoken of between them, and Kristoph backed off a little, studying the man and considering his words. Certainly, a husband would not be kept in chains. Kristoph pondered the idea a moment before speaking.

"Mostig, I have not said this to you before, but I will now," he said. "You are a man without a family... help me escape and I shall see that you are amply rewarded. You could command a fine bride with the money I would reward you with. Does this not appeal to you?"

Mostig's eyes widened. "I could not do it! Lord Alary would kill me if he discovered what I had done!"

Kristoph could see the fear in the man's eyes. "You will come with me," he assured him. "Alary would never see you again. You do not have to worry about such things. The money I could give you would keep you comfortable for the rest of your life, I assure you. Mostig, please – will you not help me?"

Mostig was staring at him with big eyes, perhaps seriously considering the offer. He was torn between his fear of Alary and the lure of a great reward. He scratched his head after a moment, watching Kristopher as the man resumed his meal.

"I... I do not know," he finally said. "It would be a terrible risk. Lord Alary has allies everywhere in the north. We would have to flee to the south."

Kristoph finished the last of the meat, chewing loudly. "And we could do that," he said, trying to sound confident because he was attempting to convince the man to betray his liege. "Once I reach my Norman brethren, you would have nothing to fear. Mayhap, you could even serve me. I have hundreds of men but you would have a place of honor among them."

Mostig liked that thought a great deal. With Alary, he had no place of honor. He was a soldier, just like all the rest. But what this Norman was promising him was appealing. He was a weak man, in truth, and simply wanted to find someplace where he belonged. Ever since he'd lost his family, that was his only desire. Now, the Norman was offering him such a thing. It was difficult to resist.

"Would... would I live in Normandy?" he asked timidly. "I have never been there, you know."

Kristoph began to feel some hope. Was it possible he could sway his guard to help him? "You could live wherever you wanted to," he said. "I intend to have lands here in England, so if you wanted to live here, you could. Or, you could go to my properties in Normandy. It would be your choice."

Mostig liked what he was hearing and he was quite seriously considering everything he'd been told. Still, he was fearful, mostly of Alary. He'd seen what the man was capable of with traitors and he was genuinely concerned that his attempt to help a prisoner might be discovered. That fear kept him from accepting Kristoph's offer.

"If I help you, I cannot do it now," he hissed, hoping the walls around them didn't have ears. "Lord Alary is discussing you with the Saxon lord right now and if we flee, they would soon catch up to us. We would not have much time to get away."

Kristoph didn't agree. "If you do not help me now, there may not be another opportunity," he said, trying not to sound too forceful because he felt that he was losing the man's interest in his offer. "If Alary sells me to the Saxon, I will be gone. How are you to help me then?"

He had a point, one that seemed to convince Mostig that the time to act was now. He was quite torn, however, with apprehension in both his expression and movement.

"If I help you, where will we go this night?" he asked. "It is very dark and there is nowhere we can run."

Kristoph sensed that the man was finally coming around to his way of thinking. Mostig seemed to be good of heart, but he was weak of will. Kristoph sat back against the straw again, thanking God for his friend Mostig. In his plans to escape, he never thought he'd have an accomplice.

"You know this area," he said. "Are there any towns nearby?"

Mostig nodded. "A few," he said. "Smaller villages."

"Then we will avoid them. When we leave, the first places Alary will search are the nearby villages. But I will tell you something; a secret."

"What?"

"I do not believe my Norman brethren have stopped following us. They would not let me go so easily. I believe they are around, somewhere. All we need to do is find them."

Mostig's eyes widened. "Are you certain?"

Kristoph shrugged. "I know them. They would not give up."

"That is an interesting bit of news."

It wasn't Mostig who replied. It was Alary, entering the livery with a pair of his henchmen with him, men who were always at his side to do is bidding. They were also the men who had beaten Kristoph in the first few days of his captivity and the men, he suspected, who held him down when Alary cut off his finger. They were mindless, brutal dogs.

Kristoph's blood ran cold when he saw them enter the livery. *He heard us!* He thought in a panic. But *how* much did he hear? Kristoph would have to be extremely careful with this situation if he wanted to survive it. All of the hope he'd been feeling drained out of him like liquid through a sieve. Now, he felt empty.

Empty and apprehensive.

As Kristoph tried to gauge just how bad his punishment was going to be, Alary looked at Mostig.

"Excellent work," he said to the man. "You have done well this night."

Kristoph looked at Mostig, unsure what Alary meant as Mostig stumbled to his feet, looking at Alary in terror.

"I did not do anything, my lord," he cried. "The Norman spoke of escape but I did not do anything!"

Alary looked very pleased. "I knew you were developing a friendship with him," he said. "I have seen it from the start. Now you have tricked him into confessing that his Norman friends have not given up the chase, after all. I knew they had not but I also knew our captive would not tell me. You have done that for me, Mostig. Well done."

Mostig was overwrought with terror. He looked at Kristoph with such horror upon him that it was palpable. "I did not...," he breathed. Then, he looked to Alary again. "I would not betray you, my lord. Forgive me!"

Alary shook his head. "There is nothing to forgive," he said. "You have shown me your true loyalties. Tell me you did this for me and I shall believe you."

Mostig was trembling as he nodded his head. "I have done this for you, my lord, I swear it."

Alary approached him, casually, putting out a hand to rest on the man's slumped shoulder. "Tell me that you love me."

"I do, my lord, most earnestly!"

Swiftly, Alary unsheathed a dagger that was at his side, a bejeweled weapon that was quite magnificent. He'd stolen it off of a dead Saxon lord a few years back and now it was at his side every moment. It was the dagger he'd used to cut off part of Kristoph's finger. Before Mostig even realized what had happened, Alary slipped the blade between his ribs and straight into his heart. Mostig was dead before he hit the ground.

With the man in a heap, Alary stood over him.

"I lied," he said, kicking the corpse. "I do *not* believe you!"

Kristoph had to admit that he was quickly reaching a greatly apprehensive state. He couldn't even think of Mostig's death. Now, he had to think about himself. He was still chained and, in a fight, he wouldn't be very effective, but he knew they were rapidly approaching that state and he intended to fight for all he was worth. He wasn't going to let Alary slip a blade between his ribs as easily as he'd done to Mostig. As Alary turned to him, he braced himself.

The moment of life or death, for him, was coming.

"So your Norman brethren are nearby, are they?" he asked, wiping the bloodied blade off on his trousers. "Where are they?"

Kristoph's gaze never left Alary's face. "I would not know," he said. "And what I told Mostig was a guess. I have not seen any of them, if that is your meaning. For if I saw them, so would you and I would not be here right now. What I expressed was a feeling and nothing more."

Alary was closing in with his two henchmen by his side, all of them looking at Kristoph with the expressions of hunters who had just sighted their prey.

"You seemed rather certain," Alary said.

Kristoph simply shook his head, trying not to appear any too leery of what was coming. "What happened to the Saxon lord Mostig spoke of?" he asked, trying to change the subject. "I thought you were going to sell me to the man for his daughter."

Alary shrugged. "His daughter was so ugly that even I could not resign you to such a life," he said. "Moreover, the man did not want to pay my price."

"I told you that my family would pay any price you asked for my release."

Alary came to a halt and his henchmen along with him. "I wonder if your Norman brethren would pay to keep you alive."

Kristoph was coming to desperately wish that he was unchained because he very much wanted to strike the first of many blows he knew were coming. He knew he was in for another beating, perhaps the worst one yet.

"Mayhap," he said casually. "But know this; if you kill me, they will hunt you down. You will never be safe. I have told you this before, Alary. It is in your best interest to keep me alive and well so that my comrades will not punish you by stripping your skin from your body while you are alive. They will make sure you suffer a more painful death than I could ever suffer, so remember that before thinking to kill me."

It was a threat, a line drawn between them that Kristoph was instructing the man not to cross. But Alary wasn't smart enough to realize it. He saw it as a threat to his safety and nothing more than that. He didn't realize that Kristoph was trying to save his life.

In fury, he struck out.

The first blow missed Kristoph because he ducked, but after that, the fight was on as Alary's two men jumped on Kristoph and began beating on a man who was severely restricted by his chains. But Kristoph was strong, much stronger than Alary had realized. In the end, he'd strangled one of the men with his chains and kicked the other one unconscious, all the while as Alary stood back and watched.

This time, Alary didn't step in to disable Kristoph. The man had taken a beating but it was clear he was ready for anything that came at him. He was strong, bound or not, and Alary backed off. He had a stronger sense of survival than most. Therefore, he left Kristoph alone that night, leaving the dead bodies of two of his men while the third, once he regained consciousness, limped from the livery and disappeared.

As for Alary, he spent the night in the tavern where it was warm and dry, pondering his next move with the Norman knight who was not so injured as he had wanted everyone to believe.

That night, the Norman knight showed his worth, and Alary realized he had a prisoner who was very capable of killing.

He would have to kill his prisoner before he was the man's next victim.

CHAPTER NINETEEN

cs

LEGIO TERTIUM AUGUSTUS

S OMEONE WAS SHAKING her.

Ghislaine ignored the gentle shaking, going so far as to shove them away, but she heard someone call her name, softly, and her eyes flew open.

Ghislaine!

There was some light now across the land in the very early dawn as she blinked, having no idea where she was or how she got here until she pulled the skirt of the cote completely away from her head and saw Gaetan bending over her. He looked pale and worried as he gazed down at her.

"Ghislaine?" he said quietly, with concern. "Thank God you are alive. What happened? How did you end up here?"

She blinked. Rolling on to her back and wincing when her right leg pained her greatly at the movement, she stared at Gaetan as if hardly believing what she was seeing. *Gaetan!* Was she dreaming? Or was he actually here, in her midst? Then, everything came tumbling down on her – the fevered wound, waking up in the smelly dank cell where she'd found herself and, most of all, waking up alone. Gaetan had promised her he would not leave her behind but he had. She was running after him to catch up with him. She must have found him and not even realized it. But now, he was here.

He was smiling at her.

Whack!

A balled fist came up and caught Gaetan right in the mouth and his head snapped back as Ghislaine struggled to sit up. She was mad enough to throw another punch at him but she didn't want to do it lying on the ground. She might even beat him to death in the process because he deserved it, in her opinion.

Her fury knew no bounds.

"That is for breaking your promise to me!" she bellowed, but there were tears on the surface. "You promised me that you would not leave me behind and you did! I had to come and find you!"

Gaetan was rocked back on his heels, a hand going to his lips and coming away with a smear of blood on them. He remained calm.

"Find me?" he repeated, confused and, frankly, rather hurt that she struck him. "What on earth are you talking about? I came to find *you*."

"But you left me! You said you would not and you did! You lied!"

Gaetan was trying to figure out why she was so irate but it occurred to him that she must not have remembered much of the past day. Her fever had wreaked havoc with her mind so there was something going on with her that he did not quite understand. She was confused and making accusations that were simply untrue. He reached out to still her as she finally managed to sit up but she yanked her arm out of his grasp, sliding away from him, not wanting to be too close to him.

In fact, the anger in her expression shocked him. He didn't like to see that where it pertained to him. "Ghislaine, I did not lie to you," he said evenly. "Why did you leave the apothecary's hut? What happened?"

She was furious and feeling ill. Moreover, her leg was killing her. "I do not know what you mean," she snapped. "I know of no apothecary."

"The man who tended your leg when you were with fever."

Ghislaine looked at him, still feeling confusion and distressed, but now she truly had no idea what he meant. Still... she thought back to the town she had fled; she *had* awoken in a smelly hovel. Was that what he meant? A shaking hand flew to her head, pushing the mussed hair out of her eyes.

"The man who tended my...?" she repeated, bewildered. Then, she looked around, seeing all of Gaetan's knights looking back at her in various stages of concern. She looked at each and every face, thinking that these did not look like men who had abandoned her. They didn't have that look about them. Her attention returned to Gaetan as she struggled for calm. "Someone tended my leg? But you tended it. You and Aramis did."

Gaetan glanced at Aramis, who was standing off to his right. Before he could reply, Aramis took a few steps towards Ghislaine and took a knee beside her.

"That was the first time," Aramis said patiently. "You began running a terrible fever and we took you in to Worcester where an apothecary cleaned out your wound again. Do you not remember?"

A little more was coming clear now but Ghislaine didn't remember any of it. It was frightening to realize that she truly had no memory of something that had happened to her. She looked at Gaetan. "Is that why my leg hurts so?" she asked.

Gaetan nodded. "It was full of poison so an apothecary cleaned it out and stitched it up again. You were sleeping after the procedure so we left to go find supper and when we returned, you were gone. Did you truly think we had abandoned you? That *I* had abandoned you?"

Now, the situation was making so much more sense. Ghislaine sighed heavily, beginning to feel quite foolish and dismayed. "I... I awoke in a strange place and I thought you had left me behind," she said. "You said that you would not, but when I awoke and you were not there... I was afraid to remain. I had to find you."

Things were becoming clear to Gaetan, too. He smiled faintly when he realized what had happened. "So you left? With your bad leg, you actually set out to find me?"

Ghislaine nodded, embarrassed. "You promised you would not leave me and I was going to find you and... you truly did not leave me behind?"

Gaetan shook his head. "Nay, little mouse. I told you I would not."

He had. But she hadn't believed him. But, as he'd proved to her since the beginning of their association, he was a man of honor. *Norman honor.* Her feelings of foolishness only increased as she noted the blood on his lip.

"I am so sorry that I struck you," she whispered. "I... I have no excuse other than I thought you had lied to me."

Gaetan's smile grew. Then, he started to laugh, turning to the men behind him who were also starting to chuckle. He wiped at his lip again but there was very little blood.

"It was a good hit," he admitted. "I supposed I deserved it if you thought I had broken my promise. But I did not, I swear it. We have been looking for you for the past several hours. Cam was following your trail but he got off task a few times when a rabbit or a fox would cross his path. But it was really Cam who helped us find you. Without him, we would still be looking for you and you would still be angry at me."

Ghislaine smiled timidly, looking at the silly dog who was sitting a few feet away, his wagging tail thumping against the ground when her attention turned to him. She shook her head at the beast.

"He followed me from town," she said. "I do not even know when he left me because it seemed as if he was always with me."

"He waited for us on the bridge. Even he knew I would come for you and he waited to show me the way."

Her smile grew, though it was still sheepish. "Then he is a good dog."

Gaetan's smile turned warm, his gaze only for Ghislaine. "Do you still despise him?"

Ghislaine let out an ironic snort. "I suppose I cannot now that he has saved me."

As if on cue, Camulos stood up and made his way over to her, wagging his big tail and licking her on the chin. Ghislaine put her arms around the dog and hugged him as Gaetan stood up, glancing over at Aramis, who did the same. He noted that Aramis was watching Ghislaine with the dog, a grin on lips that very rarely saw one.

Jealousy began to creep into Gaetan's veins but he struggled not to show it. Even though Aramis had graciously agreed to give up his pursuit of the lady, still, Gaetan didn't quite trust him. He hated that suspicion but he simply couldn't help it. Laboring to put that aside, he turned to Téo, who was standing off to his left.

"I will take the lady with me since we left her mare back in Worcester," he said. "How far from Worcester do you believe we have come?"

Téo glanced at the land around them. "At least five or six miles," he said. Then, he turned to Wellesbourne, who was standing several feet behind him. "Do you know where we are?"

Wellesbourne heard the question and looked about the landscape, trying to get his bearings.

"I think so," he said. "The lady would know better than I would, but I believe there is a road to the north that will take us to Kidderminster."

Still hugging the dog, Ghislaine heard him. She let the beast go, struggling to her feet as both Gaetan and Aramis rushed forward to help her. With Gaetan on one arm and Aramis on the other, they pulled her to her feet. When she staggered because of the pain in her leg, Gaetan swooped down and picked her up, effectively taking her away from Aramis.

But Ghislaine was unaware of the competition between them. She was in Gaetan's enormous arms and nothing felt more right or more natural. She looped an arm behind his neck to steady herself, but it was such a delicious position to be in that she nearly forgot about Wellesbourne's assessment of their location. She would have much rather lost herself in Gaetan's eyes and would have, too, had she not caught sight of Wellesbourne in her periphery. She was compelled to give the man an answer or risk looking like a besotted fool.

In Gaetan's arms, all was right in the world again.

"I truly am not even sure where we are," she said. "When I left Worcester, I crossed the river and just kept walking. You say we are five or six miles to the east?"

Wellesbourne and Gaetan were nodding. Ghislaine began to look at her surroundings. "I wonder if we are near the disputed lands," she said pensively. When Gaetan looked at her curiously, she explained. "There are lands in this area that are claimed by a tribe that calls themselves the *Tertium*. My brother, Edwin, has had some contact with them but they are very warlike and they keep to themselves. I have not known anyone who has had any contact with them other than in battle. It is possible we have entered their lands but I cannot be sure."

Gaetan was listening with interest. "*Tertium*," he repeated. *Tertium* meant "third" in Latin. "Bartholomew, have you ever heard of the *Tertium*?"

Wellesbourne nodded. "I seem to recall my father speaking of them," he said. "The lady is right; they are warlike."

"*Tertium* is a Latin word. Why would they call themselves that?"

Wellesbourne shook his head. "The Romans were all around here hundreds of years ago," he said. "Mayhap it was a name given to them by the Romans. Or it could even be a name given to them by the church; who knows? I've not heard why."

It didn't really matter but Gaetan found it curious nonetheless. However, the fact that they were warlike concerned him. "If we are near their lands, mayhap we had better leave quickly," he said. Then, he looked to Ghislaine. "You mentioned after we left Evesham that we were a day's ride from Tenebris."

Ghislaine nodded. "It is to the north. If we continue north on this road, surely it will lead to something I will recognize, for I do not recognize anything around us at the moment."

Gaetan looked at her, his face very close to hers as he held her. The mere sight of that dirty porcelain-beauty face was enough to set his heart aflutter. He was more relieved than he could express that they'd found her but he wouldn't dream of verbalizing that relief. At the moment, he was focused on getting them out of an area that was evidently either on or near disputed lands.

But his concern came too late. As he and his men turned and headed through the trees to the rest of the horses that were grazing on the side of the road, a piercing, singing sound suddenly burst overhead.

Gaetan knew that sound all too well and so did his men. It was the sound of a flying projectile, an arrow, and his warrior training kicked in. He fell to his knees, dumping Ghislaine onto the ground, and covered her with his body as two arrows hit the ground within very close vicinity. Several more sang overhead and all of the knights went to the ground, trying to protect themselves.

But it was a short flurry. When the arrows stopped flying, Gaetan leapt to his feet and pulled Ghislaine up with him, fully intending to make it to his broadsword, which was sheathed on his saddle. Around him, he could see his men unsheathing swords and daggers that were on their bodies, preparing for a fight, as the trees suddenly came alive with people.

But it wasn't an organized army; dirty savages began to advance on them in groups, bows with arrows reloaded, pointing directly at them. Gaetan was handicapped with an injured woman to protect and he pushed her to the ground even as he stood up. He didn't want her making herself a target for any further arrows that might come flying at them.

Quickly, Gaetan assessed the situation; arrows seemed to be their weapon of choice because he didn't see any swords. But every man had a bow and arrow, and each knight under his command had at least five or six of them aimed straight at him. If those arrows let loose, it would take them all down. There would be no way to fight it.

Very quickly, he could see that they were in an extremely dire situation.

Gaetan had been a commander for many years and, as Normandy's Warwolfe, it was recognized that he was the very best. Being a great commander meant that he knew when the odds were insurmountable and resistance was futile. This, unfortunately, was one of those times. They were cornered, all of them, and there was nothing they could do about it.

All they could do was surrender and pray the enemy would show mercy.

Jaw ticking with the sickening realization, he slowly lifted his hands to show that he had no weapons.

"Drop the swords," he told his men, steadily. "Put them away unless you want to die in a hail of arrows."

Du Reims, de Lara, de Winter, and de Reyne obeyed immediately. De Russe, de Moray, St. Hèver, and Wellesbourne were slower to respond. They were the battle beasts, men who refused to surrender even when it was the wise thing to do. Gaetan could see that they refused to relinquish and he barked at them.

"Drop your weapons!" he snapped.

Aramis dropped his, reluctantly, but the other three refused. The tension was growing as Gaetan had to give them the command yet again.

"I will not tell you again," he growled. "If I make it over to you, I'll break your bloody arms. The lady is without protection and every moment you refuse to lower your weapons jeopardizes her life. Now, drop your swords!"

After a moment's hesitation, the remaining three surrendered, but they were exceedingly unhappy about it. Once the weapons were all down, there was a sense of relief on Gaetan's part but also a sense of apprehension. Now, they would discover just how much mercy their attackers were willing to give.

Seated at Gaetan's feet, Ghislaine was looking at the men coming out of the trees with great trepidation. Having never had any contact with the *Tertium*, she didn't know if this was that tribe, but she suspected they might be. She watched warily as one man pushed through the others; he was dressed in what looked like a leather vest and he wore no trousers, but what looked like a short skirt made of leather strips. He was fair-haired and older, with some gray in his cropped hair. He had no bow and, in fact, looked as if he wasn't carrying any weapon at all. As a horde of his men kept the nine knights, one priest, and one lady at bay, he walked right up to Téo.

There didn't seem to be any hostility in his expression, merely curiosity. He was evidently quite interested in the mail and other things Téo was wearing. Téo stood stock-still as the man touched the mail, ran a finger over it, and even sniffed it. Then his gaze moved down to the broadsword at Téo's feet. Téo had dropped it as ordered, but the man lifted it from the ground, holding it up, inspecting it from one end to the other. He seemed to like the weapon a great deal. As he was inspecting the hilt, Camulos wandered over to the man, wagging his tail.

The man eyed the very big dog, lowering the weapon at it as if to kill him. In a panic, Ghislaine shouted.

"You will not harm that dog!" she cried, struggling to her feet and wincing with her painful leg. "Cam! Come here!"

Tail still wagging, the dog rushed over to her and she grabbed it, holding it fearfully as the man looked at her as if only just noticing her. With the sword still in hand, he followed the path of the dog straight to Ghislaine.

Gaetan was still standing next to her and his body tensed as the man was lured to Ghislaine. He didn't want to end up with ten arrows stuck in his body, but he didn't like the interest the man was showing in Ghislaine. His protective instincts took over; he had no idea what the man's intentions were but he knew what *his* intentions were. They were in a horribly precarious position but Gaetan had to take the chance – if the man got close enough, he was going to grab him. Surely the native men would lower their weapons if their leader was in danger.

At least, Gaetan hoped so. Either that, or they were all going to end up with a dozen arrows in them, like human pin cushions. He hoped it didn't come to that.

He bided his time.

The man came right up on Ghislaine as she stood there holding the dog. He looked her up and down, clearly appreciating what he saw. Gaetan watched the situation, his heart pounding in his ears, waiting for his moment to strike.

It wasn't long in coming.

When the man reached out to touch Ghislaine's dark hair, Gaetan reached out and snatched the man by the arm, yanking him against him and throwing a massive arm across his throat. By his actions and the position of his arm, his intentions were obvious and the man grabbed hold of Gaetan's arm, bracing himself so he wouldn't be strangled. But Gaetan barred his teeth at the men with the bows, showing in action and in body language that he was ready to kill.

In an instant, the tables had turned and the hunted now became the hunter.

Gaetan was brilliant that way.

"To me," he barked to his men. "Back away and get to your horses. *Go!*"

In his grip, the man in the leather skirt called to his men. "Vestra arma summittere!"

Lower your weapons!

Gaetan understood the words; it was Latin, but strangely and heavily accented. He'd never heard anything like it. He spoke to the man whose neck he was about to crush.

"Non intelligis me sermonibus?" *Do you understand my words?*

The man in his grip nodded his head, but hesitantly, as if he couldn't quite believe what he was hearing. As Gaetan's knights began backing away, seeing that they now had the opportunity to flee, Gaetan continued to hold the tribal leader by the neck. But it wasn't purely out of rage; he found that he was somewhat curious about this tribe, a seemingly very rustic group of people here in the wilds of Mercia. He was also quite curious with the man's dress. It wasn't like anything he'd ever seen before.

As he'd once told Ghislaine, it was always wise to know the language of the enemy. It was even wiser to know their ways. If Gaetan was going to conquer this land, then he wanted to know about it.

"Who are you?" he asked in Latin. "Who are your people?"

The man didn't say anything for a moment, perhaps trying to decipher Gaetan's pure Latin against the garbled tongue he spoke.

"*Legio Tertium*," he said. "This is our land."

Gaetan's brow furrowed. "*Legio Tertium*?" he repeated, more to himself. Then, he translated. "Third Legion?"

The man in his grip nodded. "You are on our lands. You do not belong here."

Gaetan could see that Téo and de Lara were standing nearby, listening. He wasn't sure who else was listening other than Ghislaine, who was standing in front of him, looking rather pale and pained. He assumed it was because they'd all had a good fright.

"We came here by accident," Gaetan said. "We came to find the lady, but mean you no harm. We were just leaving when your men attacked."

The man in his grip was looking at Gaetan's men suspiciously. "You brought your weapons."

"Of course we did. Why wouldn't we?"

"You have come to kill us!"

Gaetan shook his head. "What I do now, I do in defense of my men and of the lady," he said. "I would not have taken you hostage but you gave me no choice. You moved against us first."

The man was clearly flustered. "If you promise no harm will come to us, then let me go and I shall let you leave in peace."

Gaetan didn't know the man and he surely didn't trust him. "You will forgive me for not agreeing to that term," he said. "I have no guarantee that you will not kill us."

The man was incensed. "I could have killed you from the trees but I did not," he said. "That should show you my truthfulness."

He had a point but Gaetan was still reluctant. "I believe you," he said. "But you will forgive me for being cautious. Your men are less likely to shoot me down while you are in my grasp."

Standing a few feet in front of him, Ghislaine understood what was being said for the most part, but not all of it. The man had a very strange accent and his Latin wasn't conventional. She looked at Gaetan.

"I wonder if he speaks my language?" she asked.

The man immediately looked at her. "I do," he said. "My people know the language of trading. It is how we purchase goods with the *Saxonice*. They are too lazy to know our language, so we were forced to learn theirs."

Surprised, Ghislaine took another look at him. He wasn't unhandsome but he was rather short, at least compared to Gaetan and his men. Still, he was a strong man and seemingly very agile. She studied his queer manner of dress.

"Why did you shoot your arrows at us?" she asked. "Why did you not simply come out and speak to us? We meant you no harm."

The man eyed her. "When armed men enter our lands, we assume they are a threat," he said. "We were on a patrol when we saw these men. We must defend what is ours."

Ghislaine pondered his words. "A patrol?"

"We must protect our borders."

Ghislaine already knew that about them. Truth be told, she was quite curious about this reclusive tribe. "You have engaged my brother in battle before," she said. "This is Mercia, his territory, yet you do not swear fealty to him."

The man's brow furrowed. "Who is your brother?"

"Edwin of Mercia."

That brought a reaction. "*Nigrum Aeduini*," he muttered with disgust. "Black Edwin is your brother?"

Ghislaine nodded. "I am Ghislaine of Mercia."

"Then you are The Beautiful Maid."

Ghislaine looked a bit uncomfortable with her evident notoriety. She glanced at Gaetan, nervously, before replying. "Why would you say that?"

"Because Edwin has two sisters. You are not Edith, who is married to Harold Godwinson."

"How would you know?"

"Because I saw her once, from afar."

"You have battled Harold before."

The man nodded with perhaps a twinkle in his eye. "I have battled many Saxons before."

That was the truth. Since there was no denying her identity, Ghislaine eyed the man. "Now that you know who I am, what is your name?"

He didn't hesitate. "Antillius Decimus Shericus," he said. "These are my people and this is my land. It has been since the time of old, when the legions conquered this land."

"Are you their leader?"

Antillius nodded. "I am, as was my father before me, and his father before him," he said. Still addressing her, his gaze moved sideways to see the other knights standing around. "Who are these men you have brought with you, Lady Ghislaine?"

Ghislaine wasn't sure she should tell him. She looked to Gaetan, who was gazing back at her quite emotionlessly. He wasn't giving her any hint of what he wanted her to say. Her nervousness seemed to grow and she could feel her hands shaking. In fact, everything was shaking and she was feeling the need to sit down again because the world was starting to rock.

Camulos decided to pick that moment to move away from her. He had been standing in front of her as she held on to him, but when he moved away, everyone could see the massive bloodstain on her right leg, seeping through the bandages, the torn trousers, and her cote. It was even smeared on the dog. Ghislaine could see Gaetan's dismayed expression as he looked at her leg and she quickly looked at it, too, seeing what everyone else was seeing. Blood was everywhere. With a gasp, she suddenly toppled onto her arse.

Everyone went running.

Gaetan dropped his arm from Antillius' neck and rushed to her about the time Aramis and Téo and Lance de Reyne made it to her side. They were the closest. Blood was running everywhere and Gaetan ripped at her dirty cote, tearing a strip of material from the hem to wrap around her thigh to stem the blood.

"Bandages!" he bellowed to anyone who would listen. "Bring me bandages!"

Arrows, standoffs, and territorial tribes seemed to be forgotten as Ghislaine's bloodied leg took all of the focus. Even Antillius, now quite free, went to stand over Gaetan's shoulder as he and his men worked furiously to stop the bleeding.

"What has happened?" Antillius asked, genuinely concerned. "Why is she bleeding so? Did our arrows strike her?"

Gaetan was tying a tourniquet around Ghislaine's thigh to slow the flow of blood. "Nay," he said, grunting as he pulled it tight. "She was struck in a battle a few days ago and the wound became filled with poison. An apothecary cleaned out the poison, but that was only yesterday. The wound has not healed and the lady must have torn the stitches."

It was clear she was bleeding heavily. Without proper care, she might not survive. Antillius tapped Gaetan on the shoulder.

"Bring her," he said. "Quickly. There is no time to waste. I have a physician who will tend her."

Gaetan was clearly hesitant. "If we can stop the bleeding...."

Antillius cut him off. "Will you take such a chance?" he asked, urgency in his tone. "Come with me if you want her to live. Hurry."

Gaetan looked at the men around him; Aramis, Lance, Téo, and even Jathan had joined them. They had failed her once trying to heal the wound and because of that, Gaetan was fearful to try again. He didn't want her life in his hands when he wasn't a healer. He knew battlefield medicine, but so did every other knight. Yet, it wasn't something he did on a regular basis because he employed several physics for his men. He genuinely felt as if he had failed her the first time. Now, he was torn.

"Taking her back to Worcester will take an hour or two, at least," Aramis said, cutting into his thoughts. "She is bleeding heavily, Gaetan. She has torn her stitches wide open."

Gaetan found himself looking at the wound as Aramis peeled away the bloodied bandages. It was messy to say the least.

"There are those hunting us at Worcester," Lance put in. "They could capture us when we enter the city limits. We may not even have the chance to return her to the apothecary."

That was a very real possibility. Gaetan didn't want to return to Worcester only to be captured by the mob and separated from Ghislaine. Feeling cornered and as if he had very little choice, he turned to Antillius.

"How far is your physician?" he asked.

Antillius pointed towards the east. "Not far," he assured him. "Bandage the leg as tightly as you can and bring her. I will send my men ahead to tell our physician to be ready."

Gaetan nodded reluctantly. Then, his attention shifted to Ghislaine, who was now lying flat on her back and staring up at the sky above. She was so very pale. Leaning over her, he put an enormous palm on her forehead.

"We must take you to someone who can repair your stitches, Mousie," he said softly. "All of this activity has torn them. That is why you are bleeding."

Ghislaine's gaze turned to him and Gaetan was struck, once again, by the faith in her eyes. She trusted him, no matter what the circumstances; she didn't even have to put it into words. He knew simply by looking at her.

"I am sorry to have caused so much trouble," she said softly.

He smiled at her, lifting a hand to kiss it gently. "I was a fool to have ever left you at the apothecary. It is my fault."

This time, Ghislaine was well aware of the kiss on her hand. It was the most beautiful, tender expression she had ever experienced and she reached up, putting a hand on his stubbled cheek. It was a touch she would remember for the rest of her life.

"I should have known you would have kept your word," she murmured, her fingers caressing his skin. "Forgive me, Norman."

He gave her a lopsided grin. "It is Gaetan."

"You are a Norman."

He wasn't going to argue with her about it. Grinning, Gaetan put a big hand over her hand as she fondled his cheek, feeling the touch more deeply than he'd ever felt a woman's touch. There was something about it that went clear to his soul. Then he kissed her palm, warmth reflecting in his eyes as he looked at her.

"There is nothing to forgive," he said, kissing her palm again before lowering her hand. Then, he returned his attention to Aramis and Lance, who had finished tying off a series of very tight bandages against her bloody thigh. "Can I move her now?"

Aramis, who hadn't missed the tender scene, was feeling a great deal of disappointment and he struggled to maintain an even manner.

"Aye," he said, unable to look at either Gaetan or Ghislaine. "The bandages should hold until we can reach their physician."

With that, Gaetan bent over and scooped Ghislaine up against him, moving for his horse as Téo and Lance ran alongside him. Aramis couldn't even bring himself to do it. As he watched Gaetan carry Ghislaine away, he felt as if his heart had just been ripped out. Oblivious to Aramis' thoughts, Gaetan kept walking.

"I will follow you," he said to Antillius as he moved passed the man. "Lead the way."

Antillius nodded, watching them head to their horses before he snapped orders to his own men, who rushed back into the trees. Very shortly, those same men appeared on horseback, leading another horse for Antillius, and when the knights came off the road and headed back into the trees where the *Tertium* were waiting, the entire group tore off towards the west, through a vast meadow and disappearing into a heavy forest in the distance.

They were in *Tertium* lands now, a vast and wide place as ancient as the world itself.

CHAPTER TWENTY

☙

NE SAIS-DU PAS?

T HIS TIME, GHISLAINE remembered everything.

As blood seeped through the bindings on her right thigh, she'd ridden with Gaetan up hills and through forests, leaping across streams as they followed the swift *Tertium* on their nimble horses.

The Norman war horses, while fast, were heavy beasts, muscular like their masters, and therefore weren't as swift as the lighter horses with the long legs. Seated behind Gaetan on his animal, Ghislaine held on tightly as they traveled over unfamiliar territory.

They were deep in *Tertium* lands.

There were no roads, no landmarks, only meadows, hills, and forests in the most primal sense of the word. Ghislaine knew Mercia, or at least most of the south and east of it, but here in the west, it was a wild place, largely ignored by her brother except for a few major villages like Worcester, Birmingham, and Shrewsbury. The area they were in was positioned between the larger portion of Mercia to the north, east, and south, while to the west, Wales loomed.

This was still part of the shadowlands; that is, mysterious and dangerous territories that stretched as far as the eye could see and a part of Mercia that her brother, Edwin, had essentially turned a blind eye to.

There were too many warring and territorial tribes there, the *Tertium* included, and his focus was on Harold and the lands of his territory that he could more easily control.

Strength draining and leg hugely paining her, Ghislaine buried her face in Gaetan's back, holding him close as they traveled over the land. Gaetan was reining his horse with his left hand while the right hand held Ghislaine's right leg behind the knee, trying to keep it elevated and braced against his right hip as they traveled.

It seemed like they rode for miles and miles upon end. Ghislaine was growing groggy from the blood loss, from exhaustion in general, but suddenly, they were deep in a forest of ancient oak trees, in a clearing with a massive canopy of branches overhead and a stream that ran through the middle of it. It smelled of all things damp and leafy. There were people in the clearing. In fact, there was an entire village, with huts made out of rock that was dredged up from their farming fields and local river beds.

Deep in the forest, an entire world had sprung up.

Lifting her head when the horses slowed and they entered the outskirts of the hidden village, Ghislaine was very curious about her surroundings. People rushed out to greet their returning men but when they saw them in the company if nine very large warriors, a priest, and a lady, they seemed to back off, inherently fearful of anything from the outside. Their men had returned with what was termed in their language as an allii. *Others*. These were not people who were part of their world.

As Ghislaine saw all of the suspicious and fearful faces, she whispered to Gaetan.

"These people hate my brother," she said quietly.

Gaetan looked around at the faces of the women and children. He could see their fear, their mistrust. He was calm in his observation, assessing the situation.

"Mayhap that is true, but Antillius offered to help you even knowing who your brother was, so do not worry," he said. "Moreover, I am here. So is my sword. If they make any attempts against you, I will defend you."

Ghislaine smiled faintly, looking up at him and meeting his eyes as he looked at her over his shoulder. "You would be my champion, then?"

He had a glimmer in his eye that set her heart to racing. "Among other things."

There was something innately seductive in that reply but Ghislaine was prevented from answering when the horses came to a halt. Suddenly, Aramis was there, pulling her off of Gaetan's beast and holding her against his broad chest just as Gaetan had done. Antillius came towards them, parting the crowed and pulling along an old woman who evidently took exception to being bossed around.

Antillius was pointing to Ghislaine, explaining the situation, and once the old woman understood, she went right to Ghislaine and tossed up the edge of her cote, seeing the bloodied bandages. She didn't even pause to look at the injury; she could see that it was bad. She turned to walk away, beckoning for the lady to follow.

"This way, this way," she said, pushing through the crowd that had gathered. "Bring her this way!"

Aramis followed, as did Gaetan, Téo, and the big hairy dog, but the others remained with the horses and possessions. They were essentially in enemy territory, so no one was going to follow Gaetan and leave their assets behind to be picked over by people who were circled around them, all looking at them quite suspiciously.

As Aramis, Gaetan, Téo, and the lady disappeared into the collection of rock huts, the rest of the knights stayed very close to the horses. They were watching the inhabitants of the village as closely as the villagers were watching them. Like an odd standoff, they simply stared at one another.

Mistrust was in the air.

"Look at this place," de Moray muttered to de Lara. "This is fairly large village here beneath the trees. And look at the homes; neatly built, avenues laid out. This is not the design of barbarians."

Luc was looking around as well; with Gaetan away, he was in command. "Nay, they are not," he said. "But look at them – fair skinned, pale-haired, dressed in robes and skins. Even their manner of dress suggests some kind of civility."

As the two of them were scrutinizing the crowd, Wellesbourne walked up beside them. He, too, was watching the people surrounding them.

"My father spoke of lost tribes like this," he said, his voice low. "This is a group of people untouched by the world. They live by themselves and die by themselves. And look; did you see their monument when we came in?"

Marc and Luc hadn't. They strained to see what Wellesbourne was pointing at, finally seeing what looked like a neatly stacked pile of stones with a pole of some type rammed into the top of it. It soared several feet above the ground and, curious, the knights moved away from the crowd of gawkers and went to investigate.

Moving around the front of the monument, they could see that it was a long staff of some kind of metal, probably bronze, with several round metal discs fastened to it, discs that contained images that were faded and weathered. Near the top of the staff was a trencher-sized disc with laurel leaves carved into a circle around the edges, and in the middle of it was what looked like the figure of a goat.

It was quite fascinating. As de Moray moved in closer to touch it, de Lara spoke.

"I have seen staffs like this before," he said. "Near my father's home in Bayonne there is one in the cathedral. Look at the top – see those letters? SPQR. That has to do with the ancient legions from Rome, I believe."

"It does."

The knights turned to see Antillius walking up behind them, looking up at the large bronze staff just as they were. There was reverence in his eyes as he gazed upon it.

"My ancestors carried this staff across the sea, across England, and settled in this land," he said. "This is a shrine to those men who conquered the savage lands of Britannia but, specifically, the lands we live upon. This was the province of *Flávia Caesariensis*, the land of our ancestors. It is still our lands, although the Saxons have taken most of our territory. But not all of it; we continue to fight for what is ours but our struggle is never over. We fight for our continued way of life."

That explained a great deal about these people and how they came to live in this extremely inaccessible area. Now, the knights were coming to understand the background of this isolated tribe. It was a remarkable story.

"The Romans have not been here for hundreds of years," de Lara said. "They were in the Pyrenees, near where I was born, and all over Spain and France, but they are only a whisper of a dream now and nothing more. But here, you keep their memory alive?"

Antillius looked at the knight, a big man with a crown of black hair. "They *are* still here," he assured them quietly. "Look at my people. We are the descendants of these great men who forged their way into a cold and unfriendly country. The term *Tertium* is the name of the legion we are descended from – *Legio Tertium Augustus*. It means Augustus' Third Legion."

He pointed to the top of the staff where faded letters were etched into the bronze and the knights looked upward, trying to make out the name of the legion.

"And you have survived here, as a race, all this time?" De Lara was incredulous.

"We have."

"Your customs, your manner of speaking… this is all part of the ancestors you pay homage to?"

Antillius nodded, looking around to his people, who were starting to disburse now that the excitement of their visitors had faded. "We keep to ourselves and we protect ourselves," he said. "That is why we fired upon you when we found you within our borders. We patrol our lands constantly for invaders and when we saw you, we naturally assumed the worst. We did not know you were searching for an injured woman."

De Lara nodded. "In truth, she was looking for us but she was mistaken in both her sense of direction and her reason for searching," he said, not wanting to explain it further at this point. "Thank you for showing mercy. We shall not forget your kindness."

Antillius nodded faintly, his gaze moving from Luc to Lance, Denis to Kye, and over to Bartholomew and then Jathan. It was clear that there was something more on his mind than the history of his tribe or the injured woman.

"You are not Saxon," he finally said. "I am acquainted with those who rule these lands and you are not from here. You mentioned that you are from Spain and France?"

Now, the reason behind their appearance had been introduced and Luc was reluctant to explain too much, at least not until Ghislaine was tended and they had the opportunity to flee what would undoubtedly be angry men fearful of a Norman invasion.

In fact, as Luc pondered the situation, he knew the Normans would not leave these people alone as centuries of Saxons and Danes and Celts had evidently done. Nay, the Normans would wipe them out if they did not comply and there was some sadness in that thought. His Norman brethren would assimilate the *Tertium* until their memories, their traditions, were no more.

"We are all from France," he said after a moment. "We are here in England because we have a mission to attend to."

Antillius cocked his head curiously. "What mission?"

Luc was careful in his reply. "One of our comrades has been taken hostage," he said. It was the truth. "We are heading north to find him and free him."

"But what about The Beautiful Maid?"

"She is our guide in these strange lands."

Antillius clearly had more questions but he didn't pursue it at the moment; truth be told, he suspected that wasn't the entire truth. He found himself looking at heavily-armed seasoned knights, bigger and more fearsome than anything he'd ever seen. Surely there was more to their presence than what he was being told.

In fact, Antillius was very curious about the outside world and what went on away from his isolated life. He would often speak with the Saxons he traded with to learn such things. But before him, he saw a grand opportunity to learn more than the foolish Saxon farmers could tell him. *Warriors from France,* he thought with satisfaction. Aye, he would discover their purpose, if only to gain news of the world around him.

But something told him there was much more going on than he realized.

"Then you must be weary if you are on a mission to save your friend," he said. "Come. I will show you where you can rest. There is a corral off to the north where you can put your horses but, first, let me show you where you may sleep while you are with us."

The knights knew they couldn't refuse his hospitality. So, while St. Hèver remained with the horses, the rest of them followed Antillius to a long stone structure that turned out to be a convening hall. There were elders in the village and this was where they met to discuss any issues of concern.

Built of the same rock as the rest of the village, the convening hall had a fire pit in the center of it and a sod roof, slightly pitched, with holes near the top of the walls for smoke to escape and ventilation. It also had stone benches and faded images of pagan gods drawn on the walls that, at one time, had been painted. But the colors had faded, leaving only shadows of images, something the knights found both disconcerting and fascinating. However, it was a roof over their heads, something they hadn't had in days, and the simple comfort of it was welcome.

Antillius left his guests settling in to the convening hall while he went to seek his daughters to inform them of their guests, and then on to the elders of the village to tell them about the enormous warriors from across the sea. Certainly, they would all be interested to know what was happening on the outside, but in order for the warriors to speak more freely, they would need an incentive.

Copious amounts of alcohol, made from apples and fermented grains, were soon being prepared for the coming meal.

In vino veritas....

AFTER CAREFULLY EXAMINING the torn stitches in Ghislaine's thigh, the old woman simply removed the broken stitches and then sewed the wound up again with thread made from hemp. It was very strong but it was also painful as the woman poked the sore skin and carefully stitched.

Ghislaine sat on the floor in the old woman's neat house. It was a tiny structure with a tiny bed, a small fire pit in the center, and clutter that one would expect from an old woman living alone. Camulos, her guardian, was lying on one side while Gaetan was crouched on the other, holding her hand as the woman poked and stitched, squeezing her hand now and again as she gasped and made faces because it damn well hurt.

Aramis and Téo stood in the open door, watching the procedure, but they were both watching it from completely different perspectives. Aramis was watching Ghislaine and Gaetan, his misery gaining steam, while Téo was watching Aramis. In fact, that was the only reason he'd come. He'd seen the looks between Gaetan and Ghislaine, and subsequently Aramis and Gaetan, so he came to ensure that nothing got out of hand between Gaetan and Aramis.

It was clear that Gaetan had the lady's attention but Aramis wasn't so subtle about his interest towards her. Téo had seen this situation developing from the start and he was quite concerned for Aramis. The man didn't say much, nor did he ever react to much, but he was reacting openly to Ghislaine. At some point, Gaetan was going to have his fill of it. Therefore, Téo had come to make sure nothing happened between two men vying for the same woman.

He was dreading the moment when it did.

"How does the leg look, Gate?" he asked Gaetan.

Gaetan was watching the old woman finish up her careful stitches. "Not as bad as I thought," he said. "There was so much blood it was difficult to see, but it is not as bad as it could be."

The old woman was on her final stitch. "It will heal," she croaked in that odd Latin that Antillius also spoke. "The lady must stay still. She must rest until it heals."

Ghislaine made out most of what the old woman said. She looked to Gaetan in distress. "I cannot stay still until it heals," she said. "You must go to Tenebris and I must go with you. We cannot wait more than a day or two at most."

Gaetan patted her hand. "You will not worry about that today," he said. "Today, you will rest all day. Tomorrow, we shall discuss this further."

Ghislaine wasn't so sure. As she sat there and fretted, there was movement at the door and she looked up to see three young women approaching. Téo and Aramis, also by the door, caught sight of the young women and they immediately stood back so as not to crowd the timid women. Also, they were inherently interested in them. The women were, by all accounts, young and quite pretty.

But the young women were fearful of the big knights as they huddled near the door, eyeing the warriors while trying to gain sight of the old woman inside.

"Pullum?" one of them called. "Pater has sent us. He has told us to help you with the injured lady."

The old woman finished with the last stitch and sat there, surveying her handiwork. But she paused a moment to wave the young women in, and they darted into the tiny hut in a frightened bunch.

"Aye, I will need your assistance," she said. "This young woman has a wound that must heal. After I wrap the leg, you will assist the lady in bathing and cleaning herself. She is quite dirty and, I would presume, wishes to be comfortable. Will you tend her?"

The girls nodded, looking at Ghislaine, who was gazing back at the three of them somewhat warily. Ghislaine had very few female friends, given the fact that she had been a warrior most of her life, so female companionship was rare in her world.

In truth, it was also somewhat unwelcome. She didn't like silly women and their petty problems. But she also knew she couldn't refuse the hospitality being offered. As her gaze moved from the young women to Gaetan to see what his reaction was to all of this, the first young woman spoke again.

"I am Lygia, daughter of Antillius," she introduced herself timidly. "These are my sisters, Verity and Atia. What is your name?"

Ghislaine looked at them fearfully before her gaze moved to Gaetan. Odd how she was quite fearless in the face of men and battle, but being approached by three young women had her tongue-tied. He smiled wearily at her.

"Tell them your name," he said. "They will not bite you."

Ghislaine's focus moved back to the young women but when she spoke, it was hesitantly. "I am Ghislaine of Mercia."

Lygia was a pretty girl with soft blonde hair and a big-toothed smile. "Welcome, Ghislaine of Mercia," she said, sensing the woman's standoffishness. Without anything more to say, she turned to the old woman. "We will go and gather what we need and return shortly."

The old woman waved them off and they fled the hut, passing by Téo and Aramis as they did. They were the recipients of some rather interested expressions. In fact, Téo was still looking at them as they disappeared into the neat clusters of rock homes and only when they were out of his view did he return his focus to what was happening inside the hut. He thought one of the sisters, a tall lass with copper curls, was quite lovely, indeed, but he forced his thoughts away from her to focus on the situation at hand.

"Gate," he said, "will you have us post a guard where the lady is to be housed?"

Gaetan watched as the old woman swabbed the stitched wound with vinegar and then packed moss on top of it before beginning to bind it.

"Aye, but only on the outside," he said. "She has Cam inside to protect her and he has proven himself most worthy in that aspect. We will simply stand guard outside and be vigilant as to who comes and goes."

Gaetan patted the dog affectionately as it lay beside Ghislaine. Aramis spoke up.

"I will take the first watch."

Both Gaetan and Téo looked at him. Gaetan was becoming increasingly displeased with Aramis' boldness towards Ghislaine, struggling to keep the situation in perspective. *He said he would beg off and allow me to pursue her*, he thought. But it didn't seem that way.

"Very well," Gaetan said evenly, "but I will remain with her at present. You and Téo must go and see to the men and to your horses. I will send for you when it is time for you to stand guard."

He was effectively sending Aramis away. Téo, concerned what would happen if Aramis refused to obey, reached out to put a friendly hand on Aramis' arm to encourage him.

"Come along, *mon frère*," he said, trying to lighten the mood. "Let us see to the horses, as he says. That was quite a ride over here and I must make sure my horse didn't suffer from the terrain."

Aramis didn't say anything but his gaze lingered on Gaetan, who was staring back at him without blinking. In fact, there was hazard in Gaetan's face. Aramis could see it but, somehow, his pride wouldn't let him back down. Still, he didn't want things to escalate, at least not in front of the lady. He turned as Téo pulled at him, moving away from the hut and heading back to the area where the rest of the men were gathered.

But a coldness lingered in his wake.

It was a coldness felt by Ghislaine. She had watched Aramis and Téo move away but quickly lost sight of them. Aramis' behavior confused her.

"What is the matter with Aramis?" she asked. "Why did he look so... odd?"

Gaetan was watching the old woman wrap the leg. It was a perfect question to open up a dialogue that needed to be spoken. In spite of the fact that there was an audience to their conversation in the old woman, he doubted she would understand what he said if he said it in French. He switched to his native tongue.

"Ne sais-du pas?" he asked her softly. *Don't you know?*

Ghislaine shook her head. "Nay," she replied in his language. "What has happened? Is he angry over something? He seemed upset."

Gaetan shook his head. "He is," he said. "With me."

"Why?"

Gaetan looked at her, then. It was the perfect opportunity for him to say everything he wanted to say, everything he needed to say, and everything he was terrified to say. But if he didn't do it now, there was no telling when he would have another opportunity. There might never be another chance like this.

Therefore, he summoned his courage.

Oh, he had told women he'd cared for them in the past. He'd even told one or two that he loved them, but he hadn't meant it. He'd only done it as a means to an end. But to tell a woman he respected greatly, and wanted greatly, that he felt something for her... well, that wasn't something he'd ever done before.

At thirty years and six, Gaetan was about to be truthful to himself and to a woman for the first time in his life. He wondered if he'd be able to survive the sheer strain of it.

It was time for honesty.

"Because it seems that Aramis has developed an affection for you," he said quietly. "Have you not noticed how he is attentive towards you?"

Ghislaine's brow furrowed as the shock of his words settled. Then, her eyebrows lifted in surprise when the full impact hit her. "He *has*?" she asked, her mouth hanging open. "But... I never... I never encouraged him or thought... oh, God's Bones... he is *fond* of me?"

Gaetan could see her astonishment and, he thought, distaste. That didn't make it any easier for him to say what he needed to say.

"Aye," he said quietly. "But so has someone else."

Her eyes widened with more astonishment. "Who?"

"Me."

Ghislaine stared at him and her mouth, so recently hanging open in shock, now closed rapidly. Gaetan stared back at her, trying to read her expression, but he honestly couldn't. He had no idea what she was thinking. He was becoming embarrassed about the entire thing but, now that he'd confessed, he may as well tell her everything.

He took a deep breath.

"I am called Warwolfe," he said quietly. "I am the Duke of Normandy's most prestigious knight and I lead a contingent of the greatest knights the world has ever seen. In action and in profession, there is no one more highly regarded than I am. I am the bastard son of a great warrior and descended from the House of Vargr, the kings of Breton. Additionally, I am a man of some wealth – not only have I inherited my father's titles and lands, but from my maternal grandmother, I have inherited control of Lorient and her ports. The point is that I am a highly-regarded man of nobility with more money than most. There is great worth in that."

Ghislaine was listening to facts that Jathan, long ago, had already told her. She knew all of this already, so it wasn't a surprise. But her mind was so overwhelmed with the declaration that Gaetan was evidently romantically interested in her that Gaetan's speech was entering one ear and going out the other. *Blah, blah, blah....* He wasn't telling her what she wanted to hear, what she was dying to hear. Her fluttering heart was pounding so dramatically that she was certain it was about to burst from her chest.

God, is it really true? She thought joyfully. It was enough to bring tears to her eyes.

"I know you are a man of great worth," she finally said, her voice trembling with emotion. "Gaetan, wealth means nothing to me. It is the man beneath that means everything."

Gaetan looked at her somewhat incredulously, thinking that it sounded like she was receptive to what he was saying. *Tell her the rest, you fool!*

"I do have great wealth, but there is something more you should know," he said. Now, he was starting to stumble. "I am not married but I have... children. There are women I never married to who have provided me with children. I am not fond of these women but I will admit that I am a man who has taken comfort in women over the years. I even have women whose sole purpose in my household is to warm my bed. I am not proud of this but you must understand that I did not give thought to how a future wife might react to such things. I never thought I would marry and a wife was not of concern to me. Ghislaine, I realize that this situation might make you vastly uncomfortable and even ashamed, but I assure you, if you and I were to marry, there would only be one woman in my life, for the rest of my life, and that woman would be you."

By the time Gaetan was finished, there was an expression on his face that Ghislaine had never seen before – something of hope and desperation, of a man who was as vulnerable as he'd ever been in his life. It was enough of an expression to soften Ghislaine completely but, more than that, he was admitting everything she'd ever hoped for. This strong and handsome man, a man she'd been attracted to since nearly the beginning of their association, was confessing things she'd never thought she'd hear from him. She blinked and tears spattered onto her pale cheeks.

"This is a dream," she whispered. "It must be a dream because in my dreams is the only place you would ever say such things to me."

Gaetan couldn't tell, but he thought she might have been happy. He'd never been very good at reading women, but he thought she might – just *might* – be glad. A timid smile creased his lips.

"This is not a dream, I assure you," he said softly. "But I will admit it is my biggest fear that you will not feel that I am worthy of you."

She blinked again and more tears spilled. The brightest smile he'd ever seen nearly split her face in two.

"My sweet darling," she said earnestly. "I have never known a more worthy man. I know of your past and I know of the bedslaves. Aye, I have been told. But it is of no matter. If you say that I am to be the only woman in your life from now until forever, I believe you."

He was elated to the point of feeling lightheaded. "Truly?"

"Truly."

"Then may I know if anything I have said is agreeable to you?"

She laughed through her tears of joy. "Everything you said is agreeable," she said. "Gaetan, do you know how long I have adored you? I cannot recall when I have not. Hearing you say such things... I simply cannot believe it."

His smile turned bold and he reached out, cupping her sweet face in his two big hands. "It *is* true," he said, his heart bursting with newfound joy. "I adore you as well, my little mouse. But knowing that you return these feelings... you cannot know how happy you have made me."

"As you have made me, Gaetan."

"Are you agreeable to marrying me, then?"

"Of course, my dearest. More than you know."

With that, Ghislaine reached out, pulling him to her and Gaetan's mouth descended upon hers, tasting her lips for the first time as she responded to him. He remembered those lips from before, when she'd been sleeping. But now, there was warmth and tenderness, a potency that surged through him like wildfire. He knew she'd been married before and, because of that, he knew she wasn't a maiden, but he didn't care. He wasn't one, either. He kissed her deeply, completely uncaring that the old woman who had just finished wrapping the leg was a witness to his most private moment.

All he cared about was the moment itself.

But the old woman was being jostled around because Ghislaine's leg was moving about as Gaetan's big body overwhelmed her. The old woman thumped Gaetan on the hip because that was the body part nearest her.

"Caution, good lord," she rasped in her strange Latin. "You must be cautious of the leg!"

Gaetan didn't want to focus on the leg; he was right where he wanted to be, with Ghislaine's face trapped in his hands and his mouth on hers. But he pulled his lips away from her long enough to snarl at the old woman.

"Get out," he hissed. "Leave us."

"Be cautious of the leg!"

"I will, I will. Now, get *out!*"

The old woman looked at him, pursing her lips unhappily, but she could see that she was both unwanted and unneeded. Moreover, the lady didn't seem to be complaining about his rough treatment of her in the least. The old woman had done her job, at least for the moment, but she had a feeling the way the warrior and the lady were pawing at each other that those stitches might be torn out again before the day was finished. Surely, the lady was in pain but she didn't seem to mind. When the old woman saw the warrior plunge his tongue into the lady's mouth, she lurched to her feet with a shriek of disgust and fled her hut, slamming the door behind her.

Gaetan, his lips against Ghislaine's, simply grinned.

"We are finally without our audience," he murmured.

Ghislaine had her arms around his head, pulling the man down to her as if to never let him go.

"Excellent," she breathed. "But Cam is still here."

Gaetan could see the dog sleeping against the wall behind her. "He will pay no mind."

"He'd better not."

Her lips fused to his and Gaetan couldn't help but notice she was being quite aggressive with him, which he loved. He never imagined her arms around him could feel as good as they did. The moment she touched him, it was like it was the very first time he'd ever been touched by a woman. Nothing could have been more pure or more welcome.

"I cannot believe we are finally alone," he said as his teeth nibbled on her jawline. "I never thought we would have such a moment as this with all of those annoying men hanging around us as they do. Did they not know I have been wanting to do this to you for quite some time?"

She giggled, quickly cut off by a groan when he latched on to her tender neck. "How long?"

"Ages."

"You were not thinking of doing this when you spanked me upon the field of battle those weeks ago."

He started to laugh, but his passion was so strong that it came out as a choking sound. He simply couldn't give attention to anything other than his want for her.

"Mayhap not, but you will forgive me. I do not usually consider the battlefield a place to seduce a woman."

"I am not *any* woman."

"God help me, you are not."

Ghislaine didn't want to talk anymore. She wanted him in the worst way and she moved to unfasten the leather belt that was around his waist. Gaetan knew immediately what she meant. He was overwhelmed by the fire in his veins, the strength of which he'd never experienced, but it was a fire he'd felt before. He knew this fire that fed his manhood, not to be quenched until he was releasing himself deep into a woman's body, but he was genuinely concerned about doing anything like that with Ghislaine. She wasn't someone cheap to be used on a whim. Even as she unfastened his belt, he tore his lips from hers and looked her in the eye.

"As much as I would like to take all of you, we must be cautious of your leg," he said huskily. "Moreover... I did not tell you of my adoration for you simply to have my way with you. I told you because it was the truth."

Ghislaine yanked the belt off and it fell to the floor of the hut, heavily, because of his scabbard. "I know," she said breathlessly. "But I want you to touch me, Gaetan. I want to feel your hands upon my body. Will you make me beg, then?"

He shook his head, a smile playing on his lips. "You will never have to beg me, ever."

"Then prove it to me."

He did.

CHAPTER TWENTY-ONE

New Blood

THEIR HUT WAS shaped like a cross, with a long room that served as both an eating room and a kitchen, and then two chambers off each side where family members slept. All of the girls were in one chamber while their father, now widowed these past few years, slept in the other.

Antillius' cottage was cozy and well-kept thanks to three daughters who were as meticulous as their mother had been. This cottage was at least one hundred years old, probably more, built on the foundations of another cottage before it that had also stood for many years. The floor was hard-packed earth in the long room but in the bedchamber where Antillius slept, long ago, someone had laid down colored stones to make a mosaic. It was the portrait of a woman although no one knew exactly who the woman was. Antillius suspected it was another ancestor of his, for the woman was pale and fine-featured like he was.

Lygia, Verity, and Atia rushed into this neat little cottage on a mission. Old Pullum, the crone who was the physician of the village, had asked them to help a wounded woman, and help they would. There was very little excitement in their world so they were most eager for something new and different to accomplish, even if the lady had come with a contingent of several of the largest men they had ever seen. The men were dressed in sheets of metal, with big weapons hanging from their waists, and they were of curious interest to these isolated women.

Lygia, the eldest, was the taskmaster. She had seen twenty years and three, having lost her husband and infant daughter to a sickness two years before during a particularly bad winter. She'd moved back into the family home where her sisters, Verity and Atia, brought her some comfort. They were good sisters, even if they were a little flighty at times – Verity was tall, elegant, and with long copper curls, and Atia, the baby of the family at nineteen years, was a shorter, lighter-haired version of Lygia. But she was extremely bright, and helpful, and as Lygia gave the orders, Verity and Atia followed them precisely.

In the young women's chamber, chests were opened and items brought forth. Lygia was rushing about, finding drying linens, while her sisters were pulling forth other things needed for cleaning. Linens in hand, Lygia came to a halt in the midst of her rush.

"Why *must* the lady remain in Pullum's cottage?" she asked thoughtfully. "Why can we not bring her here? Our chamber is big enough to accommodate her. I should not like to leave the lady with old Pullum."

Verity had a bar of soft tallow soap in her hand that smelled heavily of the violets they harvested in the forest. "But Pater said we should help, not bring the lady to our home," she reminded her. "She is an *allii*, after all."

Lygia frowned at her sister. "She is a wounded woman who requires help," she said firmly. "Are you so cruel that you would leave a her with Pullum and not try to take her away from that old witch?"

"Did you see those warriors?" Atia interrupted her sisters' discussion with her rather dreamy question. "I have never seen men so tall and strong. Where do you suppose they come from? They do not look like Saxon warriors to me."

Lygia could hear the wistfulness in her youngest sister's tone. "It does not matter where they come from, dear Atia, because they are not for you," she reminded her quietly. "Phirinius is your chosen one. He would not like it if you paid attention to another man."

Atia frowned. "Phirinius is a boy. Those warriors… they are men!"

"And you will put them out of your mind," Lygia scolded, waving an impatient hand at her sister. "Gather the wash for the hair and find some clean clothes we can lend to the lady. From what I saw, she was wearing rags."

Unhappy that her conversation about the strange warriors was thwarted, Atia turned back to what she was doing, pulling forth all of the things they used when they bathed – a skin scraper to scrape away the dirt, precious oil from the almonds they collected and pressed last month, and flat ale to wash the hair. Holding up the phial of the almond oil, she looked at it in the light, noting just how much they had left.

"Lygia is right," she said. "We should simply bring the lady here. We have our tub here and Pullum has not the room for such a thing. Her cottage is very tiny. We should simply bring the lady here to tend her."

Lygia considered Atia's support a majority vote. She set the drying linens down. "Then let us go and get her," she said. "If she cannot walk, we will have one of her men carry her here."

The thought of seeing the strange warriors again had Atia heading from the chamber rather quickly. "Do you think she is a princess?" she asked. "She has many men with her. Mayhap she requires them for protection."

Verity, too, seemed to be following her sister at a clipped pace, leading Lygia to believe that Verity might think something of these handsome strangers, as well, even though she'd not said anything. She was the quiet one at times. Lygia was on the heels of her eager sisters.

"It does not matter what she is," she said. "And you will not ask her, Atia."

Atia made a face at her sister. "Can I at least ask her about her war-riors?"

"Nay!"

"Can I speak with her *at all?*"

Lygia cocked an eyebrow at her. "Only if you are polite and do not ask foolish questions."

Quitting the cottage, the young women emerged into an open area beneath the massive tree canopy. Their cottage was set off from the rest, for privacy, and they even had their own bread kiln and stock corral for their pigs and goats. But in heading towards old Pullum's hut, they had to pass by the central meeting area where the strange warriors and the lone lady had first entered, and Atia was very eager to see if those men were still around. Verity was only slightly less obvious about it, which gave her interest away completely. The two of them were searching eagerly for the strange warriors when they caught sight of the men over near the convening house. Atia grabbed hold of Verity.

"Look!" she hissed, pointing discreetly. "There they are!"

Lygia, who had been walking ahead of them at this point, came to a halt and waited for them to catch up to her. When the pair also came to a halt, gawking at the warriors in the distance, Lygia reached over and grabbed hold of Verity, pulling her and Atia along.

"Stop looking at them as if you've never seen men before," she said. "You are making fools of yourselves."

Verity was trying to walk but Atia was dragging on her, making the entire procession go quite slowly. Suddenly, their father came into view from behind the convening house and Atia began calling to him, jumping up and down and waving until Lygia grabbed hold of her.

"Stop it!" she hissed at her sister. "Are you trying to show everyone what an idiot you are?"

Atia yanked herself away from her sister and ran straight for her father who, having seen his youngest daughter waving at him, made his way towards his girls. Atia grabbed hold of his arm, pulling on him, as he smiled tolerantly at her.

"Have you gone to Pullum as I have instructed?" he asked his girls.

They nodded in unison but Lygia answered. "We have," she said.

"Pullum asked us to help bathe and tend the lady, but it would be too difficult to do it in Pullum's hut. May we bring her to ours, Pa?"

Antillius considered it. "It might be better if we put her someplace where she would not be disturbed," he said. "There would be noise in our cottage with many people walking about. There is an empty hut near the pool since the death of old Drucilla. Why not put her there? It would be quiet and peaceful."

Lygia thought that was a good idea. "I shall have the copper tub put in that cottage for her," she said. "We shall go and make her bed. Where are her possessions?"

Antillius shook his head. "With her soldiers, I would imagine," he said. "I will ask."

"About the soldiers, Pa," Atia said, hanging on his arm. "Who are they?"

Antillius knew his youngest well enough to know that she wasn't asking purely to be polite. Atia had an eye for young men and was quite enamored with the opposite sex as a whole.

"They are from France," he told her. "They have come to our lands seeking a comrade who has been abducted and they are simply passing through."

Atia was thrilled to hear they were from a mysterious, far-off land. That's what France was to the isolated young woman, something she'd only heard about in stories. "Can we speak with them, Pa?" she begged. "I would like to hear of their travels and of their home. Please, can we speak with them?"

Antillius knew that question would come, at some point. He just didn't think it would come so soon. He patted Atia on her soft cheek. "Not yet," he said. "I do not know these men. I do not know their hearts. Let me determine that they are men of good character before I permit my daughters to be around them."

Atia's face fell with disappointment. "But –!"

Antillius grasped her chin and gave her a gentle shake. "Not yet," he told her firmly. "We have allowed these men into our world but I do not trust them yet. We do not know them. You will stay away from them until such time as I deem it appropriate to have contact with them. If you do not obey me, I will take a branch to you, Atia. Do you understand?"

Atia sighed heavily, grossly disappointed. "Aye," she said. "But I have heard you speak of finding new blood for our people, Pa. You have said yourself that our numbers are less and less every year, that less babies are born. Would not men such as these bring the new blood you have spoken of?"

Antillius had, indeed, spoken of that very thing at times; after centuries of inbreeding and sickness, his people were a dying race. He knew that. He had hoped for strong husbands for his daughters to bring new bloodlines into their tribe. And it was, indeed, possible that these warriors were the new blood that he had hoped for, but it was far too early to tell. He couldn't even guess. As he told Atia, he did not know these men. He didn't know their hearts or their deeds and, until he did, he would continue to be wary of them.

"I cannot know this and you will not speak of it again," he said, kissing Atia's unhappy face before turning to his elder daughters. "I have just seen Pullum over near the kitchens and she is finished binding the lady's leg, so go and prepare the empty cottage for her. Get along with your tasks and I will see you later."

The girls nodded and he headed off, moving in the general direction of their cottage. Lygia turned in the same direction, pulling her sisters along.

"You have heard him," she said. "Let us prepare Drucilla's old cottage for our guest. Atia, did you find something for her to wear?"

Atia made a face at her sister but that face quickly changed into a fake smile when Lygia turned to look at her. Lygia knew her sister was upset with her but that couldn't be helped. Strangers in their midst had them all edgy with excitement and some fear, for it was extremely rare for them to have any visitors at all.

Truth be told, Lygia was already thinking ahead to the meal that night. She and her sisters would help supervise the meal, as daughters of the tribal chief, and she was already wondering how she was going to keep Atia from making a fool of herself over the handsome strangers.

Secretly, Lygia thought they were fairly handsome as well.

GAETAN HAD BEDDED many women in his life, but not like this.

Never, like this.

In the old woman's hut, as the sounds of a gentle rain began to fall outside, Ghislaine and Gaetan were only partially disrobed as their bodies came together in the ancient primal mating rhythm. Because of Ghislaine's bad leg, she ended up on her hands and knees, her tattered trousers down around one ankle and her cote and shift up around her shoulders as the bulk of her tender white body was laid wide for Gaetan's touch.

Her buttocks were elevated to him as he held her aloft by the hips, his manhood deep in her body as he thrust repeatedly into her, trying to keep any pounding off of her right leg. It was tricky, to be sure, and Ghislaine was contorted rather oddly, but the beauty of the moment, the sensuality of it, was beyond measure.

Having been married before, Ghislaine knew how to welcome a man's body. She knew how to move with him, and how to give him pleasure, because the moment Gaetan had entered her, she'd tightened up the muscles of her slick sheath to maximize his bliss. Gaetan had groaned with delight when he felt her body contract around him but the excitement of it, and her expert touch, very nearly threw him into a climax at the onset.

He had to still himself, slapping her buttocks gently to distract both him and her from what she was doing, but the slap against her buttocks had given Ghislaine the first of what had, so far, been two releases.

Gaetan had felt them both against his manroot, that great throbbing that signified a woman's satisfaction.

He wasn't able, at the moment, to touch any other part of her body because of the way he held her hips elevated against his, but that didn't matter at the moment. Everything he was doing below the waist, with his manhood as he ground his pelvis against her buttocks, was enough for the moment. He never knew lovemaking could be so euphoric to his heart or so satisfying to his soul.

It was heaven.

But he could feel his climax coming on and he had been for some time; it had been an effort to hold it off, to enjoy the moment. This was the woman he had fallen in love with, that he would marry, and that would bear his legitimate children. That knowledge was the most powerful aphrodisiac in the world to him.

As he carefully lowered her onto her left knee to take the brunt of her weight while he kept the right leg elevated, his left hand roamed her soft and tender body, fondling her sweet breasts, listening to her groan with pleasure. *Breasts that will nurse my children*, he thought, *but a body that belongs to me.*

Me!

He found himself wishing she would conceive his son this day; that his seed would find its mark. Surely God would listen to his prayers as he prayed for a strong son to carry on his legacy from this powerful brave woman who was very quickly consuming him.

When his hand moved to the moist junction between her legs, Ghislaine endured her third and most powerful climax yet. It was enough to throw Gaetan over the edge and he released himself deep into her body. But even then, his hips continued to move as if he didn't want the moment to end, drawing it out, savoring it, gently thrusting into her until he could thrust no more. Then, he lowered himself down next to her and very carefully took her into his arms.

Ghislaine was sure that she was only half-conscious. She was in a dream state, somewhere between life and death and utter bliss. Her eyes were partially open as she lay wrapped up in Gaetan's arms, staring at a stone wall that had pots and buckets shoved up against it. Gaetan's mouth was by her ear and he kissed it, gently.

"Considering how ill and injured you have been, I should be considered quite a brute for forcing myself upon you as I did," he murmured. "I pray you are not injured further."

Ghislaine put a hand up, holding his head against hers and savoring their closeness. "I believe I am the one who instigated it," she whispered. "I pray you do not think less of me for it."

"Think *less* of you? God, no. I think you are a goddess."

She smiled, laughing softly when she heard his gentle laughter in her ear. "Thank you," she said. "You are most kind, my lord."

"You did not answer me – I did not injure you further, did I?"

"You did not. I am no worse off than I was before."

"You really should rest. And I should see to my men."

Ghislaine sighed faintly. "I do not like the thought of you leaving me now."

He kissed her ear one last time before propping himself up so he could look at her. "Nor do I," he said, "but unless you wish to announce to the world that you bedded me, I should leave for propriety's sake. But I do intend to tell my men tonight that you have consented to be my bride. That way, when I tell them we want privacy, they will understand."

His eyes were twinkling as he said it, bringing a grin to her lips. But that smile soon faded. "What will you tell Aramis?"

Gaetan's humor quickly left him. "We had an understanding, he and I," he said. "He would permit me to express my feelings to you first. If you did not return my feelings, then I gave him permission to pursue you. I suppose now he shall simply have to accept defeat gracefully."

"And if he does not?"

"You will leave that to me."

Ghislaine simply nodded. It would be more his business than hers if Aramis was not a gracious loser because the conflict would be between them and them alone. She reached up, touching his rough cheek.

"He is a nice man," she said. "I do not wish to hurt him."

He leaned down and kissed her on the tip of her nose. "I realize that, but there are things in life we cannot control and this is one of them," he said as he pushed himself up to sit. "Now, you will stay here and rest that leg. I shall return shortly to see how you are faring."

"Promise?"

He took her hand, bringing it to his lips for a sweet kiss. "I will never leave your side if I can help it, Mousie. You must remember that. And even if I do have to leave you for a time, you will not come chasing after me. I will always return to you."

The words comforted Ghislaine deeply. She stroked his cheek, feeling like she was still living a dream. Would she wake up from this only to realize there was no spoken feelings between them? God, she hoped not. She would be shattered. At this moment, this stolen and golden moment, she was happier and more content than she had ever been in her life. She had Gaetan.

She had everything.

But any further words were cut off by a knock at the heavy oaken door. Startled, Gaetan immediately rose to his knees, pulling his trousers up and securing them in a hurry.

"Who goes?" he demanded.

There was a slight hesitation. "It is Lygia, my lord," she said nervously. "We have come to help the lady."

Gaetan wriggled his eyebrows at Ghislaine, a comical gesture, as he quickly helped her pull the skirt of her cote down. He also helped her smooth her hair and right her bodice, anything to remove the remnants of their carnal activities. When she was covered and straightened, he rose to his feet and went to the door, opening it.

Three lovely young women were standing in the entry, looking at Gaetan with some nervousness. It was Lygia who spoke again.

"I have come to take the lady to a cottage where she can rest and recover in peace," she said. "It is not far from here."

Gaetan glanced over at Ghislaine, who was sitting on the floor, leaning against the wall and trying to look quite innocent. *Who, me? Having seduced a man? Never!* He almost grinned, nearly able to read her thoughts.

"This cottage is fine for her needs," he said, letting no smile break forth at Ghislaine's attempts to play the innocent maiden. "You do not need to trouble yourselves by moving her."

"Forgive me, my lord, but this hut belongs to old Pullum," Lygia said. "It would be quite crowded for the lady, not to mention the fact that Pullum would not be the friendliest person to live with. The cottage we have prepared will be much better for her."

Gaetan looked at Ghislaine to see what her reaction was to all of this. Meeting Gaetan's eye, Ghislaine nodded somewhat eagerly at him before addressing the young women.

"It is very kind of you to do this," she said. "I will come."

Lygia moved in to help her stand but Gaetan was already there, sweeping her up into his big arms and carrying her from the cramped cottage. As Camulos trotted out on Gaetan's heels, Lygia indicated for him to follow her as Verity and Atia followed behind, taking the opportunity to inspect every inch of the massive, very handsome warrior.

Lygia could see what her sisters were doing and she was embarrassed by it. Fearful Gaetan would become wise to what her sisters were doing, she hastened to keep his attention.

"I do hope your leg is not paining you too terribly," she said to Ghislaine. "My father said that you had a battle wound."

Cradled in Gaetan's arms, Ghislaine replied. "We were ambushed while traveling," she said. "It is an arrow wound and I have managed to tear the stitches, unfortunately. Your healer was very kind to stitch the wound up again."

Lygia looked at her, greatly concerned. "What terrible fortune," she said. "Are you feeling any better now?"

Ghislaine looked right at Gaetan, struggling not to grin. "Much,

much better."

Lygia didn't miss the expressions of warmth that passed between the lady and the enormous warrior. In fact, it tugged at her heart because, once, she had looked at her husband with the same expression. Feeling sad, and perhaps even a little jealous, she turned away.

"Then I am glad," she said.

Lygia didn't say anything more after that, leading then through a series of neat rows of cottages until they reached a great pool of clear water beneath the oak trees. The stream ran right into the pool and then out another end of it to continue on, so there was a constant supply of fresh water in the pool. Women were washing their clothes on rocks on the edge of the pool while children played nearby. It was a bucolic scene as Lygia led Ghislaine and Gaetan to a cottage at the end of a row of small structures and opened the door.

"Here we are," she said. "The lady will be quite comfortable here. We have already prepared a fire for hot water and we will tend the lady while you go about your business. We shall take great care of her, my lord."

Gaetan didn't doubt the woman for a minute. She seemed sincere enough and he was comfortable leaving Ghislaine in her care. Moreover, Ghislaine could take care of herself. Even wounded, she would be able to defend herself against these three rather pale-looking women. Gaetan had great faith in her abilities; Ghislaine wasn't some foolish woman that needed looking after.

That was one of the things he admired so much about her.

Ducking under the door, Gaetan took Ghislaine right to a small bed that was built into an alcove in the one-room cottage. It was a comfortable little place, and warm with the fire in the crude hearth, and there were already two big pots of water steaming on the fire. Satisfied that Ghislaine would be well-tended, he turned to her.

"I must see to my horse and speak with my men," he told her. "I will return as soon as I can."

Ghislaine smiled, sorry to see him go, but so very glad that they had spent this precious time together. It had been one of the most moving and important moments of her life, now to know that Warwolfe, the most powerful Norman knight in the realm, belonged to her. And she belonged to him.

She loved him.

"You need not rush," she told him, glancing at Lygia and her timid sisters. "I believe I am in good hands."

Gaetan's gaze lingered on her a moment, feeling the same thing that she was feeling. He was sad to leave but so very glad they'd been able to share some time together. Something about that moment he'd shared with her seemed to make his life complete, filling him with a contentment he'd never known.

With a subtle wink meant only for her, he left the cottage, leaving Ghislaine dreaming of her heroic knight, the Norman enemy she'd finally given her heart to.

And she didn't regret any of it.

CHAPTER TWENTY-TWO

ɞ

ET PRO GLORIA DEI

GAETAN HAD NO idea what he was drinking, but whatever it was had a punch to it. Seated on the hard-packed earth floor of the convening hall around a table that was hardly taller than his knees, he leaned over in Téo's direction.

"This drink is rather potent," he muttered.

Téo, who was feeling the buzz himself, nodded. "Potent like an ax to the face," he said, peering in the wooden cup he'd been drinking from. "What is *in* this stuff?"

Gaetan didn't have a clue. All he knew was that two cups of it had made his head swim, and that usually didn't happen to him because he had a strong tolerance for drink. Wellesbourne was on the other side of him and he leaned in Bartholomew's direction.

"What is this drink?" he asked the man quietly. "You purport to know these lands. Is this some mad Mercian concoction we've been ingesting?"

Wellesbourne shrugged, but his head, too, was swimming. "It certainly seems to be."

"Two cups of this drink and already my head is rolling like the ocean waves."

"It is a cursed drink."

Next to Wellesbourne, de Lara heard the conversation. He, too, wasn't feeling so well, making it difficult when he tried to shake his head at Wellesbourne's comment. "Everything is cursed to you, Bartholomew," he muttered. "You see more omens than an old witching woman. Why is that?"

Wellesbourne eyed de Lara. "Because everything *is* cursed. How have you survived this long without knowing that?"

De Lara just laughed and took another drink from his cup, but Gaetan had stopped when he realized that the stuff was going to put him to sleep. He'd requested watered wine, or something else without such a kick to it, and a servant had brought him a bowl of juice from apples and blackberries. It was very sweet, but it was better than becoming drunk on cursed Mercian beer.

All nine knights were at the table along with Antillius and several of the elders of the village. There were even a few of Antillius' men, who seemed rather intimidated by their visitors though not unfriendly. There were one or two that still tried to strike up a conversation with them. Jathan was missing, however, because he had gone to sit with Ghislaine, taking the watch from Aramis because Gaetan didn't want the man anywhere near her until he'd had a chance to explain that Ghislaine was no longer an unpledged woman. Now, she belonged to him.

She was all he could think about.

Aramis hadn't been happy with Gaetan in the least for sending Jathan in his stead to sit with the lady while they partook of the evening meal, but he didn't argue. He simply did as he was told. But even now, he was sitting across from Gaetan, his dark and murky eyes glaring at him from across the table.

De Russe was an intimidating man when he wanted to be and it was clear that he was trying to convey his displeasure with Gaetan at the moment, but Gaetan wasn't intimidated in the least. He was, however, growing irritated, something that was magnified by that damnable drink. Therefore, Gaetan tried not to look at Aramis because he was certain if he did, the next step would see him flying over the table and wringing his friend's neck.

But he was distracted from the man when the food was brought forth, and it was quite a feast – both boiled and roast pork, pies with pork and carrots and local birds, fish in wine, and other delicacies. For people who lived such an isolated and simple life deep in the woods, it was a great display of both hospitality and prosperity, and the knights wolfed down the food before their hosts were even served. They hadn't eaten since the meal at The King's Head the night before, so they were quite eager to put food into their bellies.

Gaetan found a good deal of satisfaction with the roast pork, which had a wine sauce on it that was marvelous. There was far less conversation now that mouths were full, but Gaetan couldn't help but notice that the same women who had pledged to tend Ghislaine were also the women who were serving the knights. He wouldn't have noticed except Antillius, at the end of the table, grabbed one of them and swatted her on the behind, clearly unhappy that she was serving.

The young woman fled in tears but her two sisters were moving up and down the table, making sure the men had what they needed. Gaetan had to admit that the *Tertium* were very good hosts but he was inherently curious about them.

"Have you discovered anything about this place?" he asked Téo quietly.

Téo was well into his pork and bird pie. "Only that they are the descendants of an ancient Roman legion that settled here," he said. "Antillius is quite forthcoming about his tribe's history."

"You have spoken with him?"

Téo nodded. "When you went with the physician to tend Lady Ghislaine, the rest of us spoke with him somewhat."

Gaetan thought it might be best if he spoke with Antillius now, as the commander of the group, rather than get his information second hand. Swallowing the bite in his mouth, he leaned forward so he could address Antillius directly.

"You have my gratitude for your kindness towards my men and towards the lady, my lord," he said. "I apologize that I have not had much time to speak with you, but the lady's health was my primary concern when we arrived."

Antillius was eating but he wasn't drinking the same alcohol the knights had been served. Gaetan noticed that when a serving woman poured the same apple drink into his cup that Gaetan had requested. All things considered, it put Gaetan on edge a bit as he considered that their host may very well be trying to get them drunk. Either that, or there wasn't enough drink to go around so he was giving it all to his guests. Still, Gaetan was glad he stopped drinking so at least one of them would have a clear head.

"There is no need to apologize," Antillius said, cutting in to his suspicious thoughts. "The lady is doing better, I have heard."

Gaetan nodded. "The wound was not as bad as it looked, fortunately," he said. "Your physician was able to stitch it up and now the lady rests comfortably."

"I am glad."

Gaetan took a drink of the apple concoction. "I must also apologize for not introducing me and my men," he said. "It seems rather late for proprieties, but permit me to give introductions – I am Gaetan de Wolfe of the House of Vargr, the kings of Breton. The men you have seated around your table are de Russe of Flanders, de Reyne of Morlaix, de Moray from Rouen, de Winter of the House of Bourbon, de Lara, the Count of Boucau, St. Hèver of Normandy, du Reims of Reims, and Wellesbourne of Wales. As I told you, our comrade was abducted and we are heading north to retrieve him."

Antillius was looking around his table, rather shocked at the introductions. He was a man who soaked up information when he could get it so he knew that he had at least three men from ruling or royal families at his table, de Wolfe included. In truth, he was quite impressed.

"I am honored, my lords," he finally said. "I fear I have set a simple table for such great men."

Gaetan shook his head. "You have been a gracious host and we are grateful for what you have provided us."

Antillius banged on the table and more food suddenly appeared, filling up the tabletop with a great deal of excess. "It is my honor," he said. "And the lady – The Beautiful Maid of Mercia – although her brother is my enemy, I do not look upon her as my enemy. She is my honored guest. If you are allies of Black Edwin, I do not hold that against you."

Gaetan glanced at the men across the table; de Russe, de Moray, and St. Hèver were looking to him to see how he would respond. Gaetan thought it best to be honest with Antillius to a certain extent. He saw no harm in it.

"We are not allies of Edwin of Mercia," he said. "In fact, it is his brother Alary who has abducted our comrade."

Antillius sobered at the mention of Alary's name. "Ah," he finally said, nodding his head in a knowing fashion. "*Alary Insanus.*"

Alary the Insane. Gaetan snorted softly. "That is fitting," he said. "You know of him, then?"

Antillius nodded, but his expression was far from pleasant. "Aye," he replied, seemed hesitant, but continued. "We have had contact with him and his men on occasion. I have heard of him burning down entire villages to punish women who rejected his advances or tormenting men he wanted something from. Last year, two of our young girls wandered away and we never found them again. Saxon allies we trade with told us that it was rumored that Alary had found the girls and sold them off to the highest bidder. We tried to find the girls, but to no avail. It was as if they had vanished."

It was a disheartening tale but, given Alary's scope of evil, not surprising. "I am sorry to hear that," Gaetan said. "Has he ever tried to come to your village? It is not terribly far from his seat of Tenebris."

Antillius shook his head. "He has been in our lands but he had never come close to our home," he said, "although there are other tribes about that have attacked us from time to time."

Gaetan listened with interest, mostly for his own education on the tribes in the area. "Warring tribes?"

Antillius nodded. "Mostly," he said. "Or, they want our women. We keep a very close watch on our women. There is one tribe that tries quite frequently to steal our woman; we call them the *Homines Ossium*. No one really knows their true name, but they wear the bones of their dead ancestors in great necklaces because they believe the bones of the dead will bless them with the strength of the man the bones once served. Some of the necklaces are quite heavy and elaborate."

Gaetan wasn't sure he liked the sound of savages wearing bones. "Where do they live?"

Antillius pointed off to the east. "On the other side of the great river is a valley. They have dug holes into the sides of the hills and they live inside of them. They live like animals and they fight like animals as well. We tell our children frightening tales of the Men of Bones so that the little ones do not wander away from the village."

Gaetan wriggled his eyebrows in agreement. "It sounds as if those tales are more truth than fable," he said. "Someone told me these lands are called the shadowlands, where the land itself is cursed. Mayhap that is not far from the truth in some cases."

Antillius shook his head. "It is not, I assure you," he said. "Now, you have asked me many questions, King of the Bretons. I would like to ask you some questions as well."

Gaetan grinned. "My ancestors were the kings of Breton," he corrected. "The last time I checked, that was not my title."

"But you have one."

Gaetan nodded. "Marquis Aulerci. That is the hereditary title of the heirs of Mateudoi, the last King of the Bretons."

Antillius was clearly impressed. "You must command a great many men."

"I command enough."

"I would believe that. Which is why I would like to know why you are only traveling with nine warriors. Should you not bring more men if you are to extract your comrade from Alary's clutches?"

They were heading into an area where Gaetan wanted to be particularly careful. He didn't want to speak on how Kristoph was abducted or how they, and an entire Norman army, had come to the shores of England.

"I have two thousand men with me but Alary discovered that we were coming for our comrade and threatened his life," he said. "I left my men back in a town called Westerham. I believe my knights and I can rescue our friend. We are skilled and resourceful."

Antillius cocked his head in a dubious gesture. "I admire your bravery, my friend, but surely Alary carries more than nine men with him," he said. "Tenebris is a dark and mysterious place to the north. I do not know how many men he has there, but there will be more than just a few."

"Any Norman knight in battle is worth twenty Saxons."

"And you are confident as well."

"You've not see us fight."

Antillius grinned. Then, he laughed, looking around the table to the men who were stuffing themselves on the pork and pies. "You are as big as mountains, all of you," he said. "It would be a terrifying thing to meet you in battle. I pray that I never will."

Gaetan gave him a half-grin. "You almost did today when you ambushed us with your arrows."

Antillius waved him off. "I fear we would have lost too many men in that fight," he said. "We may have had the advantage, but in the end, I would have had to sacrifice a few. Our numbers are not so great that we can afford to lose men."

"Why is that?"

Antillius' good humor faded. "Our numbers are less and less every year," he replied. "Our people have been here for hundreds of years, de Wolfe, and we do not marry *allii* unless it is absolutely necessary. That means we marry within our tribe and, over the years, we are less and less. There are fewer babies born every year. I fear that someday we will die out completely unless we find new and worthy men to marry our women."

That comment caused every Norman but Gaetan to look straight at his food and pretend to be occupied with it, for no one wanted to get roped into a marital commitment with a father looking for worthy men for his daughters. Gaetan saw the heads go down and he laughed to himself.

"Not to worry," he told Antillius. "I am sure you will find worthy husbands for your women, in time. It would be an honor for any man to become part of your tribe, as you are excellent fighters. I could see that earlier today even though a sword was not drawn nor a weapon thrown. It is clear your men are great warriors themselves. In fact, I shall deem all of them honorary Normans. It will be a bond between your men and mine so that, in the future, we shall remember that bond and hold to it."

Antillius was greatly flattered. "We do not have allies," he said. "We have always kept to ourselves. We are quite honored by your declaration."

Gaetan held up a cup to the man as if to toast him. "And I will christen you and your family the House of de Shera, as you must have a Norman name now. Shericus is the ancient name of old, a name of great honor. De Shera is a name for a house that will evolve into greatness."

Antillius grinned, looking at his men and seeing expressions of approval. As he turned to some of the men around him to discuss the Norman honor, Gaetan turned to Téo.

"God's Bones, did I just say that?" he muttered. "Did I just completely change that man's entire world and tell him that his name was not good enough in this new Norman realm?"

Téo was indulging in a compote of berries with honey and cream; it was most delicious. "You took an ancient Roman line and made it

Norman," he said. "That is what our kind does, Gate. That is the Norman way of thinking. We take the world and change it for the better."

Gaetan pondered that, toying with his drink cup in one hand and stroking his chin with the other. But in the course of that deliberation, he noticed that de Russe was once again looking at him from across the table. His good mood fled.

"Téo," he mumbled, his eyes never leaving de Russe. "I must tell you something."

"What?"

"I have claimed Lady Ghislaine."

Téo's head came up and he looked at him curiously. "*Claimed* her? What do you mean?"

"Bodily."

That became clear in an instant and Téo's eyebrows lifted with some shock, but also with realization. Frankly, he wasn't surprised. He knew Gaetan's appetites when it came to women so it wasn't a surprise in the least. But in the same thought, he knew it was about to become quite complicated given Aramis' feelings for the woman.

Deadly, even.

"I see," he said. He set his knife down; he suddenly didn't feel like eating anymore. "Forgive me, but mayhap it was not wise to do that."

"Why not?"

"Because surely you have known that Aramis is…."

Gaetan cut him off. "Of course I know," he said. "He is sitting across the table from me, shooting daggers from his eyes as he stares me down. He and I discussed this delicate situation back in Worcester and he was most amiable then, but that has changed. He told me that he would step back and allow me to pursue the lady but his actions have said otherwise."

Téo sighed heavily. "Gate, you have been my friend for many years so forgive me for what I am about to say, but you did not need another conquest, and certainly not a conquest in the sister of Edwin of

Mercia," he said quietly. "If there was one woman you should have kept your hands from, it should have been Ghislaine of Mercia."

"I plan to marry the woman."

Now, surprise was registering across Téo's face. "Marriage?" he hissed. "What madness is this?"

Gaetan tore his eyes away from Aramis and looked at Téo. "No madness, I assure you," he said. "I do not know how it happened, but somehow I have fallen in love with the woman. I have asked her to be my wife and she has agreed. Instead of judging me for it, I should think you would be happy for me."

Téo had to make a conscious effort to close his mouth. He simply couldn't believe what he was hearing and his first reaction was that it was all a whim on Gaetan's part; Gaetan was not the marrying kind. Moreover, the man had bedslaves and everybody knew it. What would Ghislaine think about whores in her husband's house? But Téo wouldn't think to disagree with his friend in that fashion, so he kept his thoughts to himself. He knew that the right woman could change a man; perhaps that was the case.

But it was a damned surprise to him.

"I *am* happy for you," he finally said. "'Tis a shock, that's all. I never thought I would hear those words from your mouth."

Gaetan nodded as if in complete understanding. "Nor did I."

Téo shook his head, chuckling as if he still couldn't believe it, and raised his cup to Gaetan. "May you know great happiness, Gate. And your mother will be thrilled."

Gaetan smiled faintly. "Aye, Lady Dacia will be consumed with joy."

"Now to tell Aramis."

Gaetan's smile fled and he looked across the table to see that Aramis was still staring at him. He set his cup down.

"There is no time like the present," he said. "I cannot have the man competing with me for a woman who will be my wife. I would have to kill him."

Téo's blood ran cold, mostly because he knew Gaetan was not speaking figuratively. He was speaking literally. He simply nodded as Gaetan stood up and went around the end of the table, heading straight for Aramis and motioning the man to follow him outside. Aramis didn't hesitate. He was on his feet and close behind Gaetan as the two of them quit the convening hall.

But Téo wasn't happy about that. He wasn't entirely sure the private discussion wouldn't come to blows and, if that happened, the men would have to be pulled a part. He knew both men well enough to know that neither one would stop until the other one was dead, so that meant it would literally be a battle to the death. With Kristoph's life on the line, they couldn't be distracted with a situation like this. They had a mission to accomplish and time was growing short. He turned to de Winter, seated on his right.

"Get Wellesbourne and St. Hèver," he muttered. "I will get the others. Gaetan has gone outside to address Aramis on a very touchy subject and if punches are thrown, then we must be there to stop anything from escalating."

De Winter glanced at him over the rim of his cup. "You mean Lady Ghislaine?"

They all knew about it. It was possibly the worst kept secret, ever. Téo simply nodded and that was enough for de Winter. He set his cup down and did as he was asked while Téo explain the situation to de Moray, de Lara, and de Reyne.

Very quickly, the seven warriors were rising from the table and heading out of the rear of the convening hall as Antillius and his men watched them with confusion. They had no idea where they could all be going, all at once, and although Antillius thought it rather odd, he didn't follow them. He assumed they'd return.

Little could he have guessed what was really going on.

"ARAMIS, WE MUST clear the air between us. Something has happened since we last spoke at Worcester about Lady Ghislaine and it is troubling me."

In the darkness, Gaetan and Aramis faced off against one another. The village was dotted with fires this night, including one that was just outside the convening hall, creating enough light to see by. Gaetan could see Aramis' hostile expression flickering in the firelight.

"Nothing has changed," Aramis said steadily. "I told you that I would not press my suit with the lady until you did it first."

Gaetan sighed heavily. "Aye, you told me that, but look at you," he said, growing agitated. "You have been glaring at me all night and I swear if you had a sword on your person right now, you'd chase me down with it. This is not how you and I have conducted our friendship, Aramis. What has changed that you should look as if you hate me so?"

Aramis' manner was stiff; it wasn't easy for the man to talk about his feelings. That made him vastly uncomfortable. But Gaetan had a point. Perhaps, it wasn't fair not to let him in on what he was thinking.

On how much he was feeling.

"I do not hate you," he said, averting his eyes for the first time. "But I will admit... I am feeling quite inferior in this quest for Lady Ghislaine. You have everything, Gate – bloodlines, land, money, reputation. I am not so bad, you know. I have amassed a reputation for myself and my father is the Count of Roeselare. My bloodlines are older than yours, dating back centuries. When my father dies, I will have the titles and wealth that you have."

"I know that."

"And I was not born a bastard as you were."

Gaetan shrugged. "That does not matter. None of that matters."

Aramis took a deep breath, fighting for calm. "Mayhap it does not," he said, "but every time I come around Lady Ghislaine, you chase me off as if I suffer a great plague. You are purposely keeping her away from me."

Gaetan nodded. "Of course I am," he said, feeling his dander rise. "Why would I not? You have given me permission to speak to her first and I cannot do that if you are always around, always trying to turn her attention away from me. Would you not do the same if the situation was reversed, Aramis? And be honest."

Aramis opened his mouth to speak but thought better of it. He was vastly frustrated. "I suppose I would do what I had to do in order to keep her for myself."

"Then why do you fault me for it?"

"Because even if she rejects your suit, she will not know me well enough to accept mine," he said heatedly. "Am I not to be given a chance in this, Gate? Or are you doing all you can to eliminate the competition?"

"Wouldn't you?"

The question hung in the air between them and Aramis, at his limits of frustration, simply turned away. "Mayhap I would," he said. "But if I knew you were going to push me out of any contact with her, I might not have agreed to back away while you pursued her."

Gaetan could see the man's annoyance but he had no pity for him. This was a competition and Gaetan had done everything in his power to ensure he emerged the winner. He'd already won, in fact, but Aramis didn't know that.

It was time he did.

"It is over, Aramis," he said softly. "It is over and I have won."

Aramis' agitated pacing came to a halt. "What do you mean?"

"I mean that she has consented to be my wife."

Aramis didn't say anything for a moment as he attempted to digest the statement. "You have asked her?"

"I have."

Like most driven men, Aramis hated to lose. He had the same competitive instinct in him that Gaetan and the others had. That was why they got along so well with one another. The understood each other. Because of that, it was extremely difficult for him to concede defeat because he'd built up this idea in his mind of Ghislaine and of a future with her, to the point where it blurred with the reality of the situation. He simply couldn't surrender.

"You never intended to give me a fair chance," he finally said. "All of that talk in Worcester about being fearful that you were not worthy of her was just talk. You were trying to make me feel pity for you and, fool that I am, I was honorable in a situation where you were not."

Gaetan didn't like having his honor questioned and most especially not by a friend. His manner stiffened. "How was I not honorable?" he fired back. "You told me I should ask the lady if she felt something for me, or have you conveniently forgotten what you said? I am not going to speak with the lady on personal matters with you hanging over her shoulder every second of the day, Aramis. I am allowed to have time alone with her."

"But what about me?"

"There *is* no 'you' in this equation. There is only Ghislaine and me, and I will marry the woman. So, if you do not gracefully accept this situation, you will be very sorry. Is this in any way unclear?"

The situation between them was becoming quite strained. It was no longer two friends having a discussion, but two men competing for the same women. In matters of that nature, only the strong would survive and Aramis wasn't about to surrender in a case where he felt he'd been wronged.

Slowly, he approached Gaetan until he was mere inches from the man; he had the height advantage by an inch or two, but Gaetan had the power advantage. He had the strength of ten men and the skill behind his sword to back it up. As the two men gazed at one another, staring down in a deadly game, Aramis was the first to blink.

"A lady can always change her mind, you know."

Gaetan's fist came up faster than Aramis could duck. The blow caught him in the chin and he went reeling backwards. It stunned him but didn't knock him off his feet. As he charged Gaetan to retaliate, the host of knights suddenly emerged from the shadows, throwing themselves in between the battling titans.

Téo, de Lara, and St. Hèver had Gaetan while Wellesbourne, de Winter, and de Moray had hold of Aramis. De Reyne stood in between the two factions, trying to keep a distance between them.

"Nay, Gate," Téo hissed. "Not over a woman. You will not destroy what you and Aramis have over a woman. Do you hear me?"

Gaetan was beyond rage at the moment. Had his men not stopped the fight, he was quite sure he would have killed Aramis. He, too, couldn't believe it had come to this but, in the case of his heart and Ghislaine, he was willing to do anything to keep her, even destroy an old and dear friend. In fact, nothing else mattered at the moment. But he was prevented from responding when distant screams began to fill the air.

Back in the village, people were screaming and running; the knights could see them in the darkness. There was panic going on and that was enough to divert the men from their anger and set their warrior instincts on edge. No one could quite see what was happening and they began to gravitate in that direction, just a little, to see what the issue was when suddenly, a woman sprinted towards them carrying an infant against her chest.

"*Homines Ossium!*" she screamed. "They have come!"

Gaetan recognized the name of the tribe in an instant. They had only been speaking of them a few minutes earlier. The Men of Bones tribe had decided tonight was the night for another raid and all he could think about was Ghislaine, in that little cottage with only a silly dog and a priest for protection. In that instant, the warrior in him took over and he made a break for the convening hall where his possessions were. Behind him, the knights were running right along with him. They were nearly to the door when Antillius and his men emerged, great concern on their faces.

"What is happening?" Antillius demanded.

"Your Men of Bones have chosen this night for a raid," Gaetan said as he burst past him, into the hall and to the corner where all of their possessions were stored. "What is your usual procedure for a raid, de Shera?"

Antillius didn't even realize Gaetan had addressed him by his new Norman name. "We must herd the women here, to this hall," he said. "That is the only way to protect them."

Gaetan shoved his helm on his head, as did the others around him, all of them grabbing broadswords and any other weapons they could get their hands on. There was a tremendous sense of urgency in the air.

"What about the raiders?" he demanded. "Will they kill the men or are they only interested in the women?"

Antillius could only think of his daughters who, he hoped, were still in the kitchen next to the hall. "They only want the women," he said. "But they will kill the men to get to them. This is our fight, Norman. You do not have to...."

Gaetan and his men were already bursting out of the hall, running for the village that was caught up in a maelstrom of panic. As Antillius armed his men and began shouting orders, Gaetan turned to his knights.

"I am going for Lady Ghislaine," he said. "Aramis, you come with me. The rest of you find all of the women you can and bring them back to the convening hall. And if one of those raiders gets in your way... you know what to do. Do not let them get the women."

The knights nodded, securing helms and gloves. Though this raid was unexpected, they were always prepared for battle. It was what they were born to do. Téo clapped Gaetan on the shoulder as he headed into the village.

"*Et pro Gloria dei*," he said.

Gaetan responded to him. "*Et pro Gloria dei*," he said, turning to the others behind him who were preparing to charge off. "For God and Glory."

His men responded, most of them touching each other's arms or hands, which was usual with them. It was a physical touch to confirm the bond of warriors, of the words they spoke. They never went into battle without doing that. As Gaetan finished securing his helm, he turned to Aramis, standing next to him.

He didn't see the man he had been ready to kill seconds earlier. He only saw his brother.

"*Et pro Gloria dei*," he murmured.

Aramis nodded, taking a balled fist and knocking it against the hilt of Gaetan's sword and, in that gesture, Gaetan knew that everything would be well between them. There was no doubt. Brothers-in-arms superseded everything else.

Together, they raced off into the darkened village, off to save the woman they both loved.

GHISLAINE WAS ENJOYING the best sleep she'd had in weeks. Years, even. Tucked up, nice and cozy, in the little alcove bed, she was deliciously snug and warm with Camulos laying up against her, providing his doggy warmth. As she slept, it was with her arm over the once-despised dog.

Her experience with Lygia, Verity, and Atia had been a pleasant one. More pleasant than she had expected. The young women had made a very hot bath in a copper tub from the water that had been steaming over the hearth and they'd stripped her of her dirty, torn clothing and put her on a stool right in the middle of the tub. Ghislaine sat stock-still as they poured the hot water over her, making sure to be very careful with her bandaged leg, before proceeding to scrub every inch of her skin.

Ghislaine wasn't used to being treated to a bath. In fact, her baths were usually quick events, certainly not something that anyone helped her with, so to have three young women make such a ritual out of it had been very odd for her, indeed.

Sitting upon the stool, Ghislaine submitted to their scrubbing with horsehair brushes and soap that smelled of violets. Her hair was washed with flat ale and scrubbed with a bit of the soap as well. She felt she was being buffeted by powerful winds as she was subjected to the brisk scrubbing and rinsing, drying and oiling, until she was sure several layers of skin had been removed. But the truth was that it felt wonderful and, for the first time in her life, she enjoyed her sweet-smelling bath.

Perhaps there was something to this bathing ritual, after all.

After drying and brushing and braiding her damp hair, she was put into a long soft tunic with a round neck and long sleeves. Atop the tunic, the women put yet another tunic on, this one shorter so that the longer tunic beneath showed through. The bottom tunic was white while the tunic on the top was a pretty blue shade. It was even embroidered around the neck in white thread. The top tunic also had laces on the side to make it fit the wearer, so two of the women made sure the tunic fit her shapely body before piling yet one more tunic on top of her, which was more like a cloak with a soft fur lining. Ghislaine was thrilled with it. Little doe-skin slippers were placed on her feet simply to keep them warm.

Brushed, washed, combed, braided, and finally dressed, Ghislaine was helped to the bed and tucked in by the three women who then excused themselves to allow her to sleep. Ghislaine was very grateful to them.

Odd how such a simple thing as bathing made Ghislaine feel happy and content. She might even come to like such a thing. Perhaps after she and Gaetan were married, he might allow her a servant or two to help her bathe like that every single week. Maybe even every day. Her world had always been one of warfare and politics, but in that gentle hour, it took three strange women to show her what a woman was supposed to be like. She could only imagine what Gaetan would think, seeing her cleaned up for the first time and not looking like a forest urchin.

He might even like it, too.

It was to thoughts of dear Gaetan that she fell into a heavy sleep, hardly even stirring when the dog jumped onto the bed and lay down beside her. But her sleep became dreamless and heavy, until the sounds of screams began to reach into her subconscious. Even then, she didn't awaken until Camulos, alerted by the sounds, jumped off the bed and sat by the door, whining. Soon enough, someone was shaking her awake.

"My lady?" It was Jathan. "My lady, awaken!"

Ghislaine forced her eyes open but it was difficult. She could see Gaetan's priest hanging over the bed. He'd been outside the door, guarding it, but now he was inside. She was about to ask him what the matter was when another scream, this one nearby, had her sitting bolt-up right. She looked at Jathan with wide eyes.

"What is happening?" she demanded.

Jathan shook his head. "I do not know, my lady," he said, "but I am going to come inside and bolt the door. We should remain here for safety."

Ghislaine quickly nodded and Jathan pulled the heavy oaken door shut, throwing a heavy wooden bolt. The hut didn't have any windows but slits up around the top of the walls where they met the stone roof to allow for light and the ventilation of the smoke from the cooking fire. There really wasn't any way for them to know what was going on but the advantage was that it also kept them very safe, like a prison cell.

The sounds of screaming were becoming more frantic outside. They could also hear what sounded like roaring or growling of some kind. There were men speaking in a language Ghislaine couldn't quite make out. She looked at Jathan with a good deal of apprehension, hearing the sounds of a struggle going on outside.

Then there were sounds of splashing and men laughing. Ghislaine swung her legs over the side of the bed, laboring with her sore right thigh.

"I wish I had my dagger," she hissed. "I do not have a weapon at all!"

Jathan put his finger up to his lips to silence her as he reached into the belt around his waist and handed her a fairly large dagger. It was heavy and sharp, and Ghislaine felt much better with it in her hand. But she remained silent as they listened to the screaming going on outside. It was terrifying.

Suddenly, there was a great pounding at the door. Ghislaine jumped but Jathan remained calm. He had his sword leveled, prepared to defend the lady with his life, but then the pounding came again and someone was shouting his name.

"Jathan! Open this door!"

It was Gaetan. Jathan threw the bolt on the door and it burst open, nearly knocking him down. Gaetan and Aramis were in the doorway and Gaetan grabbed Ghislaine without a word, picking her up and thrusting her at Aramis, who literally dropped his sword in order to catch her. Ghislaine's dagger fell to the floor but Gaetan ignored it; he picked up the fallen sword and handed it to her instead. His expression was serious but calm.

"There are raiders in camp," he told her quickly. "They have come for the women and we must get you to safety. Can you use this sword?"

Ghislaine looked at Aramis' big broadsword, now in her hand. "Aye, I can."

Gaetan nodded swiftly. "That's a good little mouse," he said, a hint of affection in his tone. But he turned serious again in a flash. "Aramis will be your legs but you must be his sword. I will be your shield. Come now; follow me."

Together, the four of them plus the dog left the hut, out into the chaotic night where people were still screaming and running as phantoms chased them through the shadows. As they neared the end of the row of cottages that fronted the pond, a big man wearing bones all around his neck and chest jumped out and bellowed, lifting a massive club with spiked ends. Gaetan kicked the man in the gut and when he doubled over, he sliced his head clean from his body. As the head went rolling, the group continued running.

Ghislaine had to admit that she was terrified. She'd been in plenty of battles, that was true, but she'd been able-bodied and able to protect herself and fight. Now, she couldn't walk or run, and she was at a distinct disadvantage. She watched Gaetan deftly kill two more men who had charged at them and even Jathan managed to badly wound a man who had tried to club him in the head.

As they neared the kitchens that serviced the convening hall, they saw Antillius and two of his men fighting against at least four men wearing bones around their necks. One of the men had Lygia by the arm, yanking at her, as her father tried to hold on to her. Ghislaine pointed to them in a panic.

"Gaetan!" she gasped. "That is Lygia! You must help her!"

Before Gaetan could move, Aramis put Ghislaine on her feet and took his sword from her. "Nay," he said. "Gate, you take your lady to safety. I will handle these fools."

Gaetan didn't argue with him. He picked Ghislaine up again and, with Jathan running in front of them to protect their path, carried Ghislaine all the way to the convening hall where he had to beat on the door before someone opened it. Once inside the door, he set Ghislaine on her feet as Jathan and the excited dog came in after him.

"You and Jathan will guard the door," Gaetan told Ghislaine, handing her a dagger from his waist. "If anyone comes through that door that is not an ally, kill them."

Ghislaine nodded firmly. "I will, I swear it. I will not let anyone pass that is not a friend."

Gently touching her cheek in a sweet gesture, it was all Gaetan could manage before charging back out into the night to help Aramis and Antillius. Ghislaine shut the door and bolted it, looking at Jathan to see that the entire event had the priest fairly rattled. But he held his sword tightly, preparing to kill just as Gaetan had ordered. He was, after all, a trained warrior even if those duties were something he struggled with.

Now that they had reached relative safety, there was an odd stillness to it all that was unnerving. Outside, people were fighting for their lives while inside, the frightened and injured huddled. Soft weeping drew their attention and they looked around to see that the convening hall was half-full of women and children, all of them shaken and terrified.

"I will watch the door," Ghislaine told Jathan. "Mayhap you should pray with these women and comfort them."

Jathan shook his head. "If Gaetan discovers I have left my post, *I* will be the one needing prayers."

Ghislaine grinned at the man but she understood. "Very well," she said. "When things settle down, mayhap your prayers would be welcome then."

Jathan could still hear the sounds of the struggle outside. Battle, to him, never became any easier. It was all death and mayhem as far as he was concerned.

"I think I shall pray now," he said.

"I think that is a good idea."

He did.

CHAPTER TWENTY-THREE

cg

THE SLEEP OF THE DEAD

H E'D PICKED UP the pace, Kristoph was sure, because of him.
Ever since the fight outside of Warwick that had left two men
dead and another wounded, Alary had been keeping his distance from
Kristoph as they headed north at an increased pace, but certain things
had changed. Now, Kristoph found himself chained in the bed of the
provisions wagon, secured more tightly than he'd ever been before and,
since the death of Mostig, he hadn't been fed with any regularity which,
he suspected, was part of the plan. A prisoner weakened with hunger
was less likely to fight back.

But not Kristoph. He was still prepared to fight back and escape, no
matter what they tried to do to him.

Still, he had to admit that the hunger was drawing him down. He'd
last eaten yesterday morning, a bit of cold and probably rank fatty beef
that had been thrown at him. He'd sucked it down, fat and all. Anything to drink had come from the rain that had fallen off and on for the
past few days but it hadn't quenched his thirst much. It had only
prevented him from becoming completely parched.

His misery had a name these days and that name was Alary of Mercia. The first thing Kristoph planned to do when he was free was kill the

man. For every offense against him, Kristoph was going to make Alary pay many times over. Rather than thoughts of his wife and daughter keeping him alive, now thoughts of killing his captor were feeding that sense of survival.

It was something that Alary surely sensed these days if he didn't outright know it. A madman at times, he wasn't stupid. As the wagon bumped down the road on this morning that blended in to the many mornings before this as they traveled north from Harold Godwinson's defeat, Kristoph thought on his situation, on the man holding him hostage, and on what was waiting for him at the end of this road. The men were hurrying more than ever to reach Tenebris. Kristoph knew he had to escape before they reached it.

It was either that or die.

Somewhere near the nooning hour, the skies cleared and the sun came out, drying up the wet ground as well as a wet Kristoph. He'd had no protection from the rain. The wagon came to a halt at some point and the men around him began to break out rations of biscuits and wine. Kristoph was starving but he knew they wouldn't give him anything so he didn't ask; he simply looked away, trying to look anywhere that men weren't eating and drinking. Inside, his gut gnawed away painfully.

"Norman."

That was what they called him these days. *Norman.* He didn't even have a name to these people. Kristoph turned to see one of Alary's henchmen standing beside the wagon, coming in his direction. Kristoph knew the man; he was the one who had survived the fight in Warwick, although he was still showing signs of the beating Kristoph had given him. His left eye was still bruised and he was missing two front teeth. Kristoph braced himself because whenever this man was near, bad things happened. He continued to watch the man as he came closer.

"If I unchain your arms to allow you to eat, will you swear upon your oath not to fight?" the man asked, standing out of arm's length.

Kristoph's hunger was stronger than his will to resist at the moment. He nodded shortly. "I swear."

"If you break this promise, you will spend the rest of your life in chains. No one will help you."

Kristoph simply looked at the man, his blue eyes circled with malnutrition and fatigue. "I told you that I would not. I may be many things, but a liar is not among them."

The henchman hesitated for a moment before he motioned several men behind him. In a group, Alary's soldiers moved forward to both watch over Kristoph and unfasten his chains. As a result of his poor treatment and the heavy shackles, both of Kristoph's wrists and ankles were heavily chaffed and bruised. The skin was so very painful to the touch. As one of the soldier's removed the binds around his wrists while another handed him a big loaf of dirty brown bread, Alary suddenly appeared at the end of the wagon.

Kristoph saw him and he paused a moment before taking a massive bite of the bread. There was grit in it, and sawdust he thought, but it didn't matter. He was starving. As he ignored Alary and accepted a bladder of cheap wine to wash down the bread, Alary came around the side of the wagon bed.

Now, he was closer and Kristoph could no longer ignore the man. He was eating as fast as he could, fearful that Alary would grow enraged over something, anything at all, and take his food away, so he was determined to eat it as fast as he could. As he swallowed a massive bite and washed it down with the terrible wine, Alary spoke.

"I see you have recovered from killing my man back in Warwick," he said. "But you did not kill Emred. Did you recognize him?"

He was gesturing to the henchman. Kristoph knew the man by sight but not by name. Returning to his bread, he nodded. "I recognized him."

Alary watched him eat the bread like a lion devouring its prey. It was rather exciting to watch; it gave Alary a sense of power knowing he could starve this man so. Perhaps he couldn't physically defeat him, and mentally he hadn't been able to break him, but he could starve him. He could cause the man to eat as if he'd never eaten in his life. To Alary, that was a small victory.

"I have a need to speak with you, Norman," he finally said. "There are things you should know."

Kristoph was hesitant to ask the obvious question. He knew Alary was expecting him to. Therefore, he would not. "Oh?" he said.

He didn't seem concerned, which caused Alary to smile thinly. "We are nearing Kidderminster," he said. "By late tomorrow, we shall be at my fortress of Tenebris."

Kristoph had suspected they were drawing near the end of this journey simply because of the increased pace of travel. "I see," he said. "And once we reach there, then what?"

Alary leaned on the edge of the wagon. "I will not release you if that is what you are asking," he said. "I still consider you something of value even though you've yet to provide me with any real worth."

"Then why keep me?"

Alary shrugged. "I have told you why," he said. "If I keep you, the Normans are less likely to force me to their will. News travels fast. I heard last night whilst we supped in the small town of Redditch that the Normans were marching on London. Everyone is fleeing north to get away from them and I know that, sooner or later, they will come north. When they do, you will be my assurance that they will leave me in peace."

Kristoph was near the end of his bread so he wasn't hesitant to speak his mind at this point. "I told you that it would not matter. They will come and they will take your fortress whether or not I am your prisoner. Do you honestly believe they would allow one knight to divert their plans of conquest?"

Alary didn't like that answer. "You seem to have little faith in your worth."

Kristoph was becoming annoyed. "That is because I have no worth in the grand scheme of things," he snapped. "Did you really think

William of Normandy would bow down to your pathetic plans? By all that is holy, if you are going to kill me, then kill me. If you are going to fight me, then fight me. I have never seen such a foolish excuse for a man in my entire life, so if you are going to do something to me, then get on with it. I grow weary of your idiocy."

Alary wasn't used to being spoken to like that. In a fit of fury, he reached out and slapped Kristoph across the face. It was hardly a blow and Kristoph's head didn't even move from the force of it, but the sharp sound reverberated.

"I hold your life in my hands and you speak to me in such ways?" he hissed. "You are stupid, Norman. Stupid!"

Kristoph was hoping to provoke the man into unchaining him just so they could have a fair fight. At least if he was free, he would have a chance of survival. He wouldn't fight; he would run, and they wouldn't be prepared for it.

Challenge him!

"Mayhap," he said, "but you are afraid of me."

"How dare you say that!"

"Then why do you keep me chained?"

"Because you are my prisoner!"

Kristoph cocked a smug eyebrow. "Because you are afraid of what I will do if you remove these chains. That makes you a coward. Remove these restraints and prove to me that I am wrong."

Alary was so angry that his face was turning red. He landed a few more slaps on Kristoph's face.

"I do not chain you because I am afraid of you," Alary snarled. "I chain you because you are an animal and deserve to be chained. When we reach Tenebris, I am going to throw you in the vault and let you rot there!"

That wasn't exactly what Kristoph had in mind but he took heart in the fact that in order to move him to the vault, they would have to unchain him from this wagon bed. Moving under his own power meant he still had a chance to run, a chance to escape Alary to freedom. It was a chance he was willing to take because he knew that once he entered the vault, the odds of him leaving alive were stacked against him.

"We shall see," was all he said.

Enraged, Alary ordered him chained up again as the man headed back to his horse. He wanted to make it to Kidderminster by nightfall so that the following day, it would be a short trip to Tenebris where he would lock himself in. Kristoph knew this because he could hear Alary shouting to his men, declaring that there was no army in the world that could breach his walls.

They were the ravings of a madman.

As the wagon lurched forward to continue their journey, Kristoph found himself looking at the landscape, wondering where Gaetan and his brothers were but knowing in his heart that they were out there somewhere. He hoped they made their move soon, wherever they were, because once he was inside the walls of Tenebris, it would make his rescue considerably more difficult. If he couldn't escape before they were able to help him, then the situation would be dire, indeed.

If you are going to make your move, Gate, now is the time!

"YOUR ASSISTANCE AGAINST the Men of Bones was appreciated more than you can know," Antillius said. "You and your men are, indeed, great warriors."

It was early morning in the village of the *Tertium* as Antillius and Gaetan stood near one of the big outdoor fire pits where men were warming their morning meal or simply warming their bones. It had rained off and on most of the night, even after the *Homines Ossium* had been repelled, and only now were people awakening to assess the damage left by the raiders.

Gaetan had only gotten a few hours of sleep himself, staying awake until just a few hours before dawn to patrol the village and ensure that the raiders wouldn't return. Ghislaine had been moved back to her hut with Jathan to stand guard over her while Aramis had remained with Antillius' daughters because the trio seemed to have been targeted by the raiders. But the rest of Gaetan's men had patrolled the village as Gaetan did, well into the night.

This morning, the outlook was a little brighter and the damage seemingly minimal. Gaetan had just finished off a massive slab of bread slathered with the pork and wine sauce from the previous night, but he had steered clear of the "mad Mercian beer", as he called it. He had consumed the apple drink, sweet as it was, but at least it didn't make his head swim. Belly full, Gaetan now stood with Antillius, listening to the man's praise.

"We were happy to help," he replied to Antillius' statement. "You said last night that the Men of Bones raid frequently. Are there usually so many?"

Antillius nodded. "There can be," he said. "We have guards on the perimeter of our village but when the *Homines Ossium* attack, I have told them not to engage but to warn us quickly. I am afraid if they engage, they will be killed and we shall have no warning. I should not like to lose men that way. Our numbers are too few."

Gaetan understood that. "Do you have dogs?"

Antillius nodded. "A few," he said. "I saw the big dog that you have. A magnificent beast. If we had animals such as that, we would surely scare away our enemies."

Gaetan grinned. "I will tell you a secret about that dog," he said. "The only battle he is capable of is one with his tongue to your face. He will lick you until you surrender."

Antillius laughed. "He is big enough that he does not need to be fearsome," he said. "Based on his size alone, he would scare men away. You would not want to leave him with me while you went on your mission, would you? We have a few female dogs and I would love to have a few litters of pups from your beast. Mayhap more of the new blood I was speaking of last night. Even our female dogs must be given new blood if they are to survive."

Gaetan could sense the desperation in the man trying to keep his way of life from dying out. "If you promise to give me my dog back when I return from reclaiming my comrade, then I will leave him with you," he said. "But treat him well. I am quite fond of him."

Antillius was thrilled. "I will give him his own cottage and all of the female dogs he can muster the strength to mate with," he said. "He will be well taken care of until you return for him. But you… there is nothing I can do to repay you enough for what you and your men did for us last night. Usually, we lose a woman or two during those raids. That has been difficult for us to bear. But last night, when they were attempting to steal my Lygia…."

He trailed off, sickened by the idea that one of those barbarians might have captured his beloved eldest daughter. Gaetan could see the sorrow in the man's face.

"Aramis is more fearsome than any bone warrior, I assure you," he said quietly. "There was no way they could have taken Lygia from him."

Antillius nodded. "I know that now," he said. "I saw the man in action. But men such as you do not do such things from the goodness of your heart. You do it because it needs to be done, because it is your calling. But you do not do it without an expectation of a reward. You must be rewarded."

Gaetan shook his head "You rewarded us with tending Lady Ghislaine's wound, and with food and drink and shelter," he said. "What we did last night was to repay you for your hospitality."

Antillius turned to him, looking him fully in the face. "But your sword is worth more than food or healing a wounded woman," he said. "De Wolfe, I will give you and two men of your choosing my daughters as wives. Now, please hear me before you refuse – I am not asking you to remain here with them, for you are men of the world and you would not be happy spending your lives in our little village. But I do ask that you marry my daughters and beget them with child. Then you may leave and not give them another thought. All I ask is that you give my daughters your sons to bear. My people are dying, de Wolfe. You know that. We need strong warriors from your loins if we are going to survive."

Frankly, Gaetan was a little shocked at the offer but, in the same breath, he realized it was made from desperation. Antillius was a proud man with a proud heritage, so offering his daughters to strange men to essentially be broodmares must have been a humiliating experience. Therefore, he tried to be very gracious in his refusal.

"That is a most attractive offer," he said. "Your daughters are beautiful women."

Antillius nodded. "Their mother was very beautiful. They are also very smart and accomplished. They can speak several languages and each one knows how to run a house and hold. If your men marry them, I suppose they will want to take them away although I hope they will not. But that is the chance I am willing to take. They are the only things of value I have to offer you as a reward for fighting off the *Homines Ossium*, de Wolfe. Please consider it."

Gaetan was quite torn. He didn't want to insult this man who had helped them tremendously. But he certainly couldn't ask his men to marry the man's daughters just to do him a favor. It sounded as if he wanted strong half-Norman grandsons more than he actually wanted his daughters to become Norman wives.

"Truly, I have never known such generosity," he said. "And I am honored. But I am already pledged to marry and half of my men have wives, so I am not sure if those who are not married are ready and willing to take a wife, regardless of how beautiful and accomplished she is."

Antillius was embarrassed that he had practically been begging Gaetan and his men to marry his daughters. Somewhat dejected, he scratched his head and turned away.

"I understand," he said. "It is difficult for a fighting man to take a wife. But... forgive me for saying this... if your men do not wish to marry, I would not be upset if, in a month or two, one or more of my daughters discovered she was pregnant."

Gaetan was genuinely surprised. "Without a husband?"

"Without a husband."

It was a solemn suggestion. Truth be told, a month ago, Gaetan might have considered taking him up on his offer simply because his sexual appetite could be insatiable. Bedding one woman was as good as the next and if she became with child, that did not concern him. It never had. But Ghislaine had changed all of that. He couldn't even imagine touching another woman now, a very radical departure from the man before he met Ghislaine.

But he knew how desperate Antillius was to save his dying tribe. Only a despairing man would make such an offer.

"How do your daughters feel about such a thing?" he asked, somewhat gently. "To be bedded by a man, a stranger, and to hope for a child with no hope of a husband... surely that cannot be a pleasant thought to them."

Antillius shrugged. "They will do as I ask," he said. "If they do not bear children, even without a husband, then I fear their generation will be the last. We will die."

Gaetan could see his point. This was purely for survival and there was a part of him that respected that. Reluctantly, he sighed. "I will ask my unmarried knights if any of them wish to take you up on your offer," he said. "I cannot promise anything, but I will ask."

Antillius nodded, feeling increasingly ashamed with what he'd proposed. But he didn't regret it. If the *Tertium* were to survive, it was necessary.

"Thank you," he said. "Now, you will excuse me. I have duties to attend to."

Gaetan watched the man go, feeling a great deal of pity for him. As he continued to stand by the fire, his thoughts turned towards Ghislaine and wondered if she had awoken yet. He was anxious to see her, anxious to start a new day with her as part of his future. As he contemplating making the trek over to her little cottage, he caught sight of de Reyne, de Moray, and St. Hèver coming out of the convening hall where they'd tried to sleep for a few hours after patrolling most of the night. Spying Gaetan, they headed in his direction.

As those three approached, Téo, de Winter, and Wellesbourne emerged from the village. They'd kept patrolling even after the others went to bed and now, with daylight upon them, they were heading back to perhaps sleep for an hour or two after a very long night. Aramis was missing but Gaetan knew it was because the man was still with Antillius' daughters. He watched as his men came upon the fire, some of them yawning from too little sleep, some yawning from no sleep at all. It was an exhausted bunch.

"Well," Gaetan said. "I would assume everyone survived last night intact?"

The men nodded their heads to varying degrees. "At least we know now some of the indigenous people we will be facing in this forsaken country," de Moray muttered. "I am going to have to write to my father and tell him about those bone-men. It was like fighting demons straight out of hell; most frightening."

The others had to agree. "I fought one man who had an entire skull on top of his club, the teeth filed to sharp points," St. Hèver said. "The jaw was open and he kept trying to swing those teeth right at my head. That was rather traumatizing."

Coming from the man known as "The Hammer", that was saying something. De Reyne grinned at him. "Did you run from him or did you fight?"

Kye cocked his head. "I thought about running at first, but I knew he would chase me and it would not do for a man of my stature to be seen running from an enemy, so I stood my ground and gored him in the chest. In fact, I want to find that club. I will use it against our enemies and see if I cannot frighten them into surrendering with that thing."

The knights chuckled at the thought. "There mere sight of you frightens them in any case," Téo said, his gaze moving to Gaetan. "And speaking of enemies, when will we continue on to Tenebris? I am increasingly concerned that Alary and Kristoph will make it there before we will now that we have been delayed."

Gaetan nodded reluctantly. "I was thinking on that this morning," he said. "In fact, I was just going to see how Lady Ghislaine was faring, to see if she would be able to travel in the next few days."

The knights began to look at each other, glancing at one another as if there was something on their minds but they were afraid to speak it. Considering what had happened last night between Gaetan and Aramis, they knew that the lady was a very sensitive subject with Gaetan and no one wanted to be on the receiving end of a beating for speaking his mind.

But Téo wasn't afraid of that. He said what they were all thinking because it was something that needed to be addressed.

"It was forcing the lady to travel with her bad leg that caused us to end up here, Gate," he said quietly. "The lady should not be moved until her leg can heal and we cannot wait here while it does. We are close enough to Tenebris that we can continue on without her. And we should."

Gaetan looked at him. "After all she has sacrificed for us? I am surprised you would suggest such a thing."

Téo stood his ground. "What happened to the man who wanted to reach Tenebris before Alary did?" he asked, hoping Gaetan would realize there were more pressing things happening than the lady he was besotted with. "Based upon what the lady told us of her brother's lair, we decided that our only chance to save Kristoph would be to intercept them before they could reach Tenebris. We are in a prime position to do that. Would you now risk Kristoph's life for well-meaning loyalty you feel towards Lady Ghislaine?"

Gaetan's manner began to stiffen. "It is more than well-meaning loyalty and you know it."

Téo nodded patiently. "Aye, I do," he said. "I am not trying to diminish that. But we must get Kristoph before Alary takes him behind the walls of Tenebris. Gate, we can always return for the lady. Just because we leave her to go and save Kristoph does not mean we will not come back for her."

Téo was the voice of reason in all things so Gaetan had no reason not to trust him. But then he started looking around at his men and saw that they all had similar expressions on their faces; they were fully in support of what Téo was saying. He was coming to feel as if they were turning against him.

"You, too, Kye?" he asked St. Hèver. "Do you feel this way? Do you *all* feel this way?"

The subject of Gaetan's focus, Kye was very careful in his answer. "Gate, we know you feel something for the lady," he said, a man of forthrightness. "We understand you do not wish to leave her behind but, in doing so, you are jeopardizing Kristoph's life. Téo is correct – we can always come back for her. But our mission to reach Kristoph should not be dependent upon whether or not the lady is able to travel. I believe I speak for all of us when I say that we will leave this morning to continue on our mission. If you wish to go with us, all the better. But if you do not, we are going anyway."

Gaetan could see that they meant no disrespect. His men would never do that to him. But he was also coming to see that he'd been a bit of a fool when it came to Ghislaine. He had promised not to leave her behind and he swore not to break that promise to her, which had been a foolish promise in hindsight. This entire mission north had been to rescue Kristoph and now that he was in love with Ghislaine, his focus had shifted from his friend and brother-in-law to a love he'd never expected to know.

He was starting to feel very, very foolish for not seeing any of this sooner. With a heavy sigh, he was coming to understand that it was quite possible his men were right and he, in this case, might be wrong.

Had his focus really changed so much?

"I never meant to jeopardize Kristoph," he said quietly. "I hope you know that. But I suppose I felt that this mission was Ghislaine's as much as it was ours because it was her brother who abducted him. And the situation is more complex that you know. I feel enough for Lady Ghislaine that I have asked her to be my wife and she has agreed. If that is foolish, then I suppose I am a fool. All I can tell you is that she has changed my perspective on life tremendously. I never thought I would take a wife much less one I adored."

It was a difficult confession for him to make; they all knew that. Téo put a comforting hand on Gaetan's shoulder to let him know that his men respected him for his confession as the other men offered their sincere congratulations.

"It wasn't as if we couldn't guess this was coming," de Lara said with a twinkle in his eye. "If I'd been smart, I would have bet how soon you would have asked her to be your bride and taken bets from the others. I could have made a fortune."

The others grinned at him. Even Gaetan grinned, embarrassed now. "Then you can guess that is what Aramis and I were fighting over last night," he said. "I have never kept secrets from you and I am sorry if you felt I have not been forthcoming about this. But in truth, I wasn't even sure what was happening. It was hard to voice it."

De Lara clapped him on the arm. "No need to apologize," he said. "We have all had our time with women. Now, it is your time."

Gaetan was feeling a bit better, glad his men weren't making him feel as if he'd done something wrong. In fact, they were most supportive and with that support, Gaetan was starting to think a bit more clearly. He was able to see where his judgment had been a bit clouded as of late.

"You are absolutely right about Kristoph and the importance of intercepting Alary before he can reach Tenebris," he said to Kye, to the rest of them. "I agree that we should leave this morning regardless of how the lady feels. She needs to rest if her leg is to heal properly, and we have a date with her brother. That being said, gather your possessions and prepare your horses. As soon as I bid the lady a farewell and thank our host for his hospitality, we shall depart."

The men were feeling much better about the situation now that everything was out in the open. Gaetan was seeing reason and Kristoph was as good as rescued. But as they turned away to go about their business, Gaetan stopped them.

"There is something you should know in case Antillius mentions it to any one of you," he said, looking rather hesitant. "As a reward for fighting off the Men of Bones, Antillius has offered his daughters as brides to any of you who feel you may wish to accept. I told him that I would present that to you. I also told him that I would tell you that even if you do not want to marry the women, he has given you permission to bed them. Antillius is convinced that he wants strong half-Norman sons from his daughters, whether or not you are agreeable to marriage. He is a desperate man, desperate to preserve his tribe, so take the offer for what it is worth – if you wish to leave your mark upon this tribe, Antillius invites you to do so."

It was a rather shocking offer, reflected in their faces. Even Gaetan lifted his eyebrows to suggest he agreed with that shocking reaction. They'd been rewarded many times in the course of their careers, but never with something like this. They all started looking at each other to see if any one of them was going to accept the offer to impregnate one of Antillius' daughters. Téo, a married man, was looking at the unmarried ones – de Moray, St. Hèver, and de Lara who, when they realized that everyone was looking at them, waved their hands and backed away because they didn't want to be roped into a stud service.

As the knights were wrestling with the unusual proposition, Aramis appeared with two of Antillius' three daughters beside him, heading towards the convening house. There was some laughter because the girls were giggling as Aramis, a man who hardly cracked a smile, seemed to be verging on it.

Shocked at the vision before them, those who were departing came to a halt to scrutinize the women they'd only seen in the dark last night for the most part. They were very pretty women, the two younger ones, and, suddenly, de Moray, St. Hèver, and de Lara weren't so eager to run away. Lovely women had their attention. But Gaetan snapped his fingers at them.

"*After* we return from our mission," he reminded them. "Remember? Any delay could cost Kristoph."

It was a rather sarcastic reminder considering they had all but ganged up against him to impress upon him the seriousness of not waiting for Lady Ghislaine's recovery to continue with their mission. Rebuked, the knights turned around again to continue on their way as Gaetan continued to watch the approach of Aramis and the women. He leaned in to Téo.

"Is it possible that Aramis actually looks pleased?" he muttered. "I have not seen that expression on him since… well, I cannot remember."

Téo was watching as well. "If you are thinking he has forgotten all about Lady Ghislaine, then it is wishful thinking. Aramis would not forget something like that so quickly."

Gaetan was forced to agree. Aramis didn't have a fickle mind and, therefore, wouldn't transfer his affections so easily. Téo had been correct – it *had* been wishful thinking on his part. Well, one could hope, couldn't one? Clearing his throat softly, he excused himself.

"I must go and say my farewells to Ghislaine," he said. "You will tell Aramis that we depart within the hour."

A word from Téo stopped him. "Gate," he said. "It is merely a suggestion, of course, but why not leave Jathan here with the lady? He can act as her protector as well as provide her with company. You may feel better about leaving her behind if you do. And he can prevent her from trying to follow us."

Gaetan scratched his head thoughtfully. "An excellent suggestion," he said. "Although I doubt Jathan could stand up to the formidable Lady Ghislaine should she try to follow us, I will leave him with her just the same."

Leaving Téo to inform Aramis of their coming departure, Gaetan headed down through the neat stone village, inspecting it as he went along and seeing that there was, indeed, minimal damage from the raid last night. In fact, it looked as if there had been absolutely nothing amiss only hours earlier. There were women in front of their cottages, sweeping their stoops, who smiled timidly at him as he passed. Even children, playing on the avenue, came to a halt as he walked by. But one little girl, perhaps four years of age, began following him. Gaetan didn't notice her until she ran up beside him and tugged on his tunic.

Curious, he came to a halt when he saw the child. Unfortunately, he'd never been very good with children and he wasn't sure if he should speak to her or just keep walking. Not to be rude in front of all of the people who were watching him, he bent down to be more at the child's level.

"Can I be of service, my lady?"

The little girl looked at him with her enormous brown eyes, bringing up a dirty finger to point at a missing front tooth. Gaetan peered at it.

"Did you lose your tooth?"

The little girl nodded and another child, a boy of about seven or eight, ran up behind her and began to pull her away from the big knight.

"She lost it last night when she was running away from the Men of Bones," the boy said, his speech that odd mix of Latin and Saxon just like everyone else in the village. "She wanted to show you."

Gaetan fought off a grin. "That is a terrible casualty," he said. "I am sorry we could not prevent it."

The boy looked him up and down, an expression on his face suggesting he rather liked what he saw. He was used to the men around him, sometimes weak or colorless, or both, but this enormous knight in mail and leather in his midst was an example of what men could grow in to. Perhaps that was what he wanted to grow in to, someday.

"You fought with swords," the boy finally said. "I saw you."

Gaetan nodded. "We did, indeed."

"Will you teach me to fight with your big sword?"

Gaetan did smile, then; he couldn't help it. He rather liked young eager boys, willing to learn, willing to fight. But he had tasks to attend to and time was growing short, so he simply nodded his head.

"Mayhap I will, someday," he said. "In the meantime, learn to fight with the smaller blades that your men use. Understand how to use that blade before you use a bigger one. When it comes time for that, I will teach you."

The child simply grinned, brightly, and Gaetan went along his way. It was a rather nice village, he thought, peaceful when it wasn't being attacked by bone-wearing barbarians. He was starting to see why these people protected their way of life so fiercely – it was worth protecting.

Coming around the corner that led to the row of cottages where Ghislaine's hut was situated, he saw the women at the pond, washing their clothes in the early morning. As he walked by the pond, every lady turned to look at him. He felt rather on display.

Approaching Ghislaine's cottage at the end of the row, he could see Jathan sitting out in front of it, cleaning his weapon. Drawing nearer, the door of the cottage suddenly opened and Lygia appeared, closing the door very quietly behind her. She and Jathan caught sight of Gaetan at about the same time, and Jathan set his sword aside.

"Good morn to you, Gaetan," Jathan said. "'Tis a fine day."

Gaetan acknowledged the priest. "I have come to see the lady," he said. "Is she awake?"

It was Lygia who spoke. "She is not, my lord," she replied. "Her leg was paining her a great deal after she returned to her cottage last night and old Pullum gave her a potion to make her sleep. I am afraid the lady is dead to the world right now."

Gaetan was disappointed. "I see," he said. "I do not wish to wake her, but I wanted to tell her that my men and I are leaving this morning. We must finish our task and we cannot wait until her leg heals, but I wanted to reassure her that we will return for her. *I* will return for her."

"I can tell her, my lord," Lygia said. "Even if you tried to wake her now, she probably would not remember the conversation. Pullum's potions are powerful."

Gaetan was growing more disappointed by the moment. He was hoping for a sweet word and a tender kiss with Ghislaine. But as he pondered his disappointment, he noticed that Jathan had stood up and was gathering his things around him, preparing to depart with the rest of the knights.

"Nay, Jathan," Gaetan said. "You are not going. You will remain with the lady as her protector and companion until I return."

Jathan, too, now had the look of disappointment. "But… you may need me, Gate."

Gaetan shook his head. "I realize that, but it is more important to me that you remain with Ghislaine." He could see that Jathan didn't understand, so he sought to clear up the man's confusion. "It is far more important for her to remain here so that her leg may heal. Moreover, I am giving you a very important task of protecting my future wife. Will you do this for me?"

Jathan's eyes widened. "Wife?"

A glimmer of a smile appeared on Gaetan's lips. "Aye," he said. "I know it is shocking, but believe me when I tell you it is the truth. The lady and I intend to wed, so it is very important to me that you remain with her while I go to retrieve Kristoph. Please, Jathan… will you do this?"

Jathan still wasn't over his shock that Gaetan and Ghislaine were to be married, but he nodded. "Indeed," he said. "If you wish it."

"I do," Gaetan said. Then, he looked to Lygia. "I would thank you for the great care you have taken of Lady Ghislaine and for the great care you will continue to give her while I am away. Please assure her that I will return as soon as I can. And I am leaving the dog here as well. I am assuming he is in the cottage with her?"

Lygia nodded. "Passed out like a drunkard on the bed next to her, my lord."

Gaetan's grin spread. "That sounds like my dog," he said. Then, he looked at the door of the cottage. "May I take a look at her before I go? I promise I will not wake her."

Lygia nodded and very quietly opened the door, allowing Gaetan to stick his head inside. He immediately spied Ghislaine over on the cozy bed, sleeping so heavily that she was snoring. His gaze upon her was warm, wishing with all his heart that he could speak to her before he left, but it was not meant to be. He hoped she understood. It only made him want to return to her that much faster.

With a sigh, he backed out of the cottage and carefully closed the door behind him.

"It is good that she is sleeping," he said. "She needs to rest. Jathan, I will take my leave of you here. Make sure she knows I will return."

Jathan was well aware of the determination of Lady Ghislaine. "And if she tries to follow?"

Gaetan turned to look at him. "Tie her to the bed if you have to. Do not let her come after me. That is a command."

Jathan nodded his head, watching Gaetan head back in the direction he had come. He wasn't particularly thrilled at being left behind when the rest of the knights were going to rescue Kristoph but, in a sense, he understood. Someone had to stay behind to protect Lady Ghislaine and he was the logical choice.

But he wasn't happy about it.

As Jathan wrestled with his disappointment, Lygia was watching Gaetan until he disappeared from view. Then, she turned to Jathan.

"Would she really try to follow them?" she asked.

Jathan picked up his cleaning rag and resumed cleaning his blade. "My lady, you have no idea what Ghislaine of Mercia will do. I have never in my life seen a more determined or courageous woman."

Lygia thought of the rather pale woman sleeping the sleep of the dead in the cottage. Other than being quite beautiful, Lady Ghislaine didn't seem anything out of the ordinary to her. She was curious.

"Truly?" she asked. "Will you tell me why you say such things?"

Jathan looked at her, a hint of a smile on his lips. "Lady Ghislaine is worthy of the great tales told about her," he said. "In fact, some day I may write them all down. Here, now; sit down and listen. I think you will be amazed."

Jathan had been right. After the story of their trip north from the battle near Hastings, she *was* amazed.

CHAPTER TWENTY-FOUR

൬

DISTRACTION IS DEADLY

Later that morning
Outside of the village of Rock Cross; Church of St. Peter and St. Paul

"WE ARE ON the right path," Gaetan said as he dismounted his horse, speaking to his knights who were either on the ground resting or standing near the cold clear stream he'd left them by not an hour earlier. "The priest said that we are to continue up this road until we come to a larger road. The path to Tenebris will be to the east along that larger road, about half a mile. We will see the fortress on the rise through the trees."

It had taken little more than half a day since leaving the *Tertium* village to come within a few miles of Kidderminster. They knew that Tenebris was nearby but without Ghislaine's direction, they weren't sure, exactly, where it was. They needed help. Passing a farmer on their way north, the farmer directed them to the Church of St. Peter and St. Paul, a relatively new church as far as churches went, but the only one in the area other than a larger church in Kidderminster. Gaetan thanked the farmer, threw him a coin, and then continued on to the church as they'd been directed.

Coming up the road from the south, the block-steeple of the church came into view and Gaetan left his men by a stream in a thicket of trees and proceeded onward to ask the priests if they knew where Tenebris was located. His concern was that the priests might know of, or be loyal to, Alary and he didn't want word to reach Alary that nine Norman knights had been seeking him.

One knight making an inquiry would seem far less threatening.

Therefore, Gaetan went on alone, forcing himself to keep his mind on his task when all he wanted to do was think of Ghislaine. It was strange how much he missed her, considering he'd only known the woman a matter of weeks. Now, he couldn't even remember traveling without her. His arms ached to hold her but he comforted himself with the knowledge that the sooner they regain Kristoph, the sooner he would return to Ghislaine.

Under the guise of being an old friend of Alary of Mercia, Gaetan was able to extract a satisfactory answer from the solitary priest at the church and he had now returned to inform his men. Once he finished delivering the news, he brought his horse to the stream to drink, crouching down beside the animal to drink himself while his men began to gather their horses in preparation for departing.

"We shall make it to Tenebris easily before nightfall," Téo said as he pulled his horse up from greedily eating thick wet grass. "Do you intend we should remain here tonight and set out in the morning?"

Gaetan shook his head. "Nay," he said, standing up and shaking the water from his hands. "Even with the delays we have suffered, Alary was still traveling far slower than we were. We should be at least two days or more ahead of him, but we cannot be entirely certain. On the chance that he has made better time than we estimated, I will send Wellesbourne and St. Hèver into Kidderminster to watch for his party passing through. If Alary has two hundred men with him, then he will be easily spotted. Meanwhile, de Reyne and de Russe can ride head to scout out Tenebris. We need eyes on the place to see its strength and layout."

Intelligence gathering was necessary in a situation such as this and everyone agreed, for the most part. "What is the plan of attack?" de Lara wanted to know. "If Alary is carrying two hundred men, we must have something precise planned so that when he comes, we are ready."

Gaetan pulled his horse out of the stream and moved to mount the saddle. "That is what the rest of us will be doing," he said. "We will be scouting the road between Kidderminster and Tenebris to determine the best place for an ambush. That is the only way we will be able to take on a greater number."

"That is assuming Alary has not yet made it to Tenebris," de Lara said quietly.

That was the key to all of this. If Alary had already made it to his fortress, then they would have to think of something else. There was something ominous in that thought. Gaetan vaulted into the saddle and gathered his reins as his men began to do the same.

"Exactly," he said. "Let us get along with what must be done."

With that, they tore out of the thicket and back onto the road again. Beneath clear skies and a rather lovely day, they reached the main road from Kidderminster in under an hour. Suddenly, they were right where they wanted to be, on the very road they had been seeking, and Gaetan found himself looking in the direction of the city even though he couldn't see it. Still, they were here, ready to intercept Alary's army, and the moment wasn't lost on him.

They'd been waiting for it for the better part of several weeks.

Now, Gaetan's focus was where it should be as thoughts of Ghislaine were tucked away. He was on the eve of a battle and thinking of the woman he adored would only be a distraction, and every knight knew that distraction was deadly. His thoughts shifted to Kristoph and what the man must have suffered these past weeks being the prisoner of a madman.

Kristoph was strong, he knew, but even the strong had a breaking point. This was the instant where he showed Kristoph just what brotherhood meant – it meant that men were not forgotten and that the bonds of warriors were stronger than the bonds of blood.

This was that moment.

With a lesser traveled road and a heavy forest of trees to their back, the knights looked to the west where Tenebris was located. The landscape was a little hilly, but none of the bigger hills and dales they had seen further south. For the most part, it was flat. Gaetan looked from east to west along the larger road, which was heavily traveled from the ruts in it. There were, however, thick lines of trees on both sides of the road to the east, but those trees dwindled the further west the road went. In fact, he could see the trees tapering off altogether not too far to the west. Beyond was the flat lands of meadows.

"Look to the trees," he said, pointing off to the east where the trees came right up to the road. "That is where we shall make our stand, right here before the forest thins out too much. If we catch Alary and his army there, they will have nowhere to go."

Téo, Aramis, and Luc were up alongside him, looking at the landscape. "If Alary is smart, he'll have two hundred men in close quarters to protect one another while they are traveling," Luc said. "If that is the case, we use crossbows as the weapon of choice – three of us in the front, three along the flanks, and then three in the rear. We can hold an entire army hostage that way and extract Kristoph."

Gaetan nodded, looking up to the height of the trees. "That was my thinking exactly."

He spurred his horse down the road towards the trees they were discussing and his men followed. St. Hèver and de Moray entered the tree line to both the north and south side of the road, inspecting what was back in the forest, as the rest of them came to a halt about midway down a particularly dense line of trees. They were all looking about, inspecting it, noting the visibility from the road among other things. Satisfied, Gaetan was the first one to speak.

"Bartholomew and Kye will head to Kidderminster now," he said, motioning both men out of the trees and addressing them when they came near. "Remember your instructions; you are to remain out of sight. Do not let Alary or any of his men catch sight of you or we may have serious problems. Once you sight them, come back to us as quickly as you can. We will need time to prepare for their approach."

Wellesbourne and St. Hèver nodded sharply, goring their steeds forward and tearing off down the road, eastward bound for Kidderminster. As the two of them took off, Gaetan turned to Aramis and Lance.

"You two head out to scout Tenebris," he said. "Careful you are not sighted. We do not want to alert them to our presence."

Aramis nodded. "We will be cautious."

Gaetan watched them go, thundering down the road and disappearing from view when the road curved. Now, it was him, Téo, de Moray, de Winter, and de Lara. Gaetan turned to the remaining knights.

"It will be up to us to determine the best place for an attack," he said. "Go now and mark your spots. Come to me when you are ready and we shall put this plan into action."

With confidence, the others began to spread out, searching for the best place from which to launch an ambush. As Gaetan watched them go, his attention inevitably turned to the east. He wished very much that he had his entire army with him, but there was no time to spend on regrets. Nine Norman knights had to fend off two hundred Saxon soldiers and pray the Saxons didn't kill Kristoph before the knights could rescue him. That was the gist of the situation and everyone knew it. Gaetan wasn't quite sure what he would do if he saw Kristoph murdered before his eyes, before he was able to get to him.

A praying man, he began to pray very hard that it wouldn't happen.

Please, God... just give me the chance to get to him. That is all I ask....

GHISLAINE ONLY WOKE up because the dog had left her bed, jostling her when it did so. Then, he scratched at the door, wanting to be let out, so she sat up and tried to collect her wits before staggering over to the door and opening it for the dog to go out and do his doggy business. As she opened the door, however, she saw Jathan sitting against the wall of the cottage, sharpening a small dagger with a stone.

Jathan looked up, surprised, when the door opened and the dog ran past. Ghislaine smiled sleepily at him, yawning.

"Good morn," she said.

Jathan put the stone and dagger in his lap. "Good morn, my lady," he said. "Why are you awake?"

Ghislaine yawned again, looking out over the pond and the canopy above, with streams of light coming through the leaves and reaching to the earth. There were only a few people around the pond now, washing or simply sitting. In all, it was a graceful and serene scene.

"The dog awoke me," she said. "I feel as if I have been asleep for one hundred years. What day is it?"

Jathan sat forward on his stool, looking over the pond and the trees just as she was. "It is the day after your arrival here in the village," he said. "You have only been asleep seven or eight hours since last night. I thought you would sleep all day."

Ghislaine couldn't stop yawning. "Whatever that old woman gave me for the pain made me sleep." She touched her right thigh, moving it around a little. "It does not feel nearly as bad as I thought it would. There is pain, but it is not terrible. I suppose it will heal in spite of my repeated attempts to re-injure it."

She grinned and so did Jathan. "That is good to hear," he said. "Resting for the past several hours has undoubtedly helped."

"Undoubtedly."

"Shall I call Lygia and her sisters for you?"

Ghislaine shook her head, smoothing down her hair which, in spite of having slept on it, was still in a relatively neat braid. "I do not believe so," she said. "I believe I can fend for myself but I would like something to eat. Is it near the nooning meal? Mayhap I shall be in time to join Gaetan and the knights for the meal."

Jathan's smile faded. This was the moment he'd been dreading but he didn't think it would come this soon. He'd expected the lady to sleep much longer so he wasn't particularly prepared to tell her what he must. Still, she had to know. It wasn't as if he could keep it from her. Taking a deep breath, he summoned his courage.

"You cannot," he told her, seeing her turn to him curiously. "Gaetan and his men have gone on to intercept your brother. Gaetan came to tell you himself this morning, very early, but you were sleeping so peacefully that he did not want to wake you. He told me to tell you to remain here and that he would return for you as soon as he can."

Ghislaine's eyes widened as the smile vanished from her face. "He is gone?" she repeated. Then, it was as if the news hit her a second time and she suddenly grabbed Jathan's arm, squeezing it. "He *left*?"

Jathan knew this would be her reaction but, to be truthful, it frightened him. Gaetan was the only one who could control the woman and, sometimes, even he couldn't override her powerful sense of independence. He stood up even as she dug her fingers into his arm.

"He will return," he stressed. "You needn't worry. They shall find Kristoph and then they shall all return. You will see."

Ghislaine couldn't believe what she was hearing. Suddenly, she wasn't so sleepy anymore. She was shocked, appalled, and bordering on panic.

"Nay," she hissed, shaking her head as she released Jathan. "They cannot go without me. They will not survive!"

She was backing away from him, heading into the tiny cottage. Jathan followed. "Why do you say that?" he asked. "My lady, I have known Gaetan de Wolfe for many years. He is quite capable of surviving a battle, I assure you. He did it for many years before he met you."

Ghislaine yanked on the little doe-skin slippers that Lygia had given her. "Of course he did," she snapped. "But he has not survived here, in Mercia."

Slippers on, she pushed past him and began heading towards the convening house. Jathan scurried after her, doing exactly what he had been dreading – he grabbed her by the arm to physically stop her.

"My lady, wait," he said. "You cannot go after them. Gaetan gave me a direct command and if you disobey, he will punish us both. You must remain here."

Ghislaine snatched her arm away from him. "I will not remain here," she said. "I must go after him."

"You cannot!"

"I can and you will not stop me."

Jathan, beside himself, rushed at her from behind when she tried to walk away again and tackled her, grabbing her around the waist and picking her up from the ground. Gaetan had given him permission to tie her to the bed, which was exactly what he intended to do. But Ghislaine had other ideas. The moment he grabbed her, she threw an elbow back and caught him on the side of the head.

Startled from the painful blow, Jathan dropped her, but it was fortunate she didn't land on her bad leg. She plopped right down onto her left foot and she began to run, as fast as she was able with her stiff and sore thigh. But Jathan, with a bloodied ear, caught up to her again and the fight was on.

People began to come out of their cottages to watch the lady fighting off the priest who kept trying to grab her. Ghislaine didn't want to hurt the man but she was quickly growing irritated with his attempts to restrain her. She lost her patience completely when he accidentally grabbed her braid and pulled her hair, so she kicked him right in the groin with her bad leg. It was the only way she could do it since she couldn't very well balance on her right leg; therefore, it became her kicking leg. Jathan fell to the ground in anguish when she made contact.

Realizing they were attracting an audience, Ghislaine ran as fast as she could towards the convening hall in the hopes of finding Antillius. She didn't know where else to look for him. She was nearly to the long stone structure when the door to the convening hall opened and men poured forth, Antillius included. There were men by his side, speaking to him, but they quieted when they saw the lady approach.

"My lady?" Antillius went to her quickly. "What has happened? I have been told by one of my men that your priest attacked you!"

Ghislaine shook her head. "He did not attack me," she said. "He was attempting to stop me from following Gaetan and his men. My lord, did you know they had left?"

Antillius nodded. "I did, indeed," he said. "They left a few hours ago. Not long, really. Why? What is the matter?"

Ghislaine was already shaking her head, feeling a tremendous sense of urgency. She didn't have time to explain her fears but if she didn't explain them, Antillius might try to keep her here, too, and it was imperative that she follow the Normans. Therefore, she tried to remain calm as she spoke.

"I do not know how much Gaetan told you of him and his men, but they are Norman knights," she said, breathlessly. "They, and thousands of their countrymen, came to the shores of England a few weeks ago and engaged in a battle with Harold Godwinson, who was my sister's husband. I speak of him in the past because he was killed by the Normans."

Antillius and his men were looking at her with increasing shock. "Godwinson is *dead*?"

"Aye. Gaetan did not tell you?"

"He did not."

"I am sure he had his reasons, but it is true. Harold is dead."

Antillius glanced at his nervous men before replying. "Then who rules now?"

Ghislaine could see the shock reflected in their eyes at the news. She felt rather badly for telling them, as if she was essentially calling Gaetan a liar for withholding such vital information, but the reality was that she needed something from them. She was trying to lay a foundation for her argument.

"The Duke of Normandy lays claim to the throne of England now," she said. "You would have found out sooner or later and I am sure

Gaetan did not tell you because he did not want to frighten you. Do not think poorly of him; he is not an unjust man. You must believe that."

Antillius still had doubt and shock in his expression. "He told us that he had come to England to reclaim a man who had been kidnapped by your brother."

She nodded. "That is true," she said. "My brother, Alary, kidnapped Gaetan's knight after the battle. That is why they are here – to reclaim their man. It is not to take your lands from you or kill your people. Right now, all they want to do is reclaim their knight. I was their guide, directing them through these new lands to help them find their man."

Antillius' shock was fading somewhat, although the news still had him shaken. "Did your brother, Edwin, send you with them? He has no love for Alary."

Ghislaine shook her head. "Edwin has never met Gaetan or his men, nor was he at the battle where Harold lost his life," she said. "This has nothing to do with Edwin. My lord, I know you consider Edwin an enemy and I am sure that you have difficulty trusting me as well, but I must beg a favor from you."

"What?"

"You must help me save Gaetan's life."

Antillius' brow furrowed in confusion. "He does not need your help," he said. "I saw him fight off hordes of the Men of Bones last night. He and his men are the most powerful warriors I have ever seen."

Ghislaine wasn't sure how she could explain her fears to him, but she had to try. She truly felt Gaetan's life depended on it.

"Norman knights are like nothing you have ever seen on the field of battle," she said. "They are stronger, better equipped, and more skilled than anything on this earth. But that is in open battle; when it comes to the warfare our people conduct – in trees, in hiding, or covertly – Normans are extremely vulnerable. They fight head-on because that is what they know. But our people – your people, my people – do not fight that way. Right now, Gaetan has taken eight men with him and they intend to stop my brother and rescue their man. My lord, Alary has two hundred men with him who fight in this fashion. I am terrified that Gaetan and his men will walk straight into their deaths."

Antillius was listening carefully. "Surely they are not that foolish," he said. "Men like that do not live as long as they have by being foolish. I think you underestimate him."

Ghislaine tried not to appear too contrite. "I do not mean to under-estimate him," she said, "and as long as I was accompanying them, I knew I could advise them on the way our people fight. This wound in my leg? I received it when we were passing through the shadowlands, south of Worcester. Knowing what I know of the people in that area, I was able to draw them out and avert an ambush. Now… now I must avert another terrible clash, or at least try. But I have no horse and no weapons. I am asking if you will provide me with these things so I can at least help them. Please, my lord, I beseech you."

Antillius was over his shock of the situation for the most part. Now, he was pensive as he pondered her words. "If I let you go, I cannot imagine that de Wolfe would be too pleased with me," he said. "He told your priest to keep you here. Lygia told me so. Now you are asking me to let you follow him?"

Ghislaine nodded. "I will do it with or without your help, but with your help, it would be much easier."

Antillius believed her implicitly; she seemed like a rather stubborn female. He certainly didn't want to lock her up like a prisoner but he wasn't sure how else to keep her here if she wanted to follow Gaetan. He'd also heard from Lygia that Gaetan and the lady were betrothed, so he knew her request wasn't purely from concern.

It was from devotion.

Antillius had seen the way Gaetan had looked at the lady and he knew a man in love when he saw one. He could only imagine the lady felt the same thing for him, else she wouldn't be willing to risk her life so. But men in love were fickle things because he'd seen it enough to know and men like Gaetan de Wolfe couldn't truly fall in love; war was their lover, their mistress, and their life. Women like Ghislaine, while beautiful, were only an infatuation to these war creatures.

They were another conquest.

Moreover, the survival of Ghislaine's family didn't depend upon her marrying Gaetan. But the survival of Antillius' people very much depended on new blood and, with that thought, he began to formulate a plan of his own.

"Even if you go, if they are truly under attack, you cannot help them by yourself," he finally said. "You would become a casualty, too. What you need is more men."

Ghislaine nodded, trying not to look too scared or miserable in that knowledge. "I know," she said. "Gaetan has two thousand men but Alary knew we were following him and he threatened to kill his captive if Gaetan did not stop following, so Gaetan left his army at Westerham. We cannot summon them in time."

"You have not asked me if I will help."

"But I have. I asked you for a weapon and...."

He cut her off. "You did not ask me if my men would help."

Ghislaine looked at him as if the thought hadn't occurred to her. There was astonishment and hope in her eyes. "Would you?" she gasped. "If you and your men would go to help him, surely he could win. Surely he could regain his man. My lord, if the *Tertium* were to go to battle as Gaetan's army, then victory is assured."

Antillius nodded. "Mayhap," he said. "At least, Gaetan and his men would have a fighting chance against Alary and his hundreds. But even as I suggest this course of action, you must know that there is a reason behind it. I have explained such things to Gaetan but I am sure he has not spoken of it to you. You see, my lady, my people are dying out. I fear that my daughters' generation will be one of the very last unless we are able to bring new blood, new life, into our tribe. I have nearly three hundred men in the village now but in the days of my father and his father, there were thousands. If I take those three hundred men into battle against your brother, I will lose some. There is no doubt that some will die. And that is an extremely expensive price to pay. As it is now, I can never replace those men."

Ghislaine wasn't quite following his line of thought. "I am very sorry to know that, my lord," she said. "But I assure you, if you and your men go into battle for Gaetan, he will reward you greatly. Mayhap that reward will help save your people somehow."

"That is what I am hoping. But I will name my price."

"Of course, my lord. Anything you wish."

"I understand that you and Gaetan are to be married."

Ghislaine nodded, but it was with some embarrassment. She hadn't known Gaetan had told him that. "Aye," she said hesitantly. "I have agreed to be his wife."

Antillius put his hands on her shoulders in a fatherly gesture. His expression, when he looked at her, was quite serious.

"Then only you can tell him to pay my price."

"I do not understand."

Antillius eyed her a moment before continuing. "I wish for a grandson or two from a magnificent warrior like de Wolfe," he said. "I will ride into battle for you and I will help Gaetan, but I want something in return. I want you to give Gaetan permission; nay, I wish for you to *command* him to marry Lygia and give her many sons. If you truly love him, then no price will be too high to save his life. If you would like for me to help you save him, then this is my price."

That wasn't what Ghislaine had been expected. She felt as if she'd been hit in the gut, unable to breathe, unable to think. But his words settled deep and she yanked herself from his grip, hardly believing what she was hearing. It was the most horrific proposal she had ever heard in her life.

"You… you want Gaetan to…?" She couldn't even finish.

Antillius could see her revulsion, her horror, and it infuriated him. "Do you think this is a simple thing for me to ask?" he said. "That I am willing to prostitute my own daughters must speak to you of my desperation that my people should continue. Even now, old men die and new men are not born. It is rare that male children, or any children, are born these days. As a reward to Gaetan and his men for defending us against the *Homines Ossium* last night, I offered them all three of my daughters in marriage. Before you judge me, understand how difficult that was for me to do. But a desperate man will do desperate things."

Ghislaine stood there, looking at him with her eyes swimming in tears. Antillius had ceased to become their benevolent host and had now become something vile and wicked. She couldn't understand a man who would propose such a terrible bargain, something so dastardly and ignoble.

"How can you ask me to do that?" she hissed.

"If you love him, you will do what is necessary to save him. Do you wish for a dead betrothed or a living man though he may be married to someone else?"

"But what you are asking is pure madness! Are you truly so cruel?"

"You asked me to name my price, my lady. It is your choice whether or not to pay it."

"I will *not!*"

"Then de Wolfe will die."

She blinked, tears running down her face, but inside she was filled with rage. He was asking her to make a decision that would change the course of her life. Her jaw began to tick, so enraged that she was grinding her teeth.

"He saved you from those horrible raiders last night," she said tightly. "You owe him a debt!"

"And I saved you from bleeding to death. What he did last night was to repay that debt and now we are even. If you want something from me, Ghislaine of Mercia, then I want something from you. Look at you; you are injured and weak. Even if you rode to aid him, alone, you would be of little use with that bad leg. But I can offer you as many men as Alary carries to support Gaetan. He will have a far better chance of survival."

Ghislaine was struggling not to break down because she was coming to realize that she may not have a choice in all of this. If she wanted help for Gaetan, then she would have to sacrifice him in order to save him.

Oh, God, is it true? Must I do this?

"But why Gaetan?" she asked, her lower lip trembling. "Why not one of the other men?"

"Because you do not hold sway over the other men. If you ask Gaetan to marry Lygia, then he will."

"But it is not fair. What you ask is not fair."

"Time is passing, my lady. The more we discuss this, the closer Gaetan and his men come to death."

He was right. God help her, he was right. It was the first time in her life that Ghislaine had ever had to make such a choice. She had to think about Gaetan and not herself. She wanted him to survive and, in that want, she was willing to do anything. Even sacrifice her future happiness. No thoughts of her future love or future children. There would be none now. Gaetan would be married to Lygia and give her his sons. Yet, Ghislaine would remain empty. Hollow.

But Gaetan would be alive.

The decision was made.

"If that is your price, then I have little choice but to agree," she said, hating herself even as she said it. "But know that I hate you with every bone in my body for demanding such a thing. You are a wicked, wicked man."

Antillius felt as if he'd just won some great victory but in that victory was great sadness. Contrary to what the lady said, he wasn't wicked by nature, but he was determined to save his people any way he could. Perhaps in time, the lady would understand that. Perhaps not. In any case, he knew he'd made another enemy of the great Saxon family but there was nothing he could do about it. He had what he wanted.

And so did she.

"Come with me and we shall find you a suitable horse."

Ghislaine went with him, wiping tears all the way.

CHAPTER TWENTY-FIVE

THE DAY SHALL END AND
THE END SHALL BE KNOWN

KIDDERMINSTER WAS A dusty dirty town that was quite crowded, Bartholomew and Kye discovered. It was a market town, which meant farmers from all over the area brought their wares to town to find buyers for them and even at this hour, past midday, the streets were clogged with farmers, carts, animals, buyers, and everyone else in between.

In fact, Bartholomew and Kye were very surprised to see such bustle but, given the fact that they were enemy knights in Saxon territory, they didn't want to call attention to themselves as they milled through the town. The River Severn ran near Kidderminster and there was a big wooden bridge that crossed the road into the town. Down below the bridge on the riverbanks were thick trees and foliage, so the knights left their horses hidden in the undergrowth. Covering themselves with their cloaks to hide not only their mail and tunics, but also conceal their Norman haircuts and shaved faces, they headed into town.

The side of town they entered was the marketing side and it was full of people as the knights mingled with the crowds inconspicuously, keeping their eyes opened for any bulk movement of men coming through. The town itself seemed to be dirty, run-down, with collapsing buildings and people that were dressed in rags. As they moved, they saw several destitute citizens begging on the edge of the street, but the knights passed them by. They were not without sympathy for the poor but giving coinage to people who had none would attract attention they didn't want. They moved on.

Heading deeper into the town, they were struck by the smell of baking bread mingled with the smell of human waste. The road was lined with houses, with people conducting their business from their homes, and off to the north they could see the church steeple framed against the deep blue sky. They walked past a woman carrying chickens in two big cages, and passed yet another woman and her family who were herding pigs through the town.

Passing into what appeared to be the center of the town, they came upon the town well where people were drawing their water from a great pool. There was also a man selling big hollowed-out stale bread bowls filled with boiled peas and ham, and the smells lured them in. They purchased two big bread bowls and wolfed down the food, thinking Saxon food to be quite tasty. Wellesbourne managed to get it all over the front of his cloak, which made him look rather slovenly. St. Hèver rolled his eyes at him and accused him of eating like one of the many pigs they'd passed by.

Bellies full, the knights continued past the church and through the city that was really little more than clusters of wooden houses with heavy sod roofs. They seemed to be walking against traffic for the most part and as they continued walking, they could see another entrance to Kidderminster in the eastern portion of the town's wall. St. Hèver pulled Wellesbourne aside.

"Look," he hissed from behind one of those short wooden houses. "An entry into town from the east. I have been looking around but have not seen another entry, so when Alary comes through, that must be where he will come from."

Wellesbourne was looking around as well. "As I recall from being here once as a child, there is also an entry to the north on the other side of the church, but I do not think Alary would come from that direction"

"This is where he shall enter."

"Exactly."

St. Hèver scouted their location, seeing the houses spread around, the stockyards, even a cemetery across from the church. He tugged on Wellesbourne.

"Come on," he said. "I'll hide over by the eastern entrance. You find a spot near the church where you can catch a glimpse of the northern entrance just in case Alary comes in that direction. I'll get as close to the eastern entrance as I can so I can see what is coming up the road. If I see something, I'll signal you."

"How?"

"Listen for my whistle."

St. Hèver could whistle between his teeth loudly enough to puncture eardrums. Wellesbourne nodded and they split off, going to find a place to wait for a sighting of Alary's army. But it would be an uncertain wait. The army's appearance could be today, tomorrow, or even another day. Still, they were going to dig in. They were the advance team and the entire operation of rescuing Kristoph would depend on just how alert they were. Therefore, they selected their vantage points carefully and settled down.

Now, all they could do was wait.

Unfortunately, Kye realized early on in the waiting process that eating that huge meal had been a mistake. The knights were suffering from a lack of sleep and now with a full belly, it was a perfect time to sleep the afternoon away. Kye was seated against the perimeter wall of the town, a wooden wall about as tall as a man with a spiked end, and struggling to stay awake. He was wedged between a pig sty and a winter garden that had many rabbits in it, which a dog would come and chase off every so often. Then the dog would come over and sniff him before he would chase it off. That went on for a while until the dog eventually left him alone.

The afternoon continued on and the comings and goings at the wall entrance began to lag greatly. In fact, it seemed rather deserted as people returned home after a day of business. But Kye remained vigilant, watching those who were entering, on the lookout for soldiers or men with weapons. He had even stood up, several times, to peer between the slats in the wall, looking at the road that was leading into the village only to be met with a deserted scene. The road, at that time of day, remained empty.

But as time passed, Kye tried not become discouraged by the lack of an army. The knights were so terribly worked up for Alary's appearance that expectations were admittedly high. But it was very possible Alary would not show today. Perhaps he was two or three days behind them just as Gaetan had suggested. The man was traveling slowly with an army, far more slowly than knights without encumbrances were, so to expect them on this day was more than likely unreasonable.

At least, that's what Kye told himself. He had to force himself to be patient. But he settled back on his bum, leaning against the wall, and continued to watch the entrance. As the sun began to wane and the sky began to turn shades that suggested a coming sunset, he was thinking on finding Wellesbourne to see if the man had seen something worth reporting. Clearly, nothing more was going to happen this day. Just as he stood up, he thought he heard a distant rumble.

Looking up in the sky, there were clouds but nothing that implied a coming storm. But the rumble was still there, growing louder, and he turned to peer through the slats in the wooden fence. Immediately, he was met with armed men on foot, and armed men on horseback, and two wagons from what he could see coming up the road. The rumble had been from the wagons bumping over the rough road.

An army was approaching.

Kye fell to his knees again, huddling back behind the pig sty which provided him with a shield against anyone coming in through the wall entry. Certainly, this could be another army, and the truth was that he had no idea what Alary of Mercia looked like. But he did know what Kristoph looked like. It was his task to search each and every face in that approaching army to see if he spied a Norman knight he had known for several years.

Excitement filled his veins as he lay low, waiting. Meanwhile, he was praying that Wellesbourne saw the same army and was doing exactly the same as he was – laying low and trying to spot Kristoph. This was the moment they'd been waiting for. From his position behind the pig sty, Kye had a perfect view of the incoming army and it wasn't long before the leading edge of the army began to enter.

Men dressed in heavy tunics, with axes slung on their backs as well as crudely made shields, passed through the entry and continued onward. They were followed by other foot soldiers, some with helms, more than a few with what looked like Norman helms and shields. That was St. Hèver's first clue that these men might have been at the battle between Harold Godwinson and the Duke of Normandy; stolen Norman protection seemed to be peppered throughout the lines. Even one of the men on horseback, who was very well dressed with a fur cloak and well-made clothing had a sword at his side that was most definitely not Saxon.

Kye recognized the Norman workmanship.

More of the army passed through, moving at a good pace but still looking rather weary, as if they had walked a very long way. When the first of the wagons passed through, Kye struggled to see inside of it but all he could see on the flat bed were sacks and weapons and other things an army on the move might need. But then the second wagon came through. It had men around it, which blocked Kye's view of what was inside. The sides were high, also, and there were provisions piled in it; he could see barrels and sacks, food needed for the men.

Kye had to move around the pig sty so he could see what was in that wagon because the men and the provisions were blocking most of his view. As the wagon moved past him and he changed positions, he could suddenly see a man chained up in the back of the wagon and, as his heart leapt with glee, a blonde head he recognized very well. Kristoph de Lohr was chained in the back of the wagon, looking unshaven and shaggy-haired, but it was definitely him. And he was alive.

Their missing brother had been found.

Kye was so excited that he was quivering. He had to get to Wellesbourne and tell the man what he saw. And then they had to race to Gaetan and tell him that Kristoph was alive and that Alary's army was on its way. But the army was still trickling in and he didn't want to give himself away by emitting a piercing whistle. Yet, he knew the longer he waited, the more chance there was of him not being able to make his way to Gaetan before Alary did. He was almost certain that Wellesbourne was seeing the same thing from his vantage point across the road so he had to assume that the man was preparing to race back to Gaetan as well. Any delay might cost them a great deal.

Therefore, Kye began to run. Skirting through yards, over fish ponds, through horse dung, and through alleys, he raced as fast as he could, making it to the end of town well before Alary's army did and flying across the wooden bridge and to the river bank below where the horses had been left.

His horse was still where he left it, having eaten its fill of the plump grass and was now standing lazily, napping. That all ended when Kye vaulted onto the horse's back and spurred it up to the road, heading off to the east where he knew Gaetan and the others were waiting. They would have a very short amount of time to prepare their ambush and they needed all of the advance notice they could get.

Kristoph was coming. And they had to be ready.

SUNSET WAS ON the approach.

Gaetan stood on the side of the road, looking up at the sky through the canopy of trees and wondering if Ghislaine was still asleep. Perhaps she was awake by now, supping with Antillius and his three daughters, eating a good meal with a fire to keep her warm and a roof over her head.

That was the way it should be with her; the life of a fine lady and not a warrior. He knew he was going to have a fight on his hands when he told her that he didn't want her to fight any longer. He wanted her to become the wife of a great warrior, to run his household and bear his legitimate children. He hoped he could explain all of that to her before she took a stick to him.

The thought made him grin. The most beautiful woman in all the land was a ruffian in disguise. Well, not exactly a ruffian, but definitely a trained warrior. He had enough of those and didn't need another. What he wanted from her was something far less violent. He knew it would be difficult for her but he suspected she would want to please him.

Truth be told, she already did. God had been good to bring her into his life.

Forcing his thoughts away from Ghislaine, Gaetan turned back to his men who were still wandering in and out of the trees on the north side of the road. The land was relatively flat all around them but there was excellent ground cover, easily enough to hide them until they decided to come forth and ambush Alary's army.

"Gate!"

De Winter was several yards away from him to the east, now calling his name. As Gaetan headed in his direction, Denis was pointing down the road.

"Riders," Denis said. "I cannot tell who it is yet, but there are two of them. Mayhap it is Marc and Lance."

Gaetan, too, could see riders coming around the curve in the road about a half-mile down. "And it just as easily could not be them," he said, waving to the men standing on the road and trying to get a look. "Into the trees."

They scattered, disappearing into the foliate to hide themselves. Gaetan was well off the road, back behind a broad tree trunk, peering around it to see if the riders were his own men coming down the road. Soon enough, the pair came within range and he could see that it was, indeed, de Moray and de Reyne. Gaetan and the other knights wandered back out to the road.

"Well?" Gaetan demanded. "What about Tenebris? What did you see?"

As de Reyne dismounted his sweating horse, de Moray spoke. "You are not going to like this," he said. "We saw a rather small fortress with a tall wooden wall around it, a moat that we could smell from a mile away, and when we used the trees as cover to get a closer look at it, the forest around it was filled with corpses."

Gaetan's brow furrowed. "What do you mean?" he asked, confused. "As if an army had not taken away their dead?"

De Moray wearily dismounted his horse. "This, I cannot tell you," he said. "It did not look like an army to me. It was a pile of bodies, some of them so old and moldering that grass had grown up all around them and they had become part of the earth. Although the clothing remained on them, anything of value was stripped."

It sounded ghastly and Gaetan did, indeed, make a face of distaste. "God's Bones," he muttered. "Dead everywhere?"

"All around the front of the fortress from what we could see. Once we made it to the rear of the fortress, there were no more bodies."

That made absolutely no sense at all but it reminded Gaetan what Ghislaine had said of the place. "She said it was a dark and terrible place," he muttered. "Ghislaine, I mean. She said that Tenebris was very dark."

De Moray nodded, still trying to shake off what he'd seen. "More than you know," he said. "I have never seen anything like it."

The state of the fortress hinted at the darkness of the mind behind it, the man who had Kristoph's life in his hands. Gaetan couldn't shake off that sense of horror. "But what about the fortress itself?" he asked.

"Is it well guarded?"

De Reyne entered the conversation. "We saw just a few men," he said. "No more than a handful, really. There is a small motte and a keep atop it, but the fortress itself is very small."

"Is it something we can breach if needed?"

De Reyne nodded. "I have no doubt," he said. "It seemed to me that the moat flowed beneath the walls and into the compound, so that could be a relatively simple way to enter it."

De Moray grunted. "Simple, aye, but that moat was filled with unspeakable filth. I should not like to crawl through that."

Gaetan echoed that thought, but he was more pragmatic. "If we must, then we must," he said. "But you saw no evidence of an army inside of it?"

De Reyne shook his head. "Nothing at all. It seemed deserted."

There was relief in that knowledge. "Then Alary has not returned yet," he sighed, pleased. "It means he must pass along this road to get there and when he does, we shall be ready."

"Is it possible he has another property somewhere that he has gone to?" de Reyne asked. "I never heard the lady mention any other property, but it concerns me that Alary may not be returning to Tenebris at all."

Gaetan could only shrug. "That has occurred to me also, but Ghislaine seemed positive that Alary would return here and she made a point of stating that he has no other properties. Even Tenebris belongs to Edwin, but I suppose there is always a chance Alary could have stopped somewhere else or gone on to an ally's property." He paused, thinking that possibility was most disheartening. "All we can do now is wait and see. If Alary does not appear within the next week, then we may have to consider other options."

No one wanted to do that, not when they had come so far. Just as de Reyne and de Moray moved to take their horses off the road, the sounds of thundering hooves caught their attention. All eyes turned to the east to see St. Hèver riding towards them at breakneck speed.

Suddenly, everyone was on edge as St. Hèver came to a halt, kicking up rocks and dirt. His manner bordered on frantic. "Alary is coming through Kidderminster now," he said, out of breath. "He will be on us in half an hour at the very most."

The news electrified the knights. Any fatigue, or disappointment, or doubt abruptly fled as they realized the target of their search, the very bastard who had evaded them for weeks, was only minutes away.

Alary is coming!

"Did you see Kristoph?" Gaetan demanded.

St. Hèver smiled, a smile of utter relief and joy. "I did," he said "He is in the provisions wagon, surrounded by armed men. I have a feeling he may have tried to escape once or twice because he was chained to the wagon. Bless the man; he has surely given them a difficult time."

Everyone smiled at that, proud that their brother, their fellow warrior, had resisted his captors. It was such joy in a journey that had seen such fear and doubt. But it wasn't over yet. The worst of it was yet to come and they all knew it.

No one knew it more than Gaetan.

"Where is Wellesbourne?" he asked. "Did he not come back with you?"

St. Hèver shook his head. "We were separated but I know he saw the incoming army as I did," he said. "He should be coming along very shortly."

Gaetan was satisfied by that but his attention naturally swung back to the approaching army. He needed all of the information he could get in order to plan the ambush.

"Tell me everything you saw," he said. "The strength of the army, infantry and mounted warriors – everything you can think of."

St. Hèver nodded as he dismounted his steed. "It is as we were told," he said. "At least two hundred men, but what we were not told was that some of those men were mounted. I saw at least thirty mounted men, many of them carrying Norman weapons and armor. The men on foot seem to be well armed, also. There are two wagons and, as I said, the one carrying Kristoph is guarded. Moreover, they have him chained. Even when we get to him, we will have the encumbrance of those chains before we can free him completely."

Gaetan absorbed the information. "I see," he said, his mind working quickly. "Mounted cavalry, did you say?"

St. Hèver pulled off a glove so he could scratch his blonde head. "I did," he said. "I know you wanted to ambush them, Gate, but from what I saw, they have enough to repel us and then some. They could make short work of us if we go at them head-on."

Gaetan drew in a long, pensive breath and turned away. He had expected an army to have weapons, but what he hadn't counted on was the mounted warriors. That made the situation a little trickier. Now, his plans had to change in order to accommodate this news and it wasn't going to be easy. There was little time to plan a new strategy, but that's exactly what he had to do.

God help him, he had mere minutes to make a new plan to save all their lives.

Gaetan glanced at the men around him, his *Anges de Guerre*; St. Hèver "The Hammer", de Russe with his fearsome double-blades, de Reyne with his limitless bravery, and de Moray with his spear. De Winter carried *l'Espada*, the blessed blade of his Visigoth ancestors, and de Lara fought with an ax that all men feared. He was unbreakable. Finally, there was Téo, his friend and wise counsel, who wielded a morning star that decapitated enemies. These were his comrades, brothers he shared such a tremendously deep bond with, and brothers he knew would stand with him even against insurmountable odds.

This might be one of those times.

But he couldn't give up, not with Kristoph's life at stake. Still, Gaetan was starting to wonder if it was worth risking all of these lives so unfairly. These were great men, of great deeds, and he would die first before seeing any of them meet their ends. But hopefully, they wouldn't have to. His quick, experienced mind had come up with a last-ditch plan.

He could only pray it would work.

"Get into the trees on either side of the road," he told his men. "And when I say get into the trees, I mean climb into them and take your crossbows with you. Make sure you have a clear field of fire to Alary's army and make sure the knight across the road from you is not in your line of fire."

He was moving with a purpose and his men began to follow him. "What do you have in mind, Gate?" Téo asked eagerly.

Gaetan was moving into the foliage, far back where the horses were tethered. He headed to his horse in order to claim his own crossbow. "It is nearing dusk and the darkness will work to our advantage," he said. "I alone will stand on the road and block Alary's army with you men in the trees. I will tell Alary to release Kristoph or I will unleash my army, lying in wait in the trees. It will be dark enough that no one will be able to see what lies beyond the tree line, and that will be their downfall. Alary will not know that I only have eight men with me and not a thousand, and it is that fear that will force him into obeying."

"A bluff?" de Moray said as he pulled his horse in behind the others as they entered into the trees. "A brilliant suggestion, Gate. Alary will not know if you are telling the truth or not."

Gaetan reached his saddle and began to unstrap his crossbow. "Exactly," he said. "If we do not have an army with us, then we shall create one. If Alary refuses my demands, then one or more of you place a few well-aimed arrows from the trees to convince him otherwise. Listen to the conversation carefully; if it seems we are going to battle, then take out Alary and his mounted men first. If we remove the head of the beast, then hopefully his men will be directionless and scatter. I will go for Kristoph so cover me as much as you can. Is that clear?"

It was a desperate move they were planning for but there was no other choice. The situation had changed and they would have to change with it or all would be lost. The knights began preparing for the upcoming fight, removing crossbows, arrows, and making sure their broadswords were strapped to their sides. Shields, strapped to the horses, were also removed and brought forth; they would be unusable with the crossbows but if they entered into close-quarter fighting, they would be needed.

The knights were businesslike and methodical in their preparation. There was a sense of anticipation but no sense of fear; this was simply what needed to be done, the moment they had been preparing for on the long journey north. Each man was ready, willing, and able to fight to the death for Kristoph's freedom. And if Gaetan had been feeling some guilt over risking the lives of many for just one man, he needn't have worried – to each one of them, this was what needed to be done. A brother needed to be rescued and they were going to fight to the death to do it.

As they finished collecting their gear, more hooves were heard out on the road and St. Hèver rushed to the edge of the tree line to see Wellesbourne approaching. He waved the man into the trees and, together, they headed back to the rest of the men, buried deep in the shielding foliage. Wellesbourne approached and saw the preparations for battle.

"You have seen him," Wellesbourne said to St. Hèver. "Thank God you came before I did. The army was blocking my path to leave town and I had to rush round the walls to get to my horse. It took valuable time."

Gaetan, in full armor with his shield slung across his back, faced Wellesbourne. "Where was the army when you left?"

Wellesbourne was winded from his wild ride. "They were just heading to the west side of town," he said. "They are not moving slowly, as I suspect Alary wishes to make it to Tenebris by nightfall, so their pace is quick. They are more than likely thinking of the warm meal and bed that awaits them at Tenebris and not of any dangers on the road ahead."

Gaetan nodded as he digested that information. "That is good," he said, "because we intend to surround him with an army."

Wellesbourne's brow furrowed in confusion. "What army?"

Gaetan glanced at St. Hèver. "Explain it to him," he said. "I must go take my position out on the road."

Kye nodded. "Aye."

Gaetan paused before he left, looking at his men once more. Eight of the best knights in the world and he was exceptionally proud of them. He could have very well felt apprehension at this moment but he refused. He could only feel pride, honor, and determination. It was enough to bring tears to his eyes.

Men of such bravery were surely immortal.

"Alary of Mercia cannot best us," he told them in a tone that suggested pure confidence. "Although we cannot know what the end of this battle shall bring, suffice it to say that it shall end and whatever that end shall be, know that I look to each and every one of you as the bravest men I have ever known. It has been a privilege to fight at your side, good knights. It is you who have given me a sense of purpose and I shall always be grateful, no matter what comes. *Et pro Gloria dei.*"

The knights were looking at him by this time, pride and loyalty reflected in their expressions. They knew, as he did, that they were facing terrible odds. There was a very good chance that one or more of them would not make it through. But still, they were willing to risk their lives for their brother, for their comrade. There was nothing more worthwhile or noble in life.

It was the most important battle they had ever faced.

"*Et pro Gloria dei,*" Téo whispered to him.

Instead of the usual handshake, he embraced him as a brother would. In fact, all of the knights embraced Gaetan and each other. That was not usual with them but, in this case, it was vitally important to make that contact because if any of them met their deaths, then it was important for the parting to be well-made with embraces of brotherhood and of love. And those words, *For God and Glory*, were a blessing to each and every one of them, for if the end was near, then God would certainly be waiting for them. If they died, it would be with the love and devotion of their fellow knights.

It was time.

Gaetan headed out to the road, knowing that his men were taking positions in the trees behind him. Once he came through the trees and onto the road, it was dim with the setting of the sun but he knew, at any moment, he would not be alone.

He had a man to meet.

GAETAN WAS STANDING right in the middle of the road as he began to see shades of Alary's army. The sun was setting and the scenery around him ever-dimming and, true to what Wellesbourne had said, the army was moving at a clipped pace, clearly wanting to make it to Tenebris by nightfall.

Gaetan wasn't sorry he would have to disturb those plans. With his crossbow in one hand, though not raised, he simply stood there as the army entered the portion of the road where there was a dense collection of trees on both sides.

As Gaetan watched them approach, he couldn't help but notice they hadn't slowed down. He knew they saw him because men had pointed in his direction but, still, the pace remained swift. The men were noisy, kicking up dirt as they went, and the sheer rumble of many feet, hooves, and wheels gave the army a steady roar.

Wellesbourne and St. Hèver had been correct; there were many mounted warriors, heavily armed. But Gaetan held his ground, even when they came closer and he began to see facial features of the men. Not knowing what Alary of Mercia looked like since he didn't have Ghislaine to identify him, he would have to ask. As the army drew nearer still, he raised his crossbow.

The gesture was unmistakable.

"Halt!" he bellowed.

The men in the front of the army heard him and were looking at him with a mixture of curiosity and concern. But they didn't slow down; they kept coming. Gaetan was forced to encourage them to obey his command; he released his crossbow, landing the arrow right in front of one of the men on horseback. A split second after he launched his arrow, several more came sailing out of the trees, all of them landing on the road in front of the advancing army.

It was enough of a startling move to cause horses to rear up and men to come to a halt purely out of fear. But the middle and rear portion of the army kept coming, running into those who had stopped, and now there was a great commotion as the army folded up on itself because they couldn't go any further. When those in the rear tried to back up, more arrows hit the ground on the road behind them, blocking their escape.

Effectively, the army had been trapped.

Gaetan reloaded his crossbow and began to advance on the uncertain huddle of men. "Give me Alary of Mercia!" he shouted.

The men looked at each other fearfully, hissing and whispering, but Alary was not immediately produced. Gaetan advanced on them until he was about twenty feet in front of them. He leveled off his crossbow at one of the warriors on horseback.

"Give me Alary of Mercia or you men will die in a hail of arrows," he said, looking to the well-armed warrior. "And you shall be the first."

The warrior sat tall in the saddle. "I am not afraid to die."

Gaetan's answer was to let the arrow fly, right into the man's throat. He hit the ground, dying a slow and agonizing death as Gaetan reloaded.

"Know that I have a thousand men in the trees with their arrows sighted on all of you," he said loudly. "I would speak with Alary. That is all I wish. But if you do not produce him, then be prepared to die."

The confusing situation, for Alary's army, had just become deadly serious. There were more whispers about as Gaetan pointed his crossbow at another mounted warrior, who turned to run but there were so many men behind him that he couldn't. Therefore, he leapt from the saddle and hid behind his horse to protect himself. Gaetan cocked an eyebrow at the cowardly warrior.

"Is this how a Saxon fights?" he asked. "Hiding from his enemy?"

"What madness is this?"

A man suddenly came up through the center of the army but he had a very big shield in front of him. Obviously, he'd seen the arrow take down the first mounted warrior and he was smart about his approach. He looked at the man dying on the ground, his features contorted with anger.

"By what right to you kill my men?" he demanded. "Who *are* you?"

Gaetan focused on the man; he was moderately tall, and slender, with a massive scar across his face running from his left temple, across his nose, and ending by the right side of his jaw. His hair was dark and he was rather unattractive. More than that, he had a sinister look about him. Gaetan took several long moments to digest the appearance of Alary of Mercia.

"*Your* men," he said. "You must be Alary."

Alary was in no mood for whatever this man wanted. He was positively enormous, dressed in mail and heavy tunic, with a sword on his side, a kite-shaped shield slung across his back, and a wicked-looking crossbow in hand. It took him a moment to realize he was looking at a Norman knight, for no Saxon warriors dressed as this man did. The light of recognition went on and the anger on his face changed to astonishment.

"He was right," he said as if a great idea had just occurred to him. "His brethren *were* about!"

Gaetan heard him and he was fairly certain he knew what he meant. "You have something that belongs to me, *Anglais*," he said. "You took him. I want him back."

Alary kept the shield up but he took a few steps in Gaetan's direction as if to get a better look at him. "So it is true. You have come for my Norman."

"I have."

Alary seemed to be both impressed and amazed by the fact. "How astonishing that you made it this far," he said. But his eyes glittered rather knowingly. "Let me guess; my sister is with you. It was she who told you were to find me and, consequently, the prisoner I took from her. Is that it? She has asked you to avenge her?"

Gaetan wasn't surprised that Alary could figure out what was happening. The man knew he was being followed as far back as Westerham and Lady Gunnora's messenger those weeks back had clearly mentioned Ghislaine. It didn't take a great intellect to figure out that the Normans and Ghislaine must have been working together. But Gaetan didn't want to give the man any more information than he'd already guessed. They'd entered into a deadly game and Gaetan didn't want to give Alary any more ammunition against him. The man probably already knew too much.

Therefore, he played it cool.

"There is no vengeance involved," he said. "I have simply come to take my man. You will bring him forth."

Alary didn't move. He had a smirk on his face, as if he knew exactly why Gaetan was here and all of his secrets, besides. In fact, he was almost jovial.

"We will get to your man in a moment," he said. "I want to know how you and my sister found one another. Did she come to you for help? Please, tell me everything. I am most curious to know how my sister has betrayed me."

Gaetan wasn't pleased with the man's stalling tactics. He suspected there was some end to it but, at the moment, he couldn't figure out what that could be. Still, he wouldn't put it past Alary to try and undermine him somehow. He had to be vigilant.

"Your curiosity will have to wait," he said. "It is growing dark and, soon, we will be standing here in total darkness and my army in the trees will not be able to see who they are hitting with their arrows. You will lose many men if I give the word so it would be in your best interest to give me my man. That is all I have come for."

Alary looked around to the dark trees lining both sides of the road. Clearly, there were men in them, men with crossbows, but an entire army? He returned his attention to Gaetan.

"I told you not to follow me," he said. "My scouts reported that we were not followed, but your man was certain his comrades had not given up. He told me so. How did you move an entire army north and I did not know of it?"

Gaetan smiled thinly. "My men have arrows trained on you at this very moment," he said, "and that shield will only protect one side of you. If I were you, I would do as I have asked. Bring me my man. I will not ask you again. Next time, I will let my army do the asking."

There was truth to that statement. Alary could only protect one side and he lost some of his smug appearance. He backed up a bit, so there were men behind him and around him, but even those men started to move away out of fear that Alary was an arrow target. When Alary saw what was happening, his humor vanished completely. He eyed Gaetan with nothing short of pure hatred, realizing he had no choice but to bring forth his prized prisoner. If he didn't, he suspected very bad things were about to happen.

"Bring me the Norman!" he bellowed. "Bring him now!"

Back in the lines, men began to scramble. As Gaetan and Alary gazed at each other in a deadly staring game, back in the lines, Kristoph was being unchained.

Half-unconscious with hunger and fatigue, he hadn't heard what was going on at the front of the army. But he'd most definitely heard the arrows hit around them, so he knew something was happening. When the guards around him began to unchain him, he began to suspect something quite serious was afoot, but he had no idea what it was until he was brought forward through the lines of Saxon men.

Exhausted, starved, beaten, and in need of both a bath and a shave, Kristoph made his way slowly. He couldn't move very fast but he was trying. As he emerged from the army, dragged forward by two of

Alary's men, his gaze fell on Gaetan and it was all he could do to not burst into tears; he'd never seen anything so beautiful in his entire life than Gaetan de Wolfe, standing alone and facing off against an army of two hundred men. The man had the bravery of the archangels and Kristoph knew, at that moment, that he would be saved.

There was no doubt in his mind.

Gaetan, too, had never seen any sight quite so wonderful as he did when his gaze beheld Kristoph. But he wanted to burst into tears for an entirely different reason; the man looked like hell. He looked like a starved animal. Normally a muscular man of some bulk, he looked as if he'd lost half of his weight. At that moment, Gaetan's joy and shock turned into anger so deep that he was having a difficult time controlling it.

He wanted to kill.

"Kristoph," he said hoarsely. "Come here."

Kristoph moved to obey but Alary grabbed him by the arm. "Not so fast," he said. "Your man is a valuable prisoner. We must discuss his release."

Gaetan realized he was shaking with fury. "There will be no discussion. Turn him over to me or every man in your army will die, starting with you. Is this in any way unclear?"

Alary didn't like being threatened. Unsheathing a dagger at his side, the same one he'd used to cut off the portion of Kristoph's finger, he pointed the tip right at Kristoph's left kidney.

"What gives you the right to come to my country and make such demands?" he hissed. "You do not belong here, Norman. You and your kind have come here to take what does not belong to you and as long as I hold your man hostage, the Normans will do as I say!"

Gaetan could see, in that statement, that Alary was detached from the world at large. Only a fool would make such a statement. What was it Antillius had called him? *Alary Insanus.* Alary the Insane. Gaetan began to realize that there may be truth to that and his only hope would be to behave as Alary was.

Threats to a man who only understood the language of a madman.

"Holding one Norman knight against the entire Norman nation will not cause them to surrender," Gaetan said. "Give me my man and I will leave you and your army intact. Continue to threaten him as you do and my army will emerge from the trees and kill every last one of you. Now, take your dagger away from him. Kristoph, come *here*."

Alary didn't move and Kristoph, feeling the knifepoint at his kidney, knew this was the moment of truth. He could move, but he knew Alary would probably shove that dagger deep into his body if he did. He might survive it; he might not. But he was willing to take the chance. All he knew was that this was the moment when he fought back against his captor where he had been unable to fight back before. He was free and he was going to remain free.

But Gaetan had to know that and he had to be prepared. Therefore, he said the only thing he could at that moment, his blue eyes fixed on Gaetan.

"*Et pro Gloria dei,*" he said quietly.

For God and Glory.

Gaetan knew exactly what that meant. Those were words that preceded a fight, and a fight was upon them. There would be no more talk, no more negotiation. Knowing this may be their end, if they went, they would go out fighting like the knights they were. This was their battle.

Swallowing hard and bracing himself for what was to come, he nodded his head, once.

"*Et pro Gloria dei,*" he murmured.

He braced himself.

What happened after that was something Gaetan would remember for the rest of his life. It seemed as if it happened in slow motion, but it happened in the blink of an eye. Gaetan saw it and then it was gone, like a flash, and all hell broke loose as an army of men he didn't recognize came rushing out of the trees, swarming the Saxon army, and pulling men down with their bows and arrows and spears.

It was chaos. But it was chaos that saved them all.

The last thing he remembered seeing before unleashing his own crossbow was an arrow flying right at Alary's head, piercing his forehead and going all the way through to the other side. As Alary fell to the road, dead, Kristoph yanked the sword from the sheath at Alary's side and joined whatever fight this happened to be. Now, the captive had turned on the captors.

And they were going to pay.

Somewhere in the middle of it of the mass of swarming, fighting men, Gaetan caught sight of the iron staff from the monument of the *Tertium* held high above the fighting, flying once again in the face of battle as it did for its legion those centuries ago. Now, Gaetan finally realize who these men were.

The Romans, in all their glory, had arrived.

CHAPTER TWENTY-SIX

☙

WHEN YOU LOVE SOMEONE

"*G*AETAN*!*"

Gaetan heard his name screamed above the rumble of battle and he turned to see Ghislaine astride a hairy pony as she pushed through the fighting, using the bow in her hand to club men over the head with it.

In a panic, Gaetan pushed his way towards her, shoving and slashing at men, finally reaching her and pulling her off the pony. As the pony scattered, he carried Ghislaine out of the fighting, running with her into the trees, his only thought to take her to safety. He didn't even know how long he'd run, only that it seemed like forever. He was blinded with his panic to get her to safety. But Ghislaine put a hand on his face, easing him, soothing him, and bringing him back to reality.

"You can stop, Gaetan," she told him. "We are clear of the battle; all is well, I swear it. You can stop!"

He heard her words but he was still filled with terror for her safety. Slowly, he was able to come to a stop but he ended up stumbling to his knees, nearly dumping Ghislaine to the ground.

But she held on tight, arms around his neck. When they were on the moldering leaves of the forest, she finally let go, her hands going to his face.

"Are you well?" she asked urgently, eyes full of unshed tears. "Tell me you are uninjured."

Gaetan had his arms around her now, kissing her furiously as he tried to speak. "I am well," he said. "But what are you doing here? What has happened?"

Ghislaine was trying to speak but his mouth on hers made it difficult. "I had to come," she gasped. "Jathan told me that you had left and I had to come. Gaetan, I could not let you face this alone."

She finally put her hand over his mouth because he was kissing her hard enough to make her swoon. "But those men," he said, kissing her hand instead. He couldn't seem to stop kissing her. "You asked Antillius for assistance? Are those his men?"

It was so much more complex than that and Ghislaine was sick with grief at the question. How could she tell Gaetan that the price of his help was the end of their dreams? Of course, the man had to know. If she didn't tell him, then Antillius would. But she didn't want to tell him so soon. She, at least, wanted some time with him before the sorrow began.

Throwing her arms around his neck, she simply wanted to hold him against her, to remember this moment for the years to come when she was wrought with loneliness and sorrow. Squeezing her eyes shut, she fought off the tears that were threatening to rip her apart.

"We left the village a few hours after you did," she said, her throat tight with emotion. "Antillius brought all the men he could to help you. I knew this area and I suspected that you would meet Alary on this stretch of road, somewhere between Tenebris and Kidderminster, so we came up through the forest and we saw your men in the trees, watching the road. Téo and Aramis saw us and they waited with us and told us when to attack."

Now, it was all becoming clear. It was such a glorious bit of good news that Gaetan was having trouble grasping it all. He held her close.

"Your timing was perfect," Gaetan said, relief in his voice. "It could not have come at a more perfect moment. But you? You came and I did not want you to. I left orders that you should not."

"I know."

"I told Jathan to tie you to the bed if he had to."

Ghislaine was still holding him, unable to look him in the eye. "He tried," she said, somewhat remorseful. "I had to disable him."

Gaetan frowned before pulling out of her embrace, looking at her as if he wasn't sure he wanted to hear her explanation. "What do you mean 'disable' him?" he asked. "What did you do, little mouse?"

"I kicked him."

"*Where?*"

"It is a good thing he is a priest and will never want children."

Gaetan's eyebrows flew up in shock. "There?"

"Aye."

"Where did you leave the body?"

Ghislaine tried not to look too contrite. "He could not ride, so he is back at the *Tertium* village. He says you can come back for him and Camulos when the battle is over."

Gaetan knew he should scold her. But then, he started to laugh in spite of himself, his big white teeth gleaming in the weak light. "I should spank you at the very least," he said. "But I cannot muster the will. You are very determined and I adore you all the more for it."

She was glad he wasn't angry with her. But in looking at the man, into that handsome face that she'd come to know so well, the tears began to return.

"And I love you, Norman," she whispered. "I love you with all that I am. Everything I have done, I have done it because I love you. You must always remember that."

His smile turned warm, adoring. A big hand cupped her face. "I am the most fortunate man in all the world to have your love," he murmured. "As you have mine."

"Gate!"

Téo broke the tender moment, coming up behind him through the trees with Kristoph in tow. Gaetan forgot all about Ghislaine for the moment and rushed to Kristoph, throwing his arms around the man in a moment he'd been praying for since he realized Kristoph had been abducted. His brother, his friend, was finally safe, and his relief knew no limits.

"Kris," he muttered, hugging the man tightly before releasing him. "You cannot know how I have longed for this moment."

Kristoph was wearily smiling at him. "I knew you would come for me," he said. "I never had any doubt."

Gaetan put an affectionate hand on his cheek. "I am glad you did not doubt us, for it was a harrowing journey to find you." He sobered. "How is your hand?"

He meant the partially cut finger. Kristoph held up his hand to show him. "It has almost healed. I do not miss it, anyway."

"But you are well otherwise?"

"Other than the fact I could eat an entire cow by myself, I am well. But how did you happen to find me? Alary was convinced you had stopped following us, but I knew better. I knew you were around, somewhere. But how did you know?"

Gaetan pointed to Ghislaine. "It is all because of her," he said. "You *do* remember her, do you not?"

Kristoph looked at Ghislaine and his eyes widened. "Of course I do," he said, taking a few halting steps in Ghislaine's direction. "My lady protector. It was *you* who helped my comrades find me?"

Ghislaine stood up, slowly because of her aching thigh. "It was because of me that Alary took you," she said. "At first, I went to the Normans for help with vengeance in my heart. I wanted them to kill my brother for taking you away from me. But in the end, it was my own arrow that ended my brother's miserable life and I am not sorry for that. For everything he has done and all of the people he has wronged, I suppose it was the least I could do."

Her statement wasn't missed by Gaetan. "It was you who put the arrow through his skull?"

Ghislaine nodded solemnly. "Aye," she replied. "He cannot hurt anyone again. If it had to be done… it is right that I should do it. He has given our family a terrible name. We have much to atone for."

Gaetan went to her, pulling her into his arms, and Kristoph watched with some astonishment. "What's this?" he hissed. "Why do you hold that woman like that?"

Gaetan started to laugh. "Because I am going to marry her." He watched the amazement on Kristoph's face. "Do not look so surprised; you should be happy for me. Ghislaine is the only woman worthy of me, Kris, and I am not ashamed to admit that I adore her. It was a good thing her brother abducted you 'else I would have never known her."

He meant the last part a jest, but not entirely because it was true. Kristoph looked at Téo, who simply nodded with a grin, as if the joke was on Kristoph. As Kristoph struggled to absorb what he'd been told, because he had many more questions than answers, more of Gaetan's men wandered into the trees.

Aramis, de Reyne, de Moray, and de Lara all went straight to Kristoph, hugging the man just as Gaetan had, thrilled that he was alive and well. It was a tender, touching scene as men reaffirmed their bonds of friendship, of brotherhood. Joy was in the air on this dusky evening as the *Anges de Guerre* were made whole once again. A day that could have ended very badly had the best possible outcome.

There was much to be thankful for.

"The battle is over for the most part, Gate," Aramis said. "Alary's men have scattered."

Gaetan took Ghislaine by the hand. "Come along," he said. "Let us go and see to it."

Ghislaine allowed him to lead her back through the trees, with his men in tow, until they all ended up back on the road where it was now a bloody mess with scattered bodies everywhere. Off towards the west, the *Tertium* were still chasing some of Alary's men but, for the most part, the majority of them were milling around the dead and dying Saxons, stealing weapons and anything of value from their bodies.

Gaetan surveyed the brutal scene.

"Give the *Tertium* anything they want from Alary's wagons," he told his men. "They can even have the horses if they wish. I will not lay claim to anything. This was their battle, not mine. It is the least I can do."

As his men nodded, de Winter, St. Hèver, and Wellesbourne emerged from the mess, also heading to Kristoph to do exactly what the others had done. There was much hugging and rejoicing going on as their lost brother was reclaimed.

Holding tightly to Gaetan's hand, Ghislaine watched it all. As she'd seen from the beginning with the *Anges de Guerre*, there was the strength of bond between them that was more powerful than anything she had ever seen. Now they were a complete brotherhood again and the joy in the air was indescribable. It almost made all of the pain and hardship they'd suffered worth the end. Certainly, one could not experience such great joy without suffering such great pain.

But that pain was only going to get worse.

Antillius appeared with a group of his men, heading straight for Gaetan. Ghislaine stood back as Gaetan went to Antillius to extend his hand in thanks. Antillius took the man's hand and shook it.

"Words cannot express my gratitude," Gaetan said sincerely. "That you would ride to our aid... without you, it is possible that this battle would have had an entirely different outcome. Allow me to present Kristoph de Lohr, the man you risked your life for."

He introduced his knight, who nodded his head at Antillius. "I am in your debt, my lord," Kristoph said.

Antillius looked at the knight they had rescued, dirty and scruffy and beaten. "There is no debt to speak of," he said. "We have been well compensated for our efforts. Fortunately, we did not lose a man. I have a few injured, but nothing that will not heal."

Gaetan wasn't sure what he meant. "Compensated?" he asked, confused. "I do not understand."

Antillius' gaze moved to Ghislaine. "You have not told him?"

Ghislaine was back to feeling sick and miserable. When everyone looked at her, expecting an answer, she swallowed hard. She'd hoped to tell Gaetan without an audience but it seemed that was not to be.

"I… I have not," she said quietly. "There has not been time."

Gaetan didn't sense anything amiss, at least not right away. He looked at Ghislaine. "What did you pay him with? I was not aware you had any money."

Ghislaine took a deep breath, fighting to keep from breaking down. At this point, she didn't care that others were listening. All she cared about was Gaetan and how he was going to react to everything.

"I do not have money," she said. "I… I made a bargain with Antillius."

"What bargain did you make?"

Ghislaine was struggling. She tried to open her mouth but nothing seemed to come forth. Gaetan was waiting; everyone was waiting. Her heart was pounding and her knees were weak. As she opened her mouth and tried again, Antillius spoke.

"The lady was terribly grieved at the thought of your demise, as you and your men faced her brother," he said steadily. "In discussing the issue with me, she was determined to go alone and help you but I knew her help would be useless. In fact, it might even be a hindrance. I therefore offered my men in place of the army you were forced to leave behind at Westerham, but at a price."

Gaetan was listening closely but he was starting to get the feeling that there was something wrong in all of this. He was holding on to Ghislaine's hand and he could feel her trembling.

"*What* price?" he asked.

Antillius looked him in the eye. "She wanted something from me and I wanted something from her," he said. "She was willing to pay the price, although I understand that it was only to save you and your men. It was not because her heart was in this decision. She made it because she had to."

Gaetan was increasingly concerned. "Be plain, Antillius. What bargain was made?"

Antillius continued. "You will recall that I offered my daughters to you and your men this morning," he said. "You will recall why. My people are a dying race and I explained to you how important it was for my daughters to bear sons, strong sons, to continue our family. I am a desperate man, de Wolfe, but you already know that. When you and your men left this morning, there were no takers to my offer, so the lady agreed that there would be at least one taker."

Gaetan didn't like the sound of that at all. "What could she possibly agree to?"

"I agreed that I would allow you to marry Lygia in my stead," Ghislaine said hoarsely. She was looking at the ground, unable to face him. "I told Antillius that I would insist you marry Lygia so that at least one of his daughters could bear sons from a man of new blood. And your sons will be the strongest and greatest of them all."

Gaetan was horrified at the mere suggestion. "How could you agree to such a thing?" he demanded. "That you would give up –?"

Ghislaine cut him off as she burst into tears. "I had no choice!" she said. "If I did not agree, then they would not help you, and if they did not help you, you would die. Your men would all die. Do you not understand, Gaetan? I did it because I love you. I would rather have you alive and married to another than a dead memory of my life that could have been. I did it to save your life!"

Gaetan was beside himself. He looked at the top of Ghislaine's head as she stood there and wept before turning to look at Antillius. For a man that had only gratitude in his expression just moments before, now there was only hatred as he faced off against the man he'd considered an ally.

"How could you make such a bargain with her?" he hissed. "You have put her honor on the line and now mine with your unreasonable demands. How in God's name could you manipulate her like that? Because she loves me, she agreed to your demands. Only a vile man would take advantage of a woman like that."

Antillius was faced with a very angry warrior. Not that he expected otherwise. He was torn between defiance and remorse.

"When your family is dying off, see if you would not make a deal with the devil to save them," he said quietly. "I am sorry, de Wolfe. I truly am. But that was the price of my assistance. If you have any honor in you, you will abide by the lady's bargain."

Gaetan had never felt more hollow, more devastated, in his entire life. He understood Antillius' point of view; he simply didn't agree with the man's methods.

"So you would force me into a marriage with your daughter, knowing that I love another woman?" he asked, incredulous. "Surely there is another way."

Antillius was deeply pained by the grief he'd brought about. "I wish there was. This morning, I asked you if you would be willing to marry your men to my daughters but you evidently refused and did not have the decency to tell me. Therefore, I must do all I can to provide at least one of them with a good husband and to ensure the survival of my family. Please forgive me, de Wolfe, but this is something I had to do."

Gaetan simply stared at the man. As a warrior of consummate honor, Gaetan was a man who stood by his word. He had never broken his word, not to anyone. Even though he'd not made this bargain, Ghislaine had and, if he didn't go through with it, he would be destroying her credibility and his right along with it.

Oh, God... is it really true? Must I do this?

He was, therefore, at a loss; he couldn't even look at his men, knowing they heard the real reason behind the unexpected help they'd received against Alary. It was heartbreaking in so many ways because now they, too, knew his honor was on the line. They were watching him to see what he would do. Would he refuse? Or would he keep a bargain that would destroy his emotions as well as Lady Ghislaine's? His honor, especially in front of his men, was the most important thing to him. His men had to know he was unbreakable, no matter what the cost.

Realizing he had no choice, he turned away from the group, still holding Ghislaine's hand.

"Give me a moment, if you will," he muttered. "I must speak with Ghislaine."

Antillius watched the big man as he turned away, pulling a sobbing woman up against him. He almost called out to them to apologize again but he thought better of it. His apologies meant nothing. If he was truly sorry, he would have broken the bargain himself but he wasn't willing to do that. As he stood there uncomfortably, listening to the lady's weeping, a deep voice spoke.

"There is no need for Gaetan to marry your daughter, my lord."

Antillius found himself looking at Aramis, the man who had defended his daughters against the Men of Bones. He rather liked Aramis, in fact.

"Unfortunately, there is," he said to him. "Mayhap it is not the most savory bargain, but you will not interfere."

Aramis shook his head. "I must," he said. "If you are looking for a husband for Lygia, please consider me instead of Gaetan. I would consider it an honor."

Antillius looked at Aramis in surprise. In fact, even Gaetan came to a halt, having heard his knight's offer. "Aramis?" Gaetan said hesitantly. "Nay, man... you cannot do this."

Aramis turned to look at Gaetan, his dark eyes glimmering with warmth. "Do what?' he asked. "Marry a lovely accomplished woman? Are you so selfish that you would try to keep me from every beautiful woman in Mercia? I am quite serious, Gate. I spent time with Lygia and her sisters last night and Lygia is a lovely woman. I would consider it an honor to marry her in your stead."

Gaetan's mouth popped open in shock as he looked to Antillius, who was looking at Aramis with equal shock. But somewhere amongst the disbelief, hope and joy sprang forth. "Is this true?" Antillius asked. "You would actually... but why did you not say anything before now?"

Aramis cocked a dark eyebrow. "When has there been the opportunity, my lord? We have had very little time to speak that was not full of death or panic."

He had a point. Antillius looked to Gaetan, who was heading back in his direction with his attention solely on Aramis.

"Truly, Aramis?" Gaetan asked, astonished. "You would do this?"

Aramis looked at Gaetan. "Aye, I would." His gaze moved to Ghislaine, who still had tears on her cheeks even though her sobbing had come to an abrupt halt. He smiled at her. "Sometimes when you love someone, you would do anything to make them happy. Is that not so, Lady Ghislaine."

Sometimes, when you love someone... Ghislaine understood what he meant immediately. Because Aramis loved *her*, he was willing to do what was necessary to see her happy. In this case, it meant marrying Lygia so Gaetan would be freed from the bonds of Ghislaine's bargain. Rather than see Gaetan forced into marriage so he could sweep in and be a shoulder for Ghislaine to cry on, Aramis saw greater honor in seeing her happy.

Aramis was prepared to sacrifice himself for her joy.

"Oh, Aramis!" Ghislaine gasped when she realized the depths of his offer. "Thank you!"

She launched herself at Aramis, throwing her arms around the man's neck as he stumbled back from the force of the blow. Momentarily surprised by her action, he began to laugh as he timidly put his arms around her to give her a squeeze. But not too much; Gaetan was watching. In fact, when he saw the expression on Gaetan's face, he took his arms away from her to show that he wasn't touching her at all.

"See?" he said. "I am not touching her. It is she who is holding on to *me*."

Gaetan had to laugh. It was the most astonishing moment of his life, realizing that Aramis was willing to sacrifice himself for his and Ghislaine's happiness. The man he'd known for years, the man he considered to be a brother, was displaying just how extensive his loyalty was. Gaetan was humbled by the gesture, touched beyond measure. As he pulled Ghislaine off of the man, he turned to Antillius.

"Will you accept his offer, then?" he asked. "Lygia could find no greater husband than Aramis. He is one of the finest men I have ever known."

There was no doubt in Antillius' mind as to whether or not he would accept the offer. In truth, he was extremely relieved by it. Now, he didn't have to break up a man and woman who were clearly in love with each other, and Lygia would be getting a very fine husband. He looked between Aramis and Gaetan, a smile on his lips.

"I am honored by the offer," he said. "Of course I will accept it. I am sure Lygia will be quite pleased. But I have two more daughters... well, they need husbands also and...."

"The lass with the titian hair is quite beautiful," de Lara said, interrupting him. "Although I have not met her yet, I would like to. Would you introduce us, my lord?"

Antillius looked to de Lara, thrilled beyond measure. "That is Verity," he said eagerly. "I would be happy to introduce you. Thank you, my lord. Thank you ever so much."

Behind de Lara, de Moray cleared his throat loudly. "I suppose that leaves the last one for me," he said. "It would be my honor, my lord."

Antillius was astonished. His bargain with Ghislaine had only brought a husband for one daughter, but the loyalty of Gaetan's men to ensure that their liege and Lady Ghislaine were permitted to wed brought forth three marriage offers to make sure Gaetan didn't have to worry about any of Antillius' daughters. Ever. Now, they were spoken for and Antillius could not have been more delighted.

It was better than he had ever hoped for.

It was a good day, indeed.

"We shall return home on the morrow and feast," he told them all. "Let us celebrate this great victory and this fine alliance between Norman and *Tertium*. I could not ask for greater allies and fathers to a new generation of strong sons with both Roman and Norman bloodlines. Truly, they will be the greatest sons of all."

It was the ravings of a man who was extremely happy at the course the future had taken. Aramis, Luc, and Marc went to herd Antillius away from Gaetan and Ghislaine, moving with the man towards the dead on the road and turning the discussion away from the sudden betrothal of all three of them and back to the victory at hand. It was their way of giving Gaetan and Ghislaine some privacy for, undoubtedly, there was much to say between them. A future that had very nearly come to an end.

But a future that was now bright for all of them.

Around them, the other knights wandered off, including Kristoph, leaving Gaetan and Ghislaine alone in their disbelief with the turning of the tides. So much had happened that it was difficult to absorb it all. But in spite of the grief and shock they had endured, one thing was certain – they were still together and nothing could ever tear them apart. The bond they shared and the bonds of the *Anges de Guerre* were things that would never leave them. Norman or Saxon, it didn't matter. Honor was honor, and love was love, and in this new world, both had a place.

"Are you angry with me for making such a bargain, Gaetan?"

Ghislaine's soft question met his ears and he turned to look at her, that face he loved so well illuminated by the weak light as evening fell around them. Smiling, he shook his head.

"I understand why you did it," he said. "I cannot say I would not have done the same thing if the situation was reversed. I suppose it only helps me to understand the depth of your feeling for me and I am more honored than you can ever know. I am not sure what I have done in my life to be worthy of someone like you."

Ghislaine smiled, falling into his embrace when he wrapped his arms around her. "It is I who am honored," she whispered. "But thank God for Aramis. I cannot believe he would sacrifice himself so."

Gaetan held her against him, gazing down the road to see his three knights in the darkness, wandering through the dead with Antillius. "I can," he murmured. "Only a man of great honor and feeling would make such a noble sacrifice, and that is the kind of man Aramis is. He did it for you but he also did it for me. That is the bond of brotherhood, my lady, something you would not understand."

She looked up at him. "But I do," she said sincerely. "I understand that you would die for each other a thousand times over. I understand that you would make great sacrifices for each other, as Aramis and Luc and Marc just did. And I understand that they would bargain away their own happiness just so you would have the chance to live."

She meant her bargain with Antillius in her last sentence. Gaetan smiled down at her, feeling more love and contentment than he had ever known. If someone had told him those weeks ago when he came aboard his ships to the shores of Pevensey that he would have met a woman in battle that he would come to love with all his heart, he would have thought they were mad. Warwolfe was not a man prone to love, in any sense. But on this night, it was Warwolfe who finally learned that love takes many forms, the most beautiful of which were sometimes the most unexpected.

Gazing into Ghislaine's eyes, Gaetan knew that the battle for England had only been the beginning, not only for the Norman occupation of the country, but for him personally.

It was the moment that Gaetan de Wolfe's life truly began.

EPILOGUE

cs

THE BOOK OF BATTLE

Immediate Present Day

"**U**SUALLY, THESE BOARDS are a closed session, but in your case, we've made allowances."

Abigail already knew that. It was her *viva voce*, or viva, which was her final board review to determine whether or not she received her Ph.D. in Medieval History. She was here to defend her eighty thousand-word thesis that had taken her three years to write.

Sitting in a lecture hall at the University of Birmingham, she was facing a board of seven people, all of them hand selected from some of the most reputable and important Medieval and ancient historical academics in the world. She even had one guy from the Sorbonne in France whose sole focus was Medieval military battles – Hastings, Crécy, Agincourt, Towton, and everything in between. He'd been called in specifically because of the subject matter of the Battle of Hastings, but all of them had been invited to listen to something that no one had ever heard before.

The *Book of Battle.*

Abigail turned around and glanced into the audience behind her to see Queensborough and Mr. Groby sitting there, smiling encouragingly at her. Even grouchy Queenie seemed rather pleased by the whole thing. There was also another woman in the audience who'd been allowed to listen in because during the last year of Abigail's studies, Anne Smith de Wolfe, a professional genealogist and owner of a company called Digging Up Your Roots, had been a massive help to her in ironing out the history of Warwolfe and his descendants. She was married to a de Wolfe, in fact, which made all of this right up her alley.

Now, it was time for Abigail to face the music, as it were. She had seven experts in her field, who had been experts longer than she'd been alive, and she was ready to take them head-on.

"We've all had the opportunity to review your dissertation, Abby," her advisor, department head Dr. Sykes continued to speak. Then she grinned. "Of course, I've been looking at this and discussing it with you since it started, but our other panel members have only seen it as of late. I believe Dr. Sorkin wishes to begin the inquiry, so let's start."

Abigail turned to the scholar from the Sorbonne, who was looking at something on the table in front of him, his glasses halfway down his nose. When he realized the attention was on him, he glanced up at Abigail.

"The *Book of Battle*," he said in his heavy French accent. "You list this as your main source."

"Yes, sir."

"This is not a published resource."

"No, sir."

Dr. Sorkin was silent for a moment. "Young lady, if what you say is true, this source is potentially one of the biggest finds in the world of Medieval history. You *do* know that."

"Yes, sir."

"Where is the book?"

Abigail looked at Dr. Sykes, who spoke up. "It is here," she said, waving forward a department associate who had been sitting off in the shadows. "If you are worried about its authenticity, don't. We've spent the past six months having it analyzed by independent sources. I will show you the reports. It's completely authentic and we have two independent lab sources that date the book back to the era of William of Normandy's conquest. This is the real deal, gentlemen."

Dr. Sorkin was quite interested in the box the associate put on the table. In fact, they all were. As Dr. Sykes stood up and put on a pair of white gloves that were on top of the box, she spoke to Abigail.

"Abby, do you want to speak about this now?" she asked. "Because, honestly, I think this is the only thing everybody really wants to know about."

A few titters of laughter came from the panel as Abigail nodded. She was a little nervous, but she knew this subject backwards and forwards. In fact, she was rather excited to finally speak openly about something she'd been keeping to herself for the most part for the past three years. This is what she'd studied hard for and researched until she saw the material in her dreams. Sometimes, she even saw her subject in her dreams.

Warwolfe.

This was the moment Gaetan de Wolfe and his men began to shine for all the world to see.

"As you know, my dissertation is entitled *The unsung heroes of the Norman Invasion and their impact upon the Conquest,*" she said. "It has been my goal, since the beginning, to give a voice to those men who helped the Duke of Normandy conquer England. The man didn't do it all by himself and it was my goal to discover who made the biggest impact in his plans for conquest. Of course, as you know, information about the Battle of Hastings is fairly limited. There are only a few trusted sources in Barrow, Bates, Hallam, and other related scholars, but any first-hand account has been impossible to find. When I started visiting the Battle of Hastings museum a few years ago in my quest to find resources for my paper, I became acquainted with Mr. Peters Groby, who was a docent, but he had also lived in the village of Battle his entire life."

She turned to point out Mr. Groby, who lifted a hand to wave at the panel. Abigail continued to speak even though she was looking at Mr. Groby and Queensborough, seated next to him.

"The man to Mr. Groby's right is the man to whom I owe everything," she said. She'd grown quite fond of Queensborough over the past two years. "Meet Mr. Queensborough Browne, a direct descendant of Sir Anthony Browne, who was a close confident of Henry VIII. It's through Queensborough Browne that I was able to gain access to a Medieval journal that had been in his family's possession since the Dissolution of the Monasteries. This journal, which is called the *Book of Battle* because of Battle Abbey, was written by a monk named Jathan de Guerre and when you read the transcript of the *Book of Battle*, you'll see that he was probably the very first war correspondent. He gives a detailed account of not only the battle, but of a group of Norman knights known as the *Anges de Guerre*, led by a man known as Warwolfe."

By this time, Dr. Sykes had the ancient book out of its box and the assistant was passing out copies of the transcripts. They hadn't shared any of this before the viva because they had wanted this event to be the introduction of the *Book of Battle* to the world.

Dr. Sykes put the book on the table so that all of the panelists could get a look at it and, as they all stood up to see it, Abigail was essentially forgotten. For such an artifact to be presented to these historical scholars was like a drug to an addict; they were immediately filled with it, enthralled with it, and Abigail watched them as they fawned over it.

Turning her glance at Queensborough, she could see a hint of pride on the man's face. From a man who had been terrified to even show her the book those two short years ago to a man who had now gained a great deal of pride for sharing it with the world, Abigail was thrilled with the change. An old man who was able, in the twilight of his life, to find something wonderful to be proud over. She smiled at him and he winked at her.

Bring them back to life, Miss Devlin.

She was about to.

"The *Book of Battle* details the quest of Gaetan de Wolfe and his men as they went on a quest to rescue one of their comrades who had been kidnapped by a historical figure we all know as Alary of Mercia," Abigail said, talking even though no one was really paying attention to her. "Alary is also sometimes called Amary, but Jathan de Guerre definitely calls him Alary. This is an account like I've never seen before and neither has anyone else because it's very detailed. It really reads like a novel, actually. Jathan lists the men that went with de Wolfe on this quest and discusses them in fairly close detail."

One of the scholars at the table, Dr. Rapkin, was listening to her. He stepped away from the table as the others pored over the journal. "De Wolfe is a fairly well-known name in England, still," he said. "They're still the Earls of Wolverhampton, I believe."

Abigail nodded, pointing to Anne de Wolfe back in the audience. "That's Lady de Wolfe right there," she said. "She has helped me tremendously in discovering the history of the entire de Wolfe family, starting with Gaetan. We've been able to clear up a few misnomers starting with an old de Wolfe family legend that Gaetan de Wolfe met his wife, Ghislaine of Mercia, at the Battle of Wellesbourne. The truth was that Ghislaine of Mercia, the sister of Edwin of Mercia, was a warrior woman and she was at the Battle of Hastings. That's where Gaetan first met her. You'll read about it in the transcript. It was Ghislaine who helped Gaetan and his men hunt down her brother, Alary, and the Norman knight he'd abducted. The Battle of Wellesbourne didn't come until well after the Battle of Hastings. You'll also see in the transcript that one of Gaetan's men, interestingly enough, bore the name of Wellesbourne."

Dr. Rapkin nodded, very interested in this unique subject. "After reading your dissertation, I did a little research myself on the de Wolfe family. He became the Earl of Wolverhampton after the Battle of Wellesbourne."

"That is correct."

"But the de Wolfes that inherited the earldom of Warenton are a separate branch."

Abigail shrugged. "Partially," she said. "Those de Wolfes came from William de Wolfe, who was the first Earl of Warenton. William was the third son of the Earl of Wolverhampton, the man who had inherited that title through Gaetan. Since William de Wolfe was the third son, he was not in line for that inheritance. He received the title Earl of Warenton from Henry III, but he is a direct descendent of Gaetan de Wolfe."

It was clearing up some rather complicated family trees and, by now, more of the panelists were listening. "I also read about the Roman factor in your paper as it had to do with Gaetan's quest northward," Dr. Rapkin continued. "Can you please clarify how a lost Roman legion was part of the Norman conquest?"

Abigail grinned. "Well, you'll see in the *Book of Battle* that they weren't really a lost Roman legion, but merely descended from one," she said. "The leader was from the House of Shericus, but it was evidently de Wolfe who changed the name to de Shera because he felt it should be in the 'Norman fashion'. At least, that's what Jathan wrote. Anyway, several great English houses – de Lara, de Moray, and de Russe – have links to these Roman descendants because they married women from the tribe."

Dr. Rapkin rubbed at his chin thoughtfully. "And the House of de Shera? What became of them?"

Abigail glanced back at Anne once more. "With Lady de Wolfe's help, I did a little research on the House of de Shera and discovered it was de Wolfe who gave them properties up near Chester when Antillius de Shera, who was a widower, married a Norman woman," she said. "He had a few sons by her and it was the service of the sons to the Norman kings that gave them the Earldom of Coventry. The House of de Shera and the House of de Wolfe remained allies for hundreds of years after that."

It was a very neat story, all wrapped up in her dissertation and ex-plained to the last genealogical detail. Dr. Rapkin picked up a copy of the text from the *Book of Battle*, scanning it as Abigail sat there and waited for the next question. Considering the fascinating subject, it wasn't long in coming.

"De Lohr, de Russe, de Moray," Dr. Rapkin muttered as he read. "These are some of the greatest Medieval houses during that time. And all of them came with Warwolfe with the Duke of Normandy?"

Abigail nodded. "That's right," she said. "You know that Edward I named his giant trebuchet *Lupus Guerre*, which means war wolf, but I couldn't find any definitive information that stated that he actually named it after de Wolfe. But one can only assume he knew of the Normandy's greatest knight, so maybe that was his homage to de Wolfe."

Dr. Rapkin was still looking at the transcript. "It would explain a lot, actually," he said. Then he began flipping around the pages. "I saw somewhere that Gaetan and his wife had eleven children."

Abigail watched him flip around. "That's in my paper," she said. "William, Aaric, Elizabetha, Matthias, Juliana, Stefon, Dacia, Edwin, Quinton, Jarreth, and Catherine."

When he looked at her strangely for rattling off all of those names so quickly, she knew his question before he asked it.

"I have an eidetic memory. I see words," she said.

He understood. Dr. Rapkin looked back at the papers. "And they all lived into adulthood?"

Abigail nodded. "Seven sons and four girls, all of them growing up to become pretty great in their own right, but Lady de Wolfe can tell you more about that since it's her family. My focus was on Warwolfe and Ghislaine of Mercia, not their children."

Dr. Rapkin simply nodded as he went to reclaim his seat, still looking at the papers in his hand. In fact, all of them were starting to settle back into their seats and Abigail took the opportunity to plead her case before the heavy questioning started. There were a few things she wanted to clear up.

"I had someone tell me once that writing about English history like this wasn't my right because I'm not British," she said. "As I explained to him, my love of England is in my blood. I may not have been born here, but my heart is here. I didn't set out to change English history as we know it but I did want to give a voice to those men, those warriors, whose deeds and names had been lost to time. Maybe it was arrogant of me, but just maybe I actually did something that will make people look back on these knights – the *Anges de Guerre* – and appreciate them for their accomplishments. Yes, I know they conquered a nation, but it goes beyond that – these were men of great honor, and when you read the transcription of the *Book of Battle*, you'll see how much they were devoted to each other. Nowadays, we just don't see honor and duty like that. These men literally risked their lives for a colleague, just to rescue the man, and that's a kind of heroism that is largely lost these days. People have forgotten what it means to love your friends like these men loved each other. I think that's the greatest thing I took away from this whole project – the love these knights had for each other. They were the original band of brothers."

By the time she was finished speaking, the entire panel was looking at her. They were reclaiming their seats, refocusing on the task at hand even though there wasn't one of them that didn't want to run off with the *Book of Battle* and bury themselves in a room with it for the next six months. Such history, and such artifacts, were rare in their field. But even more rare was the passion from this young woman who spoke of men who had been dead for almost a thousand years as if they were her real-life heroes. That alone infused her dissertation with a glow that was difficult to describe, but one that was most worth listening to.

"Then let's talk about these men, Miss Devlin," Dr. Sorkin said, a smile playing on his lips. "You speak as if you know them personally."

Abigail was dead serious as she looked at them. "I do," she said. "Let me tell you about them."

As Abigail began to speak of Gaetan de Wolfe and his humble origins, Groby and Queensborough sat back and listened with the pride of fathers listening to their children. Abigail was articulate and intelligent, and she spoke of Warwolfe and the *Anges de Guerre* as if she knew them all personally. But, as she'd said, she did. She truly did. These weren't simply men on paper; these were men who had lived and died but, now thanks to her, they were living once again. Now, the world would know what Abigail and Queensborough knew.

The world would know the importance of the Duke of Normandy's greatest knights.

Therefore, this was a satisfying moment as well as a defining one, at least for Queensborough. He was proud; so very proud to have been part of something that brought the honored dead to life. From that old book that had remained buried in his family's artifacts, he was glad he'd been the one that allowed the story to finally be told. It gave him a sense of satisfaction he'd never known before.

"She told you she would make these men breathe again, Queenie," Groby leaned over and whispered to him. "Do you believe her now?"

Queensborough smiled, remembering those words from the day he'd first met the determined Abigail Devlin.

I'll make you proud, I swear it. I'll make these men breathe again.

She had. And somewhere in the halls of heaven, he was pretty sure Gaetan was smiling, too.

ᦲ THE END ᦳ

De Wolfe Pack Series:

The Wolfe

Serpent

Scorpion (Saxon Lords of Hage – Also related to The Questing)

The Lion of the North

Walls of Babylon

Dark Destroyer

Nighthawk

WarWolfe

ShadowWolfe

ABOUT KATHRYN LE VEQUE

Medieval Just Got Real.

KATHRYN LE VEQUE is a USA TODAY Bestselling author, an Amazon All-Star author, and a #1 bestselling, award-winning, multi-published author in Medieval Historical Romance and Historical Fiction. She has been featured in the NEW YORK TIMES and on USA TODAY's HEA blog. In March 2015, Kathryn was the featured cover story for the March issue of InD'Tale Magazine, the premier Indie author magazine. She was also a quadruple nominee (a record!) for the prestigious RONE awards for 2015.

Kathryn's Medieval Romance novels have been called 'detailed', 'highly romantic', and 'character-rich'. She crafts great adventures of love, battles, passion, and romance in the High Middle Ages. More than that, she writes for both women AND men – an unusual crossover for a romance author – and Kathryn has many male readers who enjoy her stories because of the male perspective, the action, and the adventure.

On October 29, 2015, Amazon launched Kathryn's Kindle Worlds Fan Fiction site WORLD OF DE WOLFE PACK. Please visit Kindle Worlds for Kathryn Le Veque's World of de Wolfe Pack and find many action-packed adventures written by some of the top authors in their genre using Kathryn's characters from the de Wolfe Pack series. As Kindle World's FIRST Historical Romance fan fiction world, Kathryn Le Veque's World of de Wolfe Pack will contain all of the great story-telling you have come to expect.

Kathryn loves to hear from her readers. Please find Kathryn on Facebook at Kathryn Le Veque, Author, or join her on Twitter @kathrynleveque, and don't forget to visit her website and sign up for her blog at www.kathrynleveque.com.

Made in the USA
Middletown, DE
02 November 2017